Freedom's Altar

ALSO BY CHARLES F. PRICE

Hiwassee: A Novel of the Civil War

JOHN F. BLAIR,
PUBLISHER
Winston-Salem,
North Carolina

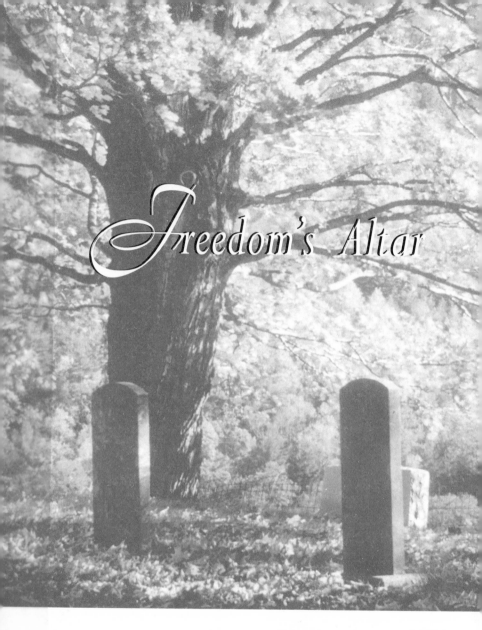

Freedom's Altar

CHARLES F. PRICE

Photograph used on dust jacket and throughout book by William A. Bake

Library of Congress Cataloging-in-Publication Data
Price, Charles F., 1938–
Freedom's altar / Charles F. Price.
p.   cm.
ISBN 0-89587-177-7 (alk. paper)
1. North Carolina—History—Civil War, 1861–1865—Influence—Fiction.
2. Afro-Americans—North Carolina—Fiction.
3. Reconstruction—North Carolina—Fiction. I. Title.
PS3566.R445F74   1999
813'.54—dc21   98–55781

$ 16.00

For *Ruth,*
who gave this book its heart

He that fights fares no better than he that does not. Coward and hero are held in equal honor, and death deals like measure to him who works and him who is idle.

Achilles
The Iliad of Homer

PART I

Necklaces

of

Fire

CHAPTER 1

The man the Curtises had once owned and whom they had called Black Gamaliel stood at the top of the lane and watched the distant figures disputing the fire down in the river bottom, where he remembered planting oats and cutting timothy. The field had grown over in weeds since he last saw it, and it looked like the white folk had tried to burn off the waste growth and the fire had got away from them. The wind was out of the south, and it was blowing the fire uphill across a shaggy pasture toward the rise where sat the big frame house and its ruined outbuildings. The white folk were flailing at it with blankets and fetching buckets of water from the river to throw on it. Their movements were jerky and awkward with panic. He set down his knapsack and leaned on his hickory staff and watched them with amusement and satisfaction mixed with an amount of pity almost too small to measure.

His name was Daniel McFee—the McFee line went as far back as anybody in the family could remember, and came from a plantation in Virginia long ago—but when the Curtises bought him he felt obstinate and wouldn't give his true name, and the judge had called him Black Gamaliel. He was a young buck at the time, nineteen years old, a prime field hand also trained as a carpenter; the judge had given seven hundred and fifty dollars for him. But no matter what the Curtises called him, he had been Daniel McFee then and had remained Daniel McFee through sixteen years of slavery, and then he'd been Daniel McFee through three years of freedom, two of them attached to the Union army; and he was Daniel McFee here today, a veteran of war and a free man, looking down on the farm where he had been in bondage, while the people he once called Marster and Mistress struggled comically to fight a fire they'd started but couldn't control. He smiled. Hadn't that been what all of Dixie had done—lit a fire that got away from them and ended by burning them out?

He settled on his rump among the bloodroot and arbutus growing on the verge of the path and filled his corncob pipe and lit it and sat smoking in the fine spring weather with his staff across his lap. The old place had suffered in the war. He looked for the barn he had helped to build but in its place saw only a heap of charred timbers covered by a net of honeysuckle and morning glory. The big house was in one piece but looked mighty shabby, with the paint flaking off of it and all the shutters and gallery railings gone and the front steps broken in. The smithy and the corncrib and the smokehouse and the chicken coop had disappeared. Across the little branch where the quarters had once stood there was nothing now but briars and wild blackberry and patches of thistle, except for the one apple tree he remembered so well. It had stood by the stoop of the cabin where he and Sukey and Sukey's Hamby had lived, and each fall he and Sukey and Hamby had eaten of its fruit, and sometimes Sukey would bake a cobbler with its apples that tasted bitter and sweet at the same time in a way no other apples ever had. He could taste those apples now as he sat. That tree had borne every year for sixteen years, but now it looked dead. Sukey's grave would be off yonder near those poplars, but he couldn't see it for the high uncut grass.

The smoke from the fire rose in several gray plumes that joined high up to form one thick column against the deep blue sky, in which a barely visible moon still shone pale as a wafer of partly melted ice. The fire was closing in around the base of the promontory on which the house stood, with its fine view of the valley of the Hiwassee and the Georgia mountains in the distance. Daniel thought the chain of fire gathered around that hill resembled a string of baubles about a woman's neck. The white folk dashed to and fro beating at the fire and fetching water from the springhouse, because it was nearer than the river now. Behind them the burnt fields smoldered and gusts of black chaff blew in the wind.

The people he had camped with two nights ago by Munday's place at Aquone came along the road above him and paused to watch with him. There were only nine of them now, and the large buck who had been a driver on a South Carolina rice plantation explained that two of them had turned off that morning to go up Shooting Creek. Daniel remembered them and sourly reflected that they had been the best two. There had never been a lot of coloreds in this part of the country, and during the war there had not been a one, for they had all run off. But now it seemed they were everywhere on the roads.

The Negro leading the white mule by a length of plowline asked, "Is this here that homeplace you was going on about, then?" Daniel confirmed that it was, and the Negro laughed. "They gone burn that place slap down, they keep on that way."

His partner with the one eye laughed too and said, "We ought to go down and help. Build a backfire in they house."

Daniel regretted even speaking to them that night at Munday's. If he had not, they wouldn't have felt encouraged to be familiar with him now. But he had been tired and lonesome for talk, even though he knew he was not of their stripe. Such trifling no-accounts were always looking to lord it over the defeated Rebels and insult folk and rob them and above all avoid work of any sort.

"It's burning itself out," he said of the fire. They saw that it was so and soon lost interest, and after a spell of pointless gabble they wandered on down the road. He did not blame such as they for savoring freedom after lifetimes of servitude. But he was ashamed of all shiftless vagabond darkies. He believed there was virtue in ambition and sin in idleness, and he thought now was the time for the colored man to prove himself worthy of the freedom the war had brought him.

He nourished an ambition in his heart which he scarcely understood but which had nevertheless drawn him all the way over the mountains from Nashville in Tennessee, twenty-two days coming. His ambition was to contract with Judge Curtis for free labor and to crop shares with him here along the Hiwassee, where he had grown to manhood as a slave. He could not explain this ambition to himself except to say that the Curtis place seemed home to him in a way that the Cobb place did not. The Cobb place at Bethel on the other side of Waynesville was where he had been born and raised, and then sold off to pay a gambling debt; it was where his mam and pap slept their last sleep.

Yet it was the Curtis farm that lay nearest his heart. Partly this was because it was where he and Sukey and Hamby had been together. But there were other reasons that were less clear. They had to do with those Curtises yonder, who for a long time had been the only family he could claim after Sukey passed and Hamby ran off, who knew him better than anyone alive, although of course they did not understand him at all. Then there was the beauty of the fields and mountains he could see now spread out before him. In the old days, when he was in bondage, the place had seemed dreary to him;

he had not been conscious of its appeal. But now it seemed so lovely that it made him ache. There was a time when he had never expected to see it again. Slowly he shook his head in wonderment. Now, after all that had happened to him, here he sat gazing down on what he could not help thinking of as home. And although everything about it was different, everything was also somehow the same. For a moment he felt as if he might sob.

But that quickly passed and was replaced by a brisk and resolute mood more appropriate to the doing of business. Rising, he knocked the coals out of his pipe against the heel of his hand and then shrugged back into his knapsack and adjusted his dusty blue forage cap, which bore the shield insignia of General Jacob Cox's Twenty-third Army Corps. Then he set off confidently down the lane, striking the ground with the point of his staff at every second step. He had long since mastered the art of seeming confident even when he wasn't, because he had promised himself never again to act the cringing servant.

Yet there were many things connected to this ambition of his that worried him, not the least of which was how to address the judge and the other Curtises and how to behave toward them, now that he was free and they were beaten and he and they were all equal before God and President Abraham Lincoln. He had already singled out the small wiry figure of the judge himself by the springhouse and was headed straight for him, and stoutly he rehearsed to himself the speech and demeanor he had studied out to his satisfaction in day after day of careful thought, all the way from Tennessee.

The judge had been as kind a master as a man could be that trafficked in human bondage and unlike most slave owners had worked alongside his Negroes and regarded them as beings possessed of souls. If this hadn't been true then Daniel's ambition would never have come upon him in the first place. But still Daniel had never yet seen a white man that believed a colored was his equal, no matter what

President Abraham had declared, and that included Judge Madison Curtis and probably President Abraham himself. Daniel hoped to show the judge respect at the same time he required it for himself. But he was aware of how difficult this would be, and despite his outward confidence he was uneasy as he came down the lane and around the base of the hill.

The judge spied him and stood unmoving, watching curiously, mopping his face with a sooty handkerchief. "I believe I know that walk," the judge declared, "even if I don't recognize that gray beard and woolly poll." He cocked his head inquiringly, like a bird looking for a worm in the ground. "Are you Gamaliel?"

Daniel approached to a distance just out of arm's reach and stopped there and replied with a degree of ceremony, "That's how you knew me, sir"—sir, that was the form of address he had chosen—"but my actual name is Daniel. Daniel McFee, to say all of it."

At first the judge seemed a little perplexed; he knit his brow and gave Daniel a shrewd look, as if he suspected Daniel were funning him. But after a moment he repeated the name. Then he nodded briskly, and that appeared to end the name business. He ran his forefinger left and right under his mustache in the old way. "Well, Daniel McFee, you can see we've made a botch of things here today and just escaped burning our ownselves down, after three years of warding off marauders that had the same notion in mind."

He was black with soot and running with sweat, and Daniel could see from his gauntness and the tremor of his hands what the war had taken out of him. But he still bantered Daniel just the same, and in spite of himself Daniel was touched, remembering how in slavery times the old man had often been freer with him than he'd been with his own kin.

The earth they stood on was scorched and ashy; it smoked around them, and the smoke stung their eyes till tears rose. So neither Daniel nor the judge could know for sure whether the other wept at this meeting, although even the possibility made Daniel a little angry both at the judge and at himself. But then nothing could change the fact that while they had been master and slave they had also been much like father and son, and it had hurt them both to the quick when Daniel ran off to freedom. Yet in spite of this bond there was a part of Daniel that hated Judge Curtis and reviled his affection, which after all went no deeper than the affection one has for a loyal dog or a good horse.

Through the blur of his tears Daniel looked past the judge into the burnt field to see who was there and saw that they were all womenfolk—he recognized the judge's wife and reckoned the rest were his daughters or daughters-in-law, all grown three years older. There was no sign of the boys he had known as Marster Andy and Marster Jack and Marster Howell. When he left the Curtises in November of sixty-two all three were in the Rebel army, but Marster Jack and Marster Andy had come home sick at heart to lay out. Now it appeared that despite their dread they'd gone back. As Daniel stood pondering their absence it struck him for the first time that when the armies disbanded they and young Marster Howell might not come home at all. Perhaps some of them were reported dead already. The thought pierced him like a knife, and all of a sudden he realized it had never occurred to him that the war could kill those gay boys off. Yet under the circumstances he did not know how to ask about them, and so he stood baffled and tongue-tied while the judge summoned his wife.

She who had always been Mistress Sarah he now gravely addressed as Miz Curtis, as he dragged off the cap he had defiantly left in place when the judge spoke to him. The handsome lively woman he remembered had faded and dwindled. She was only a wisp of a thing with a cloud of silver hair blown scraggly from fighting the fire. Like the judge the war had reduced her. And looking into her eyes Daniel knew it was true that death had taken some of the boys. Yet there was a warmth of affection in her face as she nodded to him and spoke his old name.

"He's called Daniel McFee now," the judge corrected her, so solemnly that Daniel half-suspected him of sarcasm.

"Always was," Daniel insisted.

The judge stared at him in mild astonishment; the name business wasn't finished after all. "Is that so? I thought it was a name you picked when you went to freedom. All those years I called you Gamaliel and you were Daniel McFee instead? Well, I declare."

He looked hurt and this pleased Daniel, although he dared not show it in looks. They stood awkwardly for a time, not knowing what to say next, while the others gathered round and gravely spoke to him one by one, the two eldest girls that were married—Mistress Betty, who would now be Miz Cartman, and Mistress Martha, who would now be Miz Barter—and the younger daughters—Mistresses Sarah, Polly, Julia and Rebecca, ranging in age from eighteen to ten, who would now be the Misses Curtis. Farther off, wearily leaning on a broom she'd used to beat out the flames, was Marster Andy's wife—no, *Mister* Andy's wife—Miz Salina, wearing a brown homespun dress the rim of whose skirt had burnt entirely off, leaving a fringe of char. There was no sign of Mister Jack's wife Miz Mary Jane.

Miz Curtis had been watching Daniel closely, and now she suddenly spoke up as if she'd read his mind. "You're wondering about the boys, I expect. Our Howell was killed November a year ago up near Knoxville. And Jack fell sick in Georgia last spring and was captured, and we've heard nothing of him since."

"We pray he's safe, of course," said the judge, though Daniel could see that Miz Curtis had concluded such prayers were wasted. "We pray he'll come back to us."

"I'm sorry," Daniel said, looking at his shoes. "And Mister Andy?"

"We had a letter from him some two weeks since," the judge replied. "He was in Alabama at a place called Spanish Fort and was ill with fever. He's been sickly the whole war, but he's never quit." This last was said proudly, but then at a glance from Miz Curtis the judge seemed to repent his boastfulness and looked shy. "We pray for Andy too," he finished lamely.

"I'll pray too, if I may," Daniel offered.

"We'd be obliged," Miz Curtis said with a wan smile.

There was no mention of the whereabouts of Miz Betty's Mister Bill Cartman or of Miz Martha's Mister Sanders Barter, both of whom Daniel recalled had favored Union. He didn't know how to ask about them either and so did not. But now Miz Curtis spoke up to inquire if Daniel knew the whereabouts of Sukey's Hamby or had heard aught of him; Hamby, Daniel's stepson, had vanished that first spring of the war.

Daniel looked down, viewed his shoe tops. He hated to ponder Hamby because Hamby reminded him of Sukey, and Sukey whom Daniel had loved was altogether gone. And besides, Hamby's rage at being born neither white nor black was not a pleasing memory. With Sukey gone Daniel had tried to tame Hamby, and now when any thought of Hamby came, the guilt of that failure nagged at him.

"Nome," he replied in a small voice, "I've not heard a thing of Hamby in all this time." Sadly Miz Curtis inclined her head and nodded. Sukey's Hamby was yet another casualty of the war, it seemed.

The judge cleared his throat. "Well, I see you wearing the blue. Did you take up arms, Daniel McFee, after leaving us?" With two boys gone to glory and a third still at risk and every one a Rebel, the judge had not posed a commonplace question. Asking it made him and Daniel so uneasy that they each gazed fixedly into the middle distance without seeing a thing.

"No, sir," said Daniel. "I was an orderly-like, to some officers in the Twenty-third Corps. I was with that Cumberland army two years."

Daniel supposed it was a kind of relief to the judge to learn that he had not fought. At least that was the way it seemed as he stole a glimpse of the judge's averted face.

Once more the judge cleared his throat. "I'll not pretend it ain't hard to see you, Daniel McFee, after what has gone before. And that's not just because you stole a thousand dollars in property by carrying yourself away or because you broke faith with me when I had treated you more like a friend than a servant, more like my own child than even a friend. And it's not even because you joined the enemy in a war that has ended by ruining me and killing one of my boys, if not two, or even all three." As the judge spoke Daniel regarded him sternly, to show that no tirade could discompose him. Miz Curtis turned red as a brick with embarrassment and rested a hand on the judge's sleeve as if to caution him, but he went on undeterred. "I don't reckon we can ever see eye to eye, or that I can ever willingly give you the rights you're bound now to demand." He turned his gaze back and gave Daniel an earnest look, and Daniel was surprised to see that in spite of what he had just said there did not seem to be any rage in him. Almost forlornly the judge added, "I suppose you're a Union Leaguer and a Redstring like all the nigras nowadays."

Sternly Daniel drew himself up to his full height. "Yes, sir, I am indeed." It occurred to him that he would seem less deferential wearing his cap, so he put it back on and gave it a rakish slant. "I'm dedicated to restoring the Union and making a citizen of the Negro."

The judge winced. "I hoped you'd spare me the orations. Already I regret teaching you to read and write and giving you the run of my library." He sighed and wagged his head in exasperation. "But I must admit, in spite of everything, it pleases a part of me—a perverse part, no doubt—to have you about the place again. But what in the world brings you back? This is a played-out spot, and no doubt a fount of misery for you, as the scene of your bondage." He eyed Daniel edgewise.

Daniel drew a breath and then in one turbulent burst of words related his scheme just as he had rehearsed it so many times on the road. The judge and Miz Curtis and the others all stood amazed, except for Miz Betty, who had always been the feisty one. "Well," she burst out when he had finished, "I for one am in favor of taking Gamaliel—er, Daniel—on. If he'd been with us this morning we wouldn't have nearly burnt ourselves out of house and home by mistake."

The judge colored at this; Daniel remembered well enough the pride the old man took in never shunning the basest farming chore and always doing a job better and quicker than any hand on the place. Daniel could see that the fire had degraded him, no matter that he was older now and more infirm, or that he'd had no help beyond womenfolk. Meanwhile Miz Salina spoke up too in Daniel's behalf, and then he saw Miz Sarah pass a look to the judge, and a third time the judge cleared his throat. "Well, I've that plot over by Downings Creek that used to be in hay. . . ."

"I know that piece," Daniel said at once.

Slowly and without glancing at him the judge nodded. "I could let you crop it all to yourself, and go shares on the rest. There's even an old cabin there. . . ."

"I know it too," said Daniel.

Once again the judge sighed—whether because he was sorrowful or relieved, Daniel couldn't say. "Many hereabouts are full of strong feeling," the judge mused. "They despise the Yankee and the nigra. They long for vengeance and thirst for blood." He stood with his hands on his hips, looking off toward the Georgia mountains. "But I confess I don't see how they can still feed such fires. Myself, I'm entirely out of hate. The war's drained me of it." He shifted his weight from one foot to the other and chewed one end of his mustache. "Will you take a third share of whatever crop we can make, less my cost for rations, seed, clothing, medicines and the like?"

To these liberal terms Daniel readily agreed.

"You can keep hogs, a milch cow and cattle if you can find them, and have the right of pasture on the place." The judge considered awhile longer, as if attempting to decide whether the deal was fair or not, and then nodded and said, "All right." And for the first time in nineteen years they shook hands like equals, the judge still not looking at him.

Just then Miz Betty's two boys Jimmy and Andy came running up out of the burnt field covered with soot and cinders and stood one to each side of Miz Betty and stared at Daniel out of their black faces, their big blue eyes pale as the shell of a robin's egg. Daniel remembered those boys three years younger, looking like twins— although they were not—and doing everything the same. Nothing about them had changed except they were a little bigger. Daniel said hello to them, and in unison they said hello back.

That night, after a poor supper of boiled turnips and potatoes, Madison Curtis retired to his study to prepare for evening devotionals. By candlelight he opened his Bible and searched the Scriptures for a text that might fortify the family in these trying times. But worries without number so distracted him that he could find nothing suitably uplifting.

If indeed the war was lost, as every refugee and wanderer now proclaimed, his affairs were in a condition of shipwreck. The loss of his nigras had cost him ten thousand in property. Like a good patriot he had bought Confederate bonds and the bonds of the state of North Carolina; if the South had gone smash, the former were now worthless and the latter were at risk of repudiation.

Then there was the threat of confiscation. Dire rumor said the Yankees would steal the land of the planters and parcel it out amongst the nigras; if this happened Madison Curtis and his pitiable dependents would soon be roaming the public ways in penury with all the other vagabonds. It was said that a man might ward off this fate by taking the oath, which Madison meant to do as soon as a proper Federal officer presented himself in Hayesville. Yet the Yankees might not permit even this; there were also tales that men of property might be barred from citizenship, might be imprisoned for treason.

But even if the conquerors let him keep his land and did not jail him he had no way to make a crop. The country swarmed with bandits and malefactors of every evil sort, and in three years of constant raiding they had stolen Madison blind. Left to him were one old plow and a lame mule. He had no seed nor specie to buy any. The fields were all grown over with brush and weeds, and to his chagrin Madison had learned today the folly of trying to burn a field clear with no help beyond women and girls. By forming a contract with Gamaliel—no, what was his name? Daniel, Daniel McFee—he had no doubt made an even more ludicrous blunder. How could he feed and clothe and furnish a tenant when he could not do the same for himself and his own?

Here amid the general swarm of his woes he felt one pang of special anguish. It had wounded him deeply to learn that in sixteen years' time the servant called Gamaliel had never spoken his true name to him. To Madison such reticence was unseemly and smacked of distrust and even hate, and it shocked him to think that Gamaliel might have harbored such low emotions behind a mask of loyalty and affection, year after year. He was sickened by the idea that rather than admiring him Gamaliel might have loathed him instead.

Madison was certain he had been a good and lenient master. From his youth he had believed that slavery was evil. But it was also a fixed part of the economy he had been born into; he might abhor it, but he could not do away with it. Yet it was within his power to soften it. When he began to accumulate wealth he resolved to mitigate slavery's effects in every way he could. Given the system he lived in he must rely on the labor of slaves; in these high valleys west of the Nantahalas, where population was sparse, there was no reliable free labor to be hired as there was in Macon and Haywood and Buncombe. But he resolved to treat each servant as he might an orphan child given into his care. He never sold a nigra family apart, in fact never sold any nigra at all. To the extent the customs of the country permitted, he did not make many of the distinctions others drew. He sweated with them at their tasks of labor and ate amongst them under the trees at dinnertime. He liberally granted passes for travel, permitted them to marry spouses domiciled at other places, taught them their letters, encouraged them in religion, let them rent themselves out for wages and save their money. He had even on two occasions permitted servants to buy themselves to freedom.

He shook his head in despair. Today, when Gamaliel appeared so unexpectedly, Madison had felt a surge of fondness for his old retainer; it cheered him to think that Gamaliel had come home. He'd even gently chaffed the fellow as of old. But now at the shank of the day, with his tribulations bearing him under, Madison felt desolate. Gamaliel had stood defiantly before him, not doffing his cap, gazing him straight in the eye, pointedly saying Mister and Miz instead of Marster and Mistress. The world was upside down. Menials treated generously all their lives ran away when you needed them most and then, once you were crushed in defeat, turned up full of ingratitude and spite to gloat at your misfortune. The government you had sustained with all your heart and with every cent of your fortune, and to which you had given the life of at least one of your sons, was now collapsing, and the dispersed soldiers of its beaten armies scavenged you like vultures, along with the bushwhackers and outliers and scouts marauding out of the mountains, till at last you looked with longing even to the Lincolnites, in hopes they might at least restore order and so grant you rest from the anxieties and cares that burdened your soul.

Assailed by this host of troubles Madison gave up any notion of selecting an edifying passage and instead resolved to try the old expedient of allowing the Good Book to speak of its own accord. He bent over it and opened its heavy bulk at random, cheating only to the extent that he divided it far enough toward the back to be certain of entering the more charitable New Testament, rather than the gloomy and portentous Old. His eye fell at once on the fifth chapter of the First Epistle of the apostle Paul to the Thessalonians:

> *But of the times and the seasons, brethren, ye have no need that I write unto you.*
>
> *For yourselves know perfectly that the day of the Lord so cometh as a thief in the night.*
>
> *For when they shall say, Peace and safety; then suddenly destruction cometh upon them, as travail upon a woman with child; and they shall not escape.*
>
> *But ye, brethren, are not in darkness, that that day should overtake you as a thief.*
>
> *Ye are all the children of light, and the children of the day: we are not of the night, nor of darkness.*
>
> *Therefore let us not sleep, as do others; but let us watch and be sober.*
>
> *For they that sleep sleep in the night; and they that be drunken be drunken in the night.*
>
> *But let us, who are of the day, be sober, putting on the breastplate of faith and love; and for a helmet, the hope of salvation.*
>
> *For God hath not appointed us to wrath, but to obtain salvation by our Lord Jesus Christ,*
>
> *Who died for us, that, whether we wake or sleep, we should live together with him.*

When Madison read those words a little later at evening devotionals, with the family gathered about him in the parlor, his wife Sarah bobbed quietly in her rocking chair, her mind not on the gospel at all but instead on her precious lost boys. For Sarah no comfort was to be had anymore from Scripture. Day after day she pondered her two dead sons and pined after them, and again and again she reproached herself for being a violent Rebel mother. Others she knew had urged their boys to avoid the war, to lay out, and had hidden them away from the conscript officers. But Sarah had spoken to hers of duty and honor. Proudly she'd sent Howell and Jack and Andy off to the army, and proudly she'd imagined them heroes and paragons of the Cause.

Had Sarah been less of a partisan her boys might be alive yet. But instead Howell slept in an unmarked grave in Tennessee and Jack had died a captive of the enemy—she knew this in her heart, although none had borne her the news—and poor Andy, her eldest, lay sick in far-off Alabama amid the wreck of a lost war. Where Andy was concerned Sarah also knew a kind of shame. He was a delicate and retiring sort where the others were hearty, and Sarah had always lavished on him care she thought the others did not need. Now the sons she had neglected were dead and the one she had doted on remained. She tormented herself with thoughts of how Jack and Howell might have longed for the mother's love they saw poured out only to Andy.

These were the notions in her head, not the teachings of the Word. It couldn't be part of some unknowable divine plan that her innocent boys—and all the other boys too—should die. It couldn't be that God was cruel enough to prove faith by inflicting such pain and loss. Instead she believed that God had little to do with any of it. God, she thought, was grieving at the works of man, to whom He had granted free will. It was the will of man that Howell and Jack were dead, not the will of God. Sarah was tempted to pray for God and not to Him. She thought God needed comfort just as she did.

CHAPTER 2

T he worst thing about getting wounded in the fight at
Bentonville was that he might've missed being paid.
The rumor was that after Bentonville General Johnston had used
the gold of the Confederate treasury to pay off the army. This was
supposed to have made President Davis as mad as a doused cat on
account of his wanting to use that money to continue the fight from
behind the Blue Ridge, or from Arkansas or Texas or down in the
Everglades, or maybe from someplace in Central America or
Timbuktu, so fierce and unconquerable was Old Jeff. Now that Rich-
mond had fallen the president and the cabinet were on a grand
skedaddle southward behind the lines of Johnston's army, but the
train with the treasure on it had got delayed and General Joe had
laid hold of it. Jeff Davis was a stubborn sort and didn't want to
admit to being licked, but Joe Johnston knew the war was gone up
for sure. Being a kindly soul he'd shared out the gold to his faithful
soldiers, rather than pass it on to the president. At least that's what

was being said around the Confederate hospital in Walhalla, where Oliver Price was laid up. So devoted was Oliver to General Joe that he believed that story right to the end of his long life.

Walhalla was a village of mostly German immigrants in the South Carolina upcountry, and after learning the meaning of its name—an officer told him it was called after the heaven the old-time Vikings thought they went to when they died—Oliver felt the name suited the melancholy business the war had brought down on it. The hospital was in a big white house that stood on a low hill amid a pinewoods, with a view of the mountains off to the west. A road of red sandy soil ran past it, and just down this road was a pretty church with a high steeple, Saint John's Lutheran. Now and then the womenfolk of the church came by to hand out *strudel* and raspberry-filled cookies they called *spitzbuben* and other treats. Most couldn't speak English and looked a little peculiar to Oliver on account of their braids wound above their ears; but they had kindly faces and the treats they brought were mighty tasty, so the boys all looked forward to the German ladies coming. However, many a soldier had expired in that hospital and many another was going to. But Oliver Price wasn't going to be one of them, thank God.

He could have used his portion of that gold, though. He had been paid only three times in the whole war, once in sixty-two and twice in sixty-three. He remembered that first payday fondly—sixty-five dollars and twenty-six cents he got, representing six months' service at a private's princely wage of eleven dollars a month, less seventy-four cents to cover the cost of a wooden F. J. Gardner canteen he'd lost. That was back when Confederate money was worth something. He'd sent the money home to Nancy, feeling like a bountiful provider, knowing it would buy seed for the farm and maybe some play-pretties for little Syl and little Martha. But he didn't even remember how much they'd paid him those two times in sixty-three. By then the stuff was only good for cleaning yourself up after doing your business. Last January Nancy had written him that a barrel of wheat flour cost five hundred dollars Confederate in Clayton.

The next worst thing about getting wounded was that it had happened at the very fag-end of things. Oliver had come unscathed through Kirby-Smith's march into Kentucky, the siege of Vicksburg, the battles around Chattanooga, all the fighting from Dalton down to Atlanta, even General Hood's terrible campaign on Nashville, only to fall on the last day of the last fuss. A minie ball had struck him in the right thigh and thank God missed the bone, but the medico at the little log field hospital had wanted to saw off his leg anyway, because that was all the medicos knew to do with a wounded extremity.

But it happened that just before getting hit Oliver had picked up a beautiful brass Henry's-patent repeating rifle he'd found lying on the ground next to a dead Yank officer. At once he'd thrown away his old Enfield musket in preference to the Henry, because that Henry would shoot sixteen times without reloading and its magazine was full of shiny brass cartridges. In military terms this had not been a wise thing to do, since Oliver possessed no more Henry cartridges than just the sixteen and had no means of getting others. But in medical terms it had proved a godsend, since while lying on the operating table he was able to trade the medico his Henry for his leg. He regretted losing that pretty gun but he was glad of keeping the leg.

Being an incurable optimist, Oliver also thought of some good things about being shot.

The first good thing was that he'd been wounded and not killed. The boys fell around him like persimmons shaken out of a tree when they made that charge on Mower's Yanks in the rain, and a good many of the poor fellows never got up again.

The second good thing was, it had happened in Carolina, not in a strange and scary far-off place like some he'd seen—Champion's Hill in Mississippi, or the swamps around Savannah, or the bleak hills of eastern Kentucky. Here, if he sat up on his cot and looked out the window, he could see the foothills of his own Blue Ridge in the distance, suspended in a soft haze. Not too far away lay his home at Rabun Gap, with Nancy and the younguns awaiting him, whom he had not seen since going home on his Vicksburg parole in the summer of sixty-three and whom he sorely, sorely missed. Syl would be five years old now and Martha nearly two, and Oliver sadly reflected how on account of the war he'd missed so much of the best of their growing up. Nor was there any way to measure the loss of all the delights he and Nancy might have shared.

The third good thing was, he'd been picked up by his own and not by the Yanks and so had been spared Elmira or some other awful prison. Of course the war was mostly over now, and he reckoned they'd have paroled him rather than put him in jail. But Oliver didn't want to run any risk at all on that score. He had messmates who had perished at Johnson's Island and Fort Delaware, and he dreaded the thought of lying up even a few days in such places with a festering wound that might turn gangrenous.

Yes, taking everything into account, Oliver thought himself a fortunate man. It was the Lord's own prodigious miracle that he'd survived the last three years. He'd seen some frightful things. He'd seen teams of horses hitched to a long line of blazing wagons with their manes and tails scorched off till they looked like rats, then he'd seen those horses burn alive. He'd seen a man with his leg blown away below the knee but his foot still attached by the heel-string, and he'd seen that man cut the heel-string with his pocketknife. He'd seen fellows shot clean in two, seen a man's head sitting in the crotch of a tree, seen one jasper holding his own innards in his arms. He'd seen a man shot through the head whose eyes popped out and dangled on their stalks. Right here in the Walhalla hospital, two cots over on the same row as Oliver, was a lad from Onslow County shot through the body whose pus and excrement came out of the holes in him whenever he tried to move his bowels.

Oliver felt humble and grateful to have come through it all with no more than a ball through his leg, when so many had died or been maimed so as to suffer torments the rest of their days. Mercifully he did not suspect that his wound would trouble him all his life, or that when he was seventy he would be so afflicted with sciatica, cramps, kidney trouble and rheumatism that from time to time he would have to walk with crutches or a cane and would have to seek a disability pension from the state of Georgia, because of being unable to support himself by his shoemaker's trade.

Oliver was wounded on Tuesday the twenty-first of March, which was the third day of the Bentonville scrap. The medical orderlies took him by mule-drawn wagon twenty miles over muddy roads to Mitchener's Station on the North Carolina Railroad, there being no ambulances with the army. In the wagon with him was an artilleryman with a bandage around his head who lay so quiet Oliver never knew if the jasper was alive or dead, and two boys from the Eighth Texas Cavalry who'd been hit by Mower's musket fire and were hallooing something awful. The wagon was fixed for two tiers of stretchers laid on crossbeams, and one of the Texans was right above Oliver and bled down on him the whole twenty miles as steady as a leaky spigot. That one was dead when they got to the railroad, and Oliver was so bloody by then that he looked dead too.

After that ambulance ride the trip to Greensboro on the cars seemed downright easy. Still, some of the boys in the burden car with Oliver were in truly pitiable condition, and there weren't any orderlies or nurses to care for them, and two of them passed away before the train reached Greensboro, which was a trip of about ninety miles that took twenty-two hours. This was because the track was in such poor shape that the locomotive hardly ever moved faster than a man might walk who was in a moderate hurry. At Greensboro Oliver spent the night in C.S.A. General Hospital No. 3, and the next day they put him back on the cars. That day he traveled only fifteen or twenty miles before they off-loaded him at a little place called High Point, which had a small hospital where he lay for a day and a night without anyone so much as speaking to him. Then they put him on the train again, and on Tuesday the twenty-eighth of March, one week to the day after being wounded, he was at C.S.A. General Hospital No. 11 in Charlotte. The whole time he'd been biting on his doubled-up haversack strap to keep from giving voice from the pain, and by the time he got to Charlotte he'd chewed both thicknesses of leather all the way through.

In Charlotte they finally cleaned out his wound, which by then was mortified and suppurating, and Oliver passed out. But they gave him a few drams of morphia, and in a day or two he began to improve. He'd always been tough as locust wood. On All Fools' Day he even felt robust enough to play a trick on the pretty raven-haired lady who was his nurse by pretending to have expired in the night. She was relieved to discover that he hadn't died after all but still gave him a scolding for scaring her.

On Tuesday the fourth of April, which was one week to the day after he arrived, the town of Charlotte went into an uproar because of Stoneman's Yankee cavalry raiding through the country nearby, and they put Oliver on another train, to Rutherfordton by way of the Wilmington, Charlotte & Rutherford Railroad. Now it happened that Oliver had been born twenty-eight years ago next July in the Duncan's Creek section of Rutherford County and had lived the first ten years of his life there, before his pappy removed across the Blue Ridge to Georgia, so he was not displeased to see that the fortunes of war were moving him by stages closer and closer to his home ground.

At Rutherfordton they put him in a train of ambulances headed southwest out of Stoneman's path, and this time, due no doubt to an oversight, he had an ambulance all to himself and rode in grand style. Oliver was elated to find that he was headed for the hospital at

Walhalla, which lay scant miles across Rabun Bald and the Chatuga River from the head of the Little Tennessee and home.

It took a little better than four days to travel the eighty miles to Walhalla. They went by way of Sandy Plain, and once into South Carolina Oliver kept peeking out the back of the ambulance to see the familiar rampart of the Blue Ridge rising in the west, wearing its shining wreath of sunlit mist. Down they went past the great notch of Saluda Gap and the ragged peak of Caesar's Head. *Home*, Oliver kept saying to himself while he drank in the sight of the mountains. *Home, home.*

Oftentimes fond thoughts came to Oliver of his friends the Madison Curtises, yonder in Clay County at the far corner of Carolina, beyond the Blue Ridge and the Nantahala Mountains. An honest and virtuous man was Judge Curtis, and so free of any distinctions of class that he'd welcomed Oliver into his home and granted him respect, though he was master of more than five hundred acres of fine plantation land and before the war had owned several nigras, while Oliver was but a humble cobbler.

Oliver met the judge's two oldest boys at Cumberland Gap in sixty-two when their outfits were brigaded together in Kirby-Smith's corps. Enviously he'd listened as Jack and Andy spoke with reverence of their home in the valley of the Hiwassee at the foot of the Tusquittees. There was such rapture in their talk that Oliver caught fire with a wish to see the place they held so dear. What he called his farm, at the foot of Rabun Gap, he rented from his mama on shares; he longed for a spot of ground to name his own, in a new and bountiful land.

Coming back to the army after his Vicksburg parole, he went by way of Clay County with a notion of seeing whether he might settle in this paradise when peace came. The judge took Oliver to his heart partly on account of his boys and partly because of the fineness of his soul, which saw no difference between himself and one of Oliver's ilk. And Oliver found the valley of the Hiwassee more splendid than even Jack and Andy had sworn, though much despoiled by war, for the region lay in the track of robber bands posing as regular troops. Indeed, the very day Oliver arrived, a party of bushwhackers came raiding and fetched up in Judge Curtis's dooryard and put to the ordeal his beloved wife of many years. To save her, the judge inclined them against two of his thieving tory neighbors. By this trick the Curtises were spared, but a clan of scavengers by the name of Puckett got wiped out by the raiders. Repenting himself of having caused this slaughter, the judge besought Oliver to go and warn the other bunch he'd named. Oliver done so, and afterwards he found himself cherished as much by the judge and his good woman Sarah and their six daughters as by the boys, his army pals.

It wasn't hard to say what lay behind the devotion for the Curtises in Oliver's breast. Oliver was accustomed to the scorn of men of property. All his life he'd felt their contempt. But these Curtises, for all their learning and station, took him at his own measure. The judge declared he wanted Oliver for a neighbor at war's end, just as if Oliver were a squire and not the mudsill the prosperous men of Rabun County had long ignored. To shower such regard on one so common was to Oliver an act of grace such as Jesus mentioned in the Gospels.

Oliver knew tragedy had touched the Curtises since. Just before the battle of Resaca he'd walked the whole length of the Army of Tennessee to find Jack and Andy and learned of the death of their youngest brother Howell the previous winter in a cavalry skirmish near Knoxville. Surely that had been an awful blow to the judge and Miz Sarah; its dire mark was plain on the brothers. Now nearly a year had passed and Oliver had heard not a word of the Curtises. What nagged him was that Jack looked sickly that night before Resaca, and Oliver thought from his fever and rash that he might've taken a case of the measles. What a pity it would be if the Curtises had lost Jack and Howell both, and how much harder if Andy too had fallen. Nor were the home folk themselves free of peril; Clay County still swarmed with dangerous renegades and outliers.

It was a torment not to know the situation of these kind and decent people. One of the worst features of the war was how persons one loved could suddenly vanish, never to be seen again, their fate an eternal mystery. In his nightly prayers Oliver always beseeched the Lord to shield the Curtises from harm. He also pled Jesus to grant him his dream now that the war was as good as over and lead him by-and-by into the Hiwassee Valley, where he might take up some of that rich land and farm.

The first morning in the hospital at Walhalla Oliver was awakened by a bumblebee noisily rummaging in the pearly blossoms of a laurel bush outside his opened window. He watched the bee at work, marveling that the world was allowing it the leisure so freely to sip its nectar. Oliver had seen battlefields so devastated by shellfire and musketry that not a grasshopper dared leap nor a chickadee sing, had the poor creatures even survived to ponder such acts. At Smithfield, just before they marched down to Bentonville, twenty-four men answered the roll call in Oliver's Company G of the Thirty-ninth Georgia Infantry. Oliver remembered that three years and one month before, when the company was made up at Ellijay in north Georgia, a hundred and fourteen fellows had stood in the ranks. Of that number only three were left at Smithfield besides Oliver himself. There was J. A. Bradley and there was Third Sergeant William Osborne and there was Jeremiah Sims. The other twenty were all conscripts or transfers. The rest were gone.

Mentally he reviewed their melancholy fates. John Parks, captured at Cassville. Martin Ayers, captured at Dalton. Linzey Bramblow, killed at Tunnel Hill. Alfred Bishop, dead of camp fever, Chattanooga. William Cantrell, killed at Vicksburg. George Potts, dead of measles, Chattanooga. Ben Vendergriff, deserted. Jacob White, deserted. Elbert Weaver, deserted. Sam Tucker, deserted. Leonard Hyde, deserted.

Things got so bad in Cumming's brigade that the Thirty-fourth and Fifty-sixth Georgia had to be consolidated with the Thirty-ninth just to make up enough of a crowd to call it a regiment. Otherwise it would've looked like a color guard. On the field at Bentonville the whole of Cumming's brigade had hardly added up to two hundred fellows, while in early sixty-two when Oliver joined the war a brigade was sometimes nearly two thousand strong. Even General Cumming himself was gone, shot down at Jonesborough, and there had been two other brigade commanders since. Oliver could remember four different colonels that had commanded the Thirty-ninth since J. T. McConnell, whom the boys elected at Ellijay so long ago. There might have been others, but Oliver couldn't recall them.

Death in battle had been the rarest of the perils that stalked them. Had it been less rare they might have stood things better, for a man can muster the courage to risk dying quick and in hot blood, in the fight. Oliver didn't think the fellows that deserted or laid out had done so from fear of dying in battle, but instead from fear of wasting away of camp fever or the bloody flux or pneumonia, or of starving on short rations, or freezing in the wintry blasts, or falling of heat stroke in summertime. These were the hardest fates, and not many had the grit to face them, not when the letters from home kept telling of want and hard times and were full of entreaties that a man's place was by his hearth caring for his kin.

No, if war was mostly fighting, Oliver thought the fellows would have stuck it out. The great lessons he had learned were that a fight could make men behave like gods as well as devils, and that sometimes there was a kind of glory in it to be found nowhere else. This was not something he cared to speak about but was nevertheless something he knew to be true.

At the battle of Nashville the Thirty-ninth Georgia had been in reserve behind Holtzclaw's brigade on Overton's Hill when the Thirteenth United States Colored Troops came marching up out of the fog and sleet to attack Holtzclaw's men behind their breastworks, and those Alabama jaspers commenced to scream in that high way they always did when they faced nigra troops and started shooting them down by the dozens, but still the nigras came on as calm and regular as if on parade, closing ranks as more and more of them went down, and the Alabamians screamed higher and kept on shooting, but the nigras kept coming on. The Alabamians killed five separate colorbearers, each one picking up the flag from the last and advancing it, till the final one climbed on the head log and shook it in their faces before they could shoot him too, and then Oliver saw General Holtzclaw open up both his arms wide, the right one with sword in hand, open his arms as if to embrace all those brave nigra boys his men were shooting down, and he saw General Holtzclaw weep. In that moment Oliver knew that those colored boys and General Holtzclaw were all gods together, even while those screaming Alabamians played the devil.

Oliver penned one note to Nancy and another to his mama and posted them both by a hog drover who was passing over the Blue Ridge toward Franklin. He told of his wound and gave his whereabouts, expecting he would lie up at Walhalla for a spell and the folks would want to come for a visit. But two days after this the medicos told him he was as healed as he was likely to get and said he could leave anytime. So on the following Saturday, when he looked up from his wheelchair to see his eldest brother Lit coming up the steps of the hospital gallery, Oliver was free to go home.

It seemed a queer notion, to be free and going home. The war was pretty much done now—paroled soldiers everywhere were claiming that Lee had given up in Virginia and Joe Johnston was negotiating with Sherman in North Carolina—yet no official had turned up to extract from Oliver his oath of allegiance to the United States of America. So when he left Walhalla Oliver was an unredeemed Rebel. He would remain one for the next forty-nine years, and would be buried in 1914 in the Old Methodist Church Cemetery at Sugar Valley in Gordon County, Georgia, without having cast a vote since the election of 1860. He often said that if General Carter Stevenson, his old division commander, had ever stood for office in either party he might've taken the oath and cast a ballot, since the general was the grandest man he'd ever known. But of course General Stevenson never ran, and Oliver never voted.

Lit took Oliver home in the same old farm wagon Oliver remembered loading up with hay and ears of corn and shocks of wheat before the war. The same two mules, Whitey and Old Molasses, were in the traces and looked as superior as ever. Spring was coming to the mountains, and as the road carried them into the fastnesses Oliver gazed long at the yellow plumes of the poplars and the russet of the budding chestnuts and the bright lace of the first growth on the locusts. These covered the lower slopes like a thick cloak of moss thrown over the ridges, while farther up, the high tops still showed dull gray, because the cold up there had so far kept the hardwoods bare. Up yonder the black spikes of the spruces and balsams snaggled the sky like teeth. In the forest nearby floated the cottony dogwoods and the orange blossoms of flame azaleas. White trilliums and irises blue as indigo nodded by the roadside. Laurel bloomed in the branch heads, and the new leaves of the rhododendron reached out like small white-green hands. The woods were alive with redbirds and robins and little gray juncos and jays that fussed at them from the overhanging branches. Ground squirrels dashed across the track in front of them with their tiny tails saucily erect. Somewhere nearby the mountain folk were burning off the brush to start the fresh green for the cows, and Oliver could smell the tart fragrance of wood smoke. The smoke lay a soft film over everything, and behind that film the far crags dimly glowed like old gold.

They stopped that night and camped by the road, and through a break in the trees Oliver saw in the distance the red necklaces of the fires encircling the black throats of the hills. The woods shrilled with the songs of tree frogs. All this was just as Oliver remembered, and it seemed impossible and marvelous to him that it had all stood here waiting, untouched and unchanged, while a terrible war raged around it for four long years. He had the strange feeling it had waited that way just for him. Yet now that he had survived and come back he felt a great sadness, thinking how completely the war had changed him, while the mountains he loved had remained so much the same. He suspected that he and they could never again be as they had been before, each to the other. He feared he had lost his place in their heart and would not find it again, and so for much of the trip he rode on the wagon melancholy and unspeaking.

The homeplace was nearer than Oliver's own, so they stopped off there at the top of the gap to let Oliver see his mama. He found her sunk in her bentwood rocker on the porch wearing the same exasperated scowl as always. Jane Sims Price was seventy-four and hard and bony and had been displeased about something or other since about 1811, which was when she'd married Oliver's pappy John J. at Duncan's Creek in Carolina. His dying a few years back had not relieved her any either. She spied Oliver and through the blisters of her cataracts watched him fierce as a hawk while he limped awkwardly toward the porch. Every development seemed to her a fresh affliction to join the crowd of troubles that had plagued her throughout life, and this was no exception; she regarded Oliver as sourly as if he were a case of gallstones. "Well," she declared, "I see they had to shoot you to get you to quit."

Oliver could think of no reply to that and only meted out a

respectful smile. She was not given to affection, so he shook the clawlike hand she extended and then took the empty chair next to her.

"Hit's high time," she remarked. "You already missed the best of the planting season."

Jane Price had borne twelve live children, five of them boys—Littleton the oldest, called Lit, and Michael McCurry, called Mac, and then Freddy and Archie and last of all Oliver himself. Freddy and Archie and Oliver had gone to the war. Being so much older Lit and Mac stayed back, and the conscript officers never got them. But the war proved hard on the Prices who wore the gray. Freddy died of a fever he picked up at the siege of Vicksburg, and Archie was shot in the right leg at Chickamauga and came home an invalid, and here was Oliver as good as crippled too.

Mama shook her narrow head enclosed in its calico sunbonnet. "How'll you provide for that woman and your children, now you're busted up?"

There was indignation in her sigh. To her the whole business with the Yanks was a rich man's war and a poor man's fight. She figured the slavers ought to have been the ones to bleed, not a shoemaker like Oliver and her farmer boys Freddy and Archie. At the outbreak she'd been as hard against the Yanks as any; the night before Oliver left to enroll she'd fixed him a fine going-away dinner and pronounced herself proud of him, and of Freddy and Archie too. Now she thought they were just fools that had wasted themselves. But after the last four years nobody was any longer what they'd been before, Oliver himself least of all.

While Oliver tried to think of something to say Lit came up the steps and leaned on the porch railing. Oliver asked after Nancy and the younguns, and Mama said Syl and Martha were thriving. "But that woman taken a cough last winter and ain't shook it yet." She gave Oliver a grim look. "Hit's got the death-sound to me, if you want to know." She leaned and spat a brown stream of snuff over the railing into the shrubbery.

"I don't know if it's as bad as all that," Lit said. "But she is poorly." That was Oliver's homecoming.

At first matters proved far sweeter at the place Oliver rented from his mama down by the Little Tennessee at the mouth of Darnell Creek. Syl and Martha burst out of the cabin like colts, and he took them up, one under each arm, and covered them with kisses, and when Nancy came forth dusted with cornmeal he searched close to see if what his mama had said was true, but he saw only the dazzle of her smile and the tears of joy she'd begun to shed. That night, tenderly and a little shyly, they had congress together amid the familiar rustle of the corn-shuck tick while the younguns slept outside in the empty corncrib under quilts, and in every way Nancy felt and behaved the same, and Oliver was relieved. But toward morning he awoke to find her gone from the bed, and giving in to dread he arose and went in quest of her and found her crouching by the creek with blood spattering the front of her nightgown, coughing a deep rattling cough that had in it the very note his mama had described. He knelt and drew her close, and they rocked to and fro on the bank of the creek in the morning fog, and he sang to her a little tune he had learned in Tennessee from a Toe River man:

> I had a piece of pie
> And I had a piece of puddin'
> I gave it all away
> To hug Sally Goodin.
>
> I went up a hillside
> Saw my Sally comin'
> Thought to my soul
> I'd kill myself a-runnin'.

Chapter 3

The last that Andy Curtis saw of the war was the burning sea oats and palmetto logs on the earthworks northeast of Spanish Fort, where the Yanks had broken through. It was midnight and pitch-black, and like everybody else in what was left of Ector's brigade Andy was retreating along the footbridge over the bayou. Looking back he saw the sharp tops of the sawgrass outlined like black bayonets against the fires. Beyond, the fires themselves glimmered like so many red jewels strung together, like a choker of rubies lying on a lady's bosom. By the golden trails of burning fuses Andy could follow the mortar shells as they rose slowly from the Yank positions in the east and made rainbow shapes in the sky before accelerating to descend quickly into the fort itself, and now and then another explosion would light up the black like daylight. At this distance the explosions made tender thumping noises that sounded harmless, as if a child were idly pounding on a tom-tom in the attic of a house a ways off.

As he trotted along the yielding treadway Andy smelled the salt marsh of Bayou Minette all around him. It was an agreeable fragrance after the stench of burnt powder and the acrid odor of fire that had filled the traverses, but still it was alien to his mountain-bred soul. Everything about this briny swamp outside Mobile had felt strange and ominous from the first; he was glad to be leaving it. He was also pleased that his premonition of dying at Spanish Fort— a notion which came on him so strong when he first entered the place that he could actually see his dead flesh before him, white like marble—had proved wrong. He dared entertain an idea now that he might survive this war, despite the malarial fever that continued to afflict him and despite all the powers of Yankeedom—and the Confederacy too—arrayed alike against him.

Of course he could not know that his glimpse of the fiery earthworks behind him in the night was the last he'd see of the hostilities. As far as he knew General Maury and General Gibson were going to keep on fighting for Mobile from the Blakeley fortifications and from Battery Tracy and Battery Huger and Fort Sidney Johnston and all the other emplacements around the bay. He figured this retreat was just part of a redeployment. Andy was accustomed to redeployments. Sometimes it seemed to him that all he'd done since the battle of Resaca was redeploy. He'd redeployed all the way from Resaca to Atlanta and then from Atlanta to Nashville and back, and now he was redeploying from Spanish Fort to some other place that he didn't even know about yet but whose name would soon acquire a grim resonance, just like all the others. The laughing boy he'd been before the war would have seen the joke in all these redeployments, but humor was now as far beyond his reach as peace of mind or the comfort of his body.

Presently he came to the end of the treadway at the steamboat landing on Bayou Conway. Here several burning torches had been stuck in the ground and fastened to the pier, and in their fitful light

Captain Bristol was trying to rally what remained of Company E of the Thirty-ninth North Carolina Infantry. Although Company E now consisted also of the remnants of Companies A, B, C and D, there were only two dozen or so fellows left to gather around Captain Bristol and hear him say they must board the approaching gunboat in an orderly fashion, and the boat would then carry them across to safety in Mobile.

The gunboat was the same little tinclad that had supported their position in the fortifications with fire from its twelve-pounder howitzers. Andy and the others eyed it doubtfully as it approached the landing with its sidewheels churning tracks of white foam in the black water. There were open seams in it through which you could see the glow of its fireboxes, and its smokestacks belched alarming quantities of sparks, and it made alternate wheezing and throbbing sounds that were not reassuring. But for all its flaws it was clearly an improvement over Spanish Fort, and they boarded without any delay whatsoever, they and the boys from the Washington Artillery of New Orleans and Phillips's and Lumsden's batteries, which had all been run out of the fort together.

On the crowded deck of the gunboat Andy bumped up against Danny Davis and saw in the torchlight that Danny had lost his musket. As a sergeant Andy felt compelled to upbraid Danny for this loss to the Confederate treasury. "Where-at's your weapon?" he demanded with a show of authority he didn't feel.

But after being chased out of the fort Danny was in a disagreeable frame of mind. "Go to hell," he replied. "You lost a bayonet yourownself."

Woefully this was true, and since he wasn't sure Danny would need his musket anyhow, Andy concluded not to pursue the matter after all. Instead he found himself a spot in the stern of the boat and settled there with his legs hanging over the edge and his bare feet trailing in the water. He was burning with a flareup of fever, and the cold water felt good. He hugged himself, shivering while the baleful glow of Spanish Fort receded farther and farther into the night, till it resembled a small red carbuncle set against the vast black.

Danny Davis came and sat next to him to show he bore no hard feelings. They mused awhile without speaking, and in the silence Andy's thoughts turned as always to his younger brother Jack, left behind on the field at Resaca sick with measles, from whom no further word had come in nearly twelve months' time. By chance Danny Davis had Jack in mind at this same moment, and remarked he hoped Jack would be alive to see the war end, as it now seemed it must.

Eagerly Andy nodded. He was certain Jack had survived and was waiting out the war in some Federal prison. Andy only hoped he was being well treated—there were bad stories a man could hear about those Northern pens. But there could be no doubt that Jack still lived, no doubt at all. Jack had always been the most vigorous of the Curtis brood, more alive than any two or three of the others put together. He was guileful too, and would have found a way to keep going no matter how hard his case. And besides, Andy needed him. Jack was Andy's rock. The only thing that had kept Andy from losing his nerve this last year was the notion that Jack was alive somewhere and would one day come to him grinning and tweak his nose as before and call him by his pet name Bud and ask him how he had borne up. He wanted to be able to give a good account of himself when that happened, because he was not naturally a brave man—was in fact something of a coward—and the war had scared him worse than he'd ever been scared in his life. So earnestly had he striven to win a good name that the boys in Company E voted him into the Roll of Honor for showing valor on the field of battle, another outcome he would have laughed at had he still been the heedless merry lad of peacetime. Andy had given no thought at all to the notion that Jack might be dead. It was a prospect he dared not entertain.

For four days Andy and the forty-five hundred other boys left of General Maury's force worked to dismantle the fortifications around Mobile. Why the works needed dismantling with the war just about done, nobody seemed to know; it made more sense to let the Yankees do it. Then on the twelfth of April they evacuated Mobile and marched to Cuba Station near Meridian in Mississippi.

On this march Andy saw General Nathan Bedford Forrest ride past. He knew the famous cavalryman from seeing his likeness on the cover of a magazine. Had the general not shown such a forbidding aspect—he wore a ferocious scowl, and his long white hair with black ends blew about like the coiling snakes on the head of Medusa—Andy would have been tempted to approach him and ask if he remembered his youngest brother Howell. Andy knew from a letter Howell had written home that he'd served the general as a courier during the battle of Chickamauga. This was shortly before Howell was killed at Philadelphia, Tennessee. But the sight of that awesome face reminded Andy of the tales he'd heard of Forrest's violent and unpredictable nature, so he only watched wistfully after him, thinking as Forrest doubled the column on his black stallion that a living Howell had once observed that bony powerful figure and felt that piercing gaze. Besides, he knew his urge for a foolish one. He felt it was a pity that while the dead lived on only in the memories of the living, great men like Forrest would remember none of the hundreds who'd died in their service. It remained for ordinary persons to remember the dead that the great never even noticed.

At Cuba Station Lieutenant General Dick Taylor assumed command from General Maury. Danny Davis, who knew a little about everything, said Taylor was the son of a president of the United States, General Zachary Taylor from the war with Mexico, Old Rough and Ready. One day Andy saw the new general talking in solemn fashion with Colonel Coleman, commander of the Thirty-ninth; General Dick Taylor had a dark spade beard and sad eyes and the pale coloring of a dyspeptic. But then nobody of high rank was looking very spruce these days. There were rumors everywhere that the Virginia army had quit and Joe Johnston's was nearly played out, and that Taylor's army and the army that General Kirby-Smith commanded out west were the only two Confederate forces not yet surrendered or whipped to a frazzle. If the Confederacy was indeed going up the spout all high officers had reason to fear being tried and hanged for treason by the vengeful Yanks. But as it turned out it was not their possible fates as ex-Rebels that was troubling the general and Colonel Coleman that day; in the evening Colonel Coleman called assembly and read out a notice from General Taylor saying that Abraham Lincoln had been assassinated.

There were a few cheers, but these were quickly shouted down, and the whole of the Thirty-ninth then stood wrapped in deep thought. For four years Lincoln had been the very demon of the Yankee nation, pushing the war with a fanatic determination. Yet the whole time every Southerner also sensed in him a sort of sorrowing clemency held in abatement, like that of an indulgent father awaiting the return of his wayward children. You felt that when the Union was restored Old Abe would kill the fatted calf and welcome the prodigals to his bosom. Now he was dead, shot down by a Southern man. Waiting to grasp the reins of power were all the rabid forces of abolition and radical reconstruction intent on crushing every last Rebel in all of Dixie. Thinking of this the boys in the ranks stirred uneasily.

Meantime, Colonel Coleman continued to speak out General Taylor's message: Now that Lee had yielded, the South had little hope of success. But as long as General Johnston remained in the field it was the duty of Taylor's army to fight its way to him. The president and civil authorities of the Confederate government were on their way south and needed protection. "Granting the cause for which we have fought to be lost," Colonel Coleman read, "we owe it to our own manhood, to the memory of the dead and to the honor of our arms to remain steadfast to the last."

"I'm going home," said Danny Davis.

"Me too," said Andy.

But in spite of themselves they stayed on. Colonel Coleman was keeping a close watch, and Forrest's provost troops were everywhere. And besides, a convenient opportunity never arose. It was also possible that they did hold somewhat in mind their manhood, the memory of the dead and the honor of their arms, after all. In the end it was not even necessary to skedaddle. General Taylor surrendered them to the Yankee general Canby at Citronelle, Alabama, on the fourth of May. On the ninth Andy Curtis signed his parole at Meridian, Mississippi. That same day he set off afoot for home. With him were the other Clay County fellows from Company E—Louis Atkins, J. T. Webb, John Robins, Nicholas McFalls and the Bowers cousins Tommy and Jim and Tony.

Danny Davis was from Buncombe County and planned to go home with a different party. William Crisp, another old messmate, was from Murphy and was going later with some of the other Cherokee County boys. It was sad saying good-bye after four years of hardship and danger. Memories of their lost friends Johnny Deal and Henry Jackson, Lieutenant Grear, Marcus Magaha, Moses Fulbright, Hiram Stephenson and many others were much in their minds as they parted. They also knew without saying it that nothing in their lives to come would ever be as grand and terrible as what they had just lived through, and that they could never again be the same boys they were at the start. For good or ill they were changed forever, and in a way everything that happened to them from now on would be a disappointment.

Because Andy was ill on and off with fever and none of them had money to buy passage on the stage, it was a slow tramp home. But finally, toward the end of May, they came to Blairsville in north Georgia, and on the other side of Blairsville they took the turnoff past Track Rock and Mount Eolia, so that by nightfall they were in the gap by Brasstown Bald overlooking the valley of the Hiwassee. They made camp there in the gap to wait for morning. But thinking of home and loved ones they lay sleepless with excitement all night long. Sometime past midnight Andy got up and stood watching the play of heat lightning in the sky above the Tusquittees. At every silent flash he could see the outlines of the clouds and the peaks of the far mountains. The light flickered over the features of the gap and over Andy himself and his friends. He thought of the same light flickering over his home and through its windows and perhaps awakening his wife Salina from her sleep, so that she would be watching it too, as he watched it from the gap.

Next morning they crossed into Carolina and parted company to disperse each to his own place. Andy came home just past noontime on Saturday the twenty-seventh of May. Rounding the curve in the old wagon road from Hayesville he caught sight of the house on the point of its hill, and beyond it the line of the river marked by a row of birches and sycamores thin as tatting, and back of that the gentle lift of the south bank all covered with new green, and finally in the far distance the mountains he had just crossed, each range a paler blue than the last, behind a bright veil of haze.

He stopped in the road to look. He had been strong for a very long time, much longer than he had ever thought possible. It had been a dreadful strain on him, trying to be strong when in reality he was weak. He was tired of the pretense and was glad the need for it was gone. Now he could account himself proudly to Jack when he saw him. But he need not be strong anymore. He was home. At home the others would be strong for him. Mama would be strong and Papa would be strong and Salina would be strong and Jack would be strong. And he would rest.

But his homecoming proved far from the joyous occasion he expected, for his sister Betty lay sick in the second week of typhoid fever, with the rose spots already blooming on her belly and her wits gone in delirium and her limbs jerking with convulsions. Her husband Bill Cartman had at last ventured down out of the mountains, where he had laid out the whole war hiding from the enrolling officers, but he had brought the typhoid down with him. Bill himself had been dead two days already and lay beneath a mound of red dirt in the family graveyard on the nose of the hill overlooking the river.

When Andy came along the path toward the house Salina was in the yard with Bill and Betty's two boys, showing them how to trim the boxwoods. She meant to turn their minds away from sickness and death, but they were as uninterested in sickness and death as they were in trimming boxwoods; they chased each other in and out of the double row of bushes yelling while Salina plied the shears. At first she stood and stared at Andy without knowing him, so shaggy and ramshackle was he. Then she smiled and thanked God and came to him not hurrying but in a stately way that showed she'd always been confident of his return. She was nut-brown and thin as a rail but looked strong; she hugged him with arms like iron pipes, and when she kissed him she tasted somewhat like roast lamb, as he now recalled she always had. Little Jimmy and little Andy in their identical dirty smocks took him by the legs, demanding to be picked up. Papa came out of the house looking weary and wan and grasped Andy's hand in both of his and spoke of what had happened. Then he made Andy wait on the gallery while he went inside to fetch Mama, and Mama came from the sickroom smelling of Betty's fever-sweats and stood off at a distance for fear of communicating the disease. She wept and called his name and pitifully wrung her hands in her soiled apron. Andy was stricken at the sight of her, for he remembered her withy and tough as mountain creeper, while what he saw before him was a frail old woman with her chin atremble.

She led him inside with a cloth over his mouth to the downstairs bedroom, where Betty lay insensible. He looked in at her pearly death's-head face sweating on the pillow amid a spread of soggy hair and soon came out again. On the gallery his other sisters bade him sad hello. He asked after Jack's Mary Jane and learned she'd gone home to her grandmother's in Jackson County, Georgia, with little Alec and baby Sarah. He played in a melancholy way with the Cartman boys and dandled Martha's Eva on his knee and wondered out loud where Martha's husband Sanders might be, but no one knew.

Just before suppertime a Negro came down the path and settled on his hams in the turnaround, and Andy saw with surprise that it was Black Gamaliel. Papa told him Gamaliel had come home to share-crop and had changed his name and wanted to be called Daniel McFee. Andy went out to the turnaround, and Gamaliel stood but did not remove his cap and was wearing Yankee blue from head to foot. He'd come to pay respects to Miz Cartman in her suffering, he said. It was good to see him even wearing the bluebird uniform, for Gamaliel had helped usher Andy into young manhood taking him fishing in the Hiwassee and hunting game in the wilds of the Tusquittees.

Andy had owed Bill Cartman ten dollars and seventy cents at five percent interest since April of 1860. It was a debt he'd contracted before their differences over secession divided them and Bill abandoned his family to secret himself in the high tops. But Bill wasn't going to collect now. And neither was Betty, whom Bill in his heedless way had fatally infected. So just before family devotionals Andy went into Papa's study and wrote out a new note for the loan in the names of the two Cartman boys and had Papa witness it and file it among his important papers.

At devotionals Papa read from the fourteenth chapter of the Gospel of John, the part where Jesus says God's house has many mansions and Jesus is going there to prepare a place for those that believe in Him, and also the part that talks about Jesus being the Way, the Truth and the Life. Mama wasn't present on account of sitting up with Betty, so they ended devotionals by filing down the hall to the door of Betty's bedroom, where they stood with cloths over their faces while Papa rendered a prayer.

Later Salina made up a potion out of bloodroot and sassafras for Andy's fever. While he was drinking this she dragged the old tin bathtub into the front upstairs bedroom and filled it with water heated on the wood stove in the summer kitchen. He settled gratefully into the bath and soaked his sore limbs and blistered feet while Salina gently washed him with a soapy sponge. She lingered over his long brunet hair, which she had always thought as smooth and fine as silk. She kissed his ears and chin and the lids of his eyes and finally his soft mouth. It had been a long time since Andy had felt any comfort or the soft touch of love. Sitting in his bath he began to weep, and Salina wept with him. Crouching by the tub she drew his wet head against her bosom and rocked it like a babe.

Twelve days later Betty was seized with awful abdominal pains, and two days after that she mercifully passed on. She had not recognized Andy once. Mama and the older girls washed her poor wasted body while Andy and his papa hammered together a rude coffin out of waste lumber. They buried her on the nose of the hill next to Bill. Papa conducted the ceremony in so firm and serene a manner that everyone marveled at how perfectly he'd bent to God's terrible will. Mama was a different case and was prostrated with grief and called on the Almighty in a censorious voice to show mercy and loving kindness to them that yet lived, now that He'd seen fit to carry off her eldest and the good man who'd married her, leaving two orphan boys in a merciless world. The boys themselves looked on wondering. Gamaliel—Daniel McFee—who had a fine bass voice, sang a hymn.

As Papa pronounced the benediction, they all heard a crunch of gravel in the drive and looked up to see two women riding double on an old dun mule coming slowly down to the turnaround, where they stopped and watched stolidly across the distance. They wore dresses of grimy homespun and slatless sunbonnets, and the one in front was old and smoking a pipe. "Have ye got misfortune, I wonder?" this one cried in a cawing voice like a crow. "Iffen ye do, I rejoice in hit."

To Andy's astonishment Papa regarded them impassively. Salina and the girls ignored them with an air of embarrassment. Even Mama seemed to turn a deaf ear. Appalled by what the old woman had said, Andy started to go and run them off, but Salina touched his arm and stopped him. "It's the Puckett women," she explained, "from Fires Creek. They've come before."

The Pucketts were tories. They had favored Union in the war and had raided their Rebel neighbors without pity till a gang of bushwhackers posing as Federal rangers wiped out their menfolk a year ago last fall. Andy was home on sick furlough then, and when the bushwhackers stopped by the Curtis place Papa—knowing they'd hang Andy if they found him—hid him in the springhouse and when they commenced torturing Mama sent them on to the Pucketts. He said the Pucketts were hot old Rebels secreting great riches they'd stolen from tory homes, while the Curtises were blessed Unionists that loved Old Abe. Papa's lie had saved Andy but cost the Pucketts five dead and all the treasure they'd robbed from others.

"Is hit only two that's dead yit?" the old woman jeered. "Why, two ain't nothin'."

The younger one behind her repeated in a flat voice, "Nothin'."

The old one cackled a dry laugh. "My boy was hanged up by the neck with a plowline to strangle, and me a-watchin' him kick. My youngest they cut all to pieces with knives, then they hanged him too till he shat and stunk. They shot my man so his head come open and his brains all fell out on the ground. My brother . . ."

At last Papa spoke up. "That's enough, now." Yet he could muster no real indignation, and Andy knew why; he suffered guilt for the massacre his subterfuge had brought on the Pucketts. Even as he admonished them he could not look at them, but gazed at the ground instead, ashamed.

Of course the old woman did not stop. "My brother, they shot him three times in the lungs so he was a week a-dyin'. A tapeworm twenty foot long come out of him. And my cousin, they shot him in the face till his own mother wouldn't know him. All this thanks to ye. I want to tell ye, I mean to come a-gloatin' every time fate strikes ye a blow. Ye ain't forgettin' what ye done, not whilst I live."

And the one behind her echoed, "Not whilst we live."

They waited there awhile longer rudely laughing and then turned the mule and rode slowly up the drive and away. After they had gone Papa said a prayer for them, and everyone but Andy said amen to it.

Early in June Papa wrote to Washington City asking for any news the Yankee War Department might have of Jack, who had still not come home. Toward the end of the month he received a letter from a major in the adjutant general's office reporting that Joseph T. Curtis, twenty-two years of age, prisoner no. 541, hospital no. 6252, private, Company E, Thirty-ninth North Carolina Infantry, had died of measles on June the sixth, 1864, and was buried on that date in grave no. 7954 of the city cemetery in Nashville, Tennessee. What Andy had never allowed himself to believe was now shown to be true. Jack would not be tweaking his nose and calling him Bud anymore. Andy did not know what to do with himself. To whom was he to give his accounting now?

CHAPTER 4

Mama was right, he'd missed the best of the planting season. There was a patch of sweet corn that Nancy had started as best she could, and a few rows of potatoes and cabbages and peas and snap beans. But on account of her sickness Nancy had not felt fit enough to tend things regular. The shoots looked mighty spindly to Oliver, and anyhow the rabbits and deer had been at them and a flourishing crop of weeds was threatening to swallow them up entirely. To make matters worse the parching heat and dry air felt to Oliver like a drought coming on.

Not that they'd ever made a living farming, even before the war. Oliver had a seven-year contract with his mama for a third of his corn and small grain, but now it looked doubtful whether they could even grow enough to keep themselves in provisions through the winter, much less pay Mama her due. Despairing, Oliver made an inventory of the place. In the pantry there was a crock of ginseng that

Nancy had dug in the woods last fall, which might fetch a few pennies at the market in Clayton. He found two jars of chestnuts and some ramps Nancy had picked and chopped and some galax leaves and a mess of herbs—lobelia and Solomon's-seal, bloodroot, angelica, liverwort and such. Things looked grim indeed.

Crippled as he was from his leg wound Oliver spent his first week home weeding his little patch of ground, and snaring rabbits in the evening, and using his pappy's old brass-trimmed Harpers Ferry flintlock from the War of 1812 to scare away deer, and making a thousand awkward trips back and forth on his crutch from the springhouse to water the shoots, all in hopes of saving the poor crop that Nancy had put in. Then he carried Nancy's ginseng and chestnuts and herbs into town on market day and came home that night with two dollars and fifty-seven cents in Yankee coin.

The next day he went behind the cabin and unlashed the latchstring of the plank shed he'd built in 1857 but had not entered in three long years, and stepped inside to breathe its remembered odors of dry cedar from the roof shakes and old rosin from the pine walls and raw cowhides hanging from the joists and tanned leather stacked on the shelves. He parted the oilskin curtains on the one window and let in a shaft of sunlight in which dust motes swarmed like pollinated gold. The light shone down on the table in the middle of the shed with its clutter of shoe lasts and paper patterns and folded hides, and it awoke a dull gleam in the metal of his old pegging awls and gauge knives and hammers and peg rasps, all coated with a dull film of grit. He looked at the coils of flax thread. The hog-bristle needles, a pile of maple pegs, his old lacing punch, the groundhog and squirrel hides hung on stobs driven in the walls. All of it just as he had left it when he went off to war. He wondered if he could still do a thing as innocent and needful as make a shoe, after three years of killing his fellow man.

He tore away the cobwebs and wiped the rat droppings off the table but did not disturb the blacksnake he discovered wound up in a corner, and sat down at the bench behind the table and began sorting through the dusty lasts till he found his own. Looking through his stock he chose a good piece of neck leather for heels and hip leather for soles and flank leather for the vamp and the quarters, and laid these out on the table. Then he took his pan of hollowed-out poplar wood and went down to the springhouse and filled it and brought it back and put the leather in the water to case it. The casing would take all night. So he spent awhile tidying up the table and making sure that everything he needed was to hand, then closed up the shed and went in for supper.

Next morning he set to work with the damp leather. Twirling a length of thread onto a bristle needle he sewed the quarters and the vamp together for an upper. Then he cut the insole and tacked it to the last and drew the upper over it and whanged it into place with a carved hickory arch inside. Next he cut the sole and pegged it down, putting in a double row of pegs at the shank, where the strain would be greatest. The heel he built up with layers of neck leather pegged firmly down. He floated off the ends of the pegs inside the shoe and lined the inside with kidney leather for padding, something most cobblers never bothered to do; but Oliver bore always in mind the comfort of the wearer, and before the war this rare thoughtfulness had made his brogans highly prized throughout Rabun County and the Dark Corner nearby in South Carolina. Now he punched the eyelets and with his gauging knife cut out square laces of groundhog whang and wove them through the eyelets. Then it was time for dinner. After dinner he melted beeswax and beef tallow in an iron pot in the fireplace, and while the mixture was still warm he squatted on the hearthstone and smeared the shoes with it to waterproof them.

When he tried them on the following week the shoes fit pretty well, and Oliver was satisfied; he hadn't forgot the seemly toil of a civilized man after all. Tying the ends of the laces together he slung the shoes over his shoulder and hobbled with the aid of his crutch the three miles downriver to Uncle Ernest Dawkins's place. Uncle Ernest was not his actual uncle but was so decent and wore his many years so genially that everybody in the district called him uncle. Oliver and Uncle Ernest had the exact same foot size, and any shoe that fit Oliver would fit Ernest too.

Ernest was pleased to see him, and for a spell they leaned on the rail fence discussing the drought and the late war and the doctrine of infant baptism. Then when Oliver showed him the shoes Ernest offered him a she-goat for them, and they shook hands on the trade. Oliver led the she-goat home and turned her into the pen where Nancy had kept the milch cow till it died last winter. At least they'd have milk now, and cheese—though indeed it would be rank and noisome, like the ugly beast it came from. But Oliver was content. He'd begun the good work of turning the wolf from his door.

That summer the crop that Nancy had tried to make mostly burnt up in the fields, and even though Oliver borrowed a mule from Uncle Ernest and used his old bull-tongue plow to try to start another, all he got for his trouble was three or four rows of sprouts that yellowed and died in a matter of days. The Prices subsisted on smoked venison and whatever meat Oliver could fetch in the woods—coon, possum, squirrel—and the few peas and beans and ears of corn that survived the drought. Oliver's customers nearly always bartered for their shoes, and as the summer went on he accumulated several laying hens, a rooster and another goat, and this kept them in eggs and in milk for the younguns. Mama's place and Lit's place stood higher in the gap than his own and got more rain, and they made two thin yields of corn up there, and Lit drove down in the wagon from time to time to share out what they had. But whatever Mama gave came out of Oliver's wage, and Oliver went farther into debt to her every time Lit brought something down.

The one good thing about the hot weather was that it eased Nancy's sickness, which the medico in town said was a case of consumption. Consumption was a dread word. Oliver and Nancy both knew what it meant, but by common consent they didn't speak much about it. It seemed better just to take matters as they came, day by day. She no longer suffered with coughing fits, and the light had returned to her eye, and she felt strong enough to help with the chores. In the evening she played her gourd banjo by the fire and sang the old songs she used to sing when they were courting. She had the same splendid voice, clear as fine crystal, with a delicate tremolo in it. By the first of August she was with child.

They had been married only two years when the war came, so in Oliver's eyes Nancy still seemed a bride. Because of the war they had been apart longer than they had been together. Consequently they were still learning about each other at the same time that they were preparing to part. Much of the time Oliver was angry about this because it seemed so unfair. But he was careful not to let his anger show, lest Nancy think it was she and not fate he was angry at.

They had always been more like two younguns than a married couple. They played hide-and-go-seek in the woods and without shame played blindman's bluff in the dooryard for anybody passing on the road to see. They sat on the front stoop and sang harmony at noontime. They painted Syl and Martha and themselves like wild Indians and prowled through the forest with paper knives and tomahawks in search of settlers to murder and scalp. They played totin'-over-the-mark and ant'ny over and chased each other around the cabin and plucked feathers out of the rooster's tail. Oliver made bull-roarers, and they all whirled them around their heads in the road till it sounded like a number of steam sawmills all starting up at once. They jumped rope and played hopscotch and kitty-walks-a-corner and jackstraws.

More and more that summer and fall Nancy made mention of the Widow Henslee. The Widow Henslee lived with her nine-year-old boy and two baby girls up at the head of War Woman Creek. She was a Gillespie from down on the Chatuga, and her husband had got killed at Perryville. She was a handsome woman of high color with a smiling mouth and an abundance of yellow-brown hair. Sometimes she wore a plum-red silk bow in that hair with swallow-tail ends that hung down her back. She had a dapple-gray mare that she rode astride like a man. Oliver had made shoes for her and for the boy. He felt a little guilty for the notice he had taken of her, and when Nancy began to speak of her it made him uneasy. He knew what Nancy had in mind, even though she never said it out loud. He did not want to think of that. He wanted to keep on singing and playing with his bride, taking no account of what lay in wait. So he was somewhat gruff whenever the Widow Henslee came by, or when they saw her at church, or when Nancy insisted they go and visit her at War Woman Creek.

One day early in October Oliver was limping toward home along the main street in Clayton with a poke full of hides slung over his shoulder when a young nigra came down the road and passed him by with his hands in his pockets, whistling. The nigra did not take off his hat—none of them did these days—but he did nod and smile, and Oliver smiled back. He seemed a pleasant sort of a nigra. He was a bright high-yellow and had lively blue-green eyes. There was a pigeon feather stuck jauntily in his cap. He looked pleased to be a freedman, but unlike so many of his brethren nowadays he showed no trace of hate or arrogance.

Oliver believed slavery had been a grave sin and that God had punished the South for it by causing the war to be lost. Thus the freeing of the slaves had been for Oliver a divine act that no Christian could resent without putting in jeopardy his own redemption. Oliver doubted that a nigra was the equal of a white, but he would not put as much as a straw in the way of any nigra that wanted to better his condition. So it was agreeable to meet this smiling black who seemed to bear no malice.

After the nigra passed Oliver noticed a white man following along close behind him. Something was wrong about the way this jasper looked, and as he walked by, Oliver paused and turned in the road in time to see him pull a nickel-plated pistol out of the pocket of his coat and point it at the back of the nigra's head. When he shot, the cap with the pigeon feather in it leapt straight up in the air ten feet or more and the nigra fell violently forward on his face and did not move afterwards. The white man put his pistol back in his pocket and walked on without even a pause.

The nigra lay in a widening pool of dark blood while a number of whites stood by staring. One or two laughed out loud, and Oliver saw sitting on a rock wall a man he knew to be an officer of the new county militia, who only spat out a stream of tobacco juice and smiled a slow smile. Oliver had seen a lot of men die but seldom as casually as this. Even so, he saw it as he had learned to see all the others, as a thing far removed from himself. He shifted his poke of hides and went on his way.

A few days later in Clayton the same militia officer who'd watched the killing of the nigra approached Oliver at the tanyard and invited him into the dramshop for a drink. Since Oliver was a temperance man he declined the whiskey, but out of curiosity he agreed to go with the jasper and let him speak. The man was a planter and an original Unionist who'd gone Confederate after the shooting started and before the war had owned slaves and held a public post. Back then he regarded Oliver as what fine folk would call a low-downer, and unlike Oliver's friend the generous judge Madison Curtis he would never have addressed him man to man. But like most of his kind he did have the knack of speaking to inferiors in a way that seemed confiding when such was required. He spoke this way now. So Oliver was eager to know what had changed so greatly as to make the grandee come and seek him out.

The fellow had been exempted from the army under the twenty-nigra rule of the Conscript Law till the last year of the war, when he joined Wheeler's cavalry as a staff officer. Rumor said he'd behaved poorly under fire. Oliver had also heard he'd petitioned President Johnson for a pardon, which under the Amnesty Proclamation meant he was still worth more than twenty thousand, even after suffering the losses of emancipation and war. He was a burly and expansive man with curled mustache-ends. He inquired if Oliver knew the purpose of the militia.

"I expect it's to keep order in the wake of the war," Oliver replied, "though I'll admit I ain't paid it much heed. I ain't political, you see. Since I come home my mind's been on providing for my people."

"Yes, that must be the first concern of every responsible man," the officer said with a solemn nod. "All of us are in the struggle of our lives, now that we are a conquered people."

Oliver was not much moved by whatever struggle a man worth more than twenty thousand dollars might be engaged in; he listened impassively as the officer went on. Much that he said Oliver already knew. That the government of Georgia was in the hands of tories backed by Yankee bayonets, pending the meeting of a convention and a legislature that would write a new constitution and provide for the entry of the state once more into the Union. That in the meantime the Federal military ruled. That because the Yankee troops were too few to patrol every inch of Georgia a new militia had been organized, composed mainly of native Unionists and reconciled Rebels, to help the army keep order.

"Lawlessness confronts us on every side," the officer declared. "The abusive and turbulent nigger threatens the virtue of white woman-kind and must be kept down. Servile insurrection impends. Labor must be regularized if the harvest is to be gathered, yet everywhere the nigger loiters and wanders the byways relying on the dole of the Freedmen's Bureau. Lands are confiscated; the titles to estates are in dispute; bitter lawsuits are prosecuted. Banditry flourishes. Feud and vendetta flare up."

Listening, Oliver tried to think of an instance of disorder he had witnessed since coming home. He'd heard some tales of trouble down in the Dark Corner and in the Low Country—plundering nigras, marauding outliers, fusses between tories and returning Rebels— and over in Rutherford County the outlaw Adair Gang was robbing and pillaging. But in Rabun he had neither seen nor heard of such calamities. Yet he had witnessed the shooting of the nigra on the main street of Clayton, which this same officer had seen fit to bless with his slow smile.

"What has all this got to do with me?" Oliver asked.

Indulgently the officer smirked and touched Oliver's arm; Oliver smelled the over-fragrant odor of his condescension, like the massed flowers at a church funeral on a hot day. "The men of your section speak of you with affection and respect. Your record in the war was exemplary, and you are reputed a person of excellent character. I wish to recruit you into the county militia. We are in need of good hearts and steady hands."

Oliver shrugged. "I ain't even got a horse."

"A part of the militia is infantry," the officer replied. He exam-ined Oliver with a beady eye and divined that Oliver was not con-vinced, whereat he drew his chair nearer and assumed an even more confidential mien. "Let us speak plainly, sir. It is clear that President Johnson, as a Tennessean, intends to return the South to the Union on its own terms, with the least possible disturbance of our domes-tic arrangements. Let the South but be . . . discreet till it resumes its place in the bosom of the Union and we may see our politics and our economic order returned to the condition they were in before the outbreak. Then we will again be the masters of our own fate. And when that happens it will be the end of all the talk of nigger suffrage and nigger equality one hears out of the mouths of Radicals at the North. So this period we are in is most especially critical and sensitive. During it we must seem chastened and contrite. We must make a show of tugging the forelock before our new masters."

Oliver understood little of this. But he did guess that the militia might be in the business of restoring the power of the slavers and suppressing the nigras. Nor was he such an innocent never to have heard of Charles Sumner and Thaddeus Stevens. "Ain't them Republicans in Washington City a-pushing for something a whole lot worse than you say the president wants? Ain't they likely to reconstruct us?"

"That, Mr. Price, is what makes this time so very delicate. We must proceed in such a way as not to stoke the fire burning in the belly of the Black Republican beast. The president needs our compliance to hold back the Radicals and allow his program to succeed, and we require his support to regain our freedom of action."

He tossed off his whiskey and called for another. Then he bent even closer—so close that Oliver could smell the onions stewing on his breath in the fumes of the whiskey. "I have explained the woes that beset us, which the militia is charged with relieving. In relieving them we reassure the Yanks of our . . . contrition." Here he allowed himself an ironic smile. "We also regulate the affairs of the country. This last is our special calling, you see. By night we style ourselves Regulators. By night we remedy the wrongs that by day must be borne. For, you see, during this interregnum, we must limit the gains made by the nigger, lest matters go too far to be rolled back after reunion."

The officer went on. He told what wage Oliver could earn in the militia and what kind of uniform he could wear. He said joining the militia would be a service to the white race and would win Oliver the approbation of his neighbors and the thanks of his community. But all Oliver wanted was to get out of that dramshop. He wanted naught to do with nightriding and regulation, nor with giving the South back into the hands of the same planters that had led it to war and ruin. He did not believe the country suffered from wrongs that ought to be borne by day and avenged by night. In fact he believed the South had got licked because it deserved to get licked, for having fought in a bad cause. Henceforth Dixie should bend to the judgment of the war and do whatever its conquerors demanded. Victory had given them the right. It was Oliver's own burden, and the burden of every man that had taken up arms for the Confederacy, to find a way to atone for the sin of making war in a cause that God had turned His back on.

But Oliver was not a man to sass his betters. The officer had power and always would have it, while Oliver was powerless and would remain so. The officer was not to be offended, no matter how much Oliver despised him. And so Oliver said nothing of what was really in his mind. Instead he begged to excuse himself from service in the militia on the grounds of an ailing wife and of younguns soon to be motherless, though he was quick to express himself gratified by the offer. Then he shook hands with the officer and left the dramshop and walked quickly home.

Oliver was not wise but neither was he a fool. He knew the officer had come to him because Oliver was a man with a good name among the ordinary folk that the officer hoped to turn to the benefit of the Regulators. Wielding his name the planters who ran the Regulators might attract more of Oliver's kind. As a class, poor whites hated all planters, who'd always had everything their own way. Many a simple man, even if he hated the nigras worse than he did the planters, needed a reason to make common cause with a set of

high-and-mighty slavers; and Oliver would have given them a reason. Had the Regulators not wanted to ply Oliver's name and bor-
row its value, the officer would never have spoken to him at all. It
was the old game, using the argument of race to get the low-downer
to do the planters' will. It was the whole story of the war. Maybe it
was the whole story of humankind.

All during that autumn the Regulators kept busy. One peculiar
thing about regulation in Rabun County was that there were so few
nigras to regulate; Rabun had always been mostly Unionist and anti-
slavery. Oliver doubted as many as two hundred blacks lived in all
the county. And even that number was dropping, as more and more
left out. Now that freedom had come, it seemed every nigra needed
to be on the move to some other place in hopes of finding kinfolk
that had been sold south or laying hands on ease and fortune not to
be had at home. Some Regulators thought two hundred darkies were
far too many and wished to run them all out of the district. These
were mostly peckerwoods so poor that hating coloreds was the only
way they could feel special. But others—mostly the rich and powerful planters who controlled the militia—thought two hundred were
barely enough to do the work of the county and wanted to keep
them from leaving. Some of these even thought more nigras ought
to be brought in. It showed how little the Regulators had in common, except a white skin.

Then there was the problem of regulating wages. Most freedmen
were sharecropping, but some worked for a regular wage, usually
about eight dollars a month with board and twelve without. But
nobody wanted a nigra taking in more of a wage than a white. So all
the employers had to be regulated too. It was a lot of work, and
many fine distinctions had to be made that tested the patience of the
Regulators. They rode out night after night. And the harder they

worked the worse their mood became, for most of them were not accustomed to working at all.

They began with bluster and threats. They'd turn up wearing flour sacks over their heads to make themselves look terrible, and they'd vow to punish any nigra that didn't leave—or didn't stay, whichever the case—or any employer that didn't cut the wage he paid. But as their patience wore out so did their charity. One night Oliver was awakened by a red glow on the walls of his and Nancy's bedroom. He went to the window and saw that a great fire was burning some-place downriver toward O'Day's flour mill. The fire glared and gleamed between the trunks of the trees in the woods that sepa-rated Oliver's place from O'Day's, and the column of smoke that rose from it stood crimson against the black, with an immense blood-red October moon alongside it. Oliver remembered hearing that O'Day had hired two freedmen at ten dollars a month and board.

He roused Nancy and told her to mind the younguns while he went to see what he could do. He pulled on his trousers and ran dot-and-carrying with his crutch out of the cabin and across the dooryard and through the gate into the woods, going barefoot as he had gone through most of the war, on calluses hard as tanbark. Com-ing to the edge of the woods he heard horses in the road, and he paused behind a hickory tree to watch as the Regulators cantered past in the ruddy light, fifteen or twenty of them riding four by four, filling up the road. Under their hoods they twisted their heads inquiringly this way and that. Oliver waited for the last of them to pass before going on.

Beyond the woods he found O'Day hunkered on a stump in his nightshirt holding his Bible on his lap and watching his mill burn down. His woman was with him, wearing his greatcoat. She was pacing up and down wringing her hands and praying out loud for mercy, but O'Day sat quietly not saying a thing. He had saved his pipe and was smoking it. The rim of the mill wheel was afire, but the wheel was still slowly turning, and the water it was drawing from the millrace hissed and steamed in the heat of the blaze. The fire had already got through the roof, and dozens of shakes were taking flight into the night sky like flocks of blazing bats. Tongues of gold-and-blue flame licked out of the windows and from between the timbers of the wall, and the whole place hissed and whistled like a big teakettle. Soon the mill began to sag and lean, and finally with a groan it collapsed in a burst of sparks, and after a time the wheel, still revolving, gradually tilted over and fell. Floating embers fired the grass roundabout, and presently a slender chain of flame began to spread out from the mill, like a bright gorget around a throat.

By the end of October Nancy started to show. She had a little potbelly that Oliver could just cover with one hand, although she was less than three months gone; that was how slim she had got from the sickness. After the first frost her cough came back, but it was high up in her chest and throat, not the deep and tearing cough Oliver had heard in the spring. When she coughed she brought up no blood as before, only yellow phlegm. Other than the cough and the slimness she didn't seem poorly at all. She sewed a fine quilt that fall. It was made of interlocking wedges of what seemed a hundred different colors. She and Oliver slept warm under it through the chilly nights.

Before the leaves fell she said she wanted to go and visit the Widow Henslee at War Woman Creek. Her unspoken thought was that with the hard winter coming and the baby due by spring she might not get another chance. Oliver had no wish to spend time with the Widow Henslee just now; he begrudged every moment apart from Nancy and did not want to think about how the Widow Henslee might fit into a future from which Nancy was absent. He insisted Nancy should not walk all that distance in her condition, and Nancy agreed with him but said she was bound to go anyhow, and it was up to him to figure out how. So, seeing this was a thing beyond his power to prevent, Oliver gave in. And true to his nature, once he gave in, he decided to make a lark of it.

In the barn was an old sulky of his pappy's which nobody had used in years. Oliver dragged it out and polished it up and greased the wheels. Then, using some rope and a lot of scrap leather from the shed, he made up a harness and hitched the two goats to the sulky with it. There were so many splices and knots and dangling ends in that harness it looked like those goats had run through a weaving loom. When Nancy saw it she laughed till the tears ran.

This was how they traveled up to War Woman Creek among the cuts of the old Black Mountain Railroad that had never got built, Nancy in the sulky holding Martha on her lap and Oliver and Syl afoot, leading the goats by a length of plowline. The whole way the two goats balked and bleated and stopped from time to time to butt or kick or bite each other. This made the trip longer by half a day but was so amusing nobody but Syl minded. Syl was sullen as usual, and every delay enraged him more. His dark eyes snapped with hate whenever the others laughed. Oliver didn't know what to do about Syl. The lively giggling boy he remembered from his furlough home in sixty-three had somehow vanished. In his place was this angry little devil. The Syl of former times was so full of vigor he gave off a jolly heat like a stove; this one felt heavy and cold, as if filled with lead. Maybe growing up in wartime without a pappy had done it. If so it was another sin of Oliver's, for which he feared he must atone.

The Widow Henslee fed them sweet potato pie and fresh buttermilk. When she leaned close Oliver could smell a fragrance on her like cinnamon and cloves. He could not deny that at such a time he felt a stir. But mostly he held himself apart, wearing a grave expression while the women talked and the children played, all except Syl, who sat by the hearth staring into the fire all evening. They spent the night there and after a breakfast of sausage and eggs set out for home next morning through the red-and-gold glory of the October woods.

Passing under the glowing canopy of leaves Oliver remembered how, coming home in the spring, he had feared he might have lost his place in the heart of the mountains. He was afraid the war had changed him that much. And it was true that he had changed. There was a kind of weary indifference about him now. He had seen too much, done too much. He knew things he wished he did not know. He was tired. So he disliked the Regulators but had no thought of resisting them. He was sorry for the nigras but would not help them. He regretted that the South was prostrate but thought it deserved what it had got. His mind was not on the South or the times. It was on his family and himself. All he intended was to outlast whatever came next.

But the thing he'd worried about in the spring had not come to pass. The mountains had taken him back. He and they spoke now as they always had. If he had changed, the unchanging mountains had forgiven it. They had waited not just for the war to end but for Oliver to come back to them.

PART II

The

Destroying

Angel

CHAPTER 5

One morning late in June Daniel McFee was cutting hay in the bottom next to Downings Creek when he heard running horses on the road and looked up to see a pair of riders turning off toward his cabin in a blow of dust. They were leading two fine horses, a bay and a chestnut. The men were white, and although they wore gray and butternut they were not in true uniform, and they had an unkempt and dangerous look. Robber bands were everywhere these days, and no man's life or property was safe; warily Daniel paused with the blade of his scythe touching the tops of the timothy and watched them. They drew rein in his dooryard, and one jumped down in haste and entered the cabin, while the other stayed in the saddle to hold the horses, twisting his head to look anxiously back the way they had come.

This was mischief indeed. Daniel dropped his scythe and hurried to the fence corner, where he had left his water bottle and his coat and his small Police Model five-shooter. There was precious little in the cabin anybody would want except for the possum stew he had simmering in the fireplace for his supper, but he did not mean to give up even a possum stew to any set of scavengers, so he struck out running across the new-cut hay.

The field lay lower than the cabin, and the cabin itself shielded the course Daniel took from the view of the one holding the horses; Daniel gained the back of the cabin unseen. By the woodpile he paused, hefting his pistol in his hand and considering. The Day of Jubilee may have come and Daniel McFee might be a free man according to the declarations of the national government, but he was not yet certain he could shoot a white man—even if that white man was robbing him—and expect to live. Instead he put the pistol down the back of his pants and plucked a length of locust out of the woodpile. Then he stepped around the corner of the cabin and hit the one on the horse an awful lick in the knee with it.

It sounded to Daniel like he broke the fellow's leg. The scout hallooed and let go his lead ropes, and the two led horses ran off into Daniel's hayfield. Just then the other fellow burst out of the cabin carrying a tin cup full of possum stew, and Daniel whirled and struck him across the top of the head and leveled him on the doorstone. There was a commotion coming up the road—several horses, a jingle of harness, what sounded like the clatter of saber scabbards—but Daniel had no time to pay heed to it, for the one with the broken leg had circled his horse back into the dooryard and was pulling down on him with a big army Colt's revolver. Daniel drew his five-shooter and cocked it, and he and the scout looked at each other over their sights. "A nigger with a pistol," remarked the scout, amazed.

Meantime the oncoming riders spilled off the road into the yard around them. Three or four passed into Daniel's line of vision, and he saw that although they were irregularly dressed they seemed to be Union cavalry—oddly, some were Negro and some white—and that their horses were frothy from hard riding, no doubt from chasing these very two. One of them had a voice shrill with authority, and this one shouted, "Lay down your arms, the both of you!"

Daniel heard a man dismount and come up to him crunching in heavy boots, and he uncocked his piece then and handed it over. The man who took it was wearing an unbuttoned Federal uniform blouse with a major's shoulder straps on it but also a checkered hickory shirt and corduroy pants, so he did not seem to be a regular officer. On his head was a queer lopsided cap that appeared to have been made out of haversack canvas. The cap looked idiotic, but he did not. He was of medium size and had small red freckles all over his face and a bunch of stiff red whiskers on his chin. He had the palest blue eyes Daniel had ever seen and radiated a kind of nervous vigor that made you feel agitated too. He was not armed himself, but his horse carried two pistols in pommel holsters and a Spencer carbine slung across the bow and a straight cross-guarded sword lashed under the saddle fender. He turned to the scout and demanded his weapon, and after a moment the scout shrugged and surrendered it. "My leg's broke," he complained. "This nigger broke it."

"Don't worry about it," said the man in the major's coat in his brisk way. "Something worse is going to be broke in a minute. Then your leg won't trouble you anymore."

The scout looked outraged. "You ain't a-going to *hang* me!" he cried. He smote his brow with the heel of his hand in self-reproach. "Hell, then I might as well have shot this here nigger that broke my leg."

Some of the troopers dismounted and went over to the scout Daniel had knocked down and shook him till he roused. The man in the major's coat leaned into his face. "Hello, you damned scoundrelly murdering Rebel," he said in his high voice. "I know you for Luther Turnbull, that shot down Pearly Mayhew and two of his boys last spring in Carter County, Tennessee. That hanged a family of Bigelows at the foot of Clinch Mountain this past winter. That done a dozen other atrocities of like odor."

Luther Turnbull, if that were he, looked morosely about him. "Naw," he said.

"Yes!" cried the man in the major's coat. "I know you and all your infamous kind. And last night you even shot down two of your own, up on Chunky Gal, to steal their horses. But one lived, you see. Lived and tattled. And now this brave Negro"—he turned and flourished an arm in Daniel's direction—"has vanquished you, and you've fallen into the toils of judgment."

"Naw," said Turnbull. "Who in hell are you anyhow, to threaten judgment on an innocent man?"

"I?" The man in the major's coat strutted up and down before Luther Turnbull, as if showing off his strange hat or his fine high-top boots or maybe his silver spurs with brass rowels. "I am Nahum Bellamy the Pilot. I am the scourge of all Boneyard Rebels and demon assassins and villainous robbers."

Daniel had heard this name; it belonged to a famous guide who had spent the war taking Union men and escaped slaves through the mountains to the free soil of Kentucky. It was said he was an implacable hater of Rebels, and dark tales of savagery trailed everywhere after him. Daniel observed him with awe.

"Who made you such?" Turnbull wanted to know.

This question Bellamy did not deign to answer. He blurted a few orders, and in less than two minutes' time Luther Turnbull, if indeed it were he, and the scout with the broken leg were swinging by their necks from the Spanish oak in Daniel's dooryard. "Don't worry," Bellamy said to Daniel, patting his arm in reassurance, "I won't leave 'em there. Once they've stopped jerking I'll cut 'em down and go downriver a ways with 'em and throw 'em in." With a smile that displayed a prominent gold front tooth he returned Daniel's five-shooter and then drew off his soiled gauntlet and extended a hand. "You're a man of grit, sir. I'm glad to see grit in a colored man. Glad to see the grit ain't been whipped out of the whole race yet." Daniel shook the wiry hand; it was covered with freckles too, and a lot of red-gold hair.

Two of the troopers rode out into the hayfield and caught the horses and brought them back. The bay was a stallion and the chestnut a mare. They looked like blooded stock, and their coats shone like velvet. They snorted and stamped powerfully in the dooryard, and the stallion kept biting hanks of hair out of the manes of the cavalry mounts around him.

"No way of telling now who these fine beasts belonged to, unmarked and unbranded as they be," said Bellamy, giving them an appreciative eye and whacking his gauntlet smartly against his leg. "The desperadoes that had them could have stole them anywhere from east Kentucky down to the Big Pigeon. Ordinarily I would confiscate animals of such quality and put them to the service of the government."

He rounded suddenly on Daniel and demanded to know his name. Daniel told it. "All right, Daniel McFee, I confer these horses on you, in reward for your daring in the capture of these vicious damned Rebels." He flopped the gauntlet in the direction of the Spanish oak and the two bodies rotating slowly under it. Then, putting the gauntlet in his teeth, he took a notebook and pencil from his bosom and in a scratchy hand wrote out a notice, which he then tore from the book and gave to Daniel. Daniel glanced at it. It was a certificate of confiscation for the seizure of two contraband horses from certain known Rebels and the transfer of their ownership to Daniel McFee, freedman.

Bellamy now gave Daniel a shrewd roosterlike look. "Do you own this piece of ground I see you working?"

"No, sir," Daniel replied. "I crop shares on this place."

"The day is coming when every Negro shall have his forty acres," Bellamy prophesied. "It'll be shorn from the goddamned oppressing Rebels and given over into the hands of the Negro. And the Negro will have the suffrage and cast his vote and hold the power of office and give evidence in court and all such." He seemed transported by the notion. "But till that time, take thought of your circumstances here. Property is the foundation stone of freedom. Tenantry is but one short remove from bondage its hateful self. Go to your landlord and bargain with him. Demand credit with these beasts as collateral. Get you a deed of ownership for this ground you work." He waved his gauntlet at Daniel's chest. "Then you'll be a freeholder and a citizen, the equal of all."

He motioned then to an orderly, who brought his horse close by. Catching the reins he swung into the saddle and twisted his hand into its gauntlet again. Behind him some of the troopers began cutting down the bodies of the hanged scouts. As his horse stood champing its bit Bellamy dragged off his odd cap and wiped out its inside with a red silk handkerchief and replaced it. "Are you a Hero of America, sir?" he demanded.

"I am, sir."

"Good, good. And a Union Leaguer too?"

"Yes, sir."

Quickly Bellamy nodded. "Good, good," he repeated. "These great bodies are the seedbeds of revolution, sir. Revolution, I say; a revolution of the whole order of political economy. By them shall the Negro and those who wish him well destroy all infernal Rebels and slave masters." Once more he sent down that sudden roosterlike glare. "Who is your landlord, Mr. McFee?"

Daniel told him, and Bellamy inclined his head in thought. "Curtis is a name I seem to know," he said, "and the memory, though dim, has a taint of treason about it."

Daniel told him he must be mistaken, that while Confederate in sympathy Judge Madison Curtis and his people were the most mild and charitable of white folk, Christians all.

But Bellamy did not seem to hear. "Treason," he said, "and blood." He frowned with exasperation, but his faint remembrance would not come clear, and at last he sighed. "I'll fetch it," he declared. "I never forget a noted Rebel nor forgive treason nor fail to punish the murder of them that loved Union. I smell the blood about that name; I'll fetch it."

Then he doffed his funny-looking cap and turned his horse out of the yard, and two by two the cavalry squadron trailed after him, herding along the horses of the hanged men. They left the stallion and the mare hitched to the spirit tree Daniel had made in his dooryard. Where the scouts had been hanged, two frayed rope ends dangled from the Spanish oak; Daniel got a stepladder and set it up under the tree and unwound the cut ropes from the limb and took them down. Then he carried them into the cabin and threw them in the fireplace and watched them burn to ash.

Next morning Daniel walked to the Curtis place leading the stallion and the mare and showed them to Judge Curtis. He presented the paper Bellamy had given him and explained as best he could how he'd come by it so unlikely. Then for the first time since returning he took off his cap in the judge's presence to show himself a supplicant, and offered the horses as surety in return for four hundred dollars' credit in United States money. He inquired whether on this credit the judge would sell him the ten acres he was working along Downings Creek, together with thirty more extending to the river—land once in corn but now grown up wild. He said he'd pay the judge a colt a year till he paid off the loan.

The judge regarded him impassively for a while. Their relations had been forced and unnatural ever since Daniel's return.

The judge was trying not to behave in the peremptory way of a slave master—Daniel could see this plainly—but then his natural manner was somewhat peremptory, so in order not to offend he took refuge in an even deeper reticence than was habitual with him. This made him seem cold and indifferent, although Daniel knew the opposite was true. But Daniel did not know how to bridge the gap between them without lapsing into his old servility. Most of all he was bound to maintain his pride. But he missed the easy affection they had once shared.

Presently the judge nodded with a frown and said he would have the papers drawn up, and in this way Daniel McFee became a land-owner. For a second time in their lives they shook hands, but on this occasion each looked the other squarely in the eye. Yet the look they exchanged seemed almost angry.

At no time during the conversation did Daniel suggest that the wrath of Nahum Bellamy the Pilot might hang suspended over the judge and every Curtis that lived.

During most of the war Nahum Bellamy was full of zeal. And now that the war was over he was a zealot still. But this had not always been the case. The war when it began had seemed only an expedient, not a burning cause. It simply offered him a means of escape from a shrewish wife and seven disagreeable children and a poor farmstead on a hillside so steep he could watch his watermelons break off the vine and go bounding down the slope and explode far below in the bottomlands of the wealthy.

That was in Carter County in the upper part of East Tennessee. In November of sixty-one the Union men of that district were engaged in a scheme to burn all the bridges and destroy the railroad from Chattanooga as far upcountry as they could, in order to hamper the movement of Rebel forces in the event of Federal troops coming in. Some of these men approached Nahum Bellamy, and he saw in their plot a way to vault all the way from one kind of life to another in one great leap. And not in the four years since had he given a single thought to the farm and family he had left behind. Those belonged to some other man; he, Nahum Bellamy, had become a person entirely new.

He did help burn a bridge over the Holston in Sullivan County. But of course the Federal army did not come into East Tennessee after all—at least not then—and this left all bridge burners at the mercy of the Rebels they had enraged. In consequence he spent that winter hiding out in a rhododendron hell on Pond Mountain near the head of Elk Creek with a number of other like souls, while the Rebels searched all of Carter County for them.

One of his companions that winter was a man named Ellis, and it was because of Ellis that Bellamy eventually passed from expediency to zeal. Ellis was a flaming patriot and held the union of the states holy. For him the rebellion of the South was not simply mistaken, it was sinful, it was sacrilege; the so-called Confederacy was a stink in the very nostrils of God. By firelight amid the twining ivy Ellis seemed transfigured as he spoke so; it was as if a sacred halo shone all about him.

Till then Bellamy had often exhorted but never really known an idea greater than himself. Like his daddy before him he was a lay preacher—and a spellbinder at that—who powerfully espoused the gospel. Yet so far from his daddy's faith was he that all the while he preached he disbelieved. Now he began to glimpse the outlines of a noble purpose. It helped to form this purpose that most leading Rebels seemed to be the same men of means who before the war had captured the best land and worked it with slaves, while smallholders like Bellamy glared down enviously from the stony heights. It was easy to believe they were traitors as well as tyrants and ought to be exterminated for standing in the way of the Union and depriving the colored man of equality and freedom. Bellamy began to see that by means of Ellis's grand vision the hate he had always felt could now be transfigured. In its service he could deploy all his eloquence, all his pretended fervor of the faith.

In the latter part of sixty-two Ellis and Bellamy began the work that would bring them both renown—though some would say Ellis won the renown, while Bellamy earned only infamy. This was the piloting of runaway slaves, Union loyalists and Federal soldiers escaping from Rebel prisons through the lines from East Tennessee into free Kentucky. There, the whites could join the Union army—principally the Thirteenth Tennessee Cavalry, for which Ellis and Bellamy served informally as recruiters—and the Negroes could don the golden crown of liberty.

It was a life of torment and privation almost beyond belief, going always by night over the roughest country in every kind of weather, torn by briars, plagued by thirst and hunger, nearly drowning in rivers full of mush-ice, falling headlong into some black abyss. Bellamy ate green corn and bread made of chestnut bark and drank coffee brewed from rye and water cupped out of a hoofprint in the mud. He was tracked by bloodhounds and shot at by Home Guards and run through a thistle patch barefooted by ravening Rebels. One winter night after he and his band of stampeders had lost much of their gear being skedaddled through a frozen creek by a Rebel patrol, Bellamy crafted himself a cap out of haversack canvas. It covered his ears so comfortably he continued to wear it till spring—and then ever afterwards, as a proud memento. In the time since, he'd thrashed many a would-be wit for making the mistake of reviling that cherished cap.

Because it was a calling of such dangers Bellamy began to charge more and more for his services, till some of the Union men in East Tennessee started to complain he was little better than an extortionist. Bellamy did not much care what they believed of him, but he did care what they said, because bad talk threatened to make others doubt the purity of his fervor and also it affected business. So he visited two or three in the dead of night and thereafter no more comment was heard, and in one instance a certain complainer was not seen again in Carter County, or indeed anywhere else in any part of Tennessee.

But in time, as his zeal waxed hot, Bellamy lost interest in piloting and turned his hand more and more to punishing the infernal Rebel. He and Ellis had long since parted company; Ellis now disavowed him on account of the vanished Carter County grumbler and because of certain liberties he'd seen Bellamy take against Rebel civilians in the byways of the Cumberlands. This suited Bellamy well enough, for he now thought Ellis a slacker and a man of weak moral fiber. Bellamy believed the times called for harsh measures if the villainous Rebels were to be stamped out and the sin of slavery expunged from the land.

He need never lie idle. There were Rebels aplenty flying the black flag in that country. There was the wretch Keith, of the Sixty-fourth North Carolina, who fostered the execution of thirteen men and boys at Shelton Laurel down in Bloody Madison. There was the Thomas Legion, a band of Indian savages whom the Rebels unleashed to murder and mutilate all up and down the border with Carolina. Then there were the bands of unorganized desperadoes under the command of such beasts in human form as the Virginian Bozen and the Kentuckian Duvall, and out of East Tennessee itself there were the wild gangs of Old Bill Parker and Sam McQueen, all lynchers and shooters of Unionists, old men and children alike. There was even a place they called The Boneyard on Indian Creek between Carter and Sullivan Counties, where the Rebel fiends liked to leave the corpses of their victims for their poor widows and mothers to find and mourn over. With such demonic rogues about, the grievances to be redressed were many.

But then the war ended long before the scales could be balanced. When peace came Bellamy was forced to disband the troop of like-minded souls he had assembled to deal out requital, which some in the army called Bellamy's Bummers but he had named the Seraphim to denote how they did his will. This caused him much sadness, because he and they had done the good work together for a long time.

Presently he found a way to resume it. He got his appointment in the newly established Bureau of Refugees, Freedmen and Abandoned Lands in June when General Ruger succeeded General Schofield as commander of the Military Department of North Carolina. Bellamy had been attached to Ruger's division at one time, and the general knew of his salubrious activities in the highlands. The appointment was welcomed too by General Cox, who commanded the western district of Carolina and was also an admirer. It was because he had friends in high places that Bellamy was authorized to raise an irregular company to keep order in Clay and Cherokee Counties, in lieu of the army troops or county police employed elsewhere. He called this band the Seraphim also, in memory of his beloved companions of wartime.

Indeed, there were in this company several of the original Seraphim who, like Bellamy, had decided to stay and visit retribution on the secesh. To Bellamy they were patriot heroes. Most were Negroes, either former slaves or discharged Federal soldiers; all these held every Rebel in contempt. Others were ex-Rebels who had taken the oath, or former Confederate deserters, or men who had served as Union partisans. There were twenty of them more or less, depending on the number reporting present for duty on any given day, and they were a hard but worthy lot. They would follow Bellamy into hell if he ordered it.

The two Puckett women came into Hayesville one August morning riding double on their dun mule. Dismounting in front of the old tobacco warehouse on the square, which had first been converted into a dry-goods store and now did service as a part-time office of the Freedmen's Bureau, they confronted the crowd of Negroes gathered there and with hard looks and scornful words drove them off to a respectful distance. Then with the Negroes looking curiously on they tied the mule to the hitch rail in front of the office and made as if to break into the line ahead of those waiting to do business within. Only with difficulty did one of the bureau clerks persuade them to wait their turn. Finally with bad grace they settled on the wooden steps and sat cursing all niggers and all officialdom. But in time they seemed to forget their impatience and could be seen casually smoking their pipes in the sunlight, as if they intended to lounge there indefinitely.

From his desk inside the office by the window Nahum Bellamy observed them. He had not seen them before, and no one in the office knew who they were. They looked quite conspicuous, two white women among the twenty or thirty blacks who were always waiting. Both wore sunbonnets that sagged over their faces and rough smocks made of homespun stained an uneven brown with walnut dye. They were barefooted, and their feet were black with dirt.

When they arrived Bellamy was busy mediating a disagreement between a white farmer and his black sharecropper over the terms of a labor contract. It proved a difficult matter, and he was at it for over an hour. In the six weeks since being assigned to the bureau Bellamy had already handled fifteen or twenty such and found this the most wearisome of his many tasks. The chore was doubly galling because it lay far outside his area of responsibility. He had only taken it up when it became clear there were too many cases for the field agent and his clerks—who divided their time between the Hayesville branch office and the main station in Franklin—to handle alone.

When General Ruger appointed him supervising inspector for

the district west of the Nantahalas Bellamy had hoped to spend most of his time routing out the marauders still lurking in the hills, confiscating the lands of absconded secesh and hunting down certain Rebels that had committed criminal acts against good Union men in the war. But instead most of his time was taken up with distributing food and goods to the freedmen, helping them register their marriages, working with the Freedmen's Aid Societies, the Friends, the Presbyterians and the American Missionary Association to establish schools for the Negro children—that and resolving the innumerable contract disputes. The labor controversies were the worst, because the former slaves seemed unable to comprehend the relation of a free worker to his employer—how advance payments for rations and supplies could in time consume their share of a crop, or why one-sixth was not a greater share than one-third, or why they should work for an employer offering seventy-five cents a day rather than for a former master to whom they felt obligated who offered but twenty-five. When he could, Bellamy tried to avoid the tedium and frustration of all these wrangles. But today the agent was ill, and he'd had no choice but to take them on.

It was not that he had no wish to help the blacks—he did, or believed he did. He was in fact a species of abolitionist. His mother was a Quaker, and with her milk he'd taken in the lesson of Negro equality and the brotherhood of man. His daddy, a lay preacher of the Methodist Church, had hidden and provisioned escaped slaves, and when Bellamy was a boy his daddy had sent him away to a school in Knoxville run by a classics scholar who was a hater of all bondage.

But in Bellamy himself abolitionism was more an affair of rhetoric than of the heart. As with religion, he could powerfully unleash the oratory of abolition—he was gifted with a clever and expressive tongue—but he did so without much conviction. He could sear the souls of others, but rarely could he warm his own bosom. Yes, he wanted to free the slaves. But he longed to free himself more. As one humbly born he felt himself in thrall to those born high and dearly wished to bring them down. And he'd married young—much too young—and languished under the hard burden of providing. Only after the war was well under way did he find in it the flint to his steel. And even then the fire that the war kindled was more hate for the Rebels than love of the slaves. Yet in his way he did love them.

All morning the two Puckett women loitered and smoked while the Negroes filed one by one into the office. It was almost noon when their turn came at last. They seated themselves on the two ladder-back chairs before Bellamy's desk. The younger one complained that the office smelt of niggers, but in fact the odor that now filled the room was their own. Both were toothless, and the older one had a white mustache and several long curling hairs sprouting from her chin. Bellamy was nauseated by the sight of their black and horny toenails and grimy skin. The older one asked where the army was.

"If you mean the army of the United States," Bellamy said, breathing through his mouth lest he draw in the contagion of their stench, "there are troops stationed in Asheville. The Rebel army, of course, is disbanded."

The old woman then asked if it were not true that the Freedmen's Bureau was a part of the army, and Bellamy replied that it was an arm of the War Department. "I expect," she said with a mocking smirk, "hit's your business to look after the niggers."

"The first business of the bureau *is* the relief of the Negro," Bellamy affirmed. "But we also relieve the white refugee—that is, the Southern loyalist driven from his home by the late Confederacy."

The old woman studied him with an eye as glaring and colorless as a piece of mica. "I've heard tell ye can punish Rebels that done evil to them as held to Union in the war."

"Evil," the young one repeated.

"That ye can hang such, or take their goods," the old one went on. "Is hit so?"

Bellamy nodded. "Under the right circumstances it's so. The bureau can confiscate, the army of occupation can hang."

"Then," she concluded, "I reckon if I was to tell ye of a nest of goddamned treasonous Rebels that set bushwhackers onto Union folk to kill and rob them, ye could see justice done agin them."

"Justice," repeated the younger one, nodding.

Bellamy's heart surged. He was weary of being a dull functionary beribboned in red tape, eyed with suspicion by the field agent and his chief in Franklin, Lieutenant Hawley, and by Hawley's supervisor in Asheville, Oscar Eastmond. Here again was an opportunity to do what General Ruger had promised—take to the saddle once more, breathe the free air, mete out justice to the Rebels as he had done in wartime. "Yes," he quickly said, "I have the authority to do that, or to arrange for it to be done. Who are these Rebels, and where can I find them?"

"Family name of Curtis," the older one said. "Just over yonder a ways"—she nodded eastward—"alongside the river. Living in ease in a great white house. A mean old Rebel called Madison Curtis is the head of hit."

The name awoke an echo in Bellamy's memory. It was the name spoken by the freedman Daniel McFee on the day in June when Bellamy caught and hanged the Rebel Luther Turnbull by Downings Creek, a name that Bellamy had thought familiar but whose significance he could not then recall—the name of the man for whom McFee cropped shares. "Curtis," Bellamy repeated. It was still a name he knew, steeped in bloody treason, but he could not place it.

The old one nodded. "Hot for the rebellion, they was. So hot they give three boys to the Rebel army."

Bellamy cocked his head, alert. "Can you name these soldiers?" He was a great one for names; he knew the name of every rascal in gray who had ever done a Unionist an evil turn in East Tennessee or the highlands of Carolina. He was a keeper of accounts. Now that the war was done it would be harder to continue that work, because as an officer of the bureau he was confined by narrow rules of conduct. But he regarded it as a sublime endeavor.

The old woman plucked at the hairs on her chin. "One be called Jack. That-un died. T'other be called Andrew. That-un come home."

Bellamy leaned eagerly across the desk. "What were their regiments?" Certain Confederate units bore opprobrium for the crimes they had committed against loyalists. Because of his great mission Bellamy knew every one.

"Thirty-ninth," she replied.

Disappointed, he sank back in his chair; the Thirty-ninth North Carolina had an honorable record. "There was a third son," he prompted her.

She nodded. "Howell be his name. Was in the calv'ry. Got kilt too, like t'other one."

"And his regiment?"

She pondered a moment, then said, "Folk's Battalion."

"Folk's," the younger one repeated, nodding.

Behind his heart Bellamy felt a pang of rapture like the stab of a knife. Now all at once the meaning of the Curtis name burst upon him. Folk's Battalion was the most atrocious set of Rebel assassins that ever trod the soil of East Tennessee. Indeed, it was mostly because of them—because of an act of barbarity he saw them do at Dugger's Ford on the Watauga River—that he took up his holy toil of vengeance. In December of sixty-two the battalion was raiding through Carter County with a troop of the Johnson County Home Guard, a vicious band of the rankest Rebels, and caught five good Union men who they claimed were rangers, but who in fact were only hiding in the mountains from Rebel conscript officers. Two of these unfortunates they shot down in cold blood and the other three they hanged on bent saplings so they might slowly strangle. Alone, Bellamy had watched all this from the hills above. Later he made it his business to learn the names of the Rebels who had handled the hemp for Colonel Folk that day. One of these was a private called Howell Curtis. Mastering his excitement, Bellamy lit a cigar and bade the old woman rehearse for him how this clan of Curtises had injured good Unionists in the war.

"Hit were two summers ago," she told him, exhaling across the desk an odor like death. "Party of scouts come in. Said they was for Union. Hit were a lie. Naught but a pack of thieves, they was. They come to Curtis's. To save his life and goods the old judge tolt 'em he was loyal and we-uns was Rebels. Sicked 'em onter us. They shot my man and hanged my oldest and cut my youngest boy with knives and hanged him. They shot my cousin that was this-un's man"—she tilted her head toward the young one, who nodded and favored Bellamy with a sorrowful expression of her milky eyes—"and shot my brother and robbed us of all our goods. All on account of that lie them Curtises tolt on us." Leaning forward she pressed a finger against one side of her nose and blew a dollop of snot to the floor. "Now our menfolk be all kilt and hain't nobody to revenge us."

Bellamy puffed his cigar and toyed with his whiskers while he jotted notes on a pad with a stub of pencil. He asked the names of all concerned and inquired further into the details of the awful event. The more he learned the more it seemed providential how neatly the crime of young Howell Curtis on the Watauga dovetailed with the crime of Madison his father here in the valley of the Hiwassee. Surely these were the most vile and terrible of Rebels, the one a lyncher of innocents and the other a beguiler of murderers, bringing down massacre on a Union-loving family.

Execrable dirt-eaters the Pucketts might be. But they had favored Union. And the Curtises were of the very planter class Bellamy had always loathed. He conceded that in wartime the Pucketts might have preyed on certain Rebel neighbors, as he remembered hearing it rumored, now that he knew their names. Thus the act of Judge

Curtis may have been in reprisal for some ugly deed of theirs. But even were this so, it cut no figure with Bellamy; if the Pucketts had raided they were simply brave patriots fighting behind the lines to preserve the Union.

Howell Curtis the lyncher was dead and in hell, but those who had spawned him yet lived. It would be Bellamy's charge to call them to account for their crime, and for the crime of their child too. The prospect of engaging in the good work of recompense made him feel bright and buoyant. He'd wangled his special assignment outside the normal structure of the bureau—and thus beyond the control of the field agent and Hawley and Eastmond—for a reason. He'd come down to Clay County at war's end because all those Dugger's Ford hangmen—messmates in the same company of Folk's Battalion—hailed from Clay or Cherokee. To take his revenge he needed to be near them, the four who remained now that Howell Curtis was dead. But today he could see how that would have been a sparser meal. How much more nourishing to bring down Judge Curtis too, who not only had begot evil but embodied it too.

Full of satisfaction he summoned a clerk to write out the affidavits for the Puckett women to sign. Meantime he took up a sheaf of labor contracts for review. But he basked in such pleasure at having so eminent and maleficent a set of Rebels offered up to him unsolicited that he found it hard to concentrate on the documents in hand. For a time he dreamt of the joys of the supreme authority that was his.

Presently, though, his mood darkened as he thought again of the scene he had witnessed two and a half years ago on the Watauga. Riding with Folk's Battalion that grisly day was a foul demon of a man, a captain of the Johnson County Home Guard named Roby Brown. With their necks unbroken the poor hanged Union fellows had to choke to death. In their agony they twitched and thrashed their legs in air, and this reminded Roby Brown of the movements of a jig or a reel. As they strangled he began to bow and prance before them, coarsely calling out the measures of a dance. *Swing your partner!* he would cry. *Balance all!* he would laugh. If in their torture they happened to twirl away from him at the rope's end he would rudely wrench them back, shouting, *Face your partner, goddamn you!* At these obscene antics Folk and his troopers and Brown's minions in the Home Guard clapped and guffawed.

The sight embarked Bellamy on the mission of his life. Not long after this Captain Roby Brown was found lying on his own door log with his severed head wedged between his legs. Bellamy served others of the Johnson County Home Guard in similar fashion, and dealt as harshly with every Rebel who came into his hands in all the country between the Nolichucky and the Cumberlands. He picked and led the Seraphim, his own party of avengers. But the stranglers of Folk's Battalion escaped him, as the outfit was soon transferred out of East Tennessee. However, this had not prevented him from making inquiries against the day when—he felt sure—fate would place the guilty before him. Now, it seemed, that day had come.

When the clerk was done Bellamy witnessed the marking of the affidavits by the Puckett women. He then reviewed the documents himself, and finding them in order he took each woman by a filthy hand and profusely expressed the thanks of himself and of Generals Ruger and Cox and Provisional Governor W. W. Holden for the advices they had offered the government. Today, he told them, they had played the part of patriots.

The old one glowered sternly up at him and demanded, "Hain't you a-goin' to pay us?"

Bellamy sighed. So many nowadays saw patriotism as only a commodity, and a debased one at that. The thought depressed him. But he gave each woman ten silver dollars and watched in disgust as they stuck the coins into their mouths one by one to judge by taste the value of their reward—an expedient doubtless forced on them by their absence of teeth. Then he escorted them to the door, where they descended the steps roughly, elbowing Negroes aside right and left, and untethered their mule and mounted and rode away.

It was raining the next morning when Bellamy and his new troop of Seraphim set out. Before them shrouds of mist clung to the barely visible peaks of the Tusquittees, and scrims of fog rode slowly up the lower slopes. In the fields about them the leaves of the tasseled corn shone as though waxed, and here and there amid the thick rows stood the bone-pale skeletons of girdled oaks and poplars that some farmer had thought too large to cut and burn. A smell of hickory smoke was in the air. The Hiwassee ran red as blood where they crossed it at Sanderson Ford. The wagon road was fetlock-deep in mud.

But Bellamy took no note either of the look of the morning or the conditions of travel. He was in something like a state of grace; he thought of naught but what now seemed the sacramental nature of his calling. The atrocities of these Curtises had served to set him alight. The detestation he had always harbored for the slave-owning rich he now began to see as indistinguishable from the will of heaven, just as Ellis had once insisted but Bellamy had never been able to grasp. Till this day his ardor—though it glowed white-hot—had lacked the holy fire. Now, together with the shade of the sainted John Brown, he truly understood how Great Jehovah wanted these secesh and bond masters stamped out—how to achieve this sacred end any measure, no matter how harsh, was justified. This at last was a version of the faith to which Bellamy could subscribe; in its service he could ply heart as well as tongue and avenging arm. As he rode, it seemed to him that he could feel the face of God bending close in stern approval.

But he was no common bushwhacker to come crashing up to a

house with a menacing crowd of armed men at his back. He was conscious of his position and of the need for due process and good form. One did not mete out to a noted citizen and landowner worth two thousand four hundred in property the same fate one visited on the Roby Browns of the world, whose fall few would mark. At the top of the drive that led down to the Curtis house he bade the Seraphim dismount and told them not to stir from the spot lest they hear shooting. Then he turned the head of his horse and rode down the drive toward the house.

CHAPTER 6

S arah Curtis was emerging from the root cellar with an apron full of peach-bloom Irish potatoes when she saw a man on a heavy gray horse riding slowly down the gravel drive. Despite the rain she paused to watch. The man was swaddled in a Federal army gum blanket and on his head was a shapeless contraption of a hat so absurd it made him look like an escaped lunatic. Yet everything else about him was as neat as could be, given the road mud he'd ridden through. He wore high boots of patent leather. His saddlecloth was dark blue trimmed with gold braid and had an eagle embroidered in gold at the corner. The sword scabbard fixed to his saddle sparkled brightly even in the gloom, and his horse bent its neck in a powerful arc as she stood studying. In spite of the hat the man and his horse both had a serious look.

At first Madison and Andy did not see him. They had been working to repair the front steps when the rain started and had moved up to the gallery to get out of the wet. The gallery floor was broken through in several places just like the steps, and the boards Andy had cut and trimmed from the collapsed smithy would do just as well in the one place as in the other. Not that they were anything like a perfect fit. But since Penland's sawmill had burned down in the war nobody in Clay County could lay hold of a milled board; between Shooting Creek and Peachtree all repairs looked equally make-do. Andy and Madison were prying out the last of the rotten floorboards when Sarah came to the corner of the steps and said in a flat voice, "Father Curtis."

Madison knew that tone and stood at once and turned and saw the rider in the lane. Andy rose more slowly. Unhurriedly Sarah climbed the six broad steps and dumped the potatoes into the seat of a wicker rocking chair. Then she returned to the top of the steps and with one hand wiped the damp from her hair and with the flat of the other propped herself against a stanchion. In the war years many a villain had made this same approach, and she and Father Curtis and the family had survived them all; it figured they could survive a man wearing a ridiculous hat no matter how serious he might appear. But the family had been so much stronger then. Now as she watched the strange horseman approach she felt how frail and weak she was, and how tired Madison was, and how full poor Andy was of dread.

She waited as he came steadily on. When he reached the cul-de-sac at the bottom of the drive he dismounted and decorously tethered the gray to the iron jockey, then advanced along the flagstones between the rows of boxwoods. As he did so Jimmy and Andy— dear dead Betty's two orphan boys—burst through the front door and ran to flank her. They too had often seen evil arrive on horseback in just this manner. Yet they had not fled to their hidey-holes; boldly today they advanced to meet it. Sarah was moved by this show of grit. Reaching out with both hands she touched the backs of their blond heads.

At this gesture the officer smiled, but in a cold way. The smile revealed the flash of a gold front tooth. He had a tuft of red chin whiskers shaped just like the goatee one used to see in cartoons of Old Abe. At the foot of the steps he removed his peculiar headgear to expose a coiling mass of copper-colored hair. "Good morning," he said in a bright voice. He had eyes of palest blue.

Stiffly Madison returned him a good morning. But neither Andy nor Sarah spoke. Sarah remained propped against the stanchion at the top of the steps, figuratively and literally barring the way.

"My name," the officer said to Madison, still in that sprightly voice, "is Nahum Bellamy. I hold a special commission as a major in the United States Army, and I'm a supervising inspector of the Bureau of Refugees, Freedmen and Abandoned Lands."

Sarah recognized him now. He had been present when the officer from Raleigh administered the oath of allegiance to Madison and herself and several other farmers only weeks ago in the courthouse at Hayesville. But he had forgotten.

He smiled up at them in an introductory way while the rain formed small beads on his red curls. "May I come in?" he inquired after the passing of an awkward moment showed him that he would not be invited.

"Federals have not been kind to this household in time past," Madison said with an air of stubbornness. "Yet you say you're named for the prophet Nahum of old, and if I recollect my Bible studies aright, Nahum is a word that means compassion. Are you a man of compassion, major?"

Bellamy rotated his cap in his hands and dropped his eyes to watch it turn—or perhaps, Sarah thought, to conceal a hard glint of contempt—then looked up again and gave Madison that same cold smile. "I like to think that I was once compassionate," he said. "But I fear the war's driven out my compassion. In its place is left a hunger for justice. If a man has lost his compassion, ain't justice a worthy replacement?"

Madison shrugged. "Compassion's absolute. Justice is a thing men can interpret, each according to his own lights."

The smile faded from Bellamy's face and was replaced by an expression of impatience; he was a man of action, not reflection. "If you're James Madison Curtis, sir," he said, "I have business with you." He glanced sideways at Sarah and the Cartman boys. "It's business of a grave nature." At the words Sarah felt a stab of fright.

Madison blanched but had the self-possession to give the officer an ironical half-bow. "Then we shall be formal," he said crisply. "Major Bellamy, allow me to present my wife Sarah"—Sarah offered him only a silent nod—"and my son Andrew."

At the mention of Andy's name Bellamy's gaze sharpened. Andy saw this and turned deathly pale, and Sarah observed that he commenced very slightly to tremble. He stood with a hammer in one hand and half a decayed board in the other, gazing at Bellamy transfixed, like a field mouse before a coiled snake. Bellamy sensed the fear, and it was plain that he savored it. The pale eyes watched Andy while the rain spangled his hair and pattered on his gum blanket. "Andrew Curtis," he said. He seemed to consult his memory. "You served in the Rebel army, I believe. The Thirty-ninth North Carolina, was it not?"

Miserably Andy nodded. After a moment he found a wisp of his voice and replied, "That's right." He swallowed, then added, "I took the oath in Alabama in May. I can show you my parole if you want."

Bellamy appeared to consider it. Sarah grew first afraid, then angry as she realized he was toying with Andy's terror. Here was a thug who took pleasure in inflicting torment, yet the Yankees had placed him in authority. A red rage flared behind her eyes. But all at once he seemed to dismiss Andy from his thoughts; his mood turned. He faced Madison and said, "May we go inside?"

The Cartman orphans, grasping her skirts right and left, cried, "No!"

Bellamy looked harshly at them but then appeared to reconsider and once again used his frosty smile. "And why not, young gentlemen?" he inquired with a show of amused tolerance.

"Because you're a Yankee!" shouted Jimmy.

"Because you'll hurt us!" yelled Andy.

Sarah hugged them both close while Bellamy gave an indulgent laugh. He drew his gum blanket off over his head with a flourish that showered them with droplets of water, then started up the steps.

Daniel McFee was riding Tom the bay stallion into town to buy supplies when he encountered Bellamy's troop boiling coffee over a fire in the middle of the wagon road. There were more congenial spots—the road was muddy and the rain sifted down on them through the overhanging boughs—but none that offered as good a prospect of impeding travel and annoying the farm folk. Doing such mischief was their favorite pastime, and they were always willing to undergo discomfort for the sake of it.

Daniel knew most of the Negroes from the meetings of the Union League. Some he liked; others seemed downright dangerous, and these he avoided whenever he could. As he approached, one of his chums cried affectionately, "Here come that Cumberland nigger!" and another added, "On his fancy hoss," and a peal of laughter broke out.

Daniel was popular with the blacks in the Seraphim and in the league at large, because before any other Negro in the county he had acquired his own land and was on his way to the kind of independence most only dreamed about. The Negroes gathered about him in the road to pet and admire the stallion, while the whites stood back eyeing him in a grudging way—to a Dixie low-downer, be he Reb or tory, a flourishing nigger was no happy sight, and even a Yankee might envy a horse as fine as Tom. They all wore white straw hats with two black ribbons hanging down in back, which Bellamy had bought for them on his last trip to Knoxville. This was as much of a uniform as they had. Mostly they wore castoff Union army gear. In the damp they smelled like so many wet dogs. Each carried a revolver and some carried two, and every man packed a carbine of some model slung to his saddle.

Daniel shook a few hands and traded some jibes and exchanged the obligatory secret grips and passwords with his fellow Union Leaguers; but he was troubled by a feeling that something was afoot, something beyond the usual rascality. There was an edge of excitement in the Negroes' mood and a twitchy look in their eyes. They kept glancing sideways and down off the road, as if apprehending some event below. Curious, Daniel looked that way too, and at the bottom of the lane he saw Bellamy's gray gelding hitched under the magnolias in front of the Curtis place. His stomach rolled over in dread. Turning to a Negro called Corn Dodger, who served Bellamy as a sergeant, he asked, "Where-at's Boss Bellamy?"

Corn Dodger laughed. "Gone to grind hisself up a damn ol' Rebel."

Daniel motioned toward the Curtises'. "Down yonder?"

"Yessah," Corn Dodger said. "Boss Bellamy, he got the goods on that ol' sumbitch. Gonna grind him up fine." Corn Dodger's grin widened. "Then maybe you ain't got to pay no more on that land you bought. Maybe you get to keep all the colts this here stud is gonna make. Maybe you even gonna cotch you some more land. That damn ol' Rebel, maybe he got enough land so's every nigger in this county get a piece—hell, maybe every nigger in the state." At this notion all the blacks burst out in exuberant laughter.

Daniel felt strangely numb. Bellamy must have finally proved the treason he'd smelt that day last June in Daniel's yard at the mention of the Curtis name. But what could the act have been? Daniel's first thought was that Judge Curtis would not knowingly wrong another. But then it occurred to him that it hardly mattered what had brought

Nahum Bellamy down on the judge. Whatever crime Boss Bellamy might charge against him, the judge had to know—just as Daniel knew—that he already stood guilty of the direst offense. Daniel took thought of himself, enslaved for sixteen years to the Curtises, and of Sukey, enslaved for eight, and of Sukey's Hamby and Old Jeff and Mariah and Cuffee and the other Negroes the family had kept enslaved—enslaved in kindness, yes, but enslaved all the same.

Corn Dodger and the others clamored around him; one of the Negroes pantomimed Judge Curtis sinking to his knees to beg the mercy of the Boss. Looking on, Daniel laughed with the rest, but it was a hollow laughter. He found he could not bear to think that after all their sufferings the judge and Miz Curtis and Mister Andy were to be brought to book, leaving Miz Salina, Miz Martha, the girls and the two little orphan boys bereft. If these had been his marsters they had also been his family; he had cherished them and they him. Now they were in the hands of the Boss. Daniel admired Boss Bellamy but he also feared him, and he knew absolutely that Bellamy would destroy every last Curtis given sufficient reason; he knew Bellamy had no pity in him at all. Yet he, Daniel, whom the Curtises had held in bondage, could pity them. Even if he could not pardon them he could pity them.

In his turmoil of mind he wished only to flee now from what he saw beginning to happen here. He gathered his reins to ride on, unwilling to stay till Bellamy returned, not wanting to hear him gloat. As Daniel put Tom into the road Corn Dodger shouted up at him, "This world be changin' now! Bottom rail on top, bottom rail on top!"

Yes, the world was changing. Daniel knew he must be strong enough to let it change. He must be strong enough to hate those he had once loved, who had demeaned him. But he could not be that strong today. Maybe later he would be strong. But not today. He punched Tom's ribs with his heels.

Laughing in the rain, the Negroes parted to let him pass. "League meeting tonight," one reminded him, and another yelled, "Come to the meeting!"

Corn Dodger took off his straw hat and brandished it. "Ol' Cumberland nigger," he laughed, "come to the meeting. Hear Boss Bellamy preach the gospel of the Publicans."

Blindly Daniel urged Tom into a canter and rode on toward town.

Watching Madison and Andy retire to the parlor with Major Bellamy, Sarah wondered bitterly why it was that men felt compelled to exclude women from all talk of impending calamity when, once it arrived, it descended equally on both. In fact, more often than not, it was the women who bore the brunt of whatever misfortune befell. Not that she actually wanted to hear what this calamity was. She felt full to the brim with adversity and could not bear the thought of receiving more. Yet the Yankee had dragged danger into the house like a dragon's tail. One lash of that tail could sweep away what little remained of their lives, and Sarah could sense it coiling to deliver the blow.

She marveled at the cruelty of fate. Not God, fate. She still excused God. To her, fate was not divine but mortal; it was everything that men did, collected together in one force. God would not intervene in that. People often spoke of fate as being indifferent, but to Sarah it had proved itself implacably personal. It had smitten the Curtises with especial fury, taking away three of their children, consuming their fortune, wiping out their whole way of life. Yet still it was unsatisfied. Small explosions of fury began going off inside her like strings of fireworks as she pondered this. The war had tested them hard. Now, when they were weak and beaten down, all but defenseless, defeat was going to test them too—perhaps test them harder even than the war had. Sarah doubled her fists and moaned aloud while the Cartman boys looked on dismayed. *How can we face it?* she asked herself. *With what weapons can we resist? We have nothing.*

She dashed away the tears that stung her eyes. She could not stay a moment longer breathing the same air as that insufferable Bellamy. Quickly she threw a shawl over her head and shoulders and took the two Cartman boys by the hand and to their delight led them across the gallery and down the steps into the rain and along the flagstones to the turnaround. From the cul-de-sac a path led down the hill and across the bottom toward the river. They took this path through drenched tussocks of grass between the fields, where Madison and Andy had finally managed to start a late crop of corn. The corn was stunted and as yet untasseled. In her rage Sarah could not bear to look at it; Madison had gone deep in debt for seed corn, mules, plows, everything needed to make a crop. He and Andy had toiled in the fields like nigras. And now, like as not, it was all to be swept away. Grave business, Bellamy had said. What else could it be but confiscation?

While Sarah grieved the boys were in their glory. To be taken suddenly outside in a rainstorm—contrary to all the tedious rules adults were wont to impose on boys—was a joy beyond measure. They broke free to wallow in the wet grass and stomp lustily in the mud puddles of the path. They took up gouts of muck and flung them at each other. They wrestled screaming in the mire. By the time they reached the bushwhacker's grave by the river the orphans were soaked and mud-plastered and Sarah's sodden dress and shawl clung to her.

It was not so wet under the dangling tresses of the willow tree beside the grave. The rain came through, but only in large and inter-mittent drops. Sarah spread the shawl there, and they sat looking out at the grave and beyond it at the misty foothills of the Tusquittees in the distance. Where there was no mist the air had been washed clean by the rain, and they could see every bristling leaf of every tree in the woods on the hills. The greens there were lush and vivid. Behind them the river rushed noisily by, and they could smell its odor like that of corroded metal.

The grave was overgrown with purple joe-pye weed and Queen Anne's lace. It was where Madison had buried the leader of the Yankee bushwhacker gang called the Yellow Jackets after a company of Confederates hanged him. On a raid into the valley in the late summer of sixty-three the bushwhacker—who'd lived on Downings Creek as an orphan boy—refrained from burning the Curtises out because Madison had once done him a good turn. When on a second raid the bushwhacker was caught and hanged, Madison felt obliged to give him a resting place. It was an act Sarah had understood but not condoned, for she loathed all bummers and partisans and scouts. To her the presence of the grave was a desecration. But it was in a pretty spot, and when times got bad she liked to come here and sit and take in the beauty of the valley.

"Grandma," Jimmy asked, "why did Grandpa bury the bad man here?"

"Well, honey, the bad man did Father Curtis a sort of a favor, and I think Father Curtis believed he was beholden to him."

The two boys thought awhile, then little Andy said, "So a bad man can do good things sometimes?"

Sarah shrugged. "Sometimes. But not often." She paused, then thought it might be wise to offer some advice on the point. "You can't count on it," she added.

They sat quietly for a time before Jimmy asked, "Why are there so many bad men?"

"There weren't always so many, child. This is a special time. A time that calls bad men forth. There didn't used to be many bad men atall." Sarah smiled in recollection. "Back then it was so peaceful and so good in this place that Father Curtis used to say God lived here."

"God must have moved away," Jimmy remarked.

She gave him a sorrowing look. "He did, honey."

"Is He coming back?" little Andy wanted to know.

"Who, child?"

"God. Is God coming back?"

Sarah wanted to say something of comfort but could not think a comforting thought. So all she said was, "I don't know. I hope so. But nobody can tell."

Jimmy plucked fistfuls of wet grass. "Is the man that's talking to Grandpa now going to do something bad to us?"

Grimly Sarah nodded. "I expect he means to, yes." There was no use sparing them. They had seen the war. Now they would have to see the peace.

Little Andy looked hopefully up. "You don't think he'll do Grandpa a favor?"

"No, honey, I don't," Sarah said. She sighed. "He could if he wanted to. But I don't think he wants to."

There was a long silence. Then, in the uncanny way they had, they both spoke at once and asked, "How will we stand it, Grandma?"

Again tears rose in her eyes. "I don't know, boys," she said. "Maybe God will give us the strength."

"But God moved away," Jimmy reminded her.

When Sarah and the boys returned to the house Bellamy was gone, but to Sarah his malignant spirit lingered on like a whiff of sulphur in the damp air. Madison and Andy were still closeted in the parlor. The girls stood nervously about. The sight of the muddy boys gave Salina and Martha a means of fending off worry. With cries of reproach they swooped them up and carried them off to the summer kitchen to be bathed. Sarah stood awhile before the closed door of the parlor dripping a pool of wet on the hardwood floor. But no one stirred within, and presently she went upstairs to dry herself off and change.

When she came down half an hour later Madison was standing in the hallway wearing his frock coat and silk cravat. He looked quite handsome. Quietly he said, "We'll have a family gathering in the dining room."

Sarah presumed that Bellamy by his presence had tainted the parlor, where the Curtises ordinarily met. Andy was waiting in the shorn and vacant dining room; to her disquiet Sarah could still see the ghosts of shutters, valences, chandelier, table and chairs, long since carried off by vandals. Andy stood before one of the paneless windows with his hands clasped behind his back, gazing out at the rain; Sarah could not see his face. She seated herself on an empty nail keg, and Madison stood in the near corner. Martha took the base of a butter churn with tiny Eva in her arms. Salina and the girls arranged themselves along the walls, and the newly scrubbed Cartman boys lay side by side on their tummies in the middle of the floor, propping their chins in their hands.

In a calm voice Madison began to speak. He said the Puckett women had given affidavits charging him with inciting murder and robbery during the Yellow Jacket raid. He said he faced a military trial on criminal charges at Morganton and civil lawsuits by the Pucketts in the superior court in Hayesville. Due to the unorganized state of the county the lawsuits could not be filed and tried till next spring. But the military charges were imminent, and that trial could be held at any time.

The officer, he said, had given him to understand that in the military case the government would not press for the death penalty. Confiscation would be the object instead. In the event of a conviction the Curtises' home and their farm of five hundred and fifty-one acres would become the property of the United States, to be divided into parcels and distributed to deserving freedmen. Any remaining assets would then be subject to the claims of the civil court.

They all stared, numb with horror. Andy remained standing with his back to the room, gazing out the window. Madison paused and drew a long breath. Strangely, there seemed to be a kind of serenity about him; he looked more at peace than Sarah had seen him in months. Now he settled on her a long and tender look. Meeting it, she was amazed to find that some of his tranquility passed gently into her, and against all reason she too felt something of his content.

"For two long years," Madison said, "I've lived in a torment of guilt. When I diverted the rangers it was to protect my family, but in doing so I sacrificed someone else's family. That was a great sin. Now I—we—have to pay for that sin. It may be the will of God that we pass through this ordeal without losing everything. I pray that is the case. But on the other hand it may be that we're to lose all we hold dear. If so, that too is His will, and like Job we should bow down before His justice and magnify His name. I'm sorry for the hardship this will bring down on you"—Sarah had not heard proud Madison profess himself sorry in thirty years of marriage, and the word jarred her like a blow—"but it's proper that we suffer it, and I welcome it. I believe God has brought this judgment on us, to put us right with Him. I thank Him for His blessing." He passed his forefinger back and forth underneath his mustache.

He led them in prayer then, and Sarah reverently bowed her head. But although she could share a portion of Madison's contentment she could not agree that he had earned the punishment of heaven. He had acted rightly to save his loved ones—Sarah most of all, whom the bushwhackers had harshly mistreated. The contentment she felt came from the knowledge that Madison could find solace now from the guilt that had so sorely plagued him. But she, Sarah Warren Curtis, was not disposed to submit meekly to the bullying of Nahum Bellamy and the despicable Pucketts. Despite her frailty, despite her weariness of soul, she wanted to resist. But how? And with whose help?

Madison had given up, and Andy—poor, poor Andy—was too weak to fight. So Sarah prayed. But her prayer was far different from Madison's.

That evening, at the meeting of the Union League in the office of the Freedmen's Bureau, Daniel McFee sat amid a crowd of twenty or thirty Negroes and listened partly in excitement and partly in foreboding as Boss Bellamy passionately addressed himself to the program of the Republican Party in the South. As an officer of the Freedmen's Bureau it was not the Boss's place to purvey a political line, but he had long since shown a fine disregard for such piddling restraints. He was a famous firebrand and a thundering preacher and had captured most of the Negroes of the county, who all loved a spellbinder and needed to think someone in authority held their cause at heart.

"The extermination of slavery has been achieved," Bellamy cried. "But this is only the first of many great and holy tasks that lie before us. Now we must see to it that slavery is not revived under another name, and that the slave masters and secessionists who kept you in bondage do not regain the management of affairs in the conquered states."

He stood back modestly smiling before the storm of applause that followed this remark. In the chair beside Daniel the sergeant Corn Dodger clapped his hands heavily over his head and shouted, "Hallelujah! Lord, bring the day!" The others—wage hands, sharecroppers, loiterers on the bureau dole, some of Bellamy's Seraphim—took up the chorus, and the room thundered till Bellamy quieted them with raised hands and leaned forward over the lectern with the confiding air of a man about to communicate an important secret.

"But this ain't all, my friends. Not by any means. For what good is freedom without the power to ensure it? Yes, power. Political power.

Power is what's needed." He came from behind the lectern and paced up and down before them in his agitated way. "Gentlemen, do you know the meaning of the word *revolution?*" He made a violent circular motion in the air with one hand. "It means to revolve, to overturn. In a revolution what was up goes down, and what was down goes up."

"Rebolution!" Corn Dodger yelled, and the cry was repeated till it became a chant—"Rebolution! Rebolution! Rebolution!"

Bellamy stood sweating with his hands on his hips and a fierce light burning in his eye. When the crowd quieted he went on: "We mean to revolutionize the society of the South, my friends. The tyrannical slave-owning planter class was up"—here he repeated the circular gesture—"but will be brought down. And the Negro who was down will rise up. The freedman will have the suffrage. He'll wield the power of the ballot. Black men will sit in the general assembly of the state of North Carolina and in the halls of the Congress of the United States."

"What's up goes down!" Corn Dodger cried. "What's down goes up! The last shall be first!"

There was another outburst of cheering, but quickly Bellamy stemmed it with a flourish of his hands. "Mind me," he shouted, flushing darkly, "I speak not of simply giving the Negro his political rights. I speak of wiping away every distinction of color. I speak of lifting every black man up and making him the equal of every white, so that nothing he desires and has the ability to attain can be denied him on the grounds of negritude, be it an education, a trade, a high profession or any pursuit heretofore reserved for the white. Even further, I speak of amalgamation—the mingling of the races on a basis of true equality."

Here was a vision so compelling that the Negroes of the Union League—even the bumptious Corn Dodger—fell reverently silent, transfixed by its strangeness. Was it possible that such a day might dawn?

"But there is work to do before that time comes," Bellamy went on. "There is a great disagreement between the Republican Party, which has freed the slaves, and the president, who we should remember is a Southerner and although a lover of Union is also a hater of Negroes. The president insists that the late Confederate States have never been out of the Union at all. By waging war, he says, they have only disarranged their proper relation to the whole."

With an angry shake of his head Bellamy resumed his pacing. "They may resume their place, the president contends, by the simplest of means. They must hold conventions which will write new constitutions that outlaw slavery. They must elect new leaders. That's all, my friends. The late Rebel states are to be welcomed back into the bosom of the republic without even a slap of the wrist or a jerk of the hair. Their bloody treason is to be altogether forgiven. Already we see the shape of things to come. Next month this state will elect its delegates to its convention, and the same old Confederates—and the Whigs who in former days favored Union but were always apologists for slavery—offer themselves as candidates. The same old slavers expect to resume power. This is what we may expect from the program of the president."

"No!" the crowd burst out as one. "No! No! No!"

"But the Republican Party has a far different view," said Bellamy. "We believe that when the Southern states left the Union they committed suicide. They no longer exist as states. At most they've sunk to the status of territories or conquered provinces. They can't return to the Union except they be subject to the most rigorous testing and proof, so as to secure the rights of the freedmen. We believe that a Congress dominated by Radical Republicans, not the president, should govern this process. Treason should be punished, not rewarded. The seceded states should be corrected, not coddled. For if they're coddled they'll presently resume the control of the national government which they enjoyed before secession, reducing the Republican Party to a minority. God forbid, a minority!—the Republicans, the party of Father Abraham, the party dedicated to Union and freedom and equality. The scoundrelly slave-holding Democrats and their Copperhead sympathizers and the pusillanimous old ex-Whigs will rule the nation. And in the end they'll carry the South back again to all its old evil ways."

Again the chant of "No! No!" went up. Corn Dodger shook his fist in the air. One man leapt up and did a kind of war dance in the aisle.

Bellamy drew a red handkerchief from his pocket and mopped his brow. As the room quieted he sorrowfully shook his head. "The president chose to launch his program of mild reconstruction by executive prerogative, after Congress adjourned in May. It's well advanced." He put away his handkerchief and smiled and pointed a finger at his audience. "But I assure you, gentlemen, when the Congress returns in December with its Republican majority—our Radicals and the moderates they will win over—the president's program will surely be dismantled. In its place will be the revolution I talked of. And when the revolution is done the South will be governed by the Radical Republican Party and a Negro electorate, and it'll never be the same again."

"Rebolution!" Corn Dodger yelled. "Lord, bring the day!" Several men in the crowd began a rhythmic stamping of their feet, and soon the building shook. There was another outburst of shouting—"The Day of Jubilee done come!" "Lift me up, Lord!" "Hallelujah!" The close air in the room smelled of sweaty clothes and the unwashed bodies of laboring men.

Briskly Bellamy turned and strode back to the lectern and stood waiting till the shouting and stamping died. Then he resumed. "Till then, my friends, you must attend to the great work of the Union League. Learn its ritual and catechism; inscribe its oath upon your very hearts. Study also the principles of the Republican Party, against the day when the Negro shall have the vote. Study the Constitution of the United States and learn the rights and duties of citizenship. We must be ready when our time comes, when the reconstruction of the South falls under the hand of the Republicans—under your hands."

Here Bellamy assumed a paternal air. "To be truly ready you've got to observe the obligations of freedom even as you enjoy its delights. You must honor the terms of your labor contracts. You must be industrious and responsible. You must provide for those who depend upon you. You must observe the law. You must take thought of your appearance and demeanor and show yourselves to the world as men worthy of respect." He lifted a cautionary finger. "Don't behave surly and abusive to the whites. But take care not to cringe nor whine before them either. Carry yourself in sober manly fashion. And if any white misuses you or your family, report him to me. I promise you he'll suffer."

"That's right," Corn Dodger blurted out, "give his white ass to the Boss!" And the others cried, "Boss! Boss! Boss!"

Again Bellamy stilled them with a wave of his hands. "I've spoken of all the things you need to learn. Clearly, to learn them, you must know your letters. So if you can't read and write come to the Freedmen's Bureau school and we'll teach you. You'll have to learn your figures too, lest some white get the advantage of you in the negotiation of your contracts. You must learn to speak correctly so that you may make yourself clearly understood, and the whites will begin to esteem you as a person of accomplishment. You must take care to do all these things. For if you give the whites any excuse to slight you they'll see it as a sign that they were right to believe in white supremacy, and right to enslave you. And it'll set back the time of revolution.

"The task before us is great and difficult. Make no mistake. You have very few friends among the white race, either at the North or at the South. Most whites, Yank and Rebel both, hate you and want to see you wiped off the face of the earth. Whites like me and your comrades in the Seraphim, who love and respect you, are scarce as hen's teeth. We and the leaders of the Radical Republican Party are your only friends. So between now and the time we take the reins of power in our hands, be careful not to antagonize the whites. Be cordial and polite. Smile. And think on the happy day when you'll crush them under your feet!"

Bellamy whirled his arm violently in the air. "Revolution!" he cried, and the crowd responded with another rolling chant of "Rebolution! Rebolution! Rebolution!" "With the revolution," Bellamy went on, "will come the confiscation of the land which the planters have hoarded for generations. Then every Negro will be a freeholder."

Now he resumed the confiding mood with which he had begun. He left the lectern and came to stand close before them. "But we don't have to wait so long in every case," he said, smiling. "This very day I've instituted proceedings against a noted Rebel of this county, who by his violent acts in wartime has forfeited all his rights to property." Daniel tensed, knowing it was Judge Curtis of whom he spoke. "There are men in this room who'll have his land," Bellamy said, gazing significantly down on Daniel, who felt himself shrink back instinctively from the weight of the look.

"And this is but the beginning," Bellamy continued. "Every day I make it my business to sniff out more of the detestable Rebel traitors who've abused the Unionist and the Negro. One by one I'm bringing them to account. One by one their lands are being yielded up. And with every Rebel brought to justice, freedmen will be given land. In this way we bring the revolution nigh, even before its time."

Corn Dodger bounded to his feet with a fierce whoop, and then the whole audience rose shouting. Bellamy stepped back, smiling. He was finished.

At the adjournment of the meeting he came straight to Daniel and shook his hand and bent on him that blazing pale blue eye. "Mr. McFee," he said, "I'll need you to give evidence in my case against Curtis when it comes to court."

Daniel gaped at him. What could he mean? Daniel now knew the nature of the charge. The act it alleged had happened long after he ran away to freedom. He had no knowledge of it at all. "Why, Boss," he stammered, "I've got no evidence to give."

Bellamy laughed and laid a convivial arm about his shoulders and squeezed. "You will have," he said.

Daniel did not want to acknowledge that remark or consider its implications. He let it skip off him like a flat stone off the surface of a pond. Instead he took refuge by saying, "But Boss, a Negro can't testify in court."

"Not in county or superior court—not yet," Bellamy agreed. "But he can give evidence in a military court, sure as hell."

CHAPTER 7

It was only in February of the year the war broke out that the North Carolina legislature divided Cherokee County in two and formed Clay County out of the eastern half, and due to the unrest of the war years Clay didn't get organized till 1864, and even then its boundaries weren't properly surveyed. So, on that September afternoon when the razor grinder found the dead man on the hog farm just off Settawig Road near Brasstown, nobody knew whether to send to Murphy or to Hayesville for the authorities.

The question was an important one, because the man had clearly been murdered. The razor grinder, who did an itinerant business sharpening scythe blades and scissors out of the back of a mule-drawn Concord wagon, found him lying face down in the muck of one of his hog pens with his feet sticking out through the fence. The boars had been at the top of him; but even so the razor grinder and a neighbor who happened along found a small hole in his forehead and a much larger one at the base of his skull, which showed he'd been shot from in front, with the ball passing entirely through. There were also two holes in his back where it seemed he'd been shot again after he was down. The razor grinder and the neighbor surmised the murderer had shot him and then shoved the body through the fence for the hogs to eat, which betrayed a disposition more perverse than most.

The dead man was a Confederate veteran and had been home only five months. It was his pappy's place. His pappy, who was a widower, had died in sixty-four, and after returning from the army the soldier had started up where his pappy left off. A half-wit cousin of his had been taking care of the place and despite being a simpleton had somehow contrived to keep the boars and sows and shoats hidden from the outliers and rangers all through the wartime. But when the killing happened the half-wit was off fishing and the hog farmer was alone on the place.

The razor grinder and the neighbor figured it was guerrillas. Putting the corpse in with the hogs looked for sure like a bushwhacker trick. Although matters were gradually quieting down in the wake of the peace, there were still some bad gangs of moccasin rangers lurking in the high tops of the Tusquittees and the Valley River, who had forgot there was any other way to live and came down to the settled country from time to time to steal and kill. Either that or some tory had concluded to rid the world of another Reb. Or maybe a mob of hateful nigras had done the deed—just now the whole country was plagued with unruly freedmen and nigras discharged out of the Federal army who bore ill toward every Southern white.

In the end it was Murphy they sent to, because Murphy was nearer than Hayesville. The new high sheriff of Cherokee County that Provisional Governor Holden's officers had appointed came out and took the matter in hand. But he could discover no evidence, and the killing remained a mystery. In time it was learned that the dead man was David Sprogg. When Andy Curtis learned of the murder a few days later he recognized the name. David Sprogg had been an army friend of Howell's, a bugler in Folk's Battalion. Howell had often mentioned him in letters home. He blew a sweet and mellow horn, Howell said.

That was not the only lawless incident that season. Later that same week in Murphy a party of discharged Union soldiers was passing through town singing and shouting and raising hob, as they often did nowadays. But on this occasion the noise roused a young mother, who came to the door of her house to see what the fuss was about. She was carrying her infant girl in her arms. One of the blues took a shot at her for fun, and the ball barely missed the baby's head and broke out one of the sidelights by the door. But in this case the misdoer was seen. That dusk some of the men of Murphy found him drinking in a saloon and asked him why he took that shot. In his drunkenness he mistook them and replied that he just wanted to see if he could hit the woman without aiming. So the men took him down to the Boot Lot below the old Methodist church and hanged him from the limb of an oak tree.

Under the president's amnesty proclamation fourteen classes of men were exempt from pardon and could regain their citizenship only through application. The exempted classes included high offic-ers of the military and the Confederate government and those worth twenty thousand dollars or more. Madison Curtis had once been worth much more than twenty thousand but now was worth a tenth of that or less, and it was a cold comfort to him that in losing his fortune he had gained the franchise. But he was a responsible man and considered it his solemn duty to take part in public affairs. He and Andy had sworn the oath of allegiance and were entitled to vote in the election to choose delegates for the convention that would meet at Raleigh in October to reconstruct the state.

Accordingly, on election day, Thursday the twenty-first of September, the two of them rode into Hayesville bareback on the plow mules and cast their ballots for Augustus Merrimon, the most moderate candidate. Madison had always been a man of moderation; before the war he was a Whig and opposed secession and had only supported the Confederacy after Lincoln called for troops to subjugate the South. Now he nourished hopes that after four years of war and countless thousands of dead and wounded the day of extreme political opinion was finally done. Andy had no politics himself; he wanted only to live and let live, and he figured moderation might bring that about.

But these fond expectations were destined to go glimmering. Many tories in the highlands—including some that had served with the notorious Union bushwhacker George Washington Kirk—hated Augustus Merrimon, who as an officer of the superior court in wartime had hounded all bloody marauders North and South. When the votes were counted Merrimon was badly defeated. A candidate who had been an original Unionist went to Raleigh. But still, when October came, the convention started out in moderate fashion. It repealed the secession ordinance, abolished slavery and set up the apparatus for an election in November to choose a governor, a general assembly and a set of senators and congressmen. But then under pressure from Washington City the extreme opinion Madison had so dreaded suddenly took hold. The president himself sent a written demand that the state's war debt be repudiated, and after much wrangling this was done. Among other things repudiation completed the ruin of Madison Curtis, who held thousands in state bonds.

But all this lay in the future; on election day one might still wish for moderation to prevail. Without saying so Andy also hoped that in a reconstructed North Carolina the charges lodged against Madison by Nahum Bellamy and the Pucketts might somehow be laid aside. He had written a letter to his old commanding officer, Colonel David Coleman, who before the war had been a prominent Asheville lawyer, asking him to defend Papa in the civil and military cases. Andy had a good deal of faith in Colonel Coleman, but it was unclear whether the great man would have the time to take the matter up—Andy heard that Governor Holden had appointed Coleman solicitor of the Eighth Judicial District. How much easier it would be if the charges could simply be erased by some sweeping act of pardon. But Madison himself indulged in no such forlorn hope. Secure in the belief that he merited punishment, he awaited it with stoic fortitude.

After casting their ballots that Thursday Madison and Andy took dinner at the house of Cousin Watson Curtis and then rode home. There they had a considerable shock. Sanders Barter was ensconced on the gallery bouncing his daughter Eva on his knee. At first he hardly seemed to resemble himself, so drawn and rangy was he. In former times he was inclined to corpulence, but now knobs of bone stuck out of his wrists and his neck was slim as a length of cane and the points of his shoulders poked up like a pair of sweet potatoes standing on end. Most of his teeth were gone, and he had a great thicket of beard that was rusty brown with streaks of gray in it. But it was Sanders, all right. There was no mistaking the one hazel eye and the one blue one, and the missing tip of his left thumb.

It was hard for Andy to greet him civilly, because Andy resented how Sanders had laid out while Jack and Howell and Andy himself had served. The most Andy could do was give him a nod and stand stiffly back while Papa went to him. Papa embraced him and welcomed him home and Sanders cried, and when Martha came out of the house she told in ecstacy how she'd dropped to her knees in the yard and thanked God aloud when she saw Sanders hobbling down the lane, for the joy of her husband coming home whom she'd presumed long dead. Eva commenced happily warbling then, and presently Andy turned away and went down into the yard and hunkered under one of the magnolias and tried not to listen to the joyful sounds of Sanders's homecoming. All he could think about was how Howell and Jack had died while Sanders was laying out.

Later Sanders said he'd spent most of the war way back up under Laurel Top in the wilds of the Smokies, keeping out of everybody's way, Union and Confederate. He said he lived on groundhog and squirrel and many a field mouse and ate wild berries like a bear and had even once dined on a timber rattler. He said he lived so low he became like a beast of the woods himself and nearly forgot the English language and the Methodist doctrine. He said he hadn't learned the war was over till sometime in June, when he ventured down to Quallatown to replenish his powder and shot. Then he fell sick of a fever of the lungs and likely would've died had a family of Cherokees not taken him in and cared for him. Then he started for home rejoicing in the peace but fell and broke his leg on the Roaring Fork of the Nantahala and was laid up there till his leg healed, staying with a man that had a still-house up on the Fire Gap.

Andy didn't believe a word of it. He took Papa aside and told him he was convinced that Sanders had been with the Yankee army at the very least, and at worst was bushwhacking with Kirk, and had delayed coming home for fear of reprisal.

But Papa only rested a hand on Andy's shoulder and gave him a wistful smile. "We all did what we had to, son. What each did is on his own soul, and few of us done well enough to stand in judgment on another."

Andy knew this was true for both Papa and himself as well as for Sanders, who'd done whatever he did out of love for Union. But knowing it and being reconciled to it were two different things, and

Andy didn't see how he could ever again take the hand of Sanders Barter in friendship, for the reproving ghosts of Howell and Jack would forever be rising up between them.

In a few days Sanders found himself a little farm over by Warne and rented it, and he and Martha and Eva went there to live. After that they kept to themselves most of the time, and that was plenty all right with Andy.

Inexorably as time passed Andy felt the oppressive weight of responsibility bearing down on him more and more. The perils and woes of the war years had leached out of Papa much of his old power, and now that he stood charged with crimes of which he believed himself guilty he seemed far too ready to submit to fate. This was very unlike the Madison Curtis of old, who had made his own fate and often lectured Andy on the need for fortitude, confidence, self-reliance and all other manly virtues. Andy had never found these virtues in himself but now needed them badly. There was a large empty place in the middle of the family where Papa's resolution had once been, and Andy knew if that place was ever to be filled again it was going to be his duty to do it.

Andy resented this burden more the heavier it grew. He'd come home from the war wholly spent and reckoned on Mama and Papa and Jack handling every difficulty, as they had before. But Jack was dead and Mama was as drained as Andy himself. And Papa seemed to have given up. While he still toiled around the place as hard as any man half his age, he also spent many an evening hour closeted in his study with his Bible or back numbers of the *Arator* and the *North Carolina Planter* or rocking reflectively on the gallery, as if preparing himself in spirit for his sacrifice to come. So it all descended on Andy. And with it came the awful feeling that had tormented him throughout the war—the feeling that he was not equal to the task.

It didn't help that he'd survived the war despite this feeling, because he came to see at last that he'd survived not because of anything he'd done but because his brother Jack and his messmates and his officers had looked after him and protected him and overlooked or concealed his many blunders. He possessed the gift of a winning way. In civilian life people had always liked him and because of this had done favors for him, and this continued in the army—after all, his company messmates and officers were also his friends and neighbors. So he took no credit and drew no confidence from having survived, having been a sergeant in charge of a platoon of men, having been put on the Roll of Honor. All this was the work of others. Nothing he could name was the work of Andy Curtis alone.

Yet now everyone was turning to him. And he could see in their eyes how sorry they were to have to do it. It shamed him to see that. He knew they understood very well that he was weak and timid; all his life they'd made allowances for that, Mama especially. But now they had no choice, and he had no choice either. In spite of his shortcomings he would have to act, and they would have to rely on him to act well.

Thank God for Salina. Next to Mama she was the toughest and most levelheaded of them all. She'd always been strong, but the war had made her even stronger. There was a new and harder line to her jaw; she was as wiry as a ferret and as brown as an Indian; her dark eyes were always calm and looked out levelly at the world; even her black hair had a coarser feel. And her soul was as hard as her body— she feared nothing. Andy came to depend on her as he had once depended on Papa and Mama and Jack. He did not know how a woman so strong as she could love a man as slight as himself, but she did. She loved him for what he was and did not hate him for what he was not. She supported whatever he did no matter if it turned out well or ill. He was aware of how great a gift this was. Sometimes he thought it was this, and only this, that lent him whatever power he drew on to face what was coming.

But even with Salina there was occasion for shame. Since coming home, not once had he been able to act the man with her. At first he thought it was because of his war-weariness and the fever he carried home. But after a time the fever went away and his health returned, and still he could not manage. Salina was patient and never said a word of reproach or bitterness, and Andy showed himself tender and loving in other ways, but this was not enough for either of them. Before the war—even during the war when he was home laying out or on furlough—they'd both been full of passion always. It was a large and vital part of what they had shared. But now that it had been absent for so long Andy began to worry that it would never return. And if it didn't how could he expect Salina to stay with him? And if she didn't stay what would he do without her—Salina, his strength?

Twice more in September and October the officer Bellamy came to the farm to interview Papa and Mama and Andy about the Yellow Jacket raid. In manner he was always correct and official, but he had a fidgety way about him and a sparkle of mischief in the eye that showed the pleasure he took in bullying them and inspiring fear.

"Unfortunately," he explained with his supercilious smile on the second of his visits, "there has been a delay in the filing of the charges. Major Smith of the Seventeenth Massachusetts, the superintendent of the bureau's western subdistrict, has been mustered out, and no successor has yet been named. General Heath, succeeding General Cox in military command, has only just arrived. Further, due to the disturbed condition of the mountain counties, other matters of a more pressing nature have taken precedence. Also, certain staff officers vital to the work of administration have not yet been assigned to the Morganton headquarters, and in consequence much of the paperwork of the military district is far in arrears."

But Bellamy assured the Curtises that in due time the case would indeed be brought to trial. "Doubtless," he said, "it will be heard before a military commission on charges alleging a violation of the rules of war. The commission will be composed of line officers of the army, with a president of field grade. A judge advocate will prosecute, and a recorder will defend."

Bellamy was gathering all the evidence he could, and he wished the Curtises to know that in doing so he would search as assiduously for proofs tending toward extenuation as for those tending toward guilt. "I am after all a fair man and only doing my duty"—he said this with a modest downcast of his eyes—"and have no wish at all to persecute the innocent. All the same, given the gravity of the charges, I strongly urge you to engage competent counsel."

Shortly after Bellamy's second visit Andy received a letter from Colonel Coleman saying that the condition of his affairs prevented him from taking Papa's case, but that if Madison and Andy would come to Asheville he would be pleased to consult with them and render what assistance he could—all of course entirely without charge, in honor of their long service together in the old Thirty-ninth.

Predictably Papa declined to go. Lately he'd heard that his old servant Gamaliel—Daniel McFee—had fallen deeply under Major Bellamy's influence, and this depressed him even worse than his own troubles seemed to. He'd done everything he thought right and decent to help Daniel set himself up as a free man, only to see him take the part of the enemy. Perhaps Papa had even begun to suspect that because he'd held Daniel a slave they could never be reconciled no matter what he did. In his dispirited state Papa would not lift a hand in his own defense. So Andy went up to Asheville by himself.

He had a harness that needed mending at the saddlery in Murphy, so he rode there first and boarded the mule at a stable. After handling the harness business he caught the stage that took the Western Turnpike up the Valley River, then down the Nantahala through Cheoah and up the Little Tennessee around the north end of the mountains to Franklin. From Franklin the road went on through the Cowees and Balsam Gap to Asheville. The route was out of the way, but Andy was weary of home and looked forward to different sights and new places.

The journey rewarded him as he'd hoped. Spears of goldenrod and sheaves of white and purple asters stood thick along the roadside. The fall colors were vivid as the coach rolled between the ranges. The leaves were coming off unseasonably early, and already at the foot of each maple lay a scatter of gold like fallen riches. Some of the maples were crimson on one side and yellow on the other, and many of the poplars wore crowns the color of mustard, and all the trees were shedding their gaudy plumage. The air was full of the tiny greenish yellow leaves of locust trees blowing past like confetti. The nearer slopes of the mountains were a riot of russet and Chinese red and every possible shade of brown, following the contours of the hills like a piece of tapestry or heavy brocade folded over the ridge lines. Whenever the coach stopped Andy could hear the rattle of falling acorns and walnuts in the surrounding woods. The peaks trailed plumes of cloud.

Looking out on the glorious hues of autumn Andy was aware for the first time of how much anger was welling up inside him. And it was Papa he was angry at. Papa had no right to give up now. Too many needed him and depended on him. It was selfish of him to withdraw now. It was wrong to surrender the initiative to Andy, when everybody knew that Andy was incapable of taking charge. But in a strange way, as he filled up with it, Andy drew a kind of bitter nourishment from the anger too. Somehow it seemed to make him stronger.

He arrived in Asheville in the crisp October weather feeling refreshed and confident. The stage crossed Smith's Bridge over the French Broad and came past the ruins of the Confederate armory, burnt by Michigan troops when they pillaged Asheville last April. He found the town aswarm with nigras, many of them wenches ostentatiously twirling parasols and parading about in new dresses roughly made of the gaudiest material, imitating the fine attire of the white ladies they had admired from afar in slavery times. The rest were freedmen who roamed restlessly to and fro, some in search of wives and children sold away years before, many looking for work, the most belligerent swaggering along in hopes of provoking trouble with some resentful white. Some were still in their raggedy plantation jeans and Chilhowee cloth, but others wore bits and pieces of finery— cravats, silk hats, kid gloves, coats of fine broadcloth—that former masters had given them or they had stolen. A company of the Thirty-seventh United States Colored Troops was stationed in Asheville, and Andy saw several of these drunk on the streets in uniform and bearing arms; he saw two of them stop an elderly white man on a corner and shout abuse at him and knock his hat into the gutter. Watching all this Andy thought how truly the worm had turned for Dixie's Land.

Colonel Coleman's office was in the upper story of a brick building facing the public square. It was a modest office, as befitted a lawyer rebuilding his practice after four years of soldiering. Mezzotints and lithographs of sailing ships and oceangoing steamers hung on the walls. Years ago the colonel had served in the navy of the United States; indeed, when war came, he'd taken over the Thirty-ninth only after finding he couldn't get command of a ship in Confederate service. There had been times under fire when he'd forgot himself and started shouting nautical commands, and because of this the boys had sometimes called him the Old Salt, but never to his face.

In wartime colonels and sergeants of the line are rarely on speaking terms, so although Andy and he were veterans together they did not know each other at all. Andy of course had seen the colonel almost daily, but to the colonel Andy's was but one in a blur of faces he'd glimpsed in the ranks. The colonel was a man of noted reserve, and while in the free-and-easy Rebel army any officer was likely to be accosted by any raggedy private at any time, no one had ever seen Colonel Coleman lapse into familiarity. Nor did he do so now. His handshake was firm but cold, and as Andy seated himself the colonel gave him one piercing look of his black eyes and got straight to the point.

"This Bellamy who persecutes you," he said in his sharp voice, "is something of a rum character, from what I hear. Since receiving your letter I've done some checking. It appears that during the war he engaged in a number of quite doubtful activities, and grim tales are starting to come out."

"What sort of tales, sir?"

"Tales of . . . unsound military practice. And now that he holds a position in the Freedmen's Bureau there are further complaints. Complaints of radical political activity, of fomenting discontent among the Negroes, even of promoting insurrection. I believe him a dangerous fanatic. Yet he is protected from on high. Generals Cox and Ruger created the man, after all; and now that Cox has departed, Heath supports him too."

"What can be done, sir?"

"The right man can do much, I believe. By going to the proper authorities of the military district with valid evidence of the fellow's misbehavior, I am convinced that he can eventually be brought low. The officers of the occupying army are anxious to tread lightly on the prostrate South, lest the smoldering embers of conflict flare up again before the smoke of war even has a chance to dissipate."

At this flight of oratory Andy remembered certain of the colonel's speeches before the Thirty-ninth and inwardly smiled; the boys had often suspected him of practicing his forensic gifts on them, against the day of his return to the bar.

"The man should also be exposed to his chiefs in the Freedmen's Bureau," the colonel went on. "Eastmond, the agent of the bureau here in Asheville, is something of an agitator himself, much like your Bellamy. But his superiors at the Morganton subdistrict, like the officers of the army, are hopeful of conciliating our people. The most responsible among the Yankees have no wish to antagonize us. Men like Bellamy are a curse to them, as they are to the South. If he is shown to be the vile character of his repute, not even Heath and Ruger will act to save him."

Colonel Coleman sighed impatiently and spread his hands over the mounds of paper that covered his desk. "I regret that I cannot be your advocate, but I do not have the time just now." He leveled on Andy a glaring eye. "Do you know Kope Elias?"

Andy brightened. "Yes, sir. Lawyer Elias is from my section and is well acquainted with my father. He practices law in Murphy." Then he paused, blushing. "But ain't Mr. Elias . . . ?" He did not know how to finish; Kope Elias was no more than nineteen and had been pleading cases only since the spring term of court the year before.

"Indeed," Colonel Coleman nodded. "Confessedly he is quite young and only recently admitted to the bar, but I esteem him quite as highly as I do any advocate in western Carolina. He began his practice while I was in service, but my associates on the circuit have praised him extravagantly. Furthermore, since resuming my own practice, I have had occasion to observe him in the well myself. I assure you he is an attorney of the very highest caliber. Also, because he is building his practice, I believe you will find his fees most reasonable. I have taken the liberty of writing him in your behalf. Should you visit him I believe you will find him acquainted with all the particulars of your case. If any man—other than myself—can fetch Nahum Bellamy, it is Elias."

Andy knit his brow. "If Bellamy is brought down that would end the military case. But what about the Puckett lawsuit?"

"Bellamy is the linchpin of both cases. He is the evil genius behind the Pucketts; without him they can do nothing. No reputable lawyer of the provisional court would represent them."

Colonel Coleman had a moon-shaped face half covered by a close-cropped black beard shot with silver; it frowned shrewdly, as Andy had seen it do on the battlefield when the colonel was pondering some tactical move. "Now," he said curtly, "let us address the merits of Bellamy's case against your father. Did Madison Curtis in fact dispatch rangers to rob and murder Unionists?"

Haltingly Andy explained the circumstances of the Yellow Jacket raid. Papa had acted to save Mama from torture and Andy himself from hanging, he said. The Pucketts, whom the scouts attacked, had themselves previously raided the Curtis farm and others. "It was war, sir," Andy concluded. "It was kill or be killed. That was the way it was in the battle line, and I figure it ought to have been the same way when the war came to the home folk."

Colonel Coleman made no comment on this observation. Instead he demanded, "Do you have an independent witness who can give evidence that will sustain your version of these events?"

Andy nodded. "There was a soldier staying over with us at the time, a Georgian name of Oliver Price. Papa sent him to warn one of the tory families—name of Quillen—and saved them from the bushwhackers."

The colonel cocked an inquisitive eyebrow. "These tories that were saved, will they speak for you?"

Gravely Andy shook his head. "No, sir. They were all killed sometime after."

"Then you'll need your Georgian to tell his story to Elias. And if, God forbid, the case ever comes to court, you'll need his testimony."

Andy smiled. He'd often thought of Oliver since seeing him last before the battle of Resaca. Had Oliver survived the war? It would be good to know.

It cheered Sarah Curtis's heart to see Andy start to lay a forceful grasp on things. Now and then there was a vitality to him that she had never before witnessed. Gradually after his return from seeing Colonel Coleman this new briskness was replacing the slouchy languor that had been his normal way throughout life.

Watching him one morning as he hunched at Madison's desk in the study writing his letter to Oliver Price, she thought how the bend of his elbow and the inclination of his head reminded her of the way young Madison Curtis used to carry himself in the early years of their marriage. In those days Madison did everything—from keeping the farm accounts to splitting rails to butchering hogs—with energy and precision and without any wasted motion. And that was the way Andy looked now. Curiously, it was as if they had somehow exchanged personalities—Madison had taken on Andy's mildness, while Andy bristled with his father's resolution.

Andy's determination buoyed them all up—even Madison. Based on what Colonel Coleman had said about Bellamy, Andy believed chances were good that a persuasive advocate might get a sympathetic hearing from higher Federal authorities, who held the power to dismiss the military charges or even prevent their being filed. And now they had such an advocate. Andy had stopped in Murphy to see Kope Elias, and Elias had agreed to assume Madison's defense. Madison smiled, albeit wanly, when he heard the news. "Maybe God means to spare us the worst after all," he remarked.

But still harbingers of disaster circled about them. Every few days the Puckett women appeared in the lane, riding double on their dun mule. They would walk the mule down the lane and stop in the cul-de-sac and sit there in their grimy dresses shouting abuse, till Andy went out and chased them off. Andy always had to go; Madison never stirred. Madison would rock on the gallery and allow their cries to wash over him as serenely as if they were blessings instead of curses.

Nahum Bellamy had not come back to the farm, but they saw him often on the square in Hayesville and on the roads riding at the head of his ragamuffin crowd of nigras and tories and reformed

Rebels. Often Sarah was dismayed to see that Daniel McFee was with him; on these occasions Daniel would look both shamefaced and truculent. Bellamy would tip his absurd cap and speak some fulsome greeting and bend on them a look of knowing amusement. Always Sarah fancied she smelt a kind of scorched odor about him, like the electricity that crackled in the air before a thunderstorm.

Once, after encountering him in Hayesville, she returned home with his menacing image lingering before her more disagreeably than ever. It had always seemed ironic to her that a man so foul should carry the name of a prophet of God. But till that day she had not thought to study the Scriptures themselves and see if he was in any way consonant with Holy Writ. On a sudden impulse she entered Madison's study and opened his great leather-bound Bible to the Book of Nahum in the Old Testament. Sarah was a sensible woman and while full of faith of a certain kind was very far from superstition. Yet still, as she read the prophecy of Nahum, the hairs on the backs of her arms stood up:

> And the Lord hath given a commandment concerning thee, that no more of thy name be sown: out of the house of thy gods will I cut off the graven image and the molten image: I will make thy grave; for thou art vile. . . .
> He that dasheth in pieces is come up before thy face: keep the munition, watch the way, make thy loins strong, fortify thy power mightily. . . .
> The shield of his mighty men is made red, the valiant men are in scarlet: the chariots shall be with flaming torches in the day of his preparation, and the fir trees shall be terribly shaken.
> The chariots shall rage in the streets, they shall jostle one against another in the broad ways: they shall seem like torches, they shall run like the lightnings. . . .
> The horseman lifteth up both the bright sword and the glittering spear: and there is a multitude of slain, and a great number of carcasses; and there is none end of their corpses; they stumble upon the corpses. . . .
> Behold, I am against thee, said the Lord of hosts; and I will discover

thy skirts upon thy face, and I will shew the nations thy nakedness, and the kingdoms thy shame.

And I will cast abominable filth upon thee, and make thee vile. . . .

There is no healing of thy bruise; thy wound is grievous: all that hear the bruit of thee shall clap their hands over thee: for upon whom hath not thy wickedness passed continually?

CHAPTER 8

S o delighted was Oliver Price to hear at last from his Clay County friends that he tore open the envelope the Clayton postmaster handed him and began reading Andy Curtis's letter right there at the cage of the post office, with two impatient ladies and a petulant dry-goods merchant waiting in line behind him. He'd often thought of taking pen in hand to the Curtises, or even of going out again to visit, but Nancy's taking sick had cornered all his mind. Now he beamed at the sight of Andy's scrawl.

But what he read bore him quickly from pleasure to sorrow, and from sorrow on to alarm, and when he finished his blood ran cold with dread. It cheered him to learn that Andy had made it through the war and Miz Barter had got her husband back. But poor Jack was dead after all, as Oliver had long feared. And the lively Miz Betty Cartman had passed on, together with her man, the tory Oliver had never met, and the two orphan boys Oliver remembered pretending always to be twins were left for the Curtises to raise in their old age. Worst of all, an ordeal of the most baleful sort—trouble with the Yank authorities—beset the judge, and the Curtises needed Oliver to help them out of it.

To the relief of the two ladies and the merchant Oliver soon left the post office and found himself a bench outside by the road to rest on and think. His first thought was of Nancy and her sickness of the lungs. So far she seemed to be bearing up all right. Although she'd commenced to lose weight her cough seemed no worse, and there was no blood yet in her sputum, as there'd been last spring. But he feared what would happen when the colder weather came. Were he to travel out to Clay County as Andy implored him, he might be absent when the snows fell and the cold blasts blew in December and January. How could he leave her alone at such a time, five or six months gone and tubercular? And what of Martha and Syl? Should Nancy take sickly, who would care for them?

But even as he posed each question an answer presented itself, and it was the same answer every time—the Widow Henslee. Nancy had schemed all these months just so the widow would be present when needed. Nancy's plot was drum-tight; there wasn't any give in it. It was meant for the time when Nancy was gone, but till then it was so sound that it would serve for this necessity and many another as well. The Widow Henslee was a formidable presence. She could shoe a mule, cut a cord of firewood, lay a stone wall, dig a ditch, castrate a calf and shingle a roof. As far as Oliver knew the only thing she couldn't do was make a pair of brogans. Aside from that she was as handy as Oliver himself. She'd tend to Nancy and mind the younguns and look after the place, and when Oliver got back things would likely be in an even better fix than if he'd never left.

But it wasn't just the worry of abandoning Nancy when she was frail that nagged at him. He knew Mama and some of the others thought he'd shirked his duty by going off to war, leaving his woman to fend for herself and his younguns to grow up strange to him. Not that Mama cared much for Nancy herself. Mama wouldn't even call Nancy by name—never had, in fact—nor did she miss a chance to remind Oliver that Nancy was a Garrett from down by Earle's Ford and was febrile like all the Garretts, which was Mama's way of saying she was sickly and would die young. Now that her prophecy was coming true Mama mentioned it often, with a kind of monotonous glee. No, it wasn't just his leaving Nancy that people had objected to, it was a matter of principle. Rabun County was all for Union and against slavery—Oliver couldn't think of more than twenty men from there who'd served the Confederacy—and in all the country between Tallulah Falls and Rock Mountain Gorge it was commonly thought that when the war came a man's proper place was with his own, rather than out fighting the Yanks so the rich could keep their darkies. Oliver had violated that principle, and some thought ill of him for it.

Not only that, but in going away he'd missed the closest and tenderest of times with Nancy and Syl and Martha. Then while he was gone Nancy got sick and Syl turned surly and Martha started to grow up not knowing who he was. Since coming home he'd done his best to make up for having gone away, but he'd learned to his sorrow that this in fact lay far beyond his power. He could caper with them and make them laugh for a time, but he couldn't erase the changes his absence had set deep in them. He couldn't restore Nancy's health nor heal the wounds in Syl's heart. Even wee Martha, who loved him dearly, sometimes forgot who he was and spoke of her lost pappy, saying he was far away in an army that marched everywhere but back home again.

Presently Oliver got up from his bench and started for home, leaning on the hickory staff he still used from time to time when his leg was paining him. He was an honest man and above all was honest with himself, so while he hobbled along the rutted wagon road he had to admit to another reason for his dread of leaving, a reason that lay even nearer to his heart than his worries over Nancy and the younguns. Coming home from war Oliver had made a decision to withdraw from affairs. Yanks and Rebels, nigras and Regulators, Whigs and secesh, Freedmen's Bureau agents and Copperheads were all alike to him now. He wanted to avoid every complication of the times and only live the small life God had left him. He had no wish to jolt against the hard edges of defeat and reconstruction.

Yet this was precisely what Andy Curtis wanted him to do—come out to Clay County and resist the occupiers Oliver had promised himself henceforth to obey. Oliver felt torn between an obligation to his dear friends and an obligation to himself and did not know what he should do. Without his help the Curtises would surely be ruined. But if he helped them he would be opposing the forces he had come to think of as right for having conquered the evils of slavery and disunion. He'd compound his own sin of fighting for those evils; having repented, he would backslide again into error. More, he'd be putting himself at risk when, because of Nancy and Syl and Martha, he had no right to. All this vexed him mightily, and halfway home at the foot of the Black Rocks he stopped by the roadside and knelt down under a large red oak and prayed a long while, leaning on his staff. After praying he felt a little better, although he still had no notion what to do, and he got to his feet and limped on home in the twilight.

Nancy sat close to the hearth in her cane-bottomed chair, knitting a muffler in the firelight. "Well," she said, "all I've heard since you come home from war is what fine Christian folks these Curtises be, how they never put on airs nor judged you common. Fed you at their own table like you and them was just the same. Now they're afflicted. Seems to me you owe hit to them to go and help."

Oliver was hunched on the hearth with one leg doubled under him and his bad leg straightened out while he made pegs for shoes. He paused, holding the little block of maple wood on the hearthstone with his hammer suspended over it. He knew better than to mention her sickness, because she would only throw the Widow Henslee back at him, so he spoke his truest reason.

She listened, plying her needles while he talked. Then she said, "Ain't no enterprise of man I ever heard of was altogether perfect. I figure that includes the government. Hit may be God's on the side of the Yankees like you say. But that don't mean every last Yankee's an angel out of heaven. Some's mean as sin. I expect you know that better'n me."

Oliver set the edge of his knife blade against the top of the block of maple and rapped it with the hammer and split off a slab along the grain while Nancy went on. "This Yankee pestering the Curtises sounds to me like he's abusing his office. If he is, hit ain't the work of God he's doing, hit's Satan's. Say the government's good, as you believe. Then wouldn't they want to know if he's done wrong? Seems to me you'd be right to go agin him, and the government would thank you for hit."

He took up the slab of maple and with the knife trimmed one side to a beveled edge. Nancy's needles clicked, and the wood in the fireplace snapped and whined. "You go on out there," she said. "Take Syl with you. You and him together, that'd be good. Get him to knowing you. Maybe draw some of the meanness out of him. Me and Martha can go over to War Woman Creek till you come back. And there's your mama if we need her, and Lit and Mac."

Oliver cocked his head inquiringly. "A boy going on six years old, ain't you scared I'd be exposing him to danger, with the times unsettled as they are?"

Nancy bent over her needles. "Hit's a dangerous world," she said, and paused while Oliver took thought of her condition. Then she remarked, "The child needs to learn to make his way in hit. He'll be as safe with you as anywhere."

With the knife Oliver began splitting off pegs of half an inch for soles and a little longer for heels. He made a pile of ten or twelve pegs and then picked up the block of maple and took off another slab with a tap of his hammer. Then while he trimmed the slab he reflected on what Nancy had said. When he was ready to split off another mess of pegs he paused and gazed into the fire. He didn't look at Nancy at all. After a spell he said, "You'll be all right, then."

It wasn't exactly a question but she answered it anyway, and did it with a small laugh. "I didn't last through a whole war just to peter out while you take a little trip out to Carolina." He looked up at her then, and she gave him a nod. "I'll be here when you get back."

That was it, the end of all his upset.

Next morning he borrowed Uncle Ernest's mule and rode up to the gap to tell Mama and Lit and Mac. In her grim but gleeful way Mama foretold that Nancy would die before he came home again. She said his younguns would be poor orphans then, because he wouldn't know how to take care of them and would have to give them up. She also reminded him he had a sister Tabitha twenty years older than himself who lived in Clay County with her husband, a man name of Gettys, and said Oliver ought to visit. Oliver had forgot all about Tabitha and had even gone to Clay County that one time during the war without thinking to look her up. He supposed he was obliged to go and see her now. But then in a family of twelve a man could be excused for being a stranger to brothers and sisters he'd never even met.

Lit offered to drive Oliver and Syl down the river to Franklin, where they could catch the stage out to Hayesville. They set the time for twelve days hence. Then Oliver returned home to write to Andy, saying he would come out to Clay County and do what he could to help.

After that he rode the mule across to War Woman Creek in a fit of trepidation to arrange for the Widow Henslee to take Nancy and Martha in. She welcomed him with a robust shake of the hand, and when he followed her onto the porch he found himself admiring the braids of her thick hair wound into a bun at the back of her head and the long tails of the red silk bow fixed to the bun. He smelt again that fragrance of cinnamon and cloves that always hung about her. It was a cool day, but to observe the proprieties she served him coffee and ham biscuits on the porch while they talked, and in spite of himself he soon relaxed and felt easy in her presence. He noticed that her eyes had shades of green in them. She was a confident woman, but unlike some of that kind she did not want to make a man feel small. She spoke to him in frankness but with respect too. There was a clarity between them that he hadn't noticed before, which he liked. While they talked, James her oldest and Caledonia the next youngest and little Ellen the setalong all watched him big-eyed, as if he might try and steal the spoons. The widow agreed to look after Nancy and Martha. She wished him well on his enter-prise. Then they shook hands again and said good-bye, and Oliver left War Woman Creek feeling for the first time a little regret along with his customary relief.

In a week's time Oliver got another letter from Andy enclosing forty dollars in Yank greenbacks to cover stage fare and the expenses of the trip. Three days later he borrowed the mule again from Uncle Ernest. Nancy and Martha rode, while Oliver and Syl walked. Oliver had a hard time of it on account of his leg, and by the time they got to the Widow Henslee's it would hardly bear his weight. He'd begun to worry he was going to be a cripple for the rest of his life but had said nothing of this to anybody except for Uncle Ernest, as a reason for borrowing his mule time and time again.

Martha commenced wailing when it was time for him to go. He held her tiny self close and felt her every sob like the wound of a bullet to his heart. Finally the Widow Henslee had to carry her inside so he and Nancy could say farewell in the dooryard. They hugged and kissed in what Oliver supposed was a scandalous fashion. Nancy promised to finish knitting his muffler by Christmas and said she hoped he'd be home by then, but in any case he should stay away for as long as it took to help his friends. In the end Oliver's throat closed up so he couldn't talk. He and Syl got on the mule and left. At the edge of the woods he drew rein and looked back and saw her standing in the dooryard with one hand raised. He waved at her and then spoke to the mule, and the dry November sourwood leaves closed behind him, and he could not see her anymore.

It was the fifteenth of November, a Wednesday, when Lit and Oliver and Syl started out in the wagon for Franklin. That was the same day all the Georgians who'd amnestied themselves could vote to elect representatives to Congress and the new state legislature, but since Oliver had never taken the oath, election day was of no interest to him. Lit, who was a conscientious sort, had cast his ballot before setting out; Lit said a man was bound to vote conservative if he wanted to keep the state out of the hands of the nigras. But it was a matter of indifference to Oliver if the nigras did run Georgia for a spell; they could hardly do a worse job of it than the whites had. Syl had no opinion on the question. Ever since learning that he was going over into Carolina with Oliver all he could think about was riding for the first time on a stagecoach, and the whole afternoon as they wended their way among the foothills of Cedar Cliff Mountain he bedeviled Oliver to tell him how soon they'd get to Franklin and the post office, where the mail stage awaited.

They arrived that evening at sunset, and using the money Andy had sent, Oliver and Syl put up in a hotel overnight, while Lit slept out in the wagon before returning home to the gap. But Syl wouldn't let Oliver rest that night till they'd gone down to the post office to watch the mail coach come in from the west. After that the child was in ecstacy and couldn't sleep all night long for the prospect of actually getting into a stagecoach and taking a forty-mile trip over the mountains.

Next morning when they presented themselves at the post office they found the place in an uproar. There was an old nigra who'd bought a ticket and wanted to ride inside with the whites. The conductor said he supposed the company must sell him a ticket but was under no obligation to depart from the custom of requiring nigras to travel up top with the baggage.

Aside from Oliver and Syl there were two other white passengers. From the cut of them and from their attitude Oliver deduced they were planters from out east. Loudly these two chastised the nigra for his impertinence. "Uncle," cried one of them, who carried a gold-headed cane, "you might be free, but you ain't white!"

The old nigra was wearing a moldy frock coat and a beaver hat that had seen better days. But in spite of the man's shabby look Oliver thought he had an air of dignity. He said he was a minister of the African Methodist Episcopal Church on his way to take up a pastorate in the Hickory Stand community of Clay County. He said now that Father Abraham had brought freedom a nigra had as much right as a white man to ride inside a stagecoach. "And if you please, I ain't your uncle, sah," he politely told the planter with the cane. "I'd like it if you'd call me reverend."

The two planters laughed like it was the funniest thing they'd heard in weeks. Naturally the nigra ended up on the roof of the coach, where he sat clutching his Bible to his breast, looking aggrieved but still full of dignity. Oliver and Syl got into the tonneau with the planters, who of course behaved as if they were alone once they gave Oliver enough of a study to conclude he was a low-downer. They were greatly amused by the airs the nigra preacher had put on, and as the coach started out Oliver watched them while they made jokes about the nigra and laughed and laughed, till they both wept tears of merriment.

At first Oliver was puzzled. In a land where the war had made most everybody poor these two seemed fat and prosperous. But eventually by their talk he learned they were cotton planters from down near New Bern, who although secessionist at first had turned coat when the Yankees under Burnside occupied that part of the coast in sixty-two. So, despite being slavers and having helped take the state out of the Union, they'd sold their cotton to the Yanks for shipment north and got richer than ever, while the plain folk they'd dragged into the conflict suffered and died. Now they were headed out to Murphy to invest in land, which because of the general wreck of the country could be had cheap, and which in time would make them even richer than they already were. Oliver listened while they commiserated with each other about the difficulties of forming labor contracts with ignorant freedmen, now that peace had come and taken away their slave labor.

"Why," one declared, "these niggers has got no notion atall about wage work. I had one old buck complain, 'If I'se free how come I gots to work harder den I done when I was a slave?' I've even had 'em insist on being fed and clothed and housed just like in servitude, on top of getting a wage, as if I owed 'em a living. Hell, I had one old uncle, eighty-five if he's a day, tell me, 'Massa, I don't care if I *is* free, I'se old and poorly and I ain't a-goin' to go off and work. You gots to take care of me like always.' Hell, I sent him packing. The old bastard's free. Let him make his own way."

The jasper with the cane shook his head in sympathy. "I know, I know. You heard about Maddox, I reckon, in Havelock. He had such a time with his niggers that when he finally got the crop in he chased the whole lot of 'em off the place and never paid 'em a dime." He chuckled at the idea of all those blacks done out of their shares, but then paused and looked somber. "But then he ended up in one of them freedmen's courts, and they made him pay off."

The pair sat saddened by their friend's fate till the one with the cane brightened and remarked, "You've got to admit, the one good thing about abolition is not having to care for a pack of indolent coons cradle to grave, your whole damned life. All them shirttail younguns and yard niggers and old uncles and mammies eating a man out of house and home, with nary a one hitting a lick of work in return. It broke my daddy down and put my mama early in her grave. Hell, when emancipation came, I made my people work an extra month just to pay for the clothes they had on and the food they et, that I'd bought."

"The problem now," said the other in a grave tone, "is how to get 'em to work at all. Making staple crops is nigger labor. Free whites won't do it, except maybe for your Irisher, if you can find one. But niggers are such lazy damned creatures, and now that they're free they only want to cultivate their own land and raise bacon. And if you use the lash on 'em the agents of the goddamned Freedmen's Bureau come down on you wagging the sanctimonious finger."

Oliver tried to pay them no mind, but in the close confines of the tonneau their manner pushed and prodded at him till he glared from one to the other. He kept thinking of his brother Freddy dead of a fever taken at Vicksburg and of his friend Jack Curtis dead of measles in a Nashville hospital and of any number of other boys he'd seen killed or mangled in battle or wasting away of disease in a war these two jaspers had helped fetch but then had got out of in order to enrich themselves. And he couldn't help but take thought of himself, his bad leg, the woes he'd suffered in the army, Nancy taken sick, Syl estranged from him and Martha not even remembering who he was sometimes.

Yet these planters could dismiss him with one look of contempt. He was of even less account to them than one of the darkies they were disparaging—he and all his kind. The poor white had served his purpose, fighting the planters' war; now he could be put aside. Now more and more it was the nigra all Dixie talked of. And now like many a despised low-downer Oliver resented how the nigra had been dragged to the center of the life of everyone in the South. The queer thing was, although everybody hated the nigra nobody could do without him. Nobody but folk like Oliver.

For all his resentment Oliver didn't think he hated nigras. But then he hardly understood anything about them. Till now he'd never been around them much. Before the war the few in Rabun County had stayed put on their plantations, and he only saw the ones hired out in town. But nowadays they were everywhere underfoot; a man couldn't avoid them. But even though Oliver thought them troublesome all together, in fact he mostly judged them one by one, and so far those he'd met had given him no cause to think they were any better or worse than whites. Certainly the old reverend on the roof of the coach was a better case than the two planters, black though he was. And Oliver had surely admired the grit of colored troops he'd seen on the battlefield. Because of being preoccupied with his own, Oliver had never given a lot of thought to what a nigra's life might be like. Not till today. Now it was on his mind.

The coach stopped to take on new teams at the top of the Winding Stairs. Oliver and Syl got out, and when the trip resumed they climbed up next to the driver. The change relieved Oliver's spirit considerably and altogether delighted Syl, who now could torment the driver with endless questions about the operation of the rig. The nigra reverend sat with his back to them and his legs hanging down over the boot, reading his Bible.

Oliver remembered every inch of the road from his walk through Clay County in the late summer of sixty-three, and as the coach bounced in and out of the deep ruts between the rounded hills every landmark called up fond thoughts of old. But the country seemed different now. Two years ago the place had been one lush expanse of green. Now autumn was far gone—only the oaks still held a few clusters of leaves, and the colors looked parched and dim against the black stickwork of the naked woods. Yet in spite of the dreary advance of winter Oliver could see that the country was in a fair way to recover from the desolation he'd seen in wartime. There were a few sheep in the fields and some hogs ranging free in the chestnut woods, and even so late in the season he saw cattle grazing on the balds, a scatter of black dots against the yellow-brown of the far tops. He saw great heaps of charred logs where farmers had cut and burnt the woods to clear land for cultivation in the spring, a sure sign of optimism. With a smile he remembered prophesying to the Curtises in sixty-three how richly the bounty of the land would spring forth once peace came.

But even so, not every sign of the struggle had been erased. Still on every hand he saw the blackened chimneys and fallen timbers of destroyed houses and barns, and fields gone to seed, and rootless nigras wandering hither and yon, and younguns white and black begging by the roadside. Once a small band of horsemen gathered in the distance and watched the coach pass with a close interest Oliver did not like. He knew there were robber gangs yet abroad; it was why he'd brought along his old navy revolver from the war and stuck it down the top of his trousers in the back. In the end nobody attacked the stage. But a dire misdeed was done nevertheless, which near the end of their journey Oliver and Syl confronted at a place east of Hayesville where the public road passed over the Licklog on a little wooden bridge.

The first Oliver knew of it was when the driver of the coach slowed the horses and uttered a wary noise. Oliver looked ahead and saw on the bridge itself a troop of mounted men sitting their horses in a ragged column of twos, whites and blacks together, heavily armed and all wearing the same kind of straw hat with black ribbons hanging down in back, but otherwise dressed in a mix of military gear. Ten or twelve civilians were gathered on the bridge and along the banks of the creek. All looked intently on while two nigras down in the creek waist-deep in water dragged out the sodden body of a white man. From his color the man had been dead for some time. The driver checked his team at the end of the bridge, and the two planters got out, and they all watched in silence while the nigras stretched the corpse out on the grass and a lean jasper wearing a Yank uniform and a peculiar-looking hat knelt over him. Syl was clamoring to be let down so he could get closer to the scene of the tragedy, and at first Oliver opposed him, thinking the sight of a cadaver might be too strong for a boy his age. But then he thought, *These are the times he's got to live in.* So he and Syl climbed down and advanced to the creek bank for a look, and presently the driver joined them.

Using a reverent whisper that seemed appropriate to the occasion, Oliver asked the driver who the horsemen on the bridge might be. "Officially that's the provisional Clay County police," the driver replied with a measure of sarcasm, "but in fact it's the private army of that feller yonder with the cap that looks like an accordion, Bellamy the Pilot. He's some sort of a special officer of the Freedmen's Bureau."

Oliver gave a start, hearing so unexpectedly the name of Judge Curtis's persecutor, as set out in Andy's letter. Marveling, he gazed more closely at the man, saw the glare of his coppery chin beard and, as he glanced up, the light of a very pale blue eye. What a happenstance, thought Oliver, to come across the very officer he'd traveled all this way to resist, ten minutes after setting foot in the county.

"Now that's a man," the driver was saying, nodding toward Bellamy, "if he's a-standing in your way, it'd pay you a whole lot to go the long way around him."

Down on the creek bank, Bellamy looked up from the corpse with a quick movement and said, "This was murder—two shots in the body and a cut throat. Does anyone here know him?"

There was an awkward stillness while the onlookers pondered. Then an old farmer in a torn hat spoke up. "Name's Sasser," he said. "Tom Sasser. Farrier by trade, he was."

Oliver happened to be looking at Bellamy's face in the instant the farmer spoke, and he was puzzled to see the man brighten, as if he'd had a pleasant thought. Then Bellamy barked some orders to the two nigras, and they commenced to lug the body up the bank.

But the old nigra preacher got slowly down off the back of the coach and made his way across the bridge carrying his Bible under his arm and stood at the top of the bank, and when the two carrying the corpse saw him they came to the top and laid the dead man down before him and stood back to let him pray. The preacher took off his old beaver and held it over his bosom and spoke a prayer asking the Lord to grant mercy to this poor soul hurried on to Him so untimely. Most of the whites stood by smirking. But Oliver and Nahum Bellamy both uncovered and bowed their heads till the prayer was over.

Oliver was watching for the turnout to the Curtis place by Downings Creek when Bellamy and his troop of police caught up with the coach and passed it by, going at a gallop in the direction of Hayesville. Two of the policemen rode double, and at the end of the column the dead man was lashed across the saddle of a led horse. His long wet hair dangled down close to the ground, swaying and jerking to the gait of the horse, and Oliver saw that road dirt and pebbles were collecting in it.

Watching Bellamy's gang into the distance Oliver soon noticed a big Spanish oak standing to the right of the road a quarter-mile ahead, and seeing that its top had been lightning-struck, with a surge of excitement he recognized the Curtis turnout. As he did so one of Bellamy's nigras veered out of the column and rode off that way on a big bay horse. To Oliver the horse looked blooded—mighty grand for a nigra. Idly he wondered how the jasper had come by it. Then as the stage bore down on the turnout Oliver asked the driver to let him and Syl off there by the oak. Bad leg or no, he wanted to walk that last mile.

It was the end of a long and exciting day for Syl, and now that evening was drawing on he grew tired, and his old sullen ways came over him again. As they were crossing the little bridge over Downings Creek he suddenly stopped and sat on the edge of the bridge and refused to go another step.

"Come on, son," Oliver pleaded. "It ain't far now. We'll be there directly."

Syl shook his head and whined, "I want to ride the coach some more." Then he burst into tears.

Oliver leaned on the railing of the bridge and watched the water whirl by underneath while Syl wept. Finally he said, "We come as far as we could on the coach. Now we've got to walk. It ain't far. And when we get there you'll like the people. There's two boys there, just about your age. They act and talk and dress just alike."

Syl said he didn't care. Then he quit crying and stared stonily down the winding course of the creek past the ruins of a burnt mill toward the wagon road, and said, "I hate you."

Oliver didn't say anything for some time. In the west the sun was dipping toward the summits of the hills, and somewhere an owl was hooting, and overhead the bullbats wheeled and swooped. Presently Oliver remarked, "Maybe we can change that. Maybe I can be so you won't hate me anymore."

"I bet you go off and leave me," said Syl.

Oliver crouched down next to him on the edge of the bridge but never touched him. Off in the distance dogs were barking. "I ain't a-leaving you," he said. "Not ever again."

But he could tell Syl didn't believe him. He guessed Syl feared his pappy had taken him away to this far place only to run off and abandon him. It was because he remembered Oliver going away twice before, in wartime. He feared he would be forever lost among strangers in a strange place. Oliver spoke patiently to him but could not comfort him, and after a while Syl complained he was sleepy, and Oliver lifted him gently up and set him astraddle of his shoulders and resumed his walk toward the Curtis place, and Syl wrapped his arms about Oliver's throat and fell asleep lying against the nape of his neck, hot as a warming stone.

Oliver was drenched in memory as he limped along the wagon road toting Syl on his shoulders. Here was the canebrake where he'd hid when the Yellow Jackets took the Curtis turnout, coming down from Chunky Gal to ravage the valley of the Hiwassee. There lay the scorched foundation stones of the farmhouse he'd seen burn down. And yonder stood the patch of pines where he'd lain above the Curtis place watching the marauders mistreat Miz Curtis so fearfully he nearly took his pistol and ran downhill all alone to try and stop them. He passed a hayfield and then a shack with a spirit tree in the yard covered with blue and green bottles, and beside the spirit tree a gray-bearded nigra was rubbing down the bay stallion Oliver had seen precede him on the turnout. The nigra watched with a steady vigilance till Oliver spoke him a good evening. Then the nigra nodded gravely back, and they passed on. Syl awakened and asked Oliver a dozen drowsy questions, but he heard not a one. He was remembering the fear he felt that September day, lying in the woods as the bushwhackers hurt that fine lady, and on top of the remembrance he was feeling a new fear, today's fear—the fear of getting crossways of the authorities in the act of giving aid to the Curtises.

Yet the closer he drew to the Curtis place the stronger he felt the decent force of them. Despite their station they'd taken him into their home, given him their goodwill, accorded him respect, that gift beyond price. Jack and Andy had honored him as a comrade, and the judge had invited him to come and settle as a neighbor. Now as he stood at the top of the lane, gazing down on the great white house with its rock chimney at either end of the tin-clad roof, he allowed himself to feel again his old longing to remove to this lovely valley and settle on a piece of good land and farm. It was a longing he hadn't let himself feel for a while, not since coming home from war to find Nancy poorly, because with Nancy likely to die he hadn't thought it right to let himself feel it. But now that he was here again, surrounded by the beauty of the place and soon to enfold his old friends in his arms, the longing flooded over him, and suddenly it was possible to imagine Nancy and Syl and Martha and himself coming here after all, farming by the banks of the Hiwassee, with the Curtises close at hand. And it was this notion that drove out the fear. Now he knew he had no choice, that in fact there'd never even been a choice to make at all. Come what may he must help his friends, must help them always.

PART III

The Children

of the Day

and the

Children

of the Night

CHAPTER 9

The mare was in foal at last, and Daniel wanted to pamper her. So one afternoon in November he crossed the hayfield and made his way through the little patch of woods beyond it to the plot where he had some cool-weather garden truck growing. There he gathered carrots and also turnips after tearing the greens off them. He planned to mix the carrots and turnips with some shelled corn and oats he'd already put in the manger of the horse shed; then while the mare browsed on those delights he aimed to cook the greens for his supper.

The sun was getting low in the west when he finished and started home with a poke thrown over each shoulder, one holding the turnips and carrots and the other the greens. The light was still strong and clear, although this late in the year it was not a yellow light anymore; it was cold and silvery, and it lay on a slant over the land,

and the glint of winter was in it. Daniel's breath blew clouds of wispy white as he went.

Crossing the hayfield again he saw someone walking away from him yonder in the wagon road swinging a long stick with a kink in it. The figure was so slight and slender that at first he took it for a young woman or a girl; in fact what came sadly to mind was the image of his own poor wife, slim and winsome Sukey, dead these six years. But then he noticed how the person moved with a man's rollicking swagger, and presently that gait came to seem familiar somehow. Because of this Daniel stepped from the hayfield into the road behind the walker and said a good evening to him aloud.

He turned in the road, and although he was longer and lankier than Daniel remembered, Daniel could see that it was Sukey's Hamby, grown near all the way up in the four years since he'd run off. He was the same bright copper color and still looked burnished till he shone in the sun, just as he used to. Hamby folded both hands around his staff and leaned on it laughing as Daniel approached, but the laughter did not reach his blue-gray cat's eyes, and Daniel could see that he was the same as before, only worse.

"Shit, you ol' nigger," Hamby mocked him, "ain't you lef' outa dis damn place yit?" With one hand he smote himself on the chest so the dust flew out of his clothes. "Hell, I done marched frew Gawgia wid ol' Massa Billy Sherman hisownsef. An' Souf Calina an' Noth Calina too." He laughed again. "An' you been squattin' here on yo' black ass dis whole damn time."

Daniel came abreast of him and stopped and set down his pokes in the road. He bent on Hamby a reproachful eye. Hamby's exaggerated slave talk offended him; for all Hamby's ire he'd always used good address. "Son," Daniel said, "you can speak better than that."

Hamby's copper hue darkened, and he frowned in the old way. "Don't you be callin' me son, you damn ol' nigger. You ain't my goddamn pappy no way. And I talks how I is. Dis is how I be."

Sadly Daniel saw that the torment of being born half-white into a world bound to consider him all black had led Hamby to take up his blackness in this coarse and abusive way. By Daniel's reckoning Hamby was fourteen, maybe fifteen. But his soul had got old. Hamby hawked and spat in the road. He was wearing a Union army blouse two sizes too large and a dirty blue slouch hat with a red badge on it shaped like an acorn. It hurt Daniel to see how much of Sukey's looks Hamby had. It hurt too that where Sukey had been so sweet Hamby was bitter as gall. Daniel reminded him, "I was the nearest to a pappy you had."

"Hell," Hamby said, "dat ol' man Curtis more of a pappy to me den you eber be, and him white too, and own me like a sheep." Hamby cocked his head and looked at Daniel in an inquiring way. "Why-so you neber run off? Is you such a yaller nigger you 'fraid to leave dese white folk dat helt you a slave?" The mocking smile came back. Hamby reached out and prodded Daniel in the chest with his finger. "Is you *still* a damn slave, ol' nigger?"

Daniel told of running off to Tennessee in sixty-two and joining the Twenty-third Corps, but Hamby only laughed again. "Shit, you be blackin' de white man's boots and brushin' his blue coat de whole time. Me, I'se marchin' frew Gawgia, make dem Rebels moan." He pulled a distasteful face. "You a shameful ol' nigger. Now you slavin' just like befo'."

"No, I'm a free man," Daniel told him. "I own my own land, forty acres of it." Hamby said nothing to that; instead he looked away scowling, as if he had no wish to hear such a thing. He lifted up his kinked staff and pounded the butt of it two or three times in the dirt of the road. Daniel let some moments pass and then asked Hamby why he'd come back himself.

"Hell," Hamby replied, "I come to gloat. Come to scorn dem Curtises all ruint and broke down, dat used to be so gran'."

In spite of his own grudge Daniel felt inclined to utter a reprimand, thinking of how the judge and Miz Curtis had taken Hamby in after Sukey passed. Hamby could have been their own, the way they fussed over him. Fed him at their table, as if he was white instead of mulatto and right-born instead of a child of shame. Dressed him in the clothes Mister Howell had worn when he was small. Set out to teach him his letters. Treated him warm and kindly. And him mulish and sullen first to last, hating them and hating Daniel and even hating Sukey—hating Sukey for having lain with a white man to get him. He'd finally run off, ten years old, raging all alone in the wide world. Daniel had never expected to set eyes on him again this side of paradise, had thought the awful world would tear a child like him to bits. Yet here he stood, as full of hate and bluster as ever; Hamby had proved harder than the world.

In the end Daniel didn't rebuke him, for he saw that Hamby had only done and felt the same as he himself had, only Daniel's way was milder. Instead he picked up his pokes and led the boy along the road and over the bridge and then past the Spanish oak and the spirit tree into the dooryard of the cabin, where he paused to let Hamby remark the sweep of the hayfield and the line of woods in the distance, the pasture where the bay stallion Tom pranced up and down, the horse shed with the mare peering out of it and finally the cabin itself, showing its new roof scantling and moss chinking and chimney made of river rocks. Hamby wore a serious air as he took it all in, and for once spoke not a word.

Inside, he shrugged off his blanket roll and claimed the barrel chair by the fireplace and lit up a corncob pipe and sat smoking and scowling into the fire while Daniel commenced cooking the greens. They ate them with some cold squirrel meat and pone and did not talk. After supper Daniel took the turnips and carrots out to the shed and fed them to the mare while the stallion looked on from the fence, and Hamby stood watching from the corner of the cabin. After that Hamby returned inside, and Daniel took up the broom and swept the dooryard and then gathered up a batch of corn shucks and took them to the edge of the pasture and pitched them over the fence for the stallion to eat. It was full dark when he came back in, and Hamby was lying by the fire, swaddled in his blanket, asleep.

Daniel had belonged to the Curtises for five years when the judge bought Sukey from a merchant friend of his in Asheville. The merchant's son was in love with Sukey and got her pregnant, and the merchant wanted Sukey taken far away so the son would forget his madness and resume his place in society and in the family business. Later Sukey told Daniel the son had not forced her, that he'd been tender and tremulous and sweet as sugarcane. But still she'd had no choice in the matter, and so it amounted to the same thing, even if she'd yielded easy. But she pitied the son, who was young and too innocent for the world; she said his yellow hair smelt always like fresh-cut hay warmed in the sunlight. He loved her truly and was so mad that he actually wanted to marry her and take her away somewhere like New Orleans, where he thought they could live together openly without being troubled. But the judge obliged the merchant and bought Sukey for five hundred dollars and carried her out to the Hiwassee country and made her a house servant. A year or so later the merchant came visiting, and Sukey learned that after she was sold the son went up to Warm Springs in Madison County and loaded his pockets with stones and threw himself in the French Broad River and drowned. She wept all that night, thinking of how his hair smelt and how much he loved her.

Sukey was about twenty that summer when the judge bought her. Even swelled up and duck-walking with the weight of the child she was carrying, she was so pretty Daniel's breath caught in his throat when he first saw her getting down from the judge's calash. She had almond-shaped eyes, like the eyes of the sisters of the Pharaohs Daniel had seen in the picture books in the judge's study. She bore her head royally high too, and looked everybody white or black straight in the face, not vain or haughty but just proud, as a fine horse is proud. Yet she had a mild temper and a gentle way. Her people were Cuthbertsons and came from Maryland, but she'd been calling herself Abbott after the Asheville merchant; when she came out to the Hiwassee she took the Curtis name, like Daniel and like Old Jeff and Mariah and Cuffee, the other Curtis people.

Three months after she came Sukey was confined and got Hamby. Hamby was a small knot of gold that squirmed and howled with a tiny rage, as if he already knew he'd have no place in life. He grew up full of fury. Sukey loved him, although he blamed her for making him what he was.

A year later Sukey and Daniel jumped the broomstick. Miz Curtis made Sukey a wedding dress of cream-colored taffeta covered with pink bows, and the judge gave Daniel a new pigeon-tail coat with velvet lapels and a white collar and tie. Sukey wore a pair of store-bought morocco shoes red as rubies. All the Curtises came, and the judge brought over his kinsman the Reverend Amos Curtis from Georgia to bless the union.

Daniel and Sukey had eight years together. At first Daniel tried being a pappy to Hamby, but Hamby hardened his heart against him, just as he hardened it against everyone. Hamby ran wild as a young wolf. Then the diphtheria took Sukey. After that it was plain that Daniel could never manage Hamby, so the Curtises took him in. But despite the care they lavished on him they couldn't manage him either. It was just before the war commenced when Hamby ran off.

Daniel rested by the fire watching Hamby sleep. Hamby slept the same as he'd done as a child, both fists doubled beneath his chin and his legs drawn high under him, a ball of flesh wound up tight with rage. Only his face looked soft. Daniel gazed at his face and lingered over the parts of it that were Sukey's—the full mouth with one corner that turned up, the short nose, the long eyelashes curled luxuriantly at the ends. He let himself think of Sukey then. This was something he did not often do. It was hard for him to think of Sukey because he had loved her so much, and in losing her he had lost everything that mattered to him in those days. So every time he did think of her a terrible pain would pierce his breast, and usually he would weep bitter tears.

But tonight he did not feel the pain and did not weep. Tonight he felt only mellow and wistful. He saw Sukey clearly; he heard her voice; she touched him. He remembered walking with her along the wagon road. She was collecting wildflowers in a wicker basket. She picked blue snapdragons and dogtooth violets and jack-in-the-pulpit and larkspur and painted trilliums and meadow parsnips. The mixed smells of the flowers were heady in the warmth of the springtime day. Sukey stopped in the road and gave him a long kiss. That night in the cabin she scattered the flowers on the bed, and they made love amid their many scents.

The next morning Daniel felt obliged to take Hamby over to see the Curtises. He did so reluctantly, for in recent weeks a great gulf had opened between himself and the judge, due to Daniel's association with Boss Bellamy. Daniel was wise enough to see Bellamy's flaws of excess, but he also thought that God sometimes gave great men flaws as great as their works. All the kings and prophets and judges of the Bible were such men, whom God used nevertheless. For Daniel, Boss Bellamy was great in this way. He was like Joshua conquering the land of Canaan for the children of Israel to live in, and the Curtises were like the Canaanites who must give way before the Chosen. Joshua, like Bellamy, could be cruel and sly, but God was with him anyway. God was with Boss Bellamy too. Daniel regretted that the Curtises had to suffer at his hands, but he knew their punishment to be just. He prayed for the Curtises often and besought God's mercy in their behalf. But he would not defend them or intercede for them, for that would be to put himself against the divine will.

But neither would he give evidence against them, as Bellamy insisted he ought when their case came before the army court. To testify as Bellamy wanted would be to tell a lie, for Daniel had been long gone from Clay County when the bushwhackers came. Daniel would never have spoken an untruth. Bellamy encouraged him to think of it as an act in the service of the Lord, but Daniel knew this to be wrong; winning freedom for a race of slaves might be a holy work, but it could never justify any lie. Yet Daniel did not blame Bellamy, who was borne up so high on the wings of fervor that it was easy to forgive him his blemishes. Daniel prayed for Boss Bellamy just as he prayed for the Curtises. Surely, when he stood before the mercy seat, Boss Bellamy's good works would weigh heavier in the balance than his bad. Still, Daniel had given himself over to this man, who now clouded his every thought of the judge. Leading Hamby down the lane toward the Curtises' that morning he by turns suffered pangs of remorse and of righteous anger, feeling partly the betrayer and partly the vindicator.

Hamby, of course, was overjoyed at the sight of the run-down mansion, the ruined outbuildings, the burnt barn only half rebuilt, the fallen fences on every side. "Misfortune done walloped dese Curtises!" he exclaimed. "Done knock dem on dey ass." His laugh rang brightly in the crisp air.

The sound fetched out of the house the two Cartman boys and a third boy that Daniel didn't know, who dashed in a bunch to the head of the steps and stood solemnly watching as he and Hamby approached. Making his way up the walk between the boxwoods, Daniel uttered a greeting. The two Cartmans stood silent. But the third boy turned his head toward the front door and cried, "Here's two niggers!"

Presently a stranger came forth who walked with a limp and had light hair and a walrus mustache. He spoke a word to the boy, who looked back sulking. Daniel recognized the man; he'd passed Daniel's place afoot two days before, toting a child on his shoulders—surely this same boy, Daniel reckoned. The stranger didn't speak to Daniel nor even look at him straight on; he only took the boy by an arm and hustled him inside, just as the judge and Miz Curtis came out. Miz Curtis gave Daniel a soft smile, but the judge stood frowning.

Under his glare Daniel hesitated, then wished them a good morning and quickly said, "This here's Sukey's Hamby come back again, to see you," and thrust Hamby before him to the bottom of the steps.

The judge looked perplexed to see a long and gangling Hamby. Miz Curtis yelped for joy and started down the steps with arms outspread. Slightly stooping, with his head bowed over, Hamby might have been readying himself to withstand a cyclone; he held stiff as a poker when she hugged him close. More of the family bounded out. Little Rebecca came and perched at the top of the stairs with the Cartman boys, the three of them all in a row like crows roosting on a fence, while the older girls—Sarah and Polly and Julia—remembering Hamby from before the war, tumbled happily down the steps to make a ring of jumping pinafores about him. Mister Andy came to join the judge on the gallery and looked on grinning. People loved Hamby regardless of his spite. They always had; something about the way he spoke his malice so wild and quirky inspired a kind of astounded delight. Daniel had forgot this. Now he watched amazed as Hamby stood scorning his welcome.

The judge spoke a word to Hamby, then turned and came to Daniel and asked stiffly after the mare. Daniel told him he expected her to throw the foal next March. He thought Tom had bred her at the end of April. The judge nodded and inquired when Daniel figured the foal and its dam could be separated without harm, and Daniel said not till the foal was a yearling at least. Through all this they both stood looking awkwardly at the ground. Then the judge cleared his throat as he always did before addressing a difficult matter and set eyes on Daniel for the first time, and Daniel saw the hurt in them. "Last spring, when you came back," said the judge, "I told you I didn't think I could willingly give you the rights you were bound to demand." He sighed. "That was a fool thing for me to say and to believe. I was wrong."

Daniel stirred uncomfortably. He had no wish today to wrestle with issues as large as this. "Yes, sir," was all he could think to say.

"It didn't take me long to see how wrong I was," the judge went on, scuffing at the flagstones of the path with the toe of his shoe. "Only a week or two." Ruefully he smiled. "It's amazing how quick a man can change the beliefs of a lifetime, when he sees he must. Of course it took many a blow to bring me to it. Still, I did change. A lot of others did not. And will not. There's more than one man in Clay County today would hang you sooner than give you your rights."

Stubbornly Daniel raised his chin. "Yes, sir, I know it. But I already *got* my rights, thanks to President Abraham and the Union army and the Freedmen's Bureau. Don't need any white man giving them to me."

"You're right, of course," Judge Curtis nodded. "What I mean is, when you came to me wanting land to hold free and farm, I treated with you not like the servant you were before but man to man. We struck our bargain like equals. Since then I've done all in my power to give the respect due you. To try and wipe away every trace"—here he made a scrubbing motion in the air—"every trace of our . . . former relation." He paused and drew several deep breaths, as if the effort of what he'd said had come near to exhausting him.

Nearby, the gay noise of Hamby's homecoming ceased when Hamby said something in his hard voice, and there was an ugly stillness afterward. In that quiet Daniel could hear his own heart violently beating. He sensed that Hamby had given some affront, but because the judge had leaned close to continue—and because he knew the judge was speaking from his wounded heart—he could not remark it.

"I've dealt fair with you," the judge resumed. "Never took advantage. Never demeaned you. Never played the slave master. Honored all the terms of every agreement." He turned aside then to gaze off across the river toward the line of mountains. "But in return," he said, "you act either sullen or grudging, or you give out hard looks, or you show an open resentment. Sometimes you seem to feel contempt, or even hate itself." But surprisingly he said nothing about Daniel's having taken the part of Boss Bellamy against him. He paused again to take breath, and breaking his gaze away from the far hills he impatiently wagged his head, as if the thinness of his wind annoyed him. "I know there's much for you to overcome," he went on, as Daniel became uneasily aware of Miz Curtis and the girls withdrawing quickly up the steps, and of Hamby turning away from the house with a bitter laugh. "But it was hard for me as well. Different, yes, but still hard. Losing two sons and nearly all my goods, my whole way of life."

Here Daniel saw he must break in, although he did not feel ready and was distracted by whatever it was that Hamby had done. But he knew it was time to speak out, that God had given him this opening. "Yes, sir, judge," he said as Hamby came swaggering up, "you lost a whole lot, and I'm sorry for it. But what you lost I never even had a chance to get. Because I was a slave. Because you held me in bondage."

"But," said the judge, "I was an indulgent master, was I not? You were never cruelly treated."

Hearing this Daniel felt a bolt of pity for him, and then a flare of white-hot anger. "Oh," he cried, "I was cruelly treated the worst of all ways, for you kept my freedom from me, that Almighty God in heaven meant for me to have when He made me!"

Hamby was by Daniel's side now, and Mister Andy was approaching grim-faced, but Judge Curtis took no notice of either of them. Instead he slowly nodded. "Yes," he said, flushing a dark red. "It's true. That was a wrong against you and God both. And in what I did to provide for you, and what you did to serve me, we were both degraded. But I was truly fond of you. And you of me, I think. What about that? Was that a lie?"

This was a question Daniel could not answer. But Hamby was ready with a response, which he spoke out in his coarsest speech. "Hell, ain't no nigger lub de white man dat hold him a slave. I chain you up, you gonna lub me? Shit, no. You gonna hate me from de gut. You gonna bust de chain, den bust me. Dat's what we got now, ol' man. Our chain be bust. Now we gonna bust you."

Daniel put out a hand to still him, and Andy moved in front of the judge and sternly said Hamby had spoken vulgar to the womenfolk and must go off the farm at once.

But Judge Curtis seemed to take no notice of what Hamby or Andy had said. He moved sideways past Andy and came close again to Daniel, and once more Daniel looked into his hurt eyes. "I don't think it was a lie," the judge said. "I think it was the truth. And I think if we nourish it, it can save us."

Daniel stepped back from him. This was not a notion he was prepared to consider. It seemed far too small a thing when measured against all the unrequited toil he and Sukey and the hundreds of thousands of other slaves in every part of the South had put forth so the white man could live in wealth and comfort and idleness these many generations. But he could think of nothing sensible to say in response. Instead he took Hamby—who was boisterously cursing the judge in ridicule—by the front of his blouse and dragged him down the walk to the turnaround and then up the lane to the wagon road, Judge Curtis and Mister Andy watching after.

At the top of the lane Hamby twisted out of Daniel's grasp and turned back. "My name McFee now!" he yelled down at them.

"Hamby McFee. De damn Curtis name be cast off. Ain't no Hamby Curtis no mo' in dis worl'." Daniel caught hold of him again and made as if to lead him off, but a second time Hamby broke free. "You speaks to me now," he cried, "you calls me *Mister* McFee, you hear? *Mister* McFee. Ain't no Hamby to it no mo', not for de likes ob you."

Then he rounded on Daniel with a grin. "*Now* I ready to go," he said.

These were dangerous days. Both the best and the worst of fates seemed to be bearing down on the Negro in the wake of the war, and it was hard to tell whether to be glad or fearful for the future. Daniel hoped that good would triumph, that Paul's time, the time of bondage that the apostle condoned, would pass away and Isaiah's time would come, the time foretold by the prophet when bondage and wrong would be violently overthrown. But it was just as likely— more likely all the time, in fact—that the old Confederates would regain control of affairs and set about chaining up the Negro all over again.

Rumors swept the land that the Freedmen's Bureau had received a great document bearing four seals decreeing that on the first of January the government would confiscate all the lands of the old slave owners and share them out in forty-acre parcels to every freed-man. But on the other hand, as the new legislatures of the seceded states began to meet that winter, the whites were talking more and more about the need to pass laws to hold the black man on the plantation and hedge him about with so many restrictions that in the end free labor in the South would come to look just like slavery.

Every Freedmen's Bureau school was crowded with Negroes anxious to get learning. The Union League was teaching coloreds the principles of the Republican Party and free government to make them ready to be citizens. Throughout Dixie black folk were working for whites as free laborers under contracts whose terms were enforced by the courts of the Freedmen's Bureau. Everywhere there was talk of universal manhood suffrage and the equality of the Negro before the law. But at the same time tales circulated of coloreds being murdered and mistreated in every corner of the South. Daniel heard stories of black men lynched and tortured and burnt alive, of black women ravished and whipped and maimed, of the corpses of freedmen floating in the rivers of Texas, of a whole community in Arkansas—men, women and younguns—all hanged.

This past September a general meeting of Negroes had been held in Raleigh at the same time as the whites' convention to reconstruct the state. A hundred and seventeen delegates attended. A minister from Connecticut named Hood presided, and some eminent blacks who had once been slaves in Carolina were also there, including an Ohio educator and preachers from all parts of the North. Some like A. H. Galloway of Fayetteville were former Union soldiers, and others were self-educated men like the preacher A. H. Harris of Raleigh. A barber from Fayetteville named Isham Sweat wrote the principal address. There was much debate about equality and the Negro vote, although in the end these matters were not mentioned in the resolutions the body passed. Instead it was resolved that all discrimination be abolished and abuse of Negroes be outlawed and every black be given an opportunity for learning—notions that fell short of the goals of the most radical but still would have been unimaginable months before. The resolutions were solemnly communicated to the state convention, which received them with every show of respect. Such a thing had never been before, and to Daniel it seemed a miracle as marvelous as any in Scripture.

But at the meetings of the Union League Boss Bellamy warned against indulging in false hopes. Just as he had foretold, at the elections in November, North Carolina put aside the unconditional

Unionist Holden to give the governorship to a conservative named Worth, who'd owned slaves before the war. Except in the western part of the state, said Bellamy, every newly elected legislator, magistrate, solicitor and clerk was either an ex-Rebel or a conservative, who if given half a chance would put the foot of the old slavocrats back on the neck of the colored man. Bellamy conceded that in the highlands, where black folk were scarce, the rule of the whites was mild by comparison with the rest of Carolina and the South, and that Clay County was in fact probably the mildest place of all.

"But even here," Bellamy cried one December evening, "where slave holding was rare and planters few, where poor whites are the majority, you are not safe in rights, in property or in life. For the white trash hates you worse than he does the planter, worse than he hates anybody. In the old days, no matter how miserable and impoverished and degraded he might be, the low-downer could at least count himself superior to the Negro on account of his white skin. But now that the war is over he hears talk of Negro equality, of Negroes voting and giving testimony against whites and all such, and he dreads the loss of the last vestige of his distinction—his whiteness, and the racial supremacy that he supposed it conferred on him. Believe me, he is your very nemesis."

Nor, said the Boss, should the Negro have a naive faith in the executive office of the government. "The president of the United States has been heard to say that only the whites must manage the South. He's terrified by the notion of Negro suffrage, which the Republican Party rightly brandishes over him, and he'll go to any lengths to avoid it.

"You see," explained the Boss, "the president got a nasty shock when the war ended. As a poor white himself he's always resented the power of the slavers who governed Dixie before the war, and he thought that the war had wiped those fellows out and opened the way for the poor white to ascend. But as usual the low-downer chose not to ascend. He chose instead to lounge in torpor on his skinny ass and dip snuff and drink corn whiskey and cast a lascivious eye upon his shapely sister or wanton cousin, if not upon his lamb or his cow or his pig.

"In his absence who is to control the darkie? Who is to keep the South from becoming one vast black republic? Someone must hold back the ebony tide. And who better than the old slavers, who know all the odious tricks of cruelty and oppression? They who have two hundred years' experience at the evil game. So what did the president do? He devised a liberal system of pardon and amnesty that quickly returned citizenship to all grandee slavocrats and traitors and ex-Rebels south of Mason and Dixon's Line. It is to these tyrants that he has handed over the government of the South and the fate of every freedman in it."

Daniel had learned to filter everything Boss Bellamy said through his own judgment. And he tried never to forget that Bellamy was himself a poor white who seethed with all the resentments of his class against the planters and maybe even the very Negro he toiled to aid. The one difference—and it was a saving difference—was that even if Boss Bellamy hated black folk also, like most of his kind, he hated the planters more, and this hate was sanctified by the Holy Ghost. But Daniel hadn't forgotten for a moment that, although divinely inspired, the Boss was a white man, and that any Negro must follow any white man—even the most blessed of God—only with the greatest of care.

In his continual state of anger Hamby saw this clearly and at first crudely harangued Daniel for letting himself be led by an envying and ambitious white. But after attending a meeting of the Union League and feeling for himself Bellamy's fire, Hamby forgot his doubts. Within days he joined the Seraphim and was soon seen riding proudly about Clay County at Boss Bellamy's back on a confiscated sorrel horse. The sergeant Corn Dodger became a great pal. The

Boss, said Hamby now, was the best white man he knew after Massa Billy Sherman himself, and Corn Dodger was the best nigger.

Daniel did believe that the times were indeed as the Boss described them. He'd seen the evidence himself. When the war ended and the Confederacy fell, the Rebels all seemed ready to admit their guilt and bend their necks to the yoke of the all-conquering Union. So thoroughly were they whipped that they would have accepted anything the North demanded—Negro suffrage, Negro equality, anything. But as the months passed and the lenient terms of the peace sank in, they began to see that nearly all whites North and South shared the same dread of black folk and so shared an interest in keeping them down. Thus the serpent of rebellion once more raised its head, and the Rebels began to dream again the evil dream of white supremacy and oppression of the Negro.

Even in Clay County the attitudes were hardening. One day in late December Daniel was walking home cross-country from Hayesville when two trashy whites stopped him at the footbridge over Downings Creek. One was tow-headed and the other dark, and both showed the same look in the eye that every Negro knew. They were dressed in butternut army jackets trimmed with cavalry yellow. At the head of the bridge the dark one lounged grinning against the rail and said, "Jump in that crick, nigger." Daniel gave him a respectful smile but replied that he didn't think he would. The tow-headed one was standing on the bridge itself and insisted, "Uncle, you ort to jump in."

Daniel presented his Police Model five-shooter and with his thumb drew the hammer back to full cock. "No, I won't do it," he said, "but you better." The tow-headed one didn't hesitate at all, but swung his legs over the rail and dropped in with a splash. The other took a moment to consider if he wanted to let a darkie get the better of him. Daniel pointed the five-shooter straight at his head, and he spoke an oath and ducked under the rail and jumped also. The pair of them stood in water to their waists looking warily up at him. Daniel put away his five-shooter and leaned over the rail and said, "If you're thinking of doing something about this later on, come ahead. You'll find I look out for myself."

What he said was true; he did look out for himself. But Daniel was well known in the county, and so was his association with Boss Bellamy. For seven months the Boss had run the district. In the rest of Carolina the elections may have put the old Confederates back in power, but west of the Nantahalas the Unionists were still in charge, and Bellamy was their avenging angel. Those raggedy Rebels at the bridge wouldn't be following up Daniel to do him harm, for if they did they knew the Boss would hale them into military court, and they'd end up in an army prison. But the fact they'd stopped Daniel at all showed how minds were changing in Clay County in the ways Boss Bellamy had prophesied. Daniel saw it as an evil omen.

As the days passed into December Daniel took thought again and again of the time he'd brought Hamby to see the Curtises. The memory festered like an untended wound. Part of his unease arose from the insult Hamby gave the Curtis womenfolk, that Daniel had thought unseemly—Hamby boasted he figured on marrying himself a white bitch now that he was free, and so he aimed to couple with each of the Curtis girls and sample to see which he fancied best. Yet Daniel couldn't help but feel pride that Hamby had taken the name of McFee in casting off the name of Curtis. It was the first act of Hamby's that showed he had any thought for Daniel, who was his stepfather, after all.

But Hamby was the least of what bothered Daniel. Mostly it was the recollection of the judge that caused that wound to putrefy. Daniel saw once more in his mind's eye the judge's awful anguish and heard in his ear the plea the judge had uttered. Was the judge right? Had they felt love once, each for the other? And if they had, was that love now a lie? Or was it a truth which if they held it close might save them? Daniel thought that he and the judge were but two out of millions, and if they'd once felt love it could scarcely matter now, with the millions glaring at one another in hate. But sometimes Daniel wondered whether two might not be enough. Enough to make a start. And what if every white and every colored made that same start? Might it be enough to save them all?

CHAPTER 10

When Salina Blodgett wed Andy Curtis six years ago she had done so partly in hopes his merry disposition would help brighten her own, which she had always thought too dull and earnest. By nature all the Shipleys, her mother's people, were solemn. But even among Shipleys Salina stood out by reason of her reserve. Yet she envied those who gave themselves up to fun and mischief, as Andy did in those days. Sometimes she thought of herself as imprisoned, gazing wistfully out through the bars of her reticence at a gay world she could have no part in.

Some of her standoffishness came by blood, but some also came from hardships suffered when young. Her father Jesse Blodgett died on her fourth birthday when a tulip poplar he was cutting fell on him. His farm on Greasy Creek under the Double Knobs was lost because of debt, and all during Salina's childhood her widowed mother had to work to earn a living. The Shipleys hadn't approved of the man her mother married—he made corn whiskey, and they were temperance folk—and so they gave her no help when he was gone. Consequently the mother kept a small boardinghouse in Hiawassee over in Georgia and took in other people's sewing and mending and washing. Salina's one brother died of the whooping cough while still a boy. Very early Salina began helping with the boardinghouse and the sewing and mending and washing. It was a hard life and a bitter one, and it killed her mother at thirty-two, when Salina herself was only twelve.

With her mother gone the Shipleys took pity on Salina and became willing to forgive her the wrong her mother had done. They took her in, and she grew up at her grandparents' place on Tusquittee Creek. Although she was treated more like a servant than a granddaughter, and spent much of her time doing the same chores she had done in the boardinghouse, her grandparents loved her in their stern way and gave her a good if rigorous home. They even sent her to Mr. Hicks's pay school, although most folks would've said no girl child had any need of fancy learning, given the kind of life she was going to have. The pay school was in a log cabin a ways up Tusquittee on the farm of a Mr. Alec Martin. Sitting on rough benches split out of the trunks of poplar trees Salina learned her letters and numbers, and using a goose-quill pen and pokeberry ink she learned the rules of penmanship and came to write a fair copperplate hand.

It was while attending Mr. Hicks's pay school that Salina first got to know the Curtis boys. The Curtis family was well off and could have sent the boys to an academy in some city like Asheville or Charlotte, or they could have even employed a private tutor like many another planter. But instead they chose to let the boys take a local education with Mr. John Oliver Hicks, who had a fine name as a teacher in that country. The boys were handsome and lively, and all the girls admired them. Howell was closer to Salina in age, but he was a somber sort like Salina herself, and because she sought to be free of such studied ways he couldn't have captured her fancy. Anyhow he was interested in a girl who lived over on Buck Creek almost into Macon County. Jack the middle brother was already taken with Mary Jane Coleman, the girl he would later marry. It was to Andy that Salina turned her eye.

Among the Curtis boys the usual order of things had somehow got turned on its head. Howell the youngest was the most settled, Jack was somewhat less so and Andy the oldest was as carefree as a flock of sparrows. Also, Andy was the apple of his mama's eye instead of Howell the baby, and his mama had spoilt him in the worst way. Salina didn't know then why this was so and only learned after marrying him that for all his funning Andy had a timid soul and was frightened of the harsh ways of this earth. In the beginning all she saw were his bright eyes and all she heard was his laugh.

It was a wonder he looked back at her with favor. She had feared her dour manner would put off someone as full of whimsy as he. But instead it drew him on. He liked her calm and coolness; she soothed him, who was used to the boisterous doings of the Curtis household. As for Salina, Andy warmed her like an October sun melting an early frost off the grass. She basked in his glow, and when she was with him it was possible to think of life as something to be savored, rather than something to be wary of.

When he was twenty and she was sixteen he asked for her hand. At first she feared his family might spurn her. Andy was the judge's inheritor, and the judge was bound to be careful of the blood to be mixed with his. The Shipleys might be every bit as good as the Curtises, but Salina herself bore a kind of stain because of her mother marrying that still-house man. Yet the judge raised no objection on that score. Once she got to know him Salina found that she and Father Curtis were much alike in their restraint and stood out among the robust Curtises as a cool moon in a daytime summer sky. Quite soon they drew so close they might have been bound by blood.

Andy's fire awoke an answering blaze in Salina, and after marriage they lost themselves in pleasures of the flesh such as Salina in her detachment had never imagined. She learned she could give herself up to abandon in ways that afterwards left her full of amazement and delight and even a little fear, and it was her gratitude to Andy for setting her so alight that finally began to move her toward loving him, whereas before she had only honored him in the dutiful way that matrimony required.

But soon it was clear there would be no children. Something was wrong with one or both of them, and Salina in her clear-eyed fashion assumed the fault was hers, that in her coldness she was barren, while Andy in his heat owned seed that was full of life. But even accepting the fault Salina saw no reason for regret or guilt. The life she'd lived had shown her that loss was inevitable and had to be reconciled. It was harder for Andy, who wanted a son on whom to settle his legacy, and for Father and Mother Curtis, but no one cast blame, least of all Andy, who held her close and told her it was enough for him to know that she would be with him always.

She knew now how much he needed her. She was strong and brave where he was faint. But his weaknesses didn't dismay her. To Salina they bespoke his gentle heart. She was strong enough for the both of them anyway, so they would not lack for strength when it was needed. Being strong was a virtue as common as dirt—most every man had it, and not a few women—but gentleness was a jewel rare beyond price, and this was Andy's special gift to her, and she cherished it past her power to tell.

The war when it came clouded Andy's sun forever and drove out his cheer and cooled his desire. When he returned home all that was left of him was a great fear that he might be tried again past standing, now that he'd barely stood the trial of war. His gentle heart hung cold and still inside him. Salina's loins ached for him all in vain, and there were occasions when she thought the wear of wartime might have leached out her looks and made her unlovely in his eyes, so that he no longer desired her. But in time it came clear that his fire had just gone out. So she saw that the loss of his body was something else to be reconciled, just as she'd reconciled the barrenness. But it was the silence of his heart that made her truly despair.

In those weeks after Andy came home Salina nearly gave up hope for the first time since their marrying. It seemed he was lost to her for good, and in casting about for a reason to live Salina found nothing except the teachings of the faith, which now rang hollow and unconvincing. Yet she clung fast to an unreasoning belief that he would rally—if only because she could not now imagine going on alone. She called on the stores of patience she had built up during all the years of her girlhood when times were bad and hope dim. Andy spoke not at all of these woes but looked at her always with a silent longing and apology and a deep gratitude, so she knew he fancied her still, even if he could not honor her with his body or warm her again with his heart, and this was enough to give her courage.

Then after a time a coal or two of his old ardor began to burn again, and although he still could not complete the act of love he and she found other ways to please each other that soon came to feel even closer and more dear. And although Salina still wished to know him in the old full way she found a tenderness and languor in this that was sufficient and true in itself. Besides, they both knew that it was the start of his healing, and this gave them hope.

Then when trouble came with the Freedmen's Bureau man, and Father Curtis so unexpectedly bowed down before it, something else in Andy began to stir. Salina thought it might be rage, that Andy resented Father Curtis for failing him and making it necessary for him, Andy, to act to save the family. Maybe Andy felt that Father Curtis had reneged on a lifelong understanding that Andy would never be called on in that way. Whatever it was, Andy roused and went forth. But his heart was hard now and not gentle, and seeing him in this new guise Salina hardly knew how to regard him. He was strong now, but his was not a reasoned strength nor a wise one but instead was vengeful. Andy who'd been so gentle was close now to contempt.

In that contempt lived a kind of resignation. One night in late November as they lay in bed he turned to her in the candlelight and said, "We both know I can't be a husband with you anymore. If you want your freedom I'll not stand in your way." But she only smiled at him and put her hand behind his neck and drew his head down to her and kissed him tenderly on the mouth. Then he began to weep. He wept hard, the sobs racking him till the bed shook under them. She hugged him tight till he fell asleep exhausted on her bosom, and then finally she slept too. The next morning when they awoke they made a sort of love, and for the first time in the five months since his return she felt his heart awaken.

The morning after the day Oliver Price and his son arrived from Georgia, Salina was chasing a hen to kill for supper when the hen darted among the fallen timbers of the old smokehouse, and in following it Salina stepped on a curved nail and got a deep and painful wound in the sole of her left foot. While it still bled Mother Curtis said over it the healing words of Ezekiel. After the bleeding stopped Mother Curtis cleaned the wound with turpentine and bathed it in oil of St.-John's-wort before swaddling it in a lye poultice. Then they all forgot about it in the hubbub of getting up a good supper.

The supper was a special occasion because Mr. Price was not only a friend from the wartime but had come out to Clay County at some risk to himself to give evidence in Father Curtis's behalf in the military-court case threatened by Major Bellamy. They ate fried chicken—the Cartman boys and Mr. Price's son Syl had captured the hen after Salina hurt herself—along with mashed potatoes and gravy, leatherbritches beans and stewed apples.

At supper and in the parlor afterwards Mr. Price filled the house with his large and exuberant voice. When speaking he gestured broadly and laughed often with a brazen note like that of a bugle. In his presence it was not possible to be downcast, and because of him the pall that had hung over the family for so long began to lift a little. He was a plain man with rough ways—not at all the kind of person to dine with the likes of the Curtises in ordinary times. But a simple goodness poured out of him, and Salina marveled at his joyful air, which reminded her of Andy in past days. Mr. Price spoke of his disabling in the war and of the sickness of his young wife as sprightly as if the news were good instead of bad. In his mouth the hardships of a poor cobbler's life in the sorriest corner of upland Georgia were the stuff of so many jokes and humorous tales. His surly child sat next to him giving out every sign of annoyance and contempt, yet he could not have doted more on the boy had Syl behaved like a prince anointed. Father Curtis and Andy opened to Mr. Price like flowers. Before bedtime Mother Curtis asked him to read from the Scriptures, just as he'd done the first night of his wartime visit, and he chose the same passage he'd picked then, the Beatitudes from the Sermon on the Mount in the Gospel of Luke.

Next day Salina's foot was hot to the touch and had got so sore she could only hobble through her chores like an old crippled woman. By the third day—when Daniel McFee brought Hamby over and Hamby spoke ugly to Mother Curtis and the girls—Salina was laid up in bed with her foot throbbing as if afire. Still it was nothing but a nuisance, and compared to the upset Hamby caused it deserved no notice atall. Because of Hamby's words Andy was in a fit of fury and kept threatening to ride over to Daniel's and thrash Hamby with a horsewhip. Mother Curtis seemed heartbroken that Hamby should talk so profane to folk who'd cared for him, and she couldn't think how to explain to the girls why he'd done it. By turns the girls themselves were puzzled, then angry, then seized with naughty giggles when they thought of the things Hamby said that they'd never heard before. But Father Curtis was most disturbed of all, not because of what Hamby uttered—he hadn't even heard that—but because his old servant Daniel McFee addressed to him certain words that cut his soul. Amid the general distress even the normally lively Mr. Price could only stand aside looking somber.

On the fourth day Andy and Mr. Price were to leave for Murphy to meet with lawyer Kope Elias. When Salina awoke that morning the ache in her foot had eased somewhat, but her neck had got stiff, and upon trying to take breakfast she found that it was hard for her to swallow. Although she'd intended to get up that day and do some sewing, she decided to stay abed awhile longer in hopes the stiff neck and throat trouble would go away. She thought she might be catching cold, and the rest would do her good.

Presently Andy came to say good-bye. He was nervous and a little preoccupied because of the importance of the affidavit Mr. Price was to give, and the kiss he fetched her was an absent-minded one. But in leaving he did think to turn at the bedroom door and tell her that he loved her. It was something he didn't often say, although she knew it had been true always. He left then, and after a time Salina grew drowsy and fell asleep.

"The administration of public affairs in North Carolina since the war has been a cat's cradle of competing authorities," said lawyer Elias, "and Major Nahum Bellamy has flourished amid the confusion. Had the times been normal such a creature would've been found out and disposed of long since."

Warily Oliver Price watched him. Lawyer Elias looked so young and innocent Oliver could not help but doubt his legal sense. Yet the boy spoke well enough, and there on the wall above him hung a framed parchment saying he'd learned the law under one John Lancaster Bailey, whom Andy swore was a judge renowned throughout North Carolina and ran a reputable law school in Black Mountain. Still, Oliver wasn't fully persuaded. He figured a real lawyer ought to have some white hair.

"Bellamy holds a special commission in the army—the volunteer army, not the regular service, mind you," lawyer Elias was saying. "As far as I can tell it's completely honorary, a kind of brevet rank. No one seems to know where or when he got his rank or who gave it to him—perhaps the colonel of the Federal Thirteenth Tennessee Cavalry, the regiment for which he recruited during the war. Or maybe he gave it to himself. Anyway, as of today, he's not part of any army command that I can discover, which means there's no superior officer in the military to whom he's beholden."

Oliver thought the boy had a confident air. But then most boys did. His office was small but well appointed, located on the upper floor of a respectable brick building fronting on the town's public square, with a view of the burnt courthouse that was being rebuilt. There were a convincing number of law books on his shelves, and a reassuring lithograph of Robert E. Lee and Stonewall Jackson conferring on horseback before the battle of Chancellorsville. At least the child was educated and seemed orthodox.

"Bellamy also is in the Freedmen's Bureau," lawyer Elias continued, "which is a part of the War Department but separate from it, although most of its agents are army officers, if you can follow that. And in the bureau he has a unique position, something called supervising inspector, an office otherwise unknown anywhere in the establishment. Again, how he got the post is a mystery. His name appears nowhere on the employment rolls of the bureau.

"Finally," the boy said, "somehow, Bellamy has also arrogated to himself the role of chief of the county police, which of course is a function of the civil government, and in that capacity he commands a body of armed tories, reformed Rebels and Negroes that protects all Unionists and is the terror of every old-time Whig and former Confederate in the district."

Andy nodded with an embittered smile. "Army, Freedmen's Bureau, police—the scoundrel's got us frontways and hindways."

"But it's all sham!" cried the boy, spreading his hands. "The army thought he belonged to the bureau, and the bureau thought he belonged to the army. He laid hold of the county police because of his army rank in the days of martial law just after the surrender, but I'll wager the bureau doesn't even know he's got it. And the new state government in Raleigh doesn't care. They think we're all Unionists out here anyway and don't mind a lot of tory police commanded by a mad abolitionist."

Lawyer Elias leaned forward in his chair and, resting his elbows on his desk, bent on Oliver and Andy a confiding and significant look. "I'm not without friends in the Freedmen's Bureau," he said, "and I've been making inquiries. Based on what I've learned I believe I can say with certainty that matters are about to change. You see, one reason Bellamy flourished so long was that for many months the bureau had no superintendent for its western subdistrict. There was a vacuum of authority, and Bellamy made the most of it. In October General Howard, the head of the bureau, was in Raleigh meeting with Whittlesey, that fellow from Maine who's the assistant commissioner for North Carolina. At the same time, Hawley, the chief of the bureau station in Franklin, wired Eastmond in Asheville, who in turn wired Whittlesey, asking for guidance in the Bellamy matter, as they'd grown nervous about his activities. Howard saw the wire and ordered an investigation." Here the boy broke out in a wide grin. "I'll confess that when I heard this I caused several letters to be written by prominent Union men of my acquaintance complaining of the major's misdeeds. Gentlemen," he concluded proudly, "our Major Bellamy's about to be found out."

Andy was thunderstruck to think that his nemesis could be so easily dispatched. But the boy had not yet convinced Oliver. "Even if this Bellamy does get pitched out of the Freedmen's Bureau," Oliver spoke up, "ain't he still in the army? And ain't the charges against Judge Curtis army charges? What about them?"

Indulgently lawyer Elias gazed at Oliver. "Well, Mr. Price, as I've said, I don't think Nahum Bellamy is in the army at all," he explained with a show of strained patience. "I've written the adjutant general's office at Washington City, and there's no record of his ever receiving a commission in the regular service. Nor is he in the Volunteer Reserve Corps. And since the volunteer army is mostly mustered out, if he ever did have a volunteer rank, it's probably no good now. Whatever he is, I have been able to confirm by my inquiries what Colonel Coleman surmised in his conversation with you, Andy— the army too is moving against our man. The official policy of the government is to placate the South, yet Bellamy is antagonizing our people, and complaints have been lodged against him at the district headquarters of General Heath. An officer of General Heath's staff has been detailed to look into the matter. When it is discovered that Bellamy is not a legitimate officer of either the army or the bureau I believe we'll see the end of him."

Oliver frowned in thought. "But this jasper Bellamy has already filed charges," he said. "I was in an army awhile myownself. Mind you, it wasn't as organized as the one the Yanks has got. But it had its ways. And once somebody filed papers on somebody else them papers went on up the line. Whether there was merit to 'em nor not, they got looked at. And after a spell of time wheels commenced to turn. Then sometime or other a fellow with chicken guts on his sleeves would show up ready to do a turn in court. Ain't it likely the army'll push the charges through even if Bellamy's found out?"

"Let me acquaint you with a little history, Mr. Price," the boy said in a condescending tone that made Oliver's hackles rise. "Soon after

General Ruger succeeded General Schofield in command of the Military Department of North Carolina, a dispute arose between himself and Governor Holden as to the division of responsibility between the military and the civil courts. Last September a compromise was effected. Nowadays all cases in which freedmen are concerned are under military jurisdiction, and all those alleging crimes involving whites go to civil court. Major Bellamy has tried to sue in the wrong court." He smirked at the thought of Bellamy's many missteps. "I'm afraid the man isn't much of a lawyer."

Oliver was puzzled. "I'd of thought Judge Curtis—being a judge and all—would of known if this jasper got his law wrong."

"Papa don't know all that much law," Andy explained. "He ain't a real judge. He was a justice of the peace of Cherokee County till they organized Clay in sixty-four."

"Here in North Carolina the office of justice of the peace is more political and administrative than judicial in nature," lawyer Elias intoned. "Peace justices are nominated by the local assemblymen and endorsed by the legislature. While they do run the local magistrate's court and staff the county court they also appoint and manage the officers who levy taxes, license the selling of liquor and keep the roads in repair."

"Do you mean," Andy now inquired, "there won't be a military trial?"

"Hardly," lawyer Elias replied. "As Mr. Price suggests, it will take time for the army to process the paperwork"—Oliver felt a little better now that the boy had acknowledged his point—"but in the end the authorities will determine that the military lacks jurisdiction, and the charges will come to naught. Besides, by then, Bellamy will have been discredited."

"That leaves the Pucketts," Andy reminded him.

"Yes." Now lawyer Elias looked grave. "A much more serious matter. I know Colonel Coleman advised you not to worry yourself about it, on the grounds no decent lawyer would take the Pucketts on. The colonel is a superb attorney, but I'm afraid I must disagree with him on this. There are a number of advocates in the region who are abolitionist or Unionist and would readily represent the Pucketts out of what they might construe as principle. As a matter of fact I've learned that Bellamy is even now in the process of helping the Pucketts select one such—a pleader from Carter County in East Tennessee named Johnston Barrett. Thus I believe we must prepare ourselves not for a military proceeding but for a civilian trial at the spring term of superior court."

"When you speak of superior court," said Andy, "do you mean a lawsuit or a criminal trial?"

Lawyer Elias steepled his fingers under his chin and endeavored to look mature. "No doubt you're aware the general assembly has confirmed Colonel Coleman's provisional appointment as solicitor of the Eighth Judicial District. I think we may rest assured that even if the Pucketts try to swear out a criminal complaint against your father, the colonel—as your friend—will see fit not to seek an indictment. So it's a civil action we confront."

He sat back in his chair and rubbed his hands briskly together. "So," he said, "I suggest we get started preparing ourselves." He glanced at Oliver benevolently but also with a degree of uncertainty, and it occurred to Oliver that the boy might be as suspicious of him as he was of the boy. "We'll take Mr. Price's sworn statement now," lawyer Elias went on, "and since I know its substance already I think I'm safe in saying it'll be a great help to us. But I should also mention that we'd be on much firmer ground had we some piece of corroborating testimony—evidence given by someone not identified with the Curtis family."

Oliver bristled, thinking his honesty was being questioned. "I ain't a-goin' to lie," he growled, "not even for my friends."

The boy held up both hands to placate him. "You and I and Andy know that, sir. But the plaintiffs might argue to a jury that you're inclined to the Curtises by sentiment. Our case would be a good deal stronger if we had an objective witness, a third party with no connection to the Curtises, who could confirm your version of the events. Even better, if one of the Quillens themselves could be found, who would testify that Judge Curtis sent Mr. Price to warn them . . ."

Grimly Andy shook his head. "There are no Quillenses above ground anymore."

"Ah, well," sighed lawyer Elias, "then we shall have to make do with Mr. Price." Oliver felt another spurt of dislike for the arrogant boy, but before he could think how to act on it lawyer Elias turned solemn once more and said, "Something further must be noted here, gentlemen. If we succeed in turning this matter aside, and if Major Bellamy is dismissed from his positions of authority, then take my word for it, you must beware of him. He bears the Curtises some great grudge—God knows what it is—and will not willingly lay it down. My inquiries have shown me that he's a violent and danger-ous man. His path through the war was a bloody one, strewn with vendetta and atrocity. It's entirely possible if he's frustrated in the regular courses he's taken against you that he'll resort to irregular ones."

Andy got very still as he listened, the way a ground squirrel freezes when a hawk settles into a nearby tree. Watching him, Oliver re-membered Jack Curtis once telling him that Andy was a fearful soul whom the whole family felt obliged to protect. Yet to Oliver, Andy didn't seem afraid at all; it was more like he was poised, ready to act.

Of course there was Oliver's own hide to think of. He hadn't come out to Clay County with any notion of getting himself killed by some lunatic Yank, but then keeping from getting killed was a familiar occupation with him, and he thought he could do it as well now as he'd done it those three years in the Army of Tennessee. He thought he could play that game and get himself home to Nancy too. Also, if the boy was telling it right, this Yank was a renegade and didn't represent the majesty of the Union. That meant if Oliver went against him he wouldn't be going against the government—against the right—as he'd first feared. While he pondered this, the last of his uneasy conscience cleared right up.

In the middle of the night Salina awoke with a raging thirst, and rising up in bed she poured herself a cup of water from the bedside pitcher. But when she put the cup to her lips they did not open, and to her astonishment the water poured over her chin and down the front of her nightdress. Puzzled, she tried again to drink, and again her lips would not part, and the water spilt over her. She set the glass aside and attempted to open her mouth but discovered to her surprise that it would not even budge. Her back teeth were clamped shut. In growing alarm she felt with her hands along her neck and throat and found that the muscles there stood out as tight and hard as taut rope. That was when she knew. She lay back against her pillow then and began to sweat with dread.

Lying in the darkness she thought about what was coming and was sorry that it was going to happen now, just as Andy was recovering himself and needed her more than ever. She was afraid too, of course, but mainly of not acquitting herself well when the worst of it came; she was proud and did not wish to behave in an undignified manner or in any way to revolt anyone. She feared the pain also. But she was no more afraid now of death than she had ever been. In a strange way it was as if she had always been ready for death, since as a girl it had struck so often around her. But she did regret that her time with Andy would be cut short, and when she thought of that she began softly to cry.

She did not call for help, because she knew there was no help anyone could give. After she had cried awhile she stopped and commenced praying and reciting silently to herself some of the Psalms she'd always loved. She said the Twenty-third Psalm and Psalm Seventy-seven and a part of the Sixth Psalm:

> Have mercy upon me, O Lord; for I am weak: O Lord, heal me; for my
>   bones are vexed.
> My soul is also sore vexed: but thou, O Lord, how long?
> Return, O Lord, deliver my soul: oh save me for thy mercies' sake.
> For in death there is no remembrance of thee: in the grave who shall
>   give thee thanks?

She lay praying and reciting that way, drenched in her sweats, till just before dawn, when the roosters crowed and she heard Mother Curtis begin to stir downstairs. Now she began to think of calling for help, but as soon as the notion came to her she discovered that her throat seemed to have swelled shut and she could make no sound at all, not even a moan.

By then a pain had begun at the base of her breastbone that seemed to penetrate straight through to her spine. At first it was only a mild discomfort, but very quickly it got worse, and in twenty minutes Salina was in agony from it. Then the spasms started. At first there were only a few jerks and contractions here and there, but very soon they became violent, and with each convulsion bolts of pain shot through her that were beyond bearing but which she had to bear in silence anyway, because she could not give voice.

Now her first thought of simply lying there and letting the thing take its course became ridiculous—one could not be reconciled to something as terrible as this. She thought then to get up and go to the door and go out. But now she did not seem to be able to control her body. Whenever she tried to move, her arms and legs refused to respond in the proper way; they seemed to flop uselessly about according to a queer will of their own, and presently they started to become stiff and heavy, as if turning from flesh and bone into lead. Mother Curtis hummed a tune somewhere in the house; the Cartman boys and little Syl Price dashed up and down the hallway outside her door; in the distance a cowbell clanked. Another normal day had begun entirely indifferent to what she suffered, and she thought how peculiar it was that a thing so awful could pass so unremarked. Now she started to understand how bad her dying would be, and finally she became afraid of death also.

Salina prayed for a swoon that might give relief, but instead her mind retained a horrid clarity that allowed her to feel every shock and torment. Now between convulsions she realized that her rigid neck was gradually bending backwards, till soon the crown of her head was buried deep in her pillow and her chin pointed straight up toward the ceiling. Inwardly she began to recite the Lord's Prayer, but no sooner had she started than a searing burst of pain took her in the back, and she forgot the words of her prayer as her body arched horribly upward in the middle, only her head and her heels touching the bed, and she heard her own teeth begin to crack in her mouth like popcorn.

Down below, Sarah Curtis heard the heavy thump of the bed as the convulsion shoved it hard against the bedroom wall. Curious, she left the winter kitchen and climbed the stairs to the upper hallway and knocked at Salina's door. There was no spoken answer but instead another heavy crash of the bed, so Sarah opened the door in alarm and said Salina's name and came in.

After concluding their business with lawyer Elias, Oliver and Andy stayed the night in Ramseur's Long Hotel in Murphy, planning to start home the following day. It turned cold in the night and snowed on the high tops, and when they came out of the hotel the next morning the summits of the mountains all around were bright with rime ice like delicacies made up by a confectioner, while on the lower slopes the black lacework of the bare trees stood out stark and ugly as porcupine quills against the white of the snowfall. But the sun glared low in a clear sky, and Oliver thought it a good day for a bracing ride. He'd made inquiries and had learned that his sister Tabitha and her man Gettys lived close by the road between Murphy and Hayesville, so he meant to stop off there and visit while Andy made his way home.

The Gettys farm stood near a place called Mission, named so because there used to be a Baptist missionary church there for the Cherokees before the Indians got removed. This was at the foot of the Valley River Mountains up Roach Cove, a pine holler that wound along under a bald that Andy said was named the Ammon Knob. In surprise Oliver discovered that his sister was living quite near the old Quillen place between Sweetwater and Peachtree, where he'd gone two years ago at the judge's behest to warn old Mose Quillen of the approach of the Yellow Jackets. He marveled at the ironies of war, that he'd come within a mile of his sister's home that time without knowing it.

Oliver meant to visit awhile with Tabitha and then make his own way to the Curtis place—a way he well remembered from the war. At the cutoff Andy gave Oliver directions and then continued on. Oliver rode under the shadow of the range and up the holler, his breath and the breath of the Curtis mule blowing spouts of vapor around him in the cold air. A mile or so up, he found the farm nestled in a side cove at the head of a little branch, surrounded by a woods of hemlock. The whitened hills towered over it. The peaks shone in the sun, but the farmstead lay shadow-dark on account of the heights roundabout. Oliver forded the branch and found it running black between long shards of ice as clear as polished glass.

The log house was set about with a post-and-rail fence that was mostly fallen down, and the top was missing off one of the two rock chimneys. The roof shakes had cupped and were held on with flat stones in some places and by split logs tied down with hickory withes in others. Behind the house Oliver saw an old barn and a pen with some bristly wedge-shaped hogs in it, and on the bald above, in sunlight, a few cows and some lanky sheep were grazing. William Gettys managed the farm for a landlord who lived in Orange County down in the Piedmont; he appeared to have come through the war all right but did not seem to be much acquainted with hard work.

Oliver hallooed in the dooryard, and Gettys came out, revealing himself to be a little potbellied jasper who had small eyes with pale lashes like a pig's, and a gray beard stained brown at the mouth, and a bald head that gleamed as if waxed. Oliver had written ahead from Rabun Gap and was generally expected, and Gettys asked him in.

It proved hard to imagine Tabitha a sister, since she was old enough to be Oliver's mama and shook with palsy and was nearly blind. Of course she didn't remember Oliver any more than he remembered her, because she'd left home long before Oliver was born. Awkwardly Oliver spoke of Mama and Lit and Mac and Archie, and told of Freddy's dying. After a spell Tabitha spoke of Sister Letitia, that married Noah Biggerstaff; and poor Sister Suzie, that never married, who lived in Gilmer County, Georgia; and Sister Olivine, after whom Oliver was named, that married Simon Bowden. Then Oliver related how Sister Leanna had married a man named Barnabas Baber and how Sisters Lizzie and Rachel were still at home with Mama. Tabitha reproached Oliver for not bringing Syl along so she could look on the face of her nephew. After that Gettys bestirred himself to fix a dinner, and they dined on cold pork and sweet potatoes with black coffee.

During dinner Oliver explained why he'd come out to Clay County, and his story of helping the Curtises in their trouble seemed to annoy Gettys, who had a theory that the woes of folk like himself and Oliver could be laid at the door of such as the Curtises, who'd owned slaves. "It was *us* that was kept in slavery," Gettys railed, jabbing himself in the chest with his thumb. "The niggers and their masters held us down by keeping us from our fair part in the work and yield of a rich country. Why, even now that they're free, the damn niggers take the part of their masters, and together they look down on us. You mark my words, Brother Price, giving the nigger the vote'll have but one result—it'll unify the nigger and the slaver, and they'll vote to restore the slavers to power and keep us out, just as we've always been kept out. The nigger don't hate the slaver half as much as he hates us."

For the sake of manners Oliver expressed no opinion on this, though he did find the notion right queer. Instead he spoke again of the aid he was giving the Curtises and mentioned how it would've helped had there been a live Quillen to testify in support of him. Here Tabitha amazed him by looking up from her plate and saying, "Why, there be such a Quillen living, if you want her. She's a-squattin' down at the old place by the Sweetwater. Hit's Old Mose's woman, name of Balm In Gilead."

Oliver turned into the Quillens' lane by the round stone where he'd sat two years ago to eat a lunch of fat meat and pone before going on to see Old Mose. Judge Curtis's next-to-oldest girl Miz Martha Barter had fixed the lunch for him, and even today he remembered how good that simple fare had tasted in that time of nearly constant hunger. Riding slowly up the weed-choked path between the scraggly pines, he saw ahead of him, unchanged, the clearing studded with old stumps and littered with every kind of junk; beyond it was the sideways-leaning shack made of random boards, which had a barrel chimney and a split deer hide hanging over the doorway. Oliver had the odd feeling he'd somehow gone back in time to repeat his mission of mercy to Old Mose, and he half-expected to see the old reprobate himself emerge from the hovel, shot and buried though he was. Instead several wild-looking dogs came dashing out at him and began to bark and snarl and show their fangs and bite at the heels of the mule, which paid them no mind at all but only plodded patiently, placidly on. It was a good mule.

Oliver drew rein before the doorway while the dogs bawled around him, and presently the deerskin stirred, and someone with pale eyes and lank hair looked quickly out at him and then just as quickly withdrew. He waited awhile longer, and then at last the deerskin parted again, and a stocky woman came out carrying a Sharps carbine with the hammer cocked. She was grimy, but that Sharps gleamed like silver. She spoke loudly to the dogs, and they all ceased at once, and each sat down where it was and looked on with its tongue dangling. Oliver politely raised his hands to the level of his shoulders with the palms turned toward her and asked to speak with Miz Balm In Gilead Quillen.

"Hit's me, all right," she admitted. She had a single front tooth, and all the others were gone. She wore a man's slouch hat and a butternut blouse with horn buttons and skirts of much-patched homespun hitched up and stuffed into a belt of knotted plowline. Hanks of clotted hair stuck out under the hat. She examined him with a cold gray eye. "What-for ye asking after me?"

Oliver told his name and glanced warily about at the dogs. They all gazed back in an inquiring but respectful way, and Oliver thought it mighty unlikely how obedient they were, amid the disorder of the Quillen dooryard. "Two years ago," he began, "in the early fall, I come here at the wish of Judge Madison Curtis over towards Hayesville, to warn your husband . . ."

"I recollect," she cut him off. Her voice was low and gravelly; it might have belonged to a man. The hammer of the Sharps had been at half cock, but now she wrapped a fist around it and pulled it all the way back. "He warned us, all right," she declared. "I recollect ye brung my man a writin' he done. But I reckon that jedge put them people on us, sure as he give us warnin'." Slowly she shook her head. "They missed us that time, them bad-uns. But next winter they come back. Kilt my man and all my boys. Shot one in the house and the rest right-cheer in this yard, with me and my poor gals a-watchin'." She paused, shifted her chaw of tobacco, then turned her head aside and spat. Then she looked up at him again through the sights of the carbine. "All on account of your fine jedge."

Ruefully Oliver bent his head, his hands still raised. "I know," he said. "I'm sorry. The judge is sorry too." Then haltingly he told her why he'd come. As he spoke the words he heard how lame they sounded, and he began to think he'd made a mistake in coming so impulsively. Maybe he should have waited and asked the opinion of lawyer Elias or Andy or even the judge himself. Suddenly his own errand seemed foolish to him—coming to beg the help of a Unionist widow in the cause of a Rebel who'd sent men to murder her family. The judge's having dispatched a warning now dwindled away to nothing next to the loss she'd suffered. But he'd come this far; he may as well go the whole way and trust to the Lord to touch her heart with mercy. He drew a large breath and told his mission, expecting the whole time to be shot off the mule or at the very least ordered out of the dooryard. But when he finished she uncocked the Sharps and told him to come inside, and after a moment's hesitation he did.

Every one of the dogs filed quietly in after him. They took places around the edge of the room as if by assignment and sat again and watched him with their tongues hanging out. The room was mostly dark—there were no windows and but one candle burning on a table in the middle of it—and the place stank like the den of some carrion-eating beast. Squatting motionless and silent on the dirt floor in one corner were three or four figures whose features he couldn't make out, that Oliver thought must be the Quillen daughters and widows. Now and then their eyes caught the light of the candle and reflected it back like the eyes of wolves gathered around a campfire. Oliver stood in the center of the dim space with his mouth open, so as to breathe amid the stench, uncertain what to do next. The only sound he could hear was the panting of the dogs.

Then Balm In Gilead Quillen put down the Sharps and fetched something from a mound of indeterminate matter by the doorway and brought it and laid it on the table. Oliver leaned close to see. What he saw looked like four short links of overcooked sausage. "Them's my Mose's fingers," she explained with an air of reverence. "The leader of the bad-uns hacked 'em off, one after t'other." There was no fire on the hearth, and the room was icy cold, but still Oliver began copiously to sweat. "Hit's all that's left of him," she mused. "All I got to recollect him by." In the corner one of the daughters or widows began softly sobbing, and then one by one they started to keen and wail, making a banshee noise that caused Oliver's flesh to creep.

"I heard tell he done torture on the jedge's lady too," Balm In Gilead remarked above the din, and Oliver was so distracted that he had to think whom she meant; then he saw she referred to the leader of the Yellow Jackets. He said yes, and she nodded. "I heard tell the jedge tole on us to spare his lady." Now some of the dogs pointed their muzzles upward and joined the women in their howling, till the room rang with bewailment. Oliver felt tempted to cover his ears but did not. Again he said yes, and again she nodded. "I heard tell hit torments him, what he done." Once more he said yes amid the squalling of the women and dogs.

She pulled out a chair and let herself down at the table, gazing fondly at Old Mose's fingers, and to Oliver's relief the women stopped their hallooing, although two or three of the dogs howled on. "I never cared one way or t'other myself, Union or secesh," mused

Balm In Gilead. "Nor did Mose. Mose was a damn old robber, didn't matter who he robbed, tory or Reb or who." She leaned back in the chair and looked off dreamily into the dark. "Mose had learnin' as a youngun. Said he was born of a good family. Somewheres in Old Virginny, he said. He give the boys sech pretty names on account of his learnin'. Pharsalia. Persepolis. Parsargardae." She seemed to have forgotten that Oliver was there. In the corner all the girls were crying softly now, but only one of the dogs continued to moan, and presently it quieted too.

Balm In Gilead smiled around her chaw. "He admired the jedge, Mose did. Coveted his goods and would of burnt him out, but admired him all the same. He allus said the jedge had character. Mose hadn't got no character hisself, but he seen it in others. Mose said the jedge fell short of the glory of God that day when the leader of the bad-uns hurt his lady, but then he repented after and sent to save us. And him high up and us low down."

Then she looked sharply up at Oliver and gave his face a long and serious study. After a minute or two of this she remarked, "I expect ye got character yerownself. I reckon ye be a decent man and tryin' to do right. Ain't many nowadays a body can say that about." She paused and spat on the floor, then settled back in the chair and thought awhile, chewing. Then she said, "I expect I ort to do right too."

When Andy turned off the wagon road and started down the drive toward the house, he saw Uncle Amos's rockaway and Cousin Watson's chaise parked in the turnaround and half a dozen mules and saddle horses tied to the new worm fence, and he knew something was bad amiss. He trotted the mule down the drive and dropped off at the end of the flagstone walk and let the mule go and started up the walk. Papa came out to meet him and took him firmly by the arms and told him. Andy stared at Papa as if he thought the old man had lost his mind. But in fact he was wondering if he'd lost his own. How could he be hearing such a thing, if he were not deranged? Only a madman could think his time with her was over, when it had really only just begun. He broke free and burst into the house and dashed unseeing past the crowd of relations in the parlor to mount the stairs two at a time. At the top he turned and went along the railing to the door of the room they shared.

Opening the door he glimpsed Uncle Amos at the foot of the bed wearing black broadcloth and holding his Bible open before him, with Mama seated by the headboard and a crush of weeping females all around, his sisters Martha and Sarah and his cousin Nancy Ledford and some others. But what he saw clearest was Salina lying on her side bent impossibly backward, drenched in sweat and shaking so violently that the whole bed rattled on its posts, her face turned toward him gaunt amid a spread of wet black hair and smiling the cruel smile of lockjaw.

In the grip of an agony beyond expression Salina saw him enter. Her teeth were all shattered and her neck broken and her back snapped in three places, and for four days now her bladder had been shut and her bowels locked, but her mind was clear, and when she saw him she wished that he had not come, that he hadn't seen what he now saw and would never be able to forget. She knew it would haunt him always, and if she'd had the power she'd have spared him that. But she couldn't. All she could do was look at him with love and regret. Then a searing pain stabbed deep inside her head, and a warm red cloud passed over her vision, and the pain at last began to fade away.

They buried her on a blustery day a week before Christmas. Her grave was next to Betty and Bill Cartman's on the nose of the hill overlooking the river. The sun hung low and pale in a steely sky, and the wind lashed among the crowd as if angry and rattled the dry leaves still clinging to the oaks. Uncle Amos read the ceremony. Daniel McFee, who'd put aside his differences with Madison for the occasion because Salina had always been kind, came and sang several hymns and was welcome, but the boy Hamby McFee did not come. Daniel sang "Crossing over Jordan" and "Bound for the Promised Land" and "Nearer My God to Thee." Oliver Price and his boy Syl were there, and Oliver said a prayer. Andy bore up well. But Madison and Sarah were distraught and had to be helped inside afterwards.

They'd just been put to bed when the two Puckett women turned their dun mule onto the lane above the house and rode down the drive and halted at the edge of the cul-de-sac, where the buggies were parked and the horses and mules tethered.

"Another damn Rebel soul steeped in evil done gone a-howlin' down to hell," cried the old one, "to burn eternal in the fire that don't consume nor never quit. Hit's the judgment of the Almighty on ye, nest of vipers that ye be."

And the young one said, "Vipers."

Oliver Price looked on in horror, but all the others had grown accustomed to these visitations or knew of them and only turned away in disgust. Even Andy showed no ire. The crowd began to disperse as the Pucketts sat swearing and calling down the thunder of heaven on every Curtis on the planet, till Daniel McFee of all people addressed them sharply in reproach. They cursed him for a goddamn nigger that had forgot his place but soon turned the mule and rode out again, and were gone.

CHAPTER 11

On the day after Christmas, over beyond Hanging Dog in an abandoned rock house by Boiling Springs in Cherokee County, some children playing march-around-the-level found the body of a dead man lying in the matted leaves all covered with ice. He was frozen solid on account of the cold, and it took the work of three men to lift him into a steer cart to carry him into Murphy. The way he was lying, he had one arm flung out, and after they got him in the cart he was fixed in such fashion that this frozen arm stuck straight up, as if he was pointing at something in the sky. And as the steer cart went along on its way to Murphy, with the dead fellow in it pointing heavenward, all the folk that saw it twisted their heads to look up and see what he was drawing their attention to.

In a day or two he thawed out and ceased to point and got to looking somewhat more natural, and some of his relations from down around Ebenezer came by the sheriff's office and identified him. His name was William Lark, they said. He had a little farm under Flea Mountain, where he raised hay and some corn and flax. He'd been a soldier in the Confederate army and had got captured right at the end of the war and was put in prison in Louisville, Kentucky, and had only got home last July and was sickly with a complaint of the bowels.

He left a widow and a little girl four years of age. Somebody had shot him once in the left side of the head, so close that the powder blackened him and burnt all the hair off that part of his scalp. The sheriff thought it was bushwhackers like the ones that killed that hog farmer Sprogg on Settawig Road in September and the other fellow Sasser on the Licklog in Clay County last month. If this was so then it looked for certain like the partisans favored Union, for all three of the dead ones had served in the Rebel military. Lark's pappy said his boy was a cavalryman, in Company F of Folk's Battalion. But it was strange that nobody had seen any party of riders in that country, who might've been the ones to do the bloody work.

That December the Congress at Washington City refused to seat William A. Graham and John Pool, the senators North Carolina had elected the month before. All the newly elected senators and congressmen of the other seceded states were turned out too—the Radical Republicans called them the Confederate Brigadiers, because so many of them had worn the gray or served in the Confederate House or Senate. Instead a joint committee on reconstruction was established to investigate conditions in the South. The Radicals knew President Johnson meant to let the former Rebels resume control of Dixie, and they set out to use the joint committee to prove it and besmirch him. That done, they felt they could then persuade the moderates in Congress to join them in imposing a social revolution on the unrepentant South.

When word of the move reached the old Confederacy there were howls of rage on every hand, even in places like western Carolina, where Unionism was strong but most cared nothing for the Negro and only wanted to put the war behind them and get on with their lives. But when Nahum Bellamy heard the news he fell into a state approaching ecstacy. Here was the first log thrown in the path of Johnson's evil scheme to evade the moral outcome of the war. The war had been fought for a sublime purpose, the freeing of the slave, but Johnson wanted to pretend it had been fought only to achieve the narrow political goal of reuniting the country. For a time—far too long a time—he'd succeeded in warding off the truth. But now, thanks to the vigilance of the Radicals in Congress, the truth beamed forth for all to see.

Good news was especially welcome as year's end approached, for in recent weeks the tidings had been mostly dismal. After instructing agents of the Freedmen's Bureau to set aside parcels of confiscated land to be given to Negroes, in September General Howard, the head of the Freedmen's Bureau—under orders from Johnson— issued a circular saying the land must be restored to the pardoned secesh instead. This in the face of a confident expectation by the blacks that the land would be divided among them after New Year's. Hawley in Franklin, through the Hayesville field agent, passed along the discouraging report, and of course the downcast freedmen turned at once on Bellamy, wanting to know why the bureau was breaking the promises it had made to them through him. There was little he could say except counsel them to wait—give the president and his Rebel friends enough rope, he said, and presently they'd hang themselves. But though he spoke with his usual passion they failed to catch fire, and he could tell they'd begun to harbor doubts about him for the first time since he came among them.

Also, more and more now, they were living in fear. Tales they heard of atrocities in other places left them all atremble that such might occur right here on home ground. And indeed there'd been some incidents—a gang of whites beating on an old Negro down by Jackrabbit, a farmer giving a black sharecropper thirty-nine lashes with a coachwhip on the Cold Branch, two ex-Rebels making threats on Daniel McFee. A month ago a colored boy went missing from his place at the foot of Wildcat Mountain and hadn't been seen since, and most folks thought he was dead of a lynching, for he'd once spoken saucy to a white woman in a store in Murphy.

As was his fashion Bellamy was quick to levy justice on all abusers of Negroes. The Jackrabbit crowd he'd confined in Sheriff Chastine's log jail on the red-clay hill south of the square in Hayesville, to await trial at county court. And the Freedmen's Bureau tribunal at Murphy had already laid a fine on that Cold Branch whipper. McFee had handled his own trouble, but Bellamy knew the names of the peckerwoods that rousted him and was watching them. As for the missing boy, Bellamy had reserved that matter to himself alone, since the fewer who knew of his special work of requital the slighter the chance damaging rumors would get out; besides, some of the Seraphim who hadn't been with him in wartime were shy of doings in that line and thus had to be counted unreliable. Two low-downers on Wildcat who some suspected of doing away with the missing boy had themselves vanished in the same week's time, after Bellamy sought them out. From them he got the name of a third man who, as soon as Bellamy found him, was going to vanish as well. But no matter how speedy Bellamy's actions the freedmen lived on in dread, and with good reason.

But now with the Radicals in Congress at last taking a hand it began to look as if right was going to triumph after all, just as Bellamy had consistently foretold. If a Radical Congress took away from Johnson the whole reconstruction of the South then in time the freedmen would see the land divided after all, the tormenters of Negroes punished, the planters ground down, the suffrage extended to them and the day of Negro equality dawning. Hope was springing up anew among the black folk. But most important of all—at least for Bellamy—their faith in him returned.

It was a small barnyard he was cock of. There weren't four hundred Negroes in the whole district west of the Nantahalas. But few though they might be, they were his, and he did not mean to lose them. They were but the first of many, he thought. From these seeds would grow a forest of his making, which like Birnam wood in the writings of the Bard might bestir itself to move upon the Dunsinane of the wicked slavocrats. Blessed with an uncommon schooling and a tongue of silver, he held the Negroes in the palm of his hand, because they thought him the chosen of God. He knew now that the Holy Spirit was on him, and he knew also, as with Moses in the Bible, that God would always teach him what to say. *For who hath made man's mouth? Or who maketh the dumb, or deaf, or the seeing, or the blind? Did he not have the Lord?* He could sway them; they would hear the Almighty on his tongue; he could lead them out like Gideon; they would be the sword of the Lord and of Gideon; and the wicked would go down before them like wheat at harvest time.

On the first Thursday in January the Tennessee lawyer Johnston Barrett came down from Elizabethton in Carter County, and Bellamy rode with him from Hayesville up to the ridge-top farm on Fires Creek where the Pucketts had been squatters for as long as anybody in Clay County could remember; the land they were on belonged to a speculator living some said in Philadelphia and some said Baltimore, who'd never set foot west of the Nantahalas. The speculator had an agent in Franklin who now and again cut timber on the tract and seemed willing to tolerate the Pucketts so long as they gave over an occasional hog by way of rent.

The road into the mountains was eroded and steep and in places badly washed out, and the going was slow. It was well past noon before they drew rein in the Pucketts' dooryard. Already it was clear they would have to stay the night. Barrett had many questions he needed answered before he could prepare the complaint, and while the Pucketts were great talkers, especially the old one, they seldom came directly to the point, preferring instead to maunder on hour after hour, bemoaning their many afflictions.

Barrett was an accommodating sort and stood the ordeal manfully. He perched on a milking stool at a rickety table with only the fire on the hearth for light, diligently scribbling away while the abhorrent Pucketts whined and harangued, hovering about him like buzzards circling a dying calf. But Bellamy could hardly contain his impatience and disgust and spent much of the afternoon pacing up and down outside, where the air, if cold to the bone, was at least free of the ammoniac odor of the two women. What low creatures they were, with whom he must treat. Yet he had to bear them awhile longer if the Lord's work was to be accomplished. How glad he'd be when spring came and the case was tried and he'd be quit of these two, who with their every foul breath and wheedling word reminded him of his miserable congregants of long ago in dirt-poor Carter County.

He and Barrett spent that night in the barn—a bedchamber much preferable to anything the Pucketts could have offered—and after a quick breakfast of burnt side meat and eggs fried brittle-dry they started back for Hayesville. The way was easier going down; it was eleven in the morning when they turned into the square. Barrett rode on to the hotel to eat a lunch and rest up for his trip back to Tennessee on tomorrow's mail stage. Bellamy walked his gray around two sides of the square to the Freedmen's Bureau office—and there checked up sharply in surprise when he saw the strange black gelding asleep at the hitch rail with a McClellan army saddle on its back and a *US* brand on its hip.

"He a regular-army captain," Corn Dodger said, nervously eyeing the shut door of the room where the officer had closeted himself with the field agent. "He from headquarters in Morganton, says he on a tour of inspection. Got hisself a big leather grip all full of papers and sich." Corn Dodger fidgeted, standing first on one foot and then the other. "Been closed up in there a hour already," he said. He glanced sideways at Bellamy to test his mood and see if he was right to be alarmed. "Boss, what you reckon this captain want?"

Hamby McFee leaned against the front wall paring his nails with a case knife, and two more Seraphim stood by the side door, and although they contrived to seem as casual as Hamby, Bellamy could sense their worry. They had all been riding beyond any authority for a long time now, and they waited for his answer.

He shrugged and smiled. It had always been only a matter of time. That was why he'd moved quickly. He'd done a lot in so few months—in spite of the army, in spite of Hawley and Eastmond and Whittlesey in the bureau. And he remained confident he'd do still more; he'd not rest till he brought those Curtises down. Just because some staff captain rode up from Morganton to ask a few questions didn't mean the whole game had gone up—not yet, at least.

"That captain'll talk to me sooner or later," he replied at last. "Then we'll know what he wants." He took off his canvas cap and airily threw it on his desk to show how unconcerned he was. Again he smiled. "And then we'll see if he can get it," he added, and they all laughed, even Corn Dodger.

He said his name was Whitney Callendar, and although he was only a captain he didn't salute. He said he was a West Pointer and in the war had got as far as brevet colonel and commanded his own artillery battery. Now, in peacetime, he said, he'd reverted to his regular-army rank and had the one company of the Third United States Artillery that was in North Carolina on occupation duty. The company was stationed in Charlotte under the command of his first lieutenant, and he himself was on detached service doing staff work at General Heath's headquarters. In spite of not having saluted he chatted companionably and was pleasant enough, but it was clear from his manner that he didn't regard Bellamy as a superior officer. He had an amused and slightly condescending air. Nevertheless Bellamy treated him with indulgence. There was many a slip between the cup and the lip.

They sat on opposite sides of Bellamy's desk bathed in the window's wintry light. Corn Dodger walked slowly back and forth in his heavy boots along the low railing that separated them from the public space in the front of the room, casting them anxious looks. Hamby McFee looked on with his chair tilted back against the front wall. Others of the Seraphim began wandering in to take places standing or sitting around the room, where they looked impassively on. The field agent had gone home; after his interview with Callendar he'd emerged pale and sweating and locked the door of his office and hurried out. Two clerks remained at desks that flanked the gate in the railing, and through the front door came a steady stream of freedmen that divided at the gate to go one way or the other, to take up business.

Callendar wanted to know if Bellamy was the same Nahum Bellamy that assassinated Captain Roby Brown of the Johnson County Home Guard and the Rebels Wash and Thomas Jefferson Monroe in East Tennessee in eighteen and sixty-three. He asked this in an agreeable fashion, and just as agreeably Bellamy told him yes, he was the same man. Then Callendar inquired about the killing of Old Bill Parker in Johnson County in eighteen and sixty-four, and Bellamy confirmed it was he and some other Union men that had done Bill in. In answer to more questions Bellamy also admitted to having come over on the Hudson Trail into Carolina with Captain Lyon and shot to death Turkey Trot Kirkland and his brother Jesse, as well as a man named Mashburn and another man named Hamilton and some of Colonel Will Thomas's Indians in the western part of Cherokee, and to hanging two Rebel marauders right here in Clay County, one of whom was Luther Turnbull and the other unknown, all in eighteen and sixty-five.

"And every one of these was legal too," Bellamy declared, "under the laws of war, such as they are. Which makes me wonder why you're asking."

Genially the captain inclined his head. "Simply to establish your identity, sir. Many an ugly deed was done in these mountains in the late war, by Rebs and by those that favored Union both. Mostly the army has agreed to draw a veil over it all, and I'm sure that's for the best. But even so, one has to say that the work of Nahum Bellamy the Pilot was . . . conspicuous. If you are he then it's relevant to our discussion."

Thinly Bellamy smirked. "I was diligent. I was thorough. I still am." Then he gave a dry little laugh. "Does your inquiring mean I ain't under that veil you say the army's drawed over such matters?"

Callendar arched his eyebrows and pulled a winsome face. "My dear sir, you don't need me to remind you that you are not and never were an officer of the United States Army. That was a little charade you concocted at some point behind enemy lines in the midst of war, which served certain purposes temporarily useful both to yourself and to the army. The army permitted it as long as it was expedient, but the purposes the army cared about expired at war's end. Only, due to the press of other business, the army conveniently happened to forget about you. And ever since, you've been parading about this district confidently impersonating an officer and pretending to be under military orders, which—I need scarcely remind you—is a crime.

"As for things done in war," he went on, "the veil the army has drawn will indeed cover them. It will be as if they never occurred." Mockingly he raised a hand and made the sign of the cross in the air between them. "You are shriven, sir. Go forth and sin no more. But you must put off the uniform at once. And of course you must disband your gang of ruffians and immediately cease all connection with the Freedmen's Bureau."

How smug he was! How certain that he could descend from headquarters and mete out judgments that others would obey! Bellamy found him ridiculous in his complacency and observed him now with contempt. Bending to his desk Bellamy opened a drawer and produced the sheaf of papers he'd kept ready at hand against this very eventuality. "My orders," he said, and one by one handed them over. General Ruger's order transferring him to the bureau and naming him to the special post of supervising inspector. General Cox's order confirming the appointment. General Heath's order confirming Cox's. Each general in his turn had assumed that Bellamy was a commissioned officer; God only knew to whose file the copies of these orders had gone, since Bellamy had none at headquarters. But the orders themselves stood.

Callendar glanced them over but soon tossed them back, laughing. "Nothing's as easy as hoodwinking a busy general, if you've got his eye and ear. Show me an order from the Freedmen's Bureau. Show me something Whittlesey has signed, or General Howard the commissioner. Show me a pay voucher, even." On impulse he leaned forward and rested his elbows on the desk top and assumed a confidential mien. "By the way, speaking of pay, I'm interested to know how you've managed during all these months, without a salary from either the army or the bureau." Eagerly he tapped his fingers on the walnut desk top. "Let me in on it. How'd you do it—maintain a whole police force, not to mention feed and clothe and arm yourself?"

Look at him! How vulgar he was! What could he know of the

sacrifices Bellamy had made to carry on his arduous task? Men had paid him thousands to pilot them over the mountains in the war, and thousands more in wealth had come to him as he confiscated the goods of the many Rebels he'd found out. But had he played the miser, hoarding the riches to himself? No. Nahum Bellamy was a poor man; it was the cause he'd enriched. He'd poured out money like water, so the work could go on. And here was this sly fellow crassly wanting to know how he'd filched and grafted, as if he were not engaged in sacred toil at all but was instead nothing but a contemptible sneak thief.

Callendar saw that Bellamy would not respond and so sank back in his chair with a sigh of resignation. "Ah, well. Perhaps you're simply a man of means. It can't have been the government's money, so I suppose it don't matter." He leaned forward again and consulted a penciled list lying in front of him. "Oh, yes, the charges you've preferred against this fellow James Madison Curtis. I'm authorized to tell you that under the circumstances"—here he made an ironical little bow—"the matter will not be pursued." He scanned the list top to bottom, then folded it over, folded it again and slipped it into the bosom of his blouse.

He stood then and began to collect his papers and put them into his leather grip. Beyond the railing Corn Dodger stopped his pacing and stood staring; Hamby McFee and the other Seraphim watched with the fixity of deer surprised in a forest clearing. Callendar finished packing away his documents, closed his grip and paused to give Bellamy another of his humorous looks. "If I were you, sir," he said, "I shouldn't go off anywhere and disappear, for if you do you'll be a fugitive, and every man's hand will be against you. Once I make my report I imagine some provost troops will be along for you right directly." He dipped his head toward the agent's locked office. "It may be that someone from the bureau will come asking too—if not somebody from the state's attorney general and maybe the sheriffs of Clay and Cherokee Counties." Then he burst out laughing at the absurdity of the many roles Bellamy had played.

Bellamy had stood also, and while Callendar talked he patiently tapped the edges of his sheaf of orders against the top of the desk till they were squared off. Then when the captain was through Bellamy laid the orders exactly in the middle of the desk, and crossing his arms in front of him he gazed at Callendar, looking long and cold into his black eyes, while Corn Dodger and Hamby McFee and the clerks and the waiting freedmen all stood still by the railing. In that moment it seemed to Bellamy that the light around the captain changed, turned dim like old pewter, and the captain himself darkened to the hue of bruised fruit; and Bellamy saw that God had set His mark on Whitney Callendar.

But Callendar didn't guess it. Instead he laughed again and inquired, "Do you give me the evil eye, sir?" Then he sighed. "It won't do you any good," he said, not without a touch of pity.

But it was not enough to expunge the mark and save him. Callendar took his cape from the back of his chair and put it on and picked up his hat and gloves and turned with a whirl of his cape and walked out through the gate in the railing past the watching Seraphim.

As soon as the captain stepped outside, Bellamy dispatched Hamby McFee and one of the white Seraphim named Randlett to follow him at a discreet distance and report every hour on his whereabouts. Then he shooed out the two clerks and the miscellaneous freedmen and locked the doors. He knew from the faces of the Seraphim that they thought the end had come, and he couldn't permit them to believe that; if they did they'd begin to scatter, and in a day's time he'd have no one by him at all. He wished Daniel McFee were here. They all looked up to Daniel, who could help rally them; his word was law with them. Yet no sooner had he wished it than Bellamy reminded himself that he could no longer count on the unthinking support of Daniel McFee, who unlike his stepson Hamby or Corn Dodger the sergeant had shown himself stubbornly possessed of independent judgment. By refusing to testify against the Curtises Daniel had proved that there would be occasions when he would deny Bellamy his aid on various obscure points of honor. So it was up to Bellamy alone.

Quickly he ushered the Seraphim into the back room where the meetings of the Union League were held and sat them down around the stove and gave them a fiery talk. Yes, he told them, the officer was from headquarters, and yes, he'd come to say that Boss Bellamy must cease his work and the Seraphim disband. But this officer didn't understand that Boss Bellamy operated under an authority far higher than his. Nor did the army understand it. But the officer and those who'd sent him from headquarters would soon see how puny they were, next to the power that guided the Boss. He invited the Seraphim to remember in the next days that he'd said this, for the Almighty was going to deliver them out of the hand of their enemies. God was going to work a miracle, the same as He'd wrought miracles in the olden times, to save them that believed on Him. And when the Seraphim saw this and remembered that the Boss had prophesied it, then their faith would grow great enough so as to remove mountains, and nothing and nobody could stand in their way. As he spoke he could see their temper change from fear to exaltation, and he was vain enough to marvel at his own force; it was good to see that it hadn't waned. When he finished they came roaring to their feet, and he was satisfied.

In an hour Randlett returned to say that Callendar had gone to the hotel and asked directions to the Curtis farm, and then had ridden there. He was there yet, meeting with the Curtises. No doubt the infamous Rebels were being told they would not suffer after all for their malefactions. Bellamy found a kind of sour comedy in the notion; he imagined the pathetic relief of the Curtises, thinking themselves delivered from the ordeal, and the pride Callendar would take in his role as their deliverer. How little they knew of what was in the heart of God!

In another hour Hamby McFee came in and reported that Callendar had returned to Hayesville, engaged a room at the hotel and gone straight to bed. Callendar, he said, had asked to be awakened early, for he planned to start back at daylight for Morganton.

Long before dawn Bellamy rose and ate a cold breakfast of livermush and biscuit washed down with buttermilk, then dressed not in uniform but in a pair of corduroy britches and a sack coat, and laying aside his cherished cap of haversack canvas he put on instead a plain flat-brimmed hat with a round crown. The only parts of his army gear he donned were his high boots and his gum blanket, which he'd need for warmth. Nor when he left his cabin beneath the hill where the jail stood did he saddle his favorite gray, so readily associated with him; instead he chose the rusty little sorrel that he reserved for his secret and most special enterprises, because of its sure foot and nimble ways.

Before leaving he loaded his two Colt's revolvers, six rounds to each cylinder, and capped five of the six nipples, letting down the hammer on the uncapped nipple for safety. He was careful to open the vent of each chamber with a sewing needle, so there would be no chance of a misfire. When he finished with them he slipped the pistols into the pommel holsters on either side of his saddle. Then he shoved a full magazine into the buttstock of his Spencer and secured the carbine in its loop on the saddle bow and was ready.

It was still dark when he rode out cross-country around the foot of Dan Knob and on eastward under the point of Ash Top. By the time he forded the Licklog far enough above the bridge not to be seen, the sky ahead of him was brightening behind the crags of the

Nantahalas. He kept to the woods above the public road, but in this season with the leaves off the hardwoods it was hard to stay out of sight, and he looked for patches of evergreen to hide himself in as much as he could. The flanks of Piney Top, thick with hemlock, afforded him good cover when he came to them about nine o'clock. Then the sun got over the summits and began to melt the frost that whitened all the valley. Below him lines of smoke rose from the chimneys of the farmhouses scattered along the twisting bottomlands he'd gone so high to avoid.

He crossed Pounding Mill Branch and started up the Shooting Creek drainage into Chunky Gal Mountain, staying high off the road on the left side, along the southern slopes of the Vineyard and then the Pinnacle and finally Shooting Creek Bald. As he climbed, the air grew colder and colder; it was a sunny and cloudless day, but his route was taking him up through shadowed places that were still coated with hoarfrost and rime ice. He shivered in the chill and frequently took off his gauntlets and blew on his hands to keep them warm and flexible. The little sorrel picked its way carefully along the steeps and in and out of the rocky beds of the creeks and branches, blowing plumes of condensation. There was skim ice in all the watercourses.

Finally about midday he came to the spot he'd chosen. It was just above the place where the Old Macon Trail crossed the Muskrat on a log bridge on its way down from Grassy Gap. Several big spruces had fallen there in a windstorm years ago, and their scaly trunks and branches lay in a dense tangle that a man could hide in, never to be seen from the road below. The road itself turned along a shoulder of Chunky Gal not fifty yards below the nest of downed timber, affording a lovely prospect westward into the misty valley of the Hiwassee. Most fortuitous of all, back of the deadfall and up a ravine, the ground opened out into a high meadow, and at one end of this meadow stood a ruined house. In the yard of the house there was an open well.

Bellamy tethered his horse in the ravine and unshipped the Spencer and carried it into the deadfall and settled down to wait. The deadfall lay in full sunshine, and for the first time that day warmth began to search his cold bones. He drowsed cozily in the heat.

Corn Dodger was worried, but he was also intrigued. He was worried about what that captain from headquarters might do to vex Boss Bellamy and the Seraphim, but he was intrigued to think that the Boss had promised God would make a miracle to save them. Corn Dodger wanted to see a miracle in the worst way. But he was afraid the miracle might happen out of his presence and he'd miss it. Boss Bellamy was so close to God that Corn Dodger was pretty sure when the miracle happened it would happen in the vicinity of the Boss. So he concluded to stay near the Boss. Then when God and the Boss made the miracle happen Corn Dodger would be there to see it.

Corn Dodger lived in a shack just a short distance from the Boss's cabin, so it was an easy matter to keep watch. And that morning when the Boss left out, Corn Dodger spotted him quick. Before the war Corn Dodger had belonged to a speculator that used him to track runaways. Corn Dodger could track a runaway nigger over bare rock on a moonless night. And it wasn't just niggers either. There wasn't a critter alive he couldn't trace, man or beast, devil or angel. He followed the Boss right up. But because he was so light afoot and managed his horse so easy the Boss never suspected he was there.

Once the sun got up Corn Dodger was surprised to see the Boss riding a different mount and wearing different clothes than usual. But then he thought maybe this was part of getting a miracle to happen. Maybe this was the Boss's miracle horse and his miracle clothes too. Also, it looked like the Boss was going to a special miracle place as well, high up in the hills. And when the Boss stopped and got in amongst those fallen-down spruces Corn Dodger had to admit the spot he'd picked sure enough seemed like a miracle place, perched on the edge of the mountain, looking off into the valley all wispy with fog and spotted with patches of silver where the frost lay yet. Corn Dodger tied his horse to an ash tree and stretched out behind a rock and waited with his heart in his throat, to think that at last he was going to witness a miracle wrought by the Lord God Jehovah Hisownself.

CHAPTER 12

O liver traveled home for Christmas feeling proud of himself for having scouted out Miz Balm In Gilead Quillen. Not that he gave himself any credit at all for her making up her mind to testify. The woman had done that all by herself, musing and mulling over Old Mose's fingers, while Oliver stood by quaking with misgiving. Nonetheless the Curtises hailed him for a hero. And even lawyer Elias deigned to wring his hand in thanks when he fetched Miz Quillen to the boy pleader's office to give her affidavit. To Oliver lawyer Elias in his gratitude seemed to grow some in stature and to take on a measure of seasoning not noticeable before. Thinking of that now, Oliver was level enough of head to laugh at himself, at how ready he'd been to call lawyer Elias a man and wise, simply for taking agreeable note of him.

Now he was full of thoughts of home. He longed to see Nancy and wee Martha. He'd got two letters in his time away and knew that Nancy had been pretty well, though Martha had suffered a cold. There had even been a note from the Widow Henslee enclosed in one of Nancy's, to say that Nancy indeed was prospering and wasn't fibbing to save him worry in what she wrote. The baby was carrying well, and Nancy had started to flesh out. The Widow Henslee said the baby was going to be a boy yet failed to explain how she knew this. But Oliver believed her without question.

Oliver and Syl had the mail stage to themselves between Hayesville and Franklin. It was a bright day, but coming over the top of the Winding Stairs they found the road covered with silvery bristles of hoarfrost, and from the boulders that overhung the road long icicles hung down like so many unsheathed daggers. Then the light faded and flurries of snow blew in the wind, and the rest of the day was like that, dazzling bright and then dark and snowy. High above them, when the sun was out, the peaks of the mountains glared so white it hurt the eyes to look at them, but then when the dimness came they beamed a cool silver, like chunks of the moon fallen to earth. Sometimes it also snowed when the sun shone, and then the air sparkled as with clouds of diamonds ground up fine as powder.

It had been quite a trip for Syl. Not only were there new folks to meet and new sights to see and the Cartman boys to romp with, he'd had two stagecoach rides and seen a dead man pulled out of a creek and been present at another dying and gone to a funeral broken up by madwomen, and now he was traveling home in a snowstorm. He'd have been a dull youngun for sure if all this wasn't enough to stir him. But he laughed and babbled and gave off the merry warmth Oliver remembered from of old. Oliver thought this wasn't just due to the adventures of the visit either; he guessed it was also because Syl was glad his pappy hadn't gone off and left him marooned among strangers, as he'd feared.

At Franklin Lit and Mac and Archie were there with the wagon and carried them upriver to Oliver's place by the mouth of Darnell

Creek, where Nancy and Martha and the Widow Henslee were waiting. Although only five months gone Nancy came out waddling, the great mound of her belly swaying before her, and Oliver gathered her gently in his arms to embrace her but soon sank to his knees to lay his head against the place where his son lay curled up tight and waiting. He fancied he felt a faint kick against his ear and whooped for joy. But then Martha came insisting he bear her up high and cover her with wet kisses, which he did. The Widow Henslee stood by smiling.

For Christmas Oliver gave Martha a toy that was a wooden woman in a chestnut box with a crank in the side that made the old woman work a churn. He'd bought it off a country man that was selling them in the market at Franklin. Also he gave her an apple-head doll that Miz Curtis had made up for her special. This doll had a sour and shrunk-up expression that Syl remarked reminded him of Grandma, and Oliver was forced to agree with him on that. Syl himself got a fine slingshot Oliver had made while at the Curtises' and a popgun Andy had fashioned for him out of elder wood. There were sticks of peppermint and horehound for both the younguns too.

Nancy he gave a red satin cushion in the shape of a heart trimmed all around the edge with white lace, that had letters embroidered in silver thread across the front of it saying, *Love Forever*. He'd seen that in a shop in Franklin and known at once he couldn't last another second without buying it to give to Nancy. But the finest gift and the one that came straightest from his heart was a dulcimer from the hands of Uncle Ernest Dawkins, made of many pieces of wood, some honey colored and some dark as coffee but all as delicate as could be and fitted together so cleverly the touch of a hand couldn't feel a seam. Nancy played a tune on it in the firelight and sang,

> *Possum put on an overcoat,*
> *Raccoon put on gown,*

Rabbit put on ruffled shirt,
All buttoned up and down.
Wait, Billy, wait, wait I say
And I will marry you by and by.

In the weeks after Salina died Andy went out to her grave whenever he could and settled on the flat stone of white quartz he'd placed
beside it and tried hard to talk to her. In life he had never spoken to
her as often or as directly as he wished, and this was something he
deeply regretted. Now in the hush of her death he hoped he'd be
able to find a way to reach her at last. But he couldn't. Perhaps her
spirit was present indeed and was ready to listen, as he hoped—
there was a certain stillness in the space over her grave that seemed
to suggest this—but the words wouldn't come to him. Consequently
all he did was sit dumb beside the mound of red dirt with the wooden
marker at the head of it and think again and again of the manner of
her dying. It was as if that memory stood now like a wall between
them.

Every night in his sleep Salina died over and over again, and each
time she died Andy awoke with a cry that tore his throat raw, and
then he lay sweaty and shivering till he slept once more and the
nightmare came again. Till Salina died he thought he'd seen the worst
that a man could see. But now he knew different. There had never
been a thing on any battlefield as hard as what Salina suffered. After
all, in war, everyone who took part was conscious of the sin of what
he did and mindful of earning a sure punishment to come. But Salina
was guiltless, her agony unearned. To think of this was such torment
that at times he wished he could crack his own skull open like the
shell of an egg and tear the memory and the nightmare out of his
brain by main force. If he could rid himself of them maybe he could
reach her.

Because he had to reach her. He knew he was stronger than he used to be, but he also knew that he was not yet strong enough to do without her. He needed her. He needed her just as he'd once needed Papa and Mama and Jack and Howell. No, that wasn't right—he needed her worse than he'd ever needed any of them. She was like rising ground under his feet; she'd borne him up always with her quiet resolve. Now, with Salina not only gone but beyond the reach of his soul's voice, he didn't see how he could do what he had to do in these trying days. Yet he must. Because she was gone. Gone as surely as Jack was gone and Howell was gone and Papa had lost heart and Mama had grown weary. They'd all left Andy alone to face what came.

Papa said it was the will of God. Papa said God had stripped away the props that held Andy up all his life, just so Andy would consult his own heart at last and come to trust in heaven. But if this was so, Andy wanted nothing to do with a God as cruel as that, who could kill Jack and Howell and let Salina endure such anguish, only to teach some fellow a lesson in faith and self-reliance. A God like that would have to be evil Himself.

Still it did seem that one by one all those he'd counted on had fallen away from him. By chance or by the design of providence he was on his own. This was his fate. He couldn't ward it off or run from it. It was upon him. But he was not as afraid as he'd once been. This was because of the anger. The anger that began flowing into him when Papa lost heart had deepened and darkened over the weeks and months, till he was full of it. It brimmed inside him heavy as molasses in a vat. He was mad at much that he couldn't name, but which had in it the lost war and the hard peace and the trouble that Nahum Bellamy had brought on them. He was mad still at Papa; he knew that. But mostly now it was God he was mad at.

So while he bent over Salina's grave, trying in vain to address her hovering soul, he finally came to see that it wasn't just the memory of her dying that cut him off from her, it was his own rage too. He needed the rage, yet by the side of Salina's grave it was unfit; it didn't suit. There'd never been any room in her for harsh feeling, and there was no place for it now that she was dead either, not here where she rested. Salina would never hear him as long as he held the rage. But it was the rage that kept him going now. He was bitterly conscious of the irony—what he needed to keep living in the world was the very thing that cut him off from what his heart wanted most.

The news that the Federal army would not prosecute Papa came to them in the depth of their grief for Salina, and consequently there was small occasion for relief or rejoicing, and in the end it was just as well, for as January passed into February and February into March it became clear that despite Captain Callendar's assurances Nahum Bellamy had somehow kept his place and still meant to do the Curtises injury. He came again to the farm and in his excessively polite yet insinuating fashion asked more questions about the Yellow Jacket raid. Also, Andy heard from E. G. Smith the clerk of county court that the Tennessee lawyer Johnston Barrett was readying his civil complaint against Papa with the help of Bellamy and the Pucketts. And the Pucketts themselves kept showing up in the lane on their dun mule crying abuse and threatening not only the judgment of the court but the judgment of God as well.

Nor did anything come of lawyer Elias's prediction that the Freedmen's Bureau would relieve Bellamy of his post. This was doubtless because Colonel Whittlesey was preoccupied throughout most of February with the necessity of traveling to Washington City to testify before the Joint Committee on Reconstruction.

Then on the first of March Sheriff J. P. Chastine served Papa with a copy of the Puckett complaint and a summons to appear at the spring term of superior court to answer and defend it. That same day Andy wrote a letter to Captain Callendar asking the status of the Bellamy matter and sent it to Morganton, using the address on the card the captain had left with Papa.

In two weeks Andy's letter came back accompanied by a note not from Captain Callendar at all but instead from Lieutenant A. A. Boxley, Twenty-eighth Michigan Infantry, United States Volunteers, who signed himself Assistant Adjutant General, Western District, Military Department of North Carolina. Lieutenant Boxley explained that Callendar had never returned from his tour of inspection through Clay and Cherokee Counties in early January, and that despite a thorough investigation and a diligent search of the district by the civilian authorities no explanation for his disappearance had been uncovered, and no trace of him had ever been found. It was assumed at headquarters, wrote Boxley, that Callendar had been waylaid by bushwhackers and his body disposed of. In the absence of Callendar's report it would be necessary for another officer to repeat the inspection and render his own report, but due to the press of affairs at headquarters it would be many weeks before such an officer could be spared.

Here was another development for one to rage at. But Papa only bowed his head in resignation and resorted once again to prayer. Mama, who'd fallen very quiet since Salina died, sank even deeper into a silence that no one—not Andy, not even Papa— could penetrate.

One dreary morning in early March Andy stopped in Hayesville while going down to Gainesville in north Georgia with a wagonload of dried apples, peas, honey, eggs, dried pumpkin and deer hams. He was sitting on the wagon seat talking to Cousin Watson Curtis and Captain William Patton Moore when Nahum Bellamy and some of the county police rode into the square leading a horse that had a dead man lashed across its saddle. Hamby McFee was in the file of riders and gave Andy a sharp look of notice, but Andy gave none back. Instead Andy got down from the wagon and tethered the mules, and he and Cousin Watson and Captain Moore joined the crowd that commenced to gather around the corpse.

The fellow had been dead awhile, and standing there they could see that the nape of his neck and the backs of his hands had already turned a sort of mackerel hue, except for his fingernails, which were a dark green. He wore a jacket and trousers of butternut that were covered with mud. He gave off a strong smell that kept them all back a ways. In the act of tying his gray to the hitch rail Bellamy pushed hard against Andy and elaborately excused himself and doffed his ridiculous cap, then went to the led horse and unlashed the body and laid it out on the ground face up and asked if anybody knew who it was. It was a young man; Andy judged him to be in his middle twenties. He was beardless and had front teeth that stuck out like a boomer's. There was a single bullet hole under his right eye, and although that part of his face was dented in the eyeball itself bulged out, and a lot of maggots were in it. Captain Moore sighed and said, "That's Milt Bragg."

Andy knew the name. Howell used to write home about Milt Bragg, who was in his company of Folk's Battalion in the war. Milt Bragg had the gift of mimicry, Howell wrote. He could mock the song of any bird or the bray of a jackass or the voice of any man or woman. Many a night around the campfire he'd kept the boys laughing with his tricks, especially when he imitated Colonel Folk, who had an impediment of speech that made it hard for him to say anything with the letter *l* or *r* in it. "I raid in wait fo' the wabbit," Milt would say, while the boys howled. Now here he was, with a mess of maggots in his eye.

Bellamy turned with a cold smile and gave Captain Moore a limp and scornful salute. He hated Moore for an ex-Rebel and had tried hard to find an atrocity to charge against him, but all in vain, for the captain was an honorable man. Even so, Bellamy was now engaged in an effort to confiscate the captain's farm, which lay at the head of Tusquittee. Bellamy used his most unctuous voice. "Thank you, sir. Then you'd know his family and where he lived. Perhaps you could send to notify them. The poor fellow seems to have been murdered, you see."

Captain Moore had commanded Howell's company of Folk's Battalion and knew every man in it and their people too. They'd all been neighbors before they were soldiers. He stood gazing down on Milt Bragg with tears in his eyes.

"Where'd you find him?" somebody in the crowd asked, and Bellamy replied that a farmer on Qualls Creek discovered him lying in a pasture after going to see why his cows were acting shy of the spot. "Was it bushwhackers?" another inquired, and Bellamy said yes, undoubtedly. He'd found the tracks of several horses in the soft earth of the pasture. There were still partisans in the mountains that wanted to keep fighting the war. "But we're stamping them out one by one," he reported with a confident air. "Won't be long till we've seen the last of 'em."

Captain Moore turned away then, and Andy and Cousin Watson followed him. Behind them in the ranks of the police Hamby McFee looked hard and long after Andy, as if thinking to call out to him, but Andy didn't see this, and Hamby didn't speak after all. Captain Moore crossed to the grove of maples in the middle of the square and settled heavily on a wooden bench that encircled one of the trunks and sat quietly weeping. "That's the fourth," he said, wiping his eyes with a large white handkerchief. "That's the fourth of my boys he's murdered." The captain was sentimental—as befitted a man with the nickname of Irish Bill—and was as apt to shed a tear for a fallen comrade as to gallop his horse around the square and bend down to snatch a hat from the ground, as he'd often done in high spirits before the war.

Andy leaned close in amazement. "What do you mean? Who's a murderer?"

"Milt Bragg's the fourth of my boys to be shot down since the war." The captain wiped his nose. "And I suspect that man Bellamy's the assassin."

"Why do you suspect him?" Cousin Watson wanted to know.

Into Andy's mind came like a flare of light the thought of David Sprogg, who'd been found shot to death in his hogpen over by Settawig Road last year. Howell had written home about David Sprogg just as he'd written about Milt Bragg. Sprogg was a bugler, he said. A bugler who blew a sweet and mellow horn. Andy spoke his name.

"Yes," nodded Captain Moore. "Poor Davey, he was the first. The second was Tom Sasser, our farrier. They pulled him out of the Licklog in November. Then at Christmas there was little Willy Lark, found lying in an old rock house under Hanging Dog. Willy was the third. Willy'd been in prison, came home sick. Survived the war and a Yankee prison pen only to be shot down dead at home." He turned to Cousin Watson then. "I'll tell you why I suspect Bellamy. He got his reputation in the war tracking down and killing Southern men he suspected of outrages against the tories of East Tennessee."

Andy pondered. "But why would he take after these boys? I never heard of any outrage charged against the Clay County company."

"No, you never did," the captain agreed, "because we kept it a secret among us." He paused and shook his head and then covered his face with the handkerchief. "For the shame of it."

"Shame?" echoed Andy. Shame. The word plunged into his vitals like the tines of a pitchfork. He and Cousin Watson looked at each other in dread of what they were going to hear, and although they hadn't yet heard it, and so couldn't know its nature, already they regretted what it was. For they understood what all men in time of war understand—that some things happen in war that don't bear speaking of, and so long as all who have knowledge of such things keep silent, they are allowed to look back on their war with pride and pretend to have rendered only honorable service. It was a pact soldiers made as a way of living in peacetime with the memory of what they had done in war, and it was also a way of keeping the respect of those who loved them and had no acquaintance with war. And Captain Moore was about to break the pact.

"In September sixty-two," he said, "we were ordered into Johnson County, Tennessee, to capture or disperse a party of tories said to be operating around Stone Mountain. It was hard duty. You couldn't tell tory from Rebel in that country. In the beginning I reckon they were all tories. But by the time we came in I believe those people had no allegiance atall. One side or t'other was always at their throats, and they did what they had to, trying to stay alive. Bushwhacked blues and grays both when they got the chance, and stole their goods to keep body and soul together. Little boys would bushwhack you, whose guns were longer than they were tall, and the women would tell lies, leading you into ambush."

A bit of his famous temper rose to redden the back of his neck. He gazed down at the brown patches of winter grass between his boot toes, but it wasn't the grass he was seeing. "October sixty-two," he went on, "we moved into Carter County. Our orders were to break up the Unionists there, only this time a company of the Johnson County Home Guard rode along with us, under the command of a fellow called himself Roby. I say Home Guard. But they wasn't any militia by no means. Scavengers and cutthroats is what they were. Spent the war stealing and murdering as they pleased and called it the work of patriots. Colonel Folk couldn't control those devils. Nobody could. Christmastime of sixty-two, we were in the Watauga River country, us and that Home Guard of Roby's."

Captain Moore ceased. He folded, unfolded and refolded his white handkerchief while they stood over him waiting. Across the square the crowd of gawkers was breaking up, and Bellamy's men were carrying the body of Milt Bragg into the undertaker's, as Bellamy himself stood in front of the Freedmen's Bureau office looking on in a proprietary way. While Andy watched, Bellamy seemed to sense the weight of his attention and turned slowly and stared back at him. Then he raised an arm and gave Andy an airy wave. Andy rounded away from him.

"I was fortunate," Captain Moore was saying. "I came down bad with dysentery and got a sick furlough and returned back home to mend. So I missed it. But afterwards I heard what happened. My boys told me." He stopped again and looked at the grass awhile. Then he resumed. "It was at Dugger's Ford. Bushwhackers fired on my boys. My boys skirmished with them awhile there. In the fighting we had one man killed and several wounded. We killed one of them and caught some. My boys were sick and tired of chasing rangers and brigands. They wanted to fight the Yanks, and instead they were thrashing around in the East Tennessee woods getting shot at by thieves and old men and children. Nobody liked the notion of getting killed like that. If we were going to be killed we wanted to die in battle, under the flag. So Colonel Folk tried some of them on the spot and found them guilty of murder by ambuscade and hanged them, right there by the ford of the river.

"But hanging them wasn't good enough for Roby and the Home Guard. That Roby, he toyed with them like a cat with its mouse. The way they were hanged, it didn't break their necks, and those boys was choking to death slow. And that Roby, he danced with them, and them kicking in their death throes. 'Do-si-do,' he said. 'Do-si-do.'" Once more Captain Moore paused. "Colonel Folk chose the hanging party by lot out of my company. Five of my boys did the hanging—Milt Bragg, Tom Sasser, Davey Sprogg, Willy Lark . . ."

"That's but four," put in Uncle Watson.

Captain Moore looked up at Andy. "And Howell Curtis," he said.

Andy drove on down to Gainesville in a train with his neighbors John Kitchens and Elijah Herbert, because it wasn't safe to travel the roads alone carrying goods, not with guerrilla bands still lurking in the mountains. They all went armed; Andy carried Papa's old Tennessee rifle. Besides, it was a rough trail down into Georgia, and a man often needed help getting his wagon over the bad patches. But although they suffered in the cold they made the trip safe and in good time, and in Gainesville Andy traded for some tools they needed on the farm—a crosscut saw, a drawknife, two double-bitted axes—and also got some green coffee beans, sugar, salt and enough rations to feed himself and his stock on the road back. He bought a hundred rounds of ammunition for the rifle and a Savage revolver and fifty rounds for it and a bolt of calico for Mama, all of whose dresses were nearly in rags.

On the way down and back Andy mused over what Captain Moore had said in the square at Hayesville. Andy was saddened to hear of the hangings on the Watauga and of Howell's taking part. In the boy's letters there'd been no mention of such a dreadful thing, but in a glum way Andy wasn't surprised. Everybody knew how ugly the war had got in Unionist East Tennessee. What pained him worse was the thought of how the deed must have troubled poor Howell, a simple boy with a kind heart, eighteen years of age. The fact he'd never written of it showed the degradation he felt.

How many such simple boys had the war brought to shame? Andy thought the worst part of war was not so much the boys it killed and mangled but the boys whose good hearts it blackened with the kind of shame Howell felt. That shame in turn could blight hopes and blast dreams—you might survive the war in body, but your soul would still be dead. Poor Howell hadn't lived. But the South was full of boys who had, whose souls were dead of shame. Yet because of the pact of silence they'd made they couldn't ever speak of it. So they pretended war was glorious and they'd never done anything shameful and were proud of their time in the ranks. After a while that notion came to be thought of as a truth instead of the lie it was, that they'd all agreed to subscribe to. That was why wars kept coming, Andy thought. Because everybody forgot the truth and believed the lie.

But the war the South had fought wasn't over yet. Men like Nahum Bellamy kept it going. Andy had believed Captain Moore's suspicion the moment he heard it—that Bellamy posed by day as a legitimate officer of the government and crept about the country by night on a crazed vendetta, assassinating the boys who'd hanged tories in East Tennessee. But what could be done to stop him? Whitney Callendar had tried, and now it was plain as daylight to Andy that Bellamy had murdered Callendar too, to keep the captain from giving a report that would expose his crimes. Now it would likely be months before the government moved on Bellamy again. Meantime he'd keep after his mischief. Andy didn't think for an instant Bellamy was through killing just because he'd killed his four.

In western Carolina, with no one but Unionists in power, there was little enough an ex-Rebel like Captain Moore or Andy Curtis could do to convince anyone in authority that an officer of the Freedmen's Bureau engaged in the good work of relieving the nigra was also a mad assassin. Captain Moore, his lands at risk of confiscation, had given up any thought of taking action. But Andy had not. In fact he'd begun to think it might be up to him to settle the Bellamy matter once and for all. This idea seemed of a piece with the fate he'd come to see as he waited by Salina's grave hoping to speak to her. With all his props knocked out Andy was all by himself, like it or not, able or not. Everything was his to do. This was why he'd bought that hundred rounds of rifle ammunition and that .36-caliber Savage navy model revolver.

They stopped the last night at Blairsville and took rooms in the hotel. While he slept Andy had a dream, and for the first time since

Salina died it wasn't the dream of her agony. But it was a dream of Salina. He was steeping in a tub of warm water, and she was soaping his hair. "I'm resting now," she told him. "It's over and I'm resting. But I'm not resting away somewhere in heaven, I'm resting inside of you. So you can rest too, and we'll be resting together. We'll be together like that for all of time." Then she kissed him on the mouth, and she tasted a little like roast lamb, as he remembered. He felt as if he would burst from love of her.

After having that dream he slept peacefully all night, and never again did the nightmare of her dying come. But it would be awhile yet before he could commune with her by the grave. For he was still enraged and would continue to be, at least for as long as Nahum Bellamy lived.

CHAPTER 13

The mare dropped the foal the first week in April. It was a filly with a white blaze on her face and three white stockings, and at first Daniel thought she was going to be coal black, which would have meant that Tom wasn't the sire after all. But after her coat dried and the curls smoothed out he could see that she was a bay like Tom after all. She had big melancholy brown eyes with long lashes. He wanted to name her but didn't because she belonged to the judge, and he reckoned the judge had the right to give her a name. But if he had named her he would have called her Fancy, on account of her long and slender legs like a dancer's and the way she carried herself, head up and high-stepping and looking this way and that to see who was noticing her, like a pretty woman going to a dress ball.

That afternoon he went into the stall while she was suckling and handled her all over to get her used to the feel of a man. She stopped pulling at the mare's teat long enough to nudge her soft muzzle under his arm and gently push against him two or three times. She blew her warm breath over him. He hated like the devil to give her up. But he was obliged to.

Hamby was going into town for police duty, and Daniel asked him to stop by the Curtis place on his way and tell the judge about her. "And you be civil to that old man," Daniel admonished. Seeing Hamby's sneer he knew he'd spoken in vain, that Hamby would find a way to sass the judge and pain him, no matter about Miz Salina's passing. Daniel didn't know himself why he'd even cautioned the boy. What business was it of his if Hamby was saucy with the judge? He supposed it was an old cringing habit out of slavery times, a habit he needed to root out.

Whatever Hamby said to him, the judge made no mention of it to Daniel when he rode over on his mule the next day to see the foal in the pasture. But as always nowadays when in Daniel's presence the judge kept a studied distance, although the effort of it showed in the hard angle of his jaw and the two vertical lines in his brow where his eyebrows almost met. He joined Daniel by the fence and without speaking gave him a bob of his head in greeting, and the two of them leaned side by side on the fence watching the foal greedily taking its milk from the mare. At the cross-fence Tom stood looking curiously on, his nostrils flaring at the new scent of the foal. After a time the judge remarked that it was a good-looking foal, and Daniel agreed. Then the judge said, "What'd you name her?"

"Why, I didn't name her atall," Daniel replied. "I figured she's your filly, you get to name her."

The judge shrugged and pursed his lips. "If I know you, though, you named her anyway." He glanced at Daniel sideways. "What'd you name her?"

In spite of himself Daniel smiled, though he ducked his head to hide it. Then he told him.

The judge considered. The angle of his jaw softened, and the lines in his forehead went away. Presently he ran his forefinger back and forth underneath his mustache and nodded. "Fancy it is," he said.

Daniel sneaked a glimpse of him out of the corner of his eye. The judge wore his old-time look of keeping an amusing secret. It felt good, sharing a small merriment as they used to do. For no reason he could name Daniel now remembered that pigeon-tail coat the judge gave him to wear when he and Sukey jumped the broomstick—how the judge patted and smoothed that coat across his back the first time Daniel put it on. He remembered the feel of the judge's hand passing over him.

They leaned on the fence watching the foal. Tom stamped and tossed his head and whinnied. Daniel thought of the time he'd fallen off the roof of the barn while he and the judge and the judge's boys were building it. He thought of the judge bending over him where he lay in the hot grass with his leg broken at the ankle, and the tears that ran down the judge's face. He stirred against the fence and willed away the memory. He didn't want to ponder those things from the old time. He thought there were ways of knowing that mattered and ways of knowing that didn't. The judge knew Daniel—yes, maybe even loved him—in a way that didn't matter, but Daniel knew the judge in a way that did. Besides, it was too late; too much had happened. The war, freedom, the times—they'd changed everything. It wasn't important anymore what somebody understood of somebody else in slavery. The only thing to remember was that the white man had kept the black man in bondage.

Still, it was hard to put aside all thoughts of the high regard in which the judge once held him. Daniel had been nearer to him than his own boys. With those boys the judge thought he needed to be stern, and he stood off from them so as to get their respect. But with Daniel he maintained no such distance, and when he spoke to Daniel it was always from his heart. As a slave this had been a source of some pride for Daniel—when you had no freedom it was a great thing to be the marster's favorite. But as a free man he was ashamed of ever having felt that way, of being happy to get such crumbs of affection in return for the liberty he was meant to have.

Presently the judge spoke up, and what he said made Daniel wonder if he hadn't been thinking some of the selfsame thoughts that Daniel had, about the past. "That time you and Sukey's Hamby came to the farm," he began, reddening at the memory, "you said a hard thing to me." He wasn't wrathful about it; in fact he sounded mellow and maybe a little sorrowing. The judge peeled a splinter off the fence rail in front of him and stuck it between his teeth and began to chew on it. "Hard but true," he went on. "I didn't see it that way at first, of course. Condemned you for an ingrate." He smiled at that—a small and bitter kind of a smile. "But after mulling it over I got to where I saw something I'd never seen before—that regardless of how kind a man might be, it was wrong to keep slaves, so wrong that no amount of kindness could make it right. A simple truth, you'd say. But it took all these years for the scales to drop from my eyes and let me grasp it. You see, I thought by being kind to my servants I was not only being good myself—a Christian—but also helping bring good out of the evil of slavery." He spat out the splinter and turned his head and gave Daniel a long look, a look that appealed to Daniel to understand him. "But slavery was evil, and I was evil to take part in it. It was a great sin, and I've asked God to forgive me for it. I believe He has. But I'd like to know if you could forgive me too."

Daniel was tempted to laugh in his face but was too polite to be that harsh. Instead he leaned awhile against the fence, biting his lip and thinking what to say that would be true without reviling the judge unduly. But nothing came. So he remarked, "If the Lord's forgiven you, why do you need me to?"

The judge looked away from him into the pasture, where the foal was still at suck. "I need your forgiveness before anybody's," he said, "second only to God's."

Daniel's forbearance gave way then. For the first time since knowing the judge he wanted to strike him. Forgive him? The notion was silly. How could the judge even think of forgiveness? Did he actually think he could do wrong all his life—fifty-odd years of the worst kind of wrong against his fellow man—and then wipe it all away in a moment by asking to be forgiven? Only a spoilt, selfish, pampered white man used to having his every whim satisfied—usually by some poor nigger—could think like that. Daniel's throat closed up with rage. But it left him voice enough to answer. "No, sir," he said thickly, pushing away from the rails, "I don't reckon I can forgive you atall."

He turned quickly then and started back toward the cabin, leaving the judge alone by the fence. Then all of a sudden the rage in his throat turned to sadness, and by the time he got to the cabin he was crying.

Ever since Corn Dodger disappeared back in January something had been vexing Hamby. Daniel could tell this even though Hamby wouldn't admit to worrying about anything at all if Daniel asked him straight out. At first Daniel thought Hamby was just pining after Corn Dodger, who was his favorite among the Seraphim and with whom Hamby loved to go helling around—in fact Boss Bellamy said Corn Dodger had run off because of getting a village girl in the family way. But as time went on Daniel could tell there was more eating at Hamby's soul. Hamby seemed twitchy and distracted and was having trouble sleeping of a night. Many an evening when he did sleep he'd toss and turn and murmur to himself and presently come awake with a holler, from a nightmare.

But even if Hamby wasn't longing for his lost friend, Daniel could sense that Corn Dodger did figure in whatever anguish it was that held the boy in its grip. The very day Corn Dodger disappeared was when Daniel first noticed Hamby's distress. Furthermore, the reason the Boss gave for Corn Dodger's going missing didn't sound right to Hamby—he did confess that much to Daniel—nor did it make any sense to Daniel himself. Corn Dodger loved and admired the Boss far too much to run off over something to do with a girl. Corn Dodger hadn't served with the Boss in the war—he joined him right here in Clay County after the surrender—but of all the Seraphim, even including the ones who'd fought with the Boss in East Tennessee, Corn Dodger was the most loyal and adoring and full of trust. He was like a big shambling dog that followed the Boss everywhere, so eager to please him that it was almost humorous. No, if Corn Dodger was in trouble with a girl, he'd have stayed and besought the Boss to fix it for him, and the Boss would have fixed it.

Daniel hoped some white man hadn't done away with Corn Dodger, and he thought maybe this was Hamby's worry too. Everywhere—over in Georgia across the Hiwassee in Towns County, down east in flatland Carolina, all across the South, even a time or two here in Clay itself—whites were killing off coloreds in a plague of hate. Daniel had heard of one Negro getting shot for saying good morning to a white man without being spoken to first, and of another murdered for not taking off his hat to show respect. One white man said he'd shot a darkie because he thought the niggers needed thinning out a little. It was easy enough to imagine some hateful ex-Rebel ambushing a sergeant of Boss Bellamy's high-handed Yankee police. But if this was so then why had the Boss told that tale about a pregnant wench? And why wasn't he looking for the murderer?

But the evening of the day the judge came by to see the foal, when Daniel finally learned what was tormenting Hamby, it turned out to be far more terrible than his worst imagining. Hamby had gone to bed early, and Daniel was by the fire plaiting a halter out of horsehair for the mare when he heard Hamby cry out. Daniel turned to see him sitting bolt upright on his pallet shivering, covered all over in big drops of cold sweat, with his eye-whites showing around the pupils. "De Boss," he blurted. "De Boss, he done it."

Daniel felt a queer sense of foreknowledge, as if he understood what Hamby meant without understanding at all. He laid aside the halter and went to kneel beside the pallet, taking Hamby by both arms. It was hard to believe that the fearful creature shaking in his hands was the same sassing smart-alecky Hamby. "Done what, Hamby? The Boss done what?"

Something like a convulsion passed through Hamby, made him jump and jerk in Daniel's grasp, made his teeth rattle in his head. "K-k-kilt Corn Dodger," he said.

That was what he'd known, or should have known. Daniel felt himself go very still inside. In the instant just after disbelieving what Hamby said, he found with woe that he believed it entirely. Before he spoke again he took two, three, four deep breaths. "How do you know?"

"Corn Dodger come to me," Hamby said, trembling. "De night ob de same day dat cap'n from headquarters lef' outa here promisin' to finish up de Boss down to Mo'ganton. Corn Dodger say he follow de Boss dat day. Follow him away up Chunky Gal. See him lay up in a deadfall, bushwhack dat cap'n when he ride by, drag his dead ass up a ravine, drop it down a old well. Shot dat cap'n wid dat damn old Spencer repeater, slam frew de head, whap.

"Corn Dodger, he scared fit to shit. Say he meet de Boss on de road afterwards, tell de Boss he see what he do—Corn Dodger, he a stupid damn nigger, tell dat white man dat. Den he ask de Boss why he done dat killin'. De Boss say, 'To keep faith.' Corn Dodger say, 'What kinder faith?' An' de Boss say, 'Wit' de fallen.' Corn Dodger, he ain't got no damn idea what dis mean. Den de Boss, he say to Corn Dodger, 'You dasn't speak ob dis to nobody in de worl'. And Corn Dodger, he promise. He be swearin' on his mama's own black ass. But den he come to me."

Daniel released Hamby, rocked back first into a crouch and then sat down on the hard-packed dirt floor and put his head between his two hands. He could not rid himself of the feeling that he knew what Hamby would say next, before he said it. Yet he knew nothing, nothing at all; he thought he might be the dumbest man in the world. "What makes you think the Boss killed Corn Dodger?"

Hamby drew his blanket up around him and violently shook inside it. "When Corn Dodger tell me dis we be down by dat little branch dat pass by de jail. He leave me, go up by de jail. And den I see de Boss up dere. Leanin' on de corner ob de jail. Smilin'. Take Corn Dodger by de arm. Walk off wid him. Dat be de las' anybody see ob Corn Dodger." Now Hamby began to cry. "I lub Corn Dodger but I lub de Boss too. I don't want to hurt de Boss, get him in trouble. But he kill Corn Dodger. An' now I scared he be killin' me. He see Corn Dodger talk to me. Dat be enough for him to kill dat nigger befo' de sun go down dat same day. It be enough for him to kill my ass too."

Daniel felt as numb as if he'd fallen into a pond of freezing water. Every part of him, every thought in his head, hung heavy and immovable. But at last he got his tongue to stir. "If the Boss was going to kill you," he said, "you'd be dead already. You'd have been dead the same day as Corn Dodger."

Quivering, Hamby stared at Daniel with tears rolling from his eyes, seeming not to hear. "De day after Corn Dodger disappear," he said, "de Boss see me in de bureau office an' grin. Put two fingers to his mouf, shushin' me. He go, 'Shh.' I figure he fixin' to murder me an' make my head into a soap gourd. But nothin' happen. He be watchin' me, I be watchin' him. All de time. He know I know, I know he know. But don't neither ob us say de firs' word." He gave Daniel an imploring look. "Why dat white man ain't kill me yet?"

Slowly Daniel shook his head. "Maybe he thinks because you know what happened to Corn Dodger you're too scared ever to tell on him. Maybe he even trusts you." He paused and thought some more, then added, "He's always liked you."

Hamby snorted. "Hell, he like Corn Dodger too." When he saw the grisly joke in this remark his weeping changed to a giggle of crazy laughter and then afterward changed back again to weeping. "After Massa Billy Sherman de Boss de bes' white man I know," he sobbed. "De Boss always be helpin' de colored folk. I don't mind if he shoot dat damn headquarters cap'n. But why he go an' kill dat poor nigger? Why he turn on his own? He ort to know, Corn Dodger an' me, we neber tell on him."

Why indeed? Daniel pondered what the Boss had said to Corn Dodger's question: *To keep faith with the fallen.* What fallen?

Hamby blew his nose between two fingers and wiped them on his blanket. "Even though he kill Corn Dodger I kep' his secret long as I could. I'd of kep' it longer, but I got so scared. Jus' now I had a dream. De Boss done skinned out poor Corn Dodger jus' like a damn squirrel. Helt up his bloody skin an' shook it till it splattered. Spewed blood all up on de Boss, turn him red. Den he come at me wid dat big skinnin' knife. An' he be laughin', all spewed up wid blood. Oh, Lord have mercy."

Daniel had always known that Bellamy was capable of extreme acts, but he'd fooled himself into thinking the Boss was sanctified and that if he did wrongs he did them in the service of God, the Union and the Negro race. Daniel was not a child. He knew what men did. He'd seen the war. Great change could never come without blood; that was why the war had been so terrible and why the peace that came after it was terrible too. But the blood that men spilt in the rebellion and its aftermath was let in a rage, while the blood that Bellamy spilt—Callendar's, poor Corn Dodger's—was let in cold calculation. The Boss hadn't killed to serve the cause, he'd killed to save himself.

The pity of it wrung Daniel's guts. The Boss had done such good work—raised the Negro up, protected him, given him confidence, helped educate him and get him ready to be a citizen of the republic. Like Moses he'd delivered the people out of bondage and led them through the wilderness to make them ready for freedom. Doubtless the Boss had told himself it was to preserve this sublime effort that he'd done murder, thinking the grandness of the goal would justify the bloody wrong. But Daniel knew—just as he thought the Boss must know in his heart—that it wasn't so, that the Boss had wasted the talents God gave him and instead of doing the handiwork of the Lord had done the will of Lucifer.

But worse than the pity of this was the disgust that Daniel now felt for himself. What had he done when freedom came? Strike out on his own, make his own way? No, no. Ironically enough it was the flighty Hamby, not the sober and industrious Daniel, who'd cast himself adrift in the world and made himself over into a free soul. For all his preachments of self-sufficiency Daniel had only exchanged one white master, Judge Curtis, for another, Boss Bellamy. All he'd known to do was follow after the white man. Maybe Hamby was right, that day he met Daniel on the road, to accuse him of remaining a slave. Maybe that was all Daniel knew how to be.

He watched Hamby shuddering and sobbing on his pallet. For the first time since Hamby was born it was possible now to regard him as a child, helpless before the mad gaze of fate. Of all his former rage only the coarse and exaggerated dialect he'd affected now remained to him, sounding more hollow and out of place the longer he talked. Daniel felt a surge of compassion for him. But then sternly he spoke Hamby's name. "In the morning," he said, "I'm taking you in to Sheriff Chastine. You're going to tell him what you just told me."

"No!" cried Hamby, burying his face in his blanket. "I won't! How can I hand ober de Boss to de law?"

"We have to," Daniel insisted. "The Boss, he's gone wrong. Bad wrong. He ain't helping black folk now, he's hurting them. That blood on him, it's on us too if we let him go on, knowing what we know. You and me, we're the only ones can stop him. We have to do it—if nothing else, on account of poor Corn Dodger. Who's to do for Corn Dodger now, if not us? Corn Dodger, that he killed, who loved him so."

They rode into Hayesville along the wagon road in the brilliant springtime weather. Trillium and wild ginger were blooming along the roadside, and white masses of honeysuckle hung down from the bank overhead. The bank itself was sown thick with lady's-slipper and bluets and spring beauty. In the woods beyond, they could see the soft glow of an occasional pink azalea and golden scatters of buttercups, and farther up, everywhere on the greening slopes of the Tusquittees, the dogwoods were coming into flower.

The bright and fragrant morning mocked the grimness of their mood. But as they passed the Curtis place Daniel turned in his saddle and glanced down at the farm past the masses of rhododendron that fringed the road, and he was surprised to see that the apple tree he and Sukey had cherished—that used to stand by their cabin, that he'd thought dead last spring—had impossibly put out a single branch of leaves with two or three pinkish blossoms on it. He checked Tom and sat a moment in the road taking in the unaccountable sight, while Hamby waited impatiently in the curve ahead.

Seeing those apple blossoms buoyed him up, made him think fondly of Sukey and the bittersweet taste of the cobblers she used to make. He rode the rest of the way into town feeling righter with the world than he had in quite some while. In fact he had the queer notion that he was closer now to being free—truly free—than he'd been at any time since running away from the Curtis place nearly four years ago. He couldn't guess why he felt that way, not with calamity coming down on him and Hamby like it was. But he did.

And the closer he got to town the stronger this notion grew.

They rode into the square and were about to dismount behind the courthouse when Daniel noticed a commotion over by the office of the Freedmen's Bureau—a coming and going of several men in uniform, a row of strange horses at the hitch rail, a wagon with the letters *USA QMC* stenciled on its hood, its tailgate down and two Negroes in shirtsleeves shoving wooden crates into it. Boss Bellamy was nowhere to be seen; in fact, the second sight that had so suddenly and strangely come over Daniel last evening assured him that the Boss was gone and would not return. So he and Hamby walked their horses on between the maples of the square to satisfy their curiosity.

Just as they drew rein by the wagon a large white man wearing a high silk hat and a linen duster over his clothes came out of the office and down the steps. As he approached, Daniel saw the red cord pinned to his lapel, and smiling down on the man he remarked, "These are gloomy times."

The man stopped and looked pleasantly up. He had sandy muttonchop whiskers and hazel eyes. "Yes," he replied, "but we are looking for better."

He was the first Hero of America Daniel had met since coming into Clay County. At least he seemed to be; he wore the sign. To be certain, it would be necessary to complete the password. "What are you looking for?" inquired Daniel.

"A red and a white cord," replied the man.

Daniel asked, "Why a cord?"

"Because," the man said, "it is safe for us and our families."

With Hamby looking on amazed Daniel swung down and embraced the man and under cover of his coat exchanged with him the secret grip of the Heroes. Daniel told his name, and the man said he was Colonel Hiram Willoughby, a detective in the employ of the United States War Department. "Assigned special duty to subdistrict number ten of the Freedmen's Bureau in Morganton," he explained with a confiding wink.

With his newfound gift of sight Daniel thought he understood Colonel Willoughby's presence in Hayesville, just as he'd understood many another mystery in the past twelve hours without knowing how. But it was important to confirm the guess. "For a right good spell now," he said, "me and my boy here, and many of the Negroes of the county, have had a . . . connection with Major Nahum Bellamy, that serves in the field office of the bureau here. We're all of us in the Union League together. Am I right to think it's because of the major that you've come?"

Briskly Willoughby nodded. "You are indeed." He stood a moment with his arms clasped behind his back and appeared to engage in serious thought. Then he said, "This is all very secret, you know. Very, very secret." His gaze settled on the scarlet cord Daniel wore. "But you and I are Redstrings, after all. There ought to be trust between us, because we're brothers under the sign." A moment longer he hesitated. Then he turned and barked some orders to the Negroes loading the wagon, and after that he rounded on Daniel again and motioned him and Hamby to follow. He led them across the road and into the courthouse square, to one of the circular wooden seats built around the trunks of the maples, where he sat them down and began to talk, pacing to and fro before them with his hands again clasped behind his back.

There had been complaints, he said. Complaints to the Franklin station, the subdistrict office, even the district headquarters in Raleigh. Eminent persons—Unionist and conservative alike—had complained. Bellamy, they contended, abused his office. He infected the Negroes with violently partisan feeling. He preached the program of Radical Republicanism, which the government disavowed. He abused former Confederates beyond all reason. His every practice was unsound. In response to the allegations, General Howard had authorized an investigation, which for bureaucratic reasons had languished till now.

"As Heroes of America and believers in Union," Willoughby said, "you and I are naturally in sympathy with some of the actions complained of, Mr. McFee. Doubtless, as a Union Leaguer with Bellamy, you'll hate to see him brought low, as did I—at first. But much as I dislike conceding it, though his goals are worthy, the man himself is intemperate—intemperate and . . . extreme."

Willoughby had been given charge of the inquiry ordered by General Howard. He went first to Asheville for an interview with agent Eastmond, then to Franklin to speak to Hawley, the station chief responsible for the Hayesville office. Both professed entire ignorance of Bellamy's actions but offered certain dire speculations. Willoughby had arrived in Hayesville yesterday with a squad of soldiers and two civilians, armed with every possible authority. At the bureau office he notified Bellamy of his removal, placed him under arrest and began gathering his files for shipment back to Morganton, where they would be studied at leisure for evidence of his misdeeds. The county police whom Bellamy pretended to command were summarily broken up. Then, late last evening, while Willoughby and the others were at supper, Bellamy had managed to overpower his guard and slip away. He was now regrettably at large.

"Most regrettably indeed," Willoughby was saying as Daniel and Hamby exchanged a mute look of dread, "for today in searching Bellamy's quarters we found evidence against him of the most damning character, which shows him to be not simply an official malfeasor but a bloody murderer as well." From his pocket Willoughby drew a sheet of paper with writing on it. "Here, in Bellamy's own hand," he said, "is a list of names headed, 'Those Sacrificed To Keep Faith With The Fallen.' I am informed by the sheriff of this county that each of the persons named here save one is in fact a murdered man." The colonel extended the paper for Daniel to read. "There can be not the slightest doubt whatever that Nahum Bellamy was their executioner," Willoughby declared, "for as you see he has made a line through each name and with commendable efficiency set down by each the date of his taking off." Willoughby chortled as Daniel leaned forward to see. "Your Bellamy is a man of mighty orderly habits, but I'd hardly call him wise."

There were five names on the list, each neatly struck through by a line as straight as if ruled—David A. Sprogg, Thomas R. Sasser, William M. Lark, Milton T. Bragg, Whitney Callendar. At the bottom of the page, unlined, was a sixth name—James Madison Curtis.

Grudgingly then, and under Daniel's prodding, Hamby confessed to Colonel Willoughby what he knew of the deaths of Whitney Callendar and Corn Dodger. Willoughby in turn summoned Sheriff Chastine and the magistrate. The rest of the morning was consumed by Hamby's giving his affidavit under oath in the office of the clerk of county court, while Daniel argued in vain to Willoughby that Judge Curtis was in danger and required protection. The sight of the judge's name on Boss Bellamy's list had given him an awful turn. But to his dismay Willoughby doubted him. "That name," Willoughby insisted, "is away down at the bottom of the page, and our man is such an orderly and scientific gent, if he meant to kill Curtis, he'd have put the name up with the others."

"I don't know about that," Daniel protested. "All I know is he hates the judge and is out to ruin him. Wants to confiscate his farm. Got some white trash up on Fires Creek to sue him."

Willoughby eyed him inquisitively. Daniel could see that the colonel wondered why any black should be so anxious for the welfare of a planter who'd owned slaves. But he was respectful enough of Daniel not to probe. Instead he asked, "Why does Bellamy hate this Curtis so?"

Daniel shrugged. "The Boss—Major Bellamy—he always said it was because the judge harmed some Union folk in the war. But there was more to it. Had to be. He hated the judge too much—too hard and personal—for it to be just that alone. But I don't know why it was he hated him, I just know he did. It's because he hates him that I believe he'll try and kill him before he leaves the country, now he's on the run."

But Colonel Willoughby would not be convinced. Besides, he had no men to spare to go guarding the life of some old secesh who'd done hurt to Unionists in the war.

Nor would Sheriff Chastine help when Daniel went beseeching him. Yes, he agreed, Madison Curtis had been a good man before the war. "But look what he done when the rangers come through," the sheriff said. "On account of him many a loyalist died a hard death and many a loved one suffered loss. Clay County is all for Union now, and the slavers and secesh had best look out for themselves. Them Madison Curtises is on their own."

All day long Negroes gathered on the square. They stood silent and mostly unmoving under the maples and along the edges of the roads that bounded the square, closely watching the comings and goings of the strange men at the Freedmen's Bureau office, where they had gone so often for help and counsel. By late afternoon, when Daniel and Hamby were ready to leave, forty or fifty of them had congregated, women and younguns as well as men, coming in slowly from the countryside one by one and in small groups, many afoot but some by mule and horse and wagon. They were leaving their plows in the fields and their stock untended and their tasks undone to come and stand silent vigil at the place where Boss Bellamy had always given them hope when they felt the most hopeless. In places around the square, knots of poor whites were jeering and catcalling, jubilant at the Boss's downfall, but the colored folk paid no mind. Their mood was solemn, respectful, almost reverent; they might have been present at the funeral of a great leader, which in a way they were.

Because of the disbanding of the county police Colonel Willoughby confiscated Hamby's horse and weapons. So when it was time to go he and Daniel rode out double on the stallion Tom. They passed along the lines of waiting freedmen in the square, and one by one the plaintive voices called out to them, "Ol' Cumberland nigger, where the Boss at?" "Is the Boss gone for good?" "What'll become of us colored folk now, without the Boss?" "Corporal Hamby, is the Boss dead?" Daniel couldn't think what to tell them. So again and again he only shook his head and murmured, "I can't say, I can't say." Behind him Hamby just hung his head.

Then Daniel sharply drew rein and paused in the road and took thought. In a moment more he turned Tom around and rode back along the rank of upturned faces. "We got to do for ourselves now," he told them as he passed by. "The Boss, he showed us what to do, and we can thank him for that. But he was a white man, and we don't need him now. He's gone. Colored folk got to take charge now." He stopped, turned, walked Tom slowly back the way he'd come. "Look to yourselves and do for yourselves," he said. "Don't be thinking you need somebody's help—especially any white man's help. You can do what needs doing. You got to do it."

Then they turned off the square and rode along the crest of the hill that Hayesville stood on. Before them the valley of the Hiwassee spread out green in the soft slant of the light, and on beyond the valley the royal blue rampart of the Tusquittees stood high against a turquoise sky that had thin streaks of gold in it. As dusk came on they followed the wagon road down toward Sanderson Ford and crossed the river under the weeping willows. Tom kept snorting and tossing his head, annoyed by Hamby's extra weight.

What had happened to them was so large that they knew no words to express it, and for a long time they dared not try to speak. It was not till they'd climbed out of the river bottom and into the foot-hills—when full dark was settling over the country—that at last Hamby found his voice. "Lord, the damn world's gone topsy-turvy now," he lamented, and Daniel was gratified to hear him speak for the first time not with his crude slave talk but in his own rightful voice. "What are we going to do now, old man?"

Daniel had thought hard about this. He'd meant what he told the people on the square. They didn't need the whites. They looked too much to them. That was their whole history till now, looking to the whites. But that didn't mean they ought to turn against the whites. It meant instead that the Negro had to take care of himself, just as the white man did. It meant he had to stop looking to be coddled and guided like a child. Then when he was standing on his own he and the white man would share the same condition. Then maybe they could regard one another as what they were, as what they ought to behave like—the children of the same God, brothers. He was ready with his answer. "We're going to go and tell Judge Curtis how the Boss means to kill him, that's what."

Hamby blew out his breath in a deprecating noise. "That's a crazy damn notion," he bemoaned. "Why should we do that? Ain't it bet-ter we go looking for a hidey-hole? Why, if the Boss is fixing to kill the Curtises and we go down there, maybe we'll run up on him. Maybe he'll shoot us and the Curtises both."

Daniel replied without hesitation, "He's family, the judge is. Him, Miz Curtis, Mister Andy, the girls. Those two orphan boys of Miz Cartman's."

Hamby hooted in derision. "Family, my ass. You think if some bad sumbitch was after you and me the judge would ever stir himself on our account?"

Daniel had never been surer of anything, but all he said was, "Yes." And Hamby made no more protest, only slumped against Daniel's back and sighed. Hamby was afraid of the Boss; Daniel was afraid too. But Daniel thought perhaps something else was starting to break through Hamby's fear. He surmised it might be the same thing he himself had felt yesterday, when the judge asked to be forgiven and Daniel burst so unexpectedly into tears. Whatever it was, for the first time in his life of rage, Hamby seemed to yield up his fury. He lay quietly against Daniel's back as they rode on, and now and then Tom would blow and pitch his hindquarters in annoyance, and in this way they approached the Curtises' lane in the darkness, amid the last crying of the meadowlarks.

Tom grunted and came suddenly to a stand, his ears pricked up high. Between his knees Daniel felt a tremor run along the big muscles of Tom's shoulders. Ahead, under the trees in the blackness of the road, a bit chain jingled, and Tom threw up his head and whinnied. Daniel tensed and gathered his reins as a horse spoke back from the shadows, and Tom shimmied nervously in the road, fighting at the bit. "Who's there?" Daniel sang out.

The familiar voice came back, polite and half-amused as always, "Why, Mr. McFee, it's me, Nahum Bellamy."

There was a sound of hooves on hard ground, and three riders emerged from the shadows of the trees that overhung the road. The first was the Boss, and behind him were two of the Seraphim who'd been with him in wartime, Randlett the white and a Negro Daniel knew only as Bumper. Randlett and Bumper wore the bleached straw hats of the county police, but the Boss had on civilian clothes and was riding not his gray but a small dark horse that might have been a sorrel. The Boss was smiling; Daniel could see the gleam of his gold tooth even in the dim light. Daniel turned his head and sent a hoarse whisper back to Hamby: "Slide off and run down, go warn the Curtises. Now."

He hadn't even finished speaking before Hamby dropped off over Tom's hindquarters into the rhododendron, but Tom was tired of all the unfamiliar doings around his rump and aimed a kick at Hamby and sent him sprawling with a howl out of the thicket and across the lane, and the Boss demanded, "What's that?"

Daniel saw him raise his Spencer repeater and tuck the butt of it into the cup of his shoulder. "No, no!" Daniel cried, as Hamby sprang up and ran, and now Daniel was surprised to find that he'd drawn his five-shooter and was pointing it straight at the Boss.

The Boss tracked Hamby for an instant with the Spencer before he spied the pistol in Daniel's hand and quickly turned the carbine his way. As Hamby vanished down the lane the Boss inquired in a mocking voice, "How now, Mr. McFee? Is this gratitude?" He'd let his reins fall, and his head was bent down over the breech of the Spencer, and one pale eye looked at Daniel through the open sights, unblinking.

"No, sir," Daniel said, "I reckon it's friendship." He tried to hold the pistol steady as Tom danced under him in the road. "Those people down yonder are my friends."

The Boss laughed a dry laugh. "Friends, you say. Yet they held you a slave, while I showed you freedom."

Behind him Randlett and Bumper had unslung their carbines and cocked them, so now Daniel folded his thumb over the hammer of the Police Model and rolled it back to full cock too; in dread he saw the fluted cylinder turn slowly over. He didn't want to hurt anybody—not Bumper, not even Randlett, surely not the Boss. Part of him wanted to put his arms around the Boss and succor him, fugitive that he was.

"I'm obliged for what you done that was good," Daniel told him, "but you done evil too. I can't let you do no more."

Shockingly as he spoke there was a blaze of light from the end of the Boss's gun and a deafening noise. A violent force lifted Daniel out of the saddle, and when he came down he was astraddle of Tom's rump, and Tom squealed in indignation and bolted out from under him, and he fell hard in the ruts of the road. He rolled over and sat up. Tom was turning and bucking in the middle of the road. Daniel saw Randlett stand in his stirrups and point his carbine over the bend of Tom's neck. Another flash lit the hollow; another jolt knocked Daniel spinning. Tom turned and galloped off down the wagon road.

Moving as if in a dream Daniel got to his knees. Above him on the sorrel horse the Boss leaned down from the saddle, aiming the Spencer at him one-handed, and Daniel heavily raised his arm and fired two times at the Boss's body, and at each shot a dark hole appeared in the light-colored waistcoat the Boss wore. The Boss made no sound, but his Spencer dropped into the ruts with a clatter, and the sorrel flinched to one side and carried him off the road and down out of Daniel's line of sight.

Daniel felt no pain, only a great numbness. But he knew he was hurt bad and was sorry for it. He was sorry also for having harmed the Boss. He hadn't liked seeing those holes appear.

Somehow he got his feet under him and stood. Regretfully he saw Bumper coming toward him at a run on a white horse, and he trained the pistol up at him, but Bumper suddenly threw his carbine aside and waved one hand back and forth in front of him and rode past Daniel and kept on going down the road, back toward Hayesville. There was no sign of Randlett now either. That was a large relief, for Daniel was very tired. There had been too much fuss. He lay down on his back in the road to rest.

A panting Hamby pounded on the door of the Curtis house with both his fists, making a noise like thunder. "Rouse up!" he cried. "Rouse up in there! Men have come to kill you! Old Daniel is fighting them! Come help Old Daniel! Rouse up!"

Before anybody could answer, he heard a horse trotting in the lane behind him and turned. It was a dark horse with a man in the saddle, but in the twilight Hamby couldn't tell for sure if the man was Old Daniel or the Boss or who. He came to the edge of the gallery with his heart in his throat, and using the wisp of his voice that fear had left him he called, "Old Daniel, is that you?"

The man rummaged at the front of his saddle and then dismounted in a peculiar way, by drawing his right leg over frontwards, across the pommel, and dropping off. When he did this the door of the house opened behind Hamby and spilled a beam of lamplight down between the boxwoods and lit him up, and Hamby saw that it was the Boss. The Boss's clothes were soggy with blood, and he was reeling in his high boots as if he were about to fall. But he was holding two revolvers he'd drawn from his pommel holsters, and as Hamby watched he cocked them both, one after another.

Without a thought Hamby shouted, *"Don't!"* and with a wild leap launched himself off the gallery. He landed running on the flagstones. In front of him the Boss raised one of his pistols and aimed it and fired. The ball struck Hamby a sharp blow in his upper body and turned him partway around as he ran, but his momentum was such that he careened off balance and sideways into the cul-de-sac and collided hard with the Boss. The two of them crashed into the gravel all entangled; one of the Boss's pistols sailed loose and was lost.

It was Andy Curtis who had opened the door. He saw Hamby's leap and saw Bellamy shoot him and understood everything at once—Cousin Watson Curtis had come to the farm an hour before and told him of Willoughby's mission and the finding of Bellamy's list. Now with his new Savage revolver in his hand Andy advanced to the edge of the gallery, and one thought alone was in his mind—that Nahum Bellamy must not set foot even on the steps of the Curtis house and live to tell of it. Andy felt no fear, no doubt, no hesitation, not even anger—only a calm such as comes after a great tumult of the soul has ended.

Bellamy thrashed weakly in the gravel and at last succeeded in throwing Hamby's weight off him; Hamby flopped inert, and Andy thought he was dead. Bellamy struggled to his feet and stood swaying, looking dully this way and that. Then he seemed to see Andy at the top of the steps, and a mad light kindled in his eyes. He started up the walkway holding his pistol before him with both hands, weaving and stumbling on the flagstones. Andy descended the steps and stopped at the bottom. He pointed the Savage at Bellamy and said, "Come no further, sir. Lay yourself down where you are. I'll fetch help for you."

But Bellamy came on. A black froth bubbled at his mouth, and from two small holes in his body Andy saw blood pulse forth at every heartbeat. He appeared to smile; he spoke, but the sound that came out of him was only a gurgle. Andy drew back the hammer of the Savage and prepared to shoot. But then Bellamy stopped, sank to his knees, pitched over on his face.

Andy went on down the walkway and knelt where Bellamy lay. Behind him Papa and Cousin Watson burst out of the house. Cousin Watson came to join Andy, but Papa had heard what Hamby said, and he broke through the boxwoods and ran up the lane toward the road. He ran hard, like a young man, digging deep in the loose gravel. "Daniel!" he cried, "Oh, Daniel, Daniel!"

Bellamy was trying to talk. Andy got down on hands and knees and put his ear next to him. Bellamy said, "God is jealous, and the Lord revengeth, and is furious." Then he said, "I have kept faith."

Daniel's mam always said she was a queen in Africa. She behaved like one for sure. All the Negroes on the place at Bethel would bow down to her. She told them not to tell, and they didn't. But when they were out of sight of the white folks they bowed down to her and did whatever she said.

After he came to the Curtises', corn shuckings were Daniel's favorite time. Whenever anybody shucked a red ear the judge would give him a silver dollar. At night after the shucking there would be a wrestling match between Daniel and Cuffee or sometimes even Old Jeff—who was in good shape for his age—to see who was the best. Lay-by was another fine time. Mistress Sarah always fixed a big dinner, and everybody ate all the barbecue and cake they could hold. Lots of nights there would be candy pullings. The people got a week off at Christmas. The judge gave everybody a new pair of shoes, and then each person got a special gift. One year the judge gave Daniel a fine English shotgun to go bird hunting with, even though it was against the law for a Negro to have a firearm. Daniel remembered going fishing with Marster Andy and Marster Jack and Marster Howell. He remembered fashioning forked sticks to put inside the walls of his cabin to fend off evil spirits. He remembered reading books in the judge's study. All those books. All those stories about people and places far away. That was against the law too, a Negro reading.

He remembered how Sukey smelled, how she tasted, how she felt. He remembered making love with her on a bed of flowers. He remembered her apple cobblers. He remembered marrying her in that pigeon-tail coat. He remembered her morocco shoes. And he remembered helping build that barn.

Lying in the road, he was confused. He thought he must have fallen off the roof of the barn just now, instead of years ago, because he was lying on the ground in the same way and the judge was bending over him just as he'd done then. And the judge was weeping.

They buried Daniel in the little graveyard by the grove of poplars where Sukey and Old Jeff rested, just opposite the aged apple tree with its one sprig of pink blossoms.

Hamby recovered from his wound and took up Daniel's forty acres on Downings Creek and farmed it. But he didn't use Daniel's cabin;

instead he lived on at the Curtis place for many years. The 1870 census found him there but got his age wrong and for some reason recorded him as Robert instead of Hamby McFee. He was there also when Madison died in 1874 and when Sarah followed two years later. He was there in 1880 too, although again the census taker got his name wrong—called him McAfee instead of McFee. There was another error also. Whereas in 1870 Hamby had been termed a mulatto and not related, in 1880 he was mistaken for a white and called a cousin.

Chapter 14

The Widow Henslee got a granny woman to tend Nancy through the last of her lying-in. Her name was Granny Grindstaff, and she claimed to have helped birth more than three hundred babies while losing but one mother—"that died afore I got thar," she said—and two infants who were stillborn. She was a little crookbacked sprig of a thing and had lost most of her hair. What hair was left she wore drawn back to a tiny bun at the rear of her head, and through the thin white hair you could see her pale scalp all shiny and spotted with brown blemishes. She moved with the aid of a knobby cane and walked everywhere she went—in Nancy's case all the way across the divide from Estatoah Falls. But she never seemed tired, although after a long trek sometimes you could hear her breath rattling in her chest like dried peas in a gourd. She wore a white apron over her homespun dress and a white kerchief on her head. She had hands curled like a hawk's talons. She claimed to be a hundred and two years old.

Granny Grindstaff confirmed the Widow Henslee's opinion that the baby was a boy. Furthermore she announced that he would rise high in the world and be the admiration of many. Starting the first of February she came by once a week to check on Nancy and dose her with ginger tea and a mixture of sulphur and something called wine of cordia, that had a pleasant odor something like cedar wood. Sometimes if Nancy was feeling low Granny would put asafetida in her mouth before going into the house to keep from getting sick herself.

The Widow Henslee visited every Sunday with her younguns and every Wednesday by herself, leaving her boy and the two girls with a neighbor woman. On Wednesdays she would stay over and Oliver would sleep on the porch in the weather, wrapped in a quilt just as in his soldier days. Oliver got more and more accustomed to having the Widow Henslee around and in fact began to look forward to her visits. Although Nancy was holding up fine she was very weak and couldn't do much around the house, and the Widow Henslee when she came would cook and clean and mend and mind the younguns. But that wasn't the only reason Oliver looked forward to seeing her. He'd got accustomed to her ways and liked them. Martha adored her, and even Syl got so he'd come and sit beside her chair of an evening while she did the sewing and darning.

It no longer vexed Oliver that the closer the Widow Henslee got to them the nearer drew the time when Nancy had to die. Nancy had got so reconciled to passing on that Oliver came to accept it with somewhat better grace. Where before he'd been angry, now he was only sad and regretful. Nancy said God loved her so much He wanted her to come home and be with Him, and although she was sad to be leaving Oliver and Martha and Syl she was pleased to think how soon she would get to see the Lord Jesus. Besides, if God was taking one life, He was giving a new life too, and Nancy would be in that life. She wouldn't be gone at all; she'd be living on in the soul of that baby boy.

Of course Oliver worried she might pass away before giving birth, but Nancy assured him she would never let that happen. "I may be poorly," she said, "but I'm still in charge of some things."

The doctor said she might go at any time; on the other hand, consumption being the tricky thing it was, she might last a year or more. It was hard to believe she was as sick as the doctor said. Except for the weakness and the shallowness of her breathing she seemed as lively as ever. Now and then she'd even call for the dulcimer Uncle Ernest had made for her. She didn't have the wind to sing anymore, but she could still play like an angel. Oliver would sit by the bed and hum along as best he could, and if he knew the words he would sing full-voiced,

> *A hundred months have passed, Lorena,*
> *Since last I held that hand in mine,*
> *And felt the pulse beat fast, Lorena,*
> *Though mine beat faster far than thine*

or

> *Come Father, come Mother, come riddle us both,*
> *Come riddle us both as one,*
> *And tell me whether to marry fair Ellen*
> *Or bring me the brown girl home*

and always, at the last,

> *Blest be the tie that binds*
> *Our hearts in Christian love,*
> *The fellowship of kindred minds*
> *Is like to that above.*

Nancy's labor started one Thursday morning in April before the Widow Henslee had left for War Woman Creek. While the widow tended Nancy, Oliver borrowed a horse and buggy from the miller O'Day and drove over to Estatoah Falls to fetch Granny Grindstaff. He was in something of a state. He'd been upriver at Clayton selling shoes the day in eighteen-sixty when Syl was born, and three years later when Martha came he was a prisoner of the Yankees at Vicksburg, so he had no experience whatever in the matter of childbirth. He watched doubtfully while Granny filled a poke full of herbs and pieces of tree bark and packets of seeds and bundles of dried leaves—to boil for decoctions, she said. Oliver didn't know what a decoction might be but was afraid to ask. Granny also put in a bar of Castile soap, a vial of camphor, several small bottles of patent medicines and some folded linens, and when they got to the house she asked Oliver for a bucket of hog's lard. Oliver wasn't sure how hog's lard figured in the business, but he got her some anyway. Then Granny told Oliver to fetch a knife and an ax, and that was when his faith in her faltered. He said he could understand maybe needing a knife, but an ax was altogether out of the question. But Granny explained she needed the knife to put under Nancy's pillow and the ax to put under her bed, in order to cut the pains. Seeing the logic in this Oliver hastened to comply.

During the labor he and Syl and Martha stayed outside. Every few minutes, while the younguns watched entranced, Oliver would load his pappy's War of 1812 musket with bullets made of hair and shoot them into the side of the barn. This was done at Granny's direction, to scare off the witches and evil spirits. When he'd used up all his hair bullets Oliver poured gunpowder into the knotholes of the old maple in the dooryard and set the tree off with a match.

It was night before the baby came. The younguns were asleep in the corncrib, and Oliver was worn out with worrying. The Widow Henslee came out and told him it had been a long labor but an easy one and Nancy was fine and it was a boy indeed.

When he went inside he saw Nancy lying in the bed looking much smaller than she ought and holding in the crook of her arm a naked wrinkled little baby. The baby looked older to him than Granny Grindstaff. Nancy was white and spent, but she smiled her old bright smile at him. He came to the bed and knelt down and put one arm around her damp head and with his other hand cupped the soft warm head of the baby. Granny cut the cord with a pair of shears and tied it with twine, and the baby howled. The Widow Henslee had a shovel stuck in the stove with a piece of cloth on it. When the cloth was scorched she took it out, and Granny plucked it off the shovel blade and cut a hole in it with the shears and laid it over the baby's waist and pulled the stump of the navel cord through it while Oliver knelt by the bed watching.

Granny greased a cloth with mutton tallow and gave it to the widow, who scorched it on the shovel blade as she'd done before. Then Granny took the scorched cloth and bound it tight around the baby's belly—to keep him from rupturing, she said. There was a wooden bowl by the bed filled with the afterbirth. Granny told Oliver to make himself useful by taking the bowl outside and burying what was in it, and he did. He got sick doing it and puked. But nobody saw him, so his shame was his alone. They named the boy James Littleton, after Oliver's departed uncle James and his brother Lit on Rabun Gap.

One morning at the end of March, high up in the Tusquittees at the head of Fires Creek, where the Puckett place stood behind its stake-and-rail fence with the timbered mountainside rising behind it up toward the peak of Nigger Head, the old Puckett woman, whose name was Minnie Lee, crossed the dogtrot into the log kitchen to fix breakfast. There to her disgust she found a large raccoon crouching in the middle of the trestle table. Apparently it had come in through the window, whose oilskin covering she noticed was torn in two.

Although the weather was unseasonably mild the raccoon shivered as if it were cold, and it regarded her in mellow fashion, even hopefully, so that Minnie Lee could imagine that it wished to be taken up and warmed. But she was in no mood to tolerate such a varmint in her kitchen at breakfast time. So she seized a broom and swatted the raccoon with it. At the first lick the raccoon only stirred in a sluggish way and crouched down lower on the table. But at the second lick it snarled and took hold of the head of the broom with its two hands and then quick as a flash darted right up the broomstick and bit Minnie Lee in the face and splashed her all over with its hot saliva.

Minnie Lee's screams and curses fetched the young Puckett, who was her daughter, from the sleeping quarters across the dogtrot. The daughter's name was Rhonda Salvation. When Rhonda Salvation rushed into the kitchen the raccoon was huddled on the packed-earth floor by the fireplace, where it had landed when it jumped off Minnie Lee. Rhonda Salvation didn't see it—she was gaping in shock at the sight of Minnie Lee, whose nose had been torn mostly off—till the raccoon darted out and sank its teeth in her ankle. Rhonda Salvation shrieked and grabbed up a skillet and hit the raccoon with it as hard as she could, and the raccoon let go and stood looking up at her blinking, as if it couldn't understand why she'd attacked it. Then it ambled casually out the door, as if nothing at all had happened.

But something surely had happened, for that raccoon was mad. The Pucketts did not suspect this. Like most folks they associated rabid animals with the dog days of August and never thought to keep a madstone by them at other times of the year, least of all at the end of winter. They thought the raccoon had only bitten them because it was cornered and Minnie Lee had thrashed it with her broom. Pretty soon they forgot all about it.

Forty-two days later, at the end of April, the East Tennessee lawyer Johnston Barrett made his way up Fires Creek to prepare the Pucketts for their testimony at the trial of their lawsuit against Judge Curtis, scheduled for the spring term of superior court. By then Minnie Lee had already got sick and was passing through the first stages of hydrophobia. Although Rhonda Salvation had stitched her mother's nose back together with sewing thread, and it had nearly healed up, the place continued to throb and tingle and ache; then Minnie Lee came down with a fever and sore throat and began to suffer bouts of nausea. While that was going on, her whole face started to go numb.

When lawyer Barrett arrived, Minnie Lee was confined to her bed. The nerves in her skin had got so raw she felt like she'd been flayed alive. She'd stripped herself naked because she could no longer abide the touch of clothing on her body, but still the feel of the mattress on her back was such a torment that she continually writhed in agony, and as she flopped and twisted on the bed the great mass of her flesh shifted and shook like so much gelatin. Since any light at all seared her eyes with unbearable pain, the windows of the room were covered with blankets, and she suffered on in darkness.

For all these reasons Rhonda Salvation could not let lawyer Barrett go in to see Minnie Lee. Instead she made him squat on an upended barrel in the dogtrot. Here he tried to discuss the case with Rhonda Salvation while she sat opposite him languidly chewing her snuff stick. But of course Rhonda Salvation had no notion of the lawsuit—she had little enough notion of anything at all, lawyer Barrett discovered—and besides, Minnie Lee kept howling like a demon in the bedroom and distracting him. Naturally he couldn't guess her trouble, and Rhonda Salvation herself knew no more than that her mama was sickly. Beginning to fear for his prospects in court, lawyer Barrett begged Rhonda Salvation to let him send up a doctor. But Rhonda Salvation said the Pucketts never had no truck with doctors; they used treatments and conjurations of their own. That evening lawyer Barrett returned chapfallen to town with a promise to return when Minnie Lee felt better.

But Minnie Lee wasn't going to feel any better, and now Rhonda Salvation herself began to notice a burning in her ankle where the raccoon had nipped her. Within days she too was down with fever, a raw throat and a vicious stomach upset. When lawyer Barrett returned to the head of Fires Creek in a week's time he was horrified to find Rhonda Salvation rolled up naked in the dogtrot, foaming at the mouth, smeared with her own ordure and shaken by violent convulsions, and Minnie Lee, unclothed also, lying crossways on her bed in the darkened sleeping quarters, beaten bloody by her mad daughter, paralyzed and dying—a glimpse into hell indeed.

Sarah Curtis rocked on the lower gallery churning butter and enjoying the brilliant May morning. It was still early, and yonder in the bottom where the sun had not yet reached, fog was rising off the river like wisps of goose down. Beyond the river a band of new light lay along the crests of the hills, and as the sun rose higher that light broadened down the slopes into the bottom and lit the top of the fog as it lifted. Blue mountains stood behind the rim of hills, and as Sarah gazed at them she felt something start to melt away that had long sealed her off from them without her knowing it—maybe some membrane of dread that the war had drawn over her—and then the mountains spoke to her in the old way and began to lend her some of their old grace for the first time in a very long while. This was a gift whose worth she remembered now, after having let herself forget it for years. Thankfully she drank it in.

Hamby McFee lay next to her on the cot Andy had carried out for him to rest on, although Hamby allowed himself little enough rest, tugging and worrying as he did at the dressing on his wounded shoulder. Hamby was smoking his pipe and scowling. He'd worn that scowl off and on ever since coming to warn of danger that night nearly three weeks ago and getting himself shot. In taking the part of the Curtises against Nahum Bellamy he'd surprised himself even more than he had the Curtises, and he was far from sure of having done the right thing. Now and then he'd sigh and wag his head in wordless self-reproach. There had even been times since the shooting when fits of anger would take him, and he'd curse them all for slave masters and hypocrites, and himself for a fool who'd known no better than to save them from a fate they deserved. But Sarah felt no call to correct or reprove him. Hamby had shown them his true heart that night in the turnaround.

Madison had been walking with the two Cartman boys down by the bushwhacker's grave on the river, and now through drifts of rising fog Sarah saw them coming back. She paused in her churning to watch as they approached. Madison looked quite small, almost frail— he seemed to dwindle a little more each day as his woes bore him down—but still he held himself ramrod-straight and walked in the graceful way she'd always admired, with a spring in his gait that made him appear to slightly sway at each step, like a sapling in a breeze. He wore his black frock coat and hat, and when the sunlight touched him it glared on the white front of his starched shirt. The boys ran wild circles around him in the new grass. As Sarah watched, somehow the grace the mountains had lent her made her feel the world grow oddly bigger, more full of light, and Madison and the boys seemed like flyspecks in its great space but were also lit by a glow that gave them a special value, made them dazzle bright as gold. All of a sudden and utterly without reason it became possible for Sarah to believe again in hope.

Not that she was ready to conclude, as Madison had, that God was active in the matter of Nahum Bellamy. Madison thought the Almighty put Daniel McFee in Bellamy's road that night. He felt it was God, through Daniel, who struck Bellamy down. Furthermore he took this as a sign that God had at last forgiven him his sin of the wartime. Sarah was pleased for Madison's sake that he'd come to see things so. But for her, God remained afar off. She didn't think He intervened in mortal affairs. She thought He'd made the world and set it spinning in the heavens, and that was all. Mankind did the rest, and God looked on sorrowing. She wondered if this was heresy or blasphemy—it surely didn't fit the Methodist discipline. But only in this way could she be reconciled to the evil of the earth and the pain of life. Only in this way could she abide the loss of Jack and Howell, who in her silly pride she'd sent away to war, and of dear Betty and poor Bill Cartman and sweet Salina, all carried off by sickness, and now of Daniel McFee too, shot down by a lunatic for the sake of others.

No, Sarah didn't think God had taken a hand. What happened was, a few people in the world had given the best that was in them. Daniel had. So had Hamby. Andy had. Oliver Price had. And so had Madison himself. Together they'd done just enough good to turn aside some of the bad. Not all of it, just some of it—enough. Maybe this was sufficient to justify hope. She was glad Madison thought himself forgiven. But to her way of thinking it was hardly likely that God had taken any notice at all of what Madison or any other man did in the war, so great had been the horror of it. Likely He'd turned His face away in shame instead. Anyhow, Sarah believed that Madison did right, not wrong, the day the bushwhackers came, and had no need of forgiveness. What he'd done was out of regard for her and Andy. So now she would have hope. She would have hope in the best that was in a few good folk.

Andy came out of the house wearing his linen traveling coat and carrying a carpetbag; he and Madison were leaving soon in Uncle Amos's rockaway for Murphy, where they would meet Oliver Price, arriving tomorrow on the mail stage from Franklin. The three would confer in Murphy with lawyer Elias before coming on to Hayesville, where trial of the Pucketts' lawsuit would begin next week.

Andy asked Hamby how he was feeling.

Hamby heaved a sigh of regret. "It looks like I'm going to live after all, even though I *am* the dumbest damn nigger ever born and deserve to die. Go fetch your gun and do up the job proper."

But he broke off what might have become a tirade when Polly and Rebecca came up from the summer kitchen bearing a tea service, which they set on the floor beside him. Ever since the shooting the girls had been spoiling him scandalously, but till today he'd always rebuffed them with outbursts of swearing—which Sarah inwardly deplored but the girls seemed to overlook. Indeed, Sarah sometimes worried lest the girls get coarsened by Hamby's hard ways. But so far as she could tell they were unaffected. And now for a wonder Hamby meekly rose partway off his cot to let Polly plump up his pillows while Rebecca poured him a cup of tea. His scowl remained, and he puffed furiously on his pipe, but when Rebecca handed him his tea he actually thanked her. Andy and Sarah exchanged looks of amazement.

But the decorum proved short-lived. After taking a sip of tea Hamby spied Madison advancing up the walk between the boxwoods and remarked, "Here comes Simon Legree. Maybe I can get *him* to shoot me."

Sarah and Andy and the girls laughed. While the Cartman boys threw pieces of gravel at one another behind him in the turnaround, Madison paused at the foot of the steps and passed his forefinger back and forth under his mustache. "It's good to hear laughter on the place again," he declared, "even though I gather it's at my expense." Then he glanced at Andy's carpetbag. "I see you're ready. I'll get my grip and be back in a minute."

He started up the steps, and Sarah watched him come and thought how they'd been man and wife for thirty years, how together they'd made nine children and seen three of them taken away, how they'd started with nothing and by dint of hard work got prosperous and then because of war lost most everything, how they'd endured, the two of them—how he had helped her bear the evil of life. As he passed her she let go the dasher and caught his sleeve. "Be careful," she said.

It was court week in Murphy, the first since the war, and because of lawsuits pending between Union men and secesh—cases like the Pucketts', rising out of wartime outrages—bad blood was everywhere, talk of vendetta was on each tongue, fear lingered in the air like a bad odor. Because the court circuit began in Murphy and worked its way east to Asheville there had as yet been no session anywhere, and no one knew what to expect, though most feared the worst. Madison rested his calloused palm over her hand and smiled down at her and nodded, and went on.

Yesterday Sanders Barter had driven over from Warne with Martha and Eva to be with Sarah and the children while the other menfolk went to Murphy. Just now Sanders was out at the woodpile splitting stove wood. Standing at the top of the steps waiting for Papa, Andy became aware of the sound of Sanders chopping wood over by the north side of the house. *Whock, whock*, went Sanders's ax. At first he paid only the slightest heed, but after a while the noise became somehow insistent, and presently he thought perhaps he knew why this was so. He'd been communing in secret with the shade of his departed Salina—the wall between them had fallen the night Bellamy died, and so Salina could understand him now and speak back into his most inward ear, although she used no language known to man, and he could not have told afterward anything she'd said—and lately when they spoke, the image of Sanders had come up between them. It was a sorrowing image, and the sight of it troubled Andy every time. Now as he heard the sound of Sanders chopping wood the same image returned, and as always when seeing it he felt a twinge of guilt. Partly to ward off this feeling he took up his carpetbag and descended the steps and walked out to the cul-de-sac, where the horse and rockaway stood waiting. He stowed his bag and began idly checking the harness and hitch, waiting for Papa to come. *Whock, whock*, went Sanders's ax.

Then without really intending it Andy found himself walking around the house to where the woodpile was. He paused by the corner to watch. With expert strokes Sanders was splitting lengths of wood, one blow for each piece of poplar or the harder locust. The back of his shirt was dark with sweat. Every time he swung the ax a small grunt escaped him. Andy watched him split six or eight lengths before Sanders became aware of him and turned.

Things had not been right between him and Sanders since Sanders came back after the surrender and Andy suspected him of toryism and bushwhacking. But now with Salina's words in him Andy saw Sanders in a different light. He remembered building fences with Sanders along the Franklin road, driving cows with him to pasture up on the Double Knobs, taking turns plowing the bottomland by the river with him behind his old mule Jehosophat.

Even then Sanders loved Union and hated slavery, wouldn't own a nigra, scolded Andy for holding men in bondage, urged him to make Papa set them free. Whatever he'd done in war—even if he'd only laid out in the Smokies like he claimed—Sanders had done it from his soul, just as Jack and Howell had, just as Andy himself had. Whether he'd ridden with Kirk or hid in the woods the whole four years to keep from serving the Confederacy he hated, Sanders had been true to himself the same as Andy and his brothers. It was honor either way. And if they deserved respect then so did he.

Sanders looked at Andy in a wistful manner and dragged off his hat and spoke the first words he'd uttered to him since coming home the summer before. And what he spoke of was Salina, as if she'd been communing with Sanders too and was on his mind, just as she was on Andy's. "I always favored your Salina," he said. "But I knew you bore me ill and so I never come to her funeral, so as not to offend." He stood there with one hand on the haft of the ax and the other clutching his old hat, and his eyes swam with tears. "I'm right sorry," he choked, "right sorry. . . ." But he couldn't finish whatever he meant to say and only stood there weeping.

Andy went to him and put his arms around him and drew him close, and Sanders pressed his brushy beard to Andy's cheek and kissed him and wet him with his tears.

After Madison and Andy left, Sarah let Martha spell her at the churn. She stood on the gallery pressing her hands into the small of her back to ease the cramps she always got working the dasher. Julia and young Sarah had come out to bid the menfolk farewell, and now they settled on wicker stools on either side of Hamby in hopes of interesting him in singing some songs, as it was known he had a fine baritone voice now that it had changed. But Hamby wanted no part of singing and lay sullenly smoking his pipe while the girls struck up a rendition of "Barbry Allen." Sarah leaned against a stanchion enjoying the song and watching the boys playing in the cul-de-sac.

After a while she noticed that in romping by the river Jimmy had got mud smeared all over the hind part of his nearly worn-out velveteen sailor suit, which he would transfer to the furniture as soon as he returned inside. She called the boys to her and told Jimmy to change into something clean.

"Then I got to change too," little Andy declared.

Sarah sighed. She thought it was queer the way the two insisted on dressing and acting alike, even though they were almost two years apart in age. She knew people gossiped about them. But their pa had encouraged it in them because it amused him, and after he went into the mountains Betty had grudgingly let it go on—partly because it reminded her of Bill, Sarah guessed. Often Sarah pondered whether she should try to change them, but somehow she'd never been able to feel she had the right. It was something the boys themselves had started for reasons of their own; Sarah figured they'd grow out of it when they were ready, and till then they deserved to be let alone. But still she was curious. She wondered if they knowingly did what they did. Could they say in words why they behaved so? Impulsively—surprising herself—she made bold to ask, "How come you boys must always do everything the same?"

She expected them to hesitate in confusion, but instead Jimmy spoke right up in answer. "If we always do the same then we'll be safe."

"If we don't," Andy explained, "bad things will happen to us."

Eagerly Jimmy nodded. "Things like happened to Uncle Jack and Uncle Howell and Ma and Pa."

"And Aunt Salina and Uncle Daniel," added Andy.

Again Jimmy nodded. "And when the bushwhackers came and hurt you and stole our goods, and the tories run off the stock and burnt the crops."

"All them bad things happened," Andy said, "but nothing ever happened to Jimmy and me."

"On account of us keeping the charm, Grandma," Jimmy pointed out.

He seemed anxious to make her understand. And of course she did. This was how they'd got by. It was how they'd all got by. Each of them had found a thing to believe in, to keep themselves from going mad with fear. Madison had relied on God; Sarah had relied on a few good hearts; the boys had relied on their charm of being always the same. So she smiled and rested a hand on each towhead. "I see," she said. "Well, go on inside and change."

They rushed past her into the house, and the front door banged shut behind them. Sarah moved to the edge of the gallery and let herself down easy because of her rheumatism and sat with her feet on the first step and her hands dangling by the wrists over her knees. She was tired. She listened to the sound of the girls singing.

CHAPTER 15

I t didn't seem right to go. Not now, not with Nancy so
sick. Ever since having the baby she'd sunk lower and
lower, seeming to dwindle before Oliver's eyes, getting smaller and
more pale every day, till she looked like a little porcelain doll lying
there in the bed. It was as if the birthing had pulled a cork in her
somewhere and the life was draining steadily out.

By night she sweat big greasy drops of foul-smelling sweat and
coughed up bloody gobs of tissue, and after every spell of coughing
she found it a little harder to draw breath. Leaning close Oliver could
hear the faint gurgle of the water in her lungs every time she ex-
haled. Her voice faded to the merest whisper, and she was weak as a
kitten. She had no strength even to play the gourd banjo or Uncle
Ernest's dulcimer for Oliver to sing along. She was Oliver's play-
mate no more.

Wee James Littleton was thriving, but Nancy had no milk for
him in her poor flat breasts, and Granny Grindstaff got him a wet
nurse, a woman that lived farther up Darnell Creek who had an

infant of her own. The Widow Henslee moved in to care for Nancy and brought her younguns with her, and the cabin got so crowded Oliver had to live on the porch all the time now. Thanks to the wet nurse and Granny Grindstaff and the Widow Henslee, Nancy got all the care she needed. But it was time for Oliver to return to Carolina for the Curtis trial, and it looked to him like Nancy was going to die any minute. Mama had come to visit and after sniffing at Nancy's mouth declared Nancy wouldn't last a week; she said this standing over Nancy's bed so Nancy could hear.

Oliver was ashamed of having gone off to war and left Nancy alone so much of the short time they'd been married. It had been hard on her, raising the younguns, trying to farm the place, worrying all the while about whether he'd get killed or come home all crippled up and useless. Oliver suspected a more thoughtful husband would have done a lot better by a woman as fine as Nancy. But he reckoned he was just a fool that had no notion of what a responsible husband owed his wife.

He'd thought it was right and dutiful to go chasing off to war, but it turned out to be wrong, and he hadn't understood this till it was much too late. And all that time Nancy was alone staving off the cruelties of the world. He'd tried to make amends since coming home but didn't feel like he had; Mama especially assured him he'd fallen far short of his duty. So he didn't want to be gone away to Clay County when Nancy departed this life—especially not then. If that happened he didn't think he could stand it.

Yet the cause of the Curtises would likely fail if he didn't show up in that Hayesville courtroom. Lawyer Elias said the testimony of Miz Balm In Gilead Quillen by itself probably wouldn't be enough to sway the jury, that Oliver himself was the key witness. It was his evidence, given in person and not by deposition, that would win the case and save the Curtises from ruin. But how could he leave now?

He couldn't guess whom to turn to for advice. Before, he'd always gone to Nancy herself. That's what he did last November when he dreaded going out to Carolina, and she'd set him right about that. Nobody had ever seemed to him as wise as she. But it didn't feel right to pester her now, when she was sinking. Besides, he thought it would be unfair to pose her such a hard question in her weakened state, to force her to choose between taking leave of life with him by her side or maybe crossing over alone. How could she choose? How could he even set her such a choice? He felt like an awful sinner ever to consider it.

There was the Widow Henslee, of course. The widow had a decided opinion on most anything a man could name, from what sign to plant corn under to how to dig a well. But although Oliver had got pretty used to the widow by now he still felt shy about approaching her on a question as private as this.

No matter how he tried to avoid it his mind kept coming back again and again to Nancy. He reproached himself with how mean it was to think of vexing her, how heartless and unfeeling. But in the end that was exactly what he did. There was nobody he trusted more. He needed straight talk; straight talk was what Nancy always gave him. And what better occasion for straight talk than a time when life hung in the balance?

He had to bend close to hear. She spoke a few words at a time, and in between she gasped for the wind to say what came next. "You give them folks your word. Didn't you? Word of honor. They're a-counting on. You ain't a-going back on that." She stopped to rest, and he took her hand and waited till she was ready to go on. She smiled up at him. "Hit's why I liked you. That you kept your word. Your word of honor." She commenced to cough, and he fetched a rag for her to spit into, and it came away red. After that she couldn't speak, didn't have the breath for it. He waited, holding her moist hand. It felt like the hand of a small child.

In time she was ready again. "Hit was honor," she said in her wisp of voice. "Always was. You had hit. The others didn't. Hit made you go to the war. When most laid out. Made you stay. That last year. When most run off. Made you help them Curtises. When you'd rather not. When hit warn't safe. I was proud." Another siege of coughing racked her. He folded the rag and held it out, and she spat more red into it and lay back gasping. He thought they ought to quit now, that it was too hard on her.

"Let's wait," he said as tears filled his eyes. But she shook her head; she didn't want to stop.

Her tiny hand tightened in his. "Proud," she repeated, gazing up at him with a sudden fierceness. "Proud." She ceased and lay panting, then in a minute or two resumed. "They say the fine folk. Is the only ones. Has honor. Rich-uns. Not common ones. Like us. But you got hit. So you got to go. Help them Curtises. I'll try. And be here. When you. Get back." Once more she stopped, coughed red into the rag, sank back, rested.

Oliver wiped his tears on the rough sleeve of his shirt. He spoke her name and spoke it again. Weakly she smiled up at him. "If I pass. While you're gone. Hit's God's will. Ain't mine. I mean to hold on. Till you come home. So's I can kiss you." Then she squeezed his hand again, and in another moment she was asleep.

At first Oliver refused to take Syl along. He'd heard there might be riots breaking out at court openings around the western part of Carolina and thought it was no time to take a six-year-old into that country. But Syl implored him—he wanted to ride the stage, and play with the Cartman boys again, and see Mister Andy and Granny Sarah and the judge, and eat Granny Sarah's marble cake, and look for Indian relics down by the Indian mound, and go fishing in the Hiwassee, because last time it was too cold and he couldn't. He also said he wanted to see the old nigger Daniel McFee and ride that big horse of his that he got to ride last time, but Oliver had to tell him the sad news in Andy's last letter, that Uncle Daniel was killed.

Syl mused awhile and then remarked on how often folks died sudden up there. He was thinking of the dead man they'd seen dragged out of the creek on the wagon road going into Hayesville, and of Andy's wife Salina, whose funeral he'd attended, and now of Uncle Daniel. Pondering this, Oliver chose not to mention that Daniel McFee had slain that Bellamy jasper too, lest it make the Hiwassee country seem a field of blood indeed. Because by then he'd talked it over with Nancy and decided to take the boy after all. The last trip had done Syl a world of good—brightened him up, helped him start to trust a little in Oliver and feel easy in his company. Syl could stay home at the Curtises' on court day; if there was any trouble he'd miss it.

But in making this calculation Oliver and Nancy were thinking of Clay County alone and didn't reckon on the Pinckney Rollins mail stage pulling into Murphy in the middle of court week for Cherokee, which is just what happened. Coming along the road from Franklin on a sunny afternoon, Oliver thought the outskirts of Murphy seemed unnaturally quiet. The place had a Sunday look to it—the shops closed up, nobody much on the streets, no younguns playing in the yards of the houses. Somewhere a bell was tolling. They came up the hill into the center of town and passed along one side of the square, and Oliver glanced out the window of the coach as it drew up before the Long Hotel and saw with a bolt of alarm that the part of the square in front of the new courthouse was crowded with grim-faced jaspers, several of whom were toting shotguns or rifles. Quickly he stuck his head out the near-side window and as the driver jumped down from the box asked him what the trouble was.

The driver approached and crossed his arms on the sill, obviously pleased to oblige. "Well," he said with an eager smile, "you've got your Tathams that was Rebels in the war, and you've got your Morrows that was Union men. Or it could be the Tathams was Union and the Morrows secesh—whatever 'twas. Now, while the war was on, one of these Morrows kilt a Tatham, or maybe it was a Tatham kilt a Morrow, I forget which. Or maybe a Morrow insulted a Tatham woman or a Tatham plucked an old Morrow's beard. Some such aggravation. Anyhow, after the surrender, one or t'other sued, or maybe both of 'em sued. That-ere case is on for trial today. These fellows you see is all Tathams and Morrows and their friends and relations—interested parties, you might say."

Oliver knew a bad fix when he saw one and at once began to rage at himself for so thoughtlessly exposing Syl to danger. Anxiously he scanned the gallery of the hotel, but he saw no sign of Andy or Judge Curtis or lawyer Elias. Syl was peering out the window at the men with guns in the square. Wide-eyed, he wondered aloud if somebody was liable to get shot. Brightly the driver replied, "I wouldn't be atall surprised. I see a lawyer a-standin' yonder whose light one of them Morrows is a-promisin' to put out."

Maybe the driver was exaggerating; maybe nothing was going to happen after all. But it didn't look that way to Oliver, and he wasn't going to take even the smallest chance that Syl might get hurt. The thing to do was hustle the boy to safety. Looking out past Syl and across the square, he could see the yellow building where lawyer Elias had his office. That was the place to go. It was made of brick, and the office was on the second level, and if shooting started and they lay flat on the floor they likely wouldn't get hit.

Oliver shoved open the door on the side facing the hotel with the driver still grinning at the window. The driver stumbled backward swearing as Oliver and Syl got out. Oliver barked at him, "Fetch down my bags," and the jasper stood there grumbling it wasn't his job to rustle the passengers' plunder, that the company had a nigger for that. So Oliver climbed up on the boot himself and rummaged around on top till he found his cowhide grip and Syl's little rattan case, then dropped down again with the driver frowning at him and took Syl by the hand and set off.

The bell they'd heard on the way in kept tolling. They crossed the square, passing through the rear edge of the crowd. Oliver saw several small boys dodging in and out, and any number of dogs, but no womenfolk except one or two of the naughty kind. Several of the men were red in the face and wild of eye, and as Oliver passed he smelt whiskey on them. But others stood by looking uncertain or scared. Over in front of the courthouse two fellows had squared off yelling; Oliver heard one call the other a damned tory son of a bitch. A fellow strolled by selling packets of roasted peanuts. Somebody told a joke, and there was a burst of laughter. Oliver saw a man leaning against a tree with a bowie knife stuck in the top of his boot. A drunk man sat on the ground holding a demijohn to his breast like a babe. Of the guns Oliver saw, every one was capped.

On the other side of the square they ducked into lawyer Elias's building. Upstairs they found the office unlocked and empty. They went in and sat down to wait, and here it was very quiet except for the ticking of an old clock on the mantelpiece and the sound of the bell tolling in the distance. In only a few minutes lawyer Elias and Judge Curtis and Andy came in; they'd been waiting in the lobby of the hotel and seen Oliver and Syl get out of the coach and head for the office.

"You were right to make haste," said lawyer Elias, settling behind his desk and mopping his brow with a handkerchief. "The town's in an ugly mood." He explained about the Morrows and the Tathams and said the Tathams' lawyer was a young man named Boone, who one of the Morrows—Jim Morrow, it was—had warned not to show up on court day on pain of death. But Boone was on the square and carrying a pistol, daring Jim Morrow or any other Morrow or partisan of a Morrow to try and keep him from his constitutional duty.

The men in the square were all armed. Many were drunk, and most were ready to take the part of one side or another "as soon as a spark is struck," as lawyer Elias put it.

Syl could hardly contain his delight. "I'm going to see a shooting!" he proclaimed, to nobody in particular. He kept running to the window and peering out in hopes of witnessing the first pull; Oliver kept going and fetching him back.

Andy spoke up in favor of leaving town at once to get Syl out of the way, and Judge Curtis agreed. Lawyer Elias couldn't go, as he had a case to try in Murphy once things quieted down. "But you folks go on home," he urged. "I'll follow along once my matter here is disposed of. I'll stop by and collect Mrs. Quillen on the way. With your permission, Judge Curtis, we'll confer in your home when I arrive." So it was agreed.

The Curtises had left their horse and rig at a livery just off the northwest corner of the square, behind the house of a man named Hennessee. It was too risky to go there by the most direct way, diagonally across the square, so they decided to retreat one block off the square and then skirt three sides of it, approaching the livery from behind. Syl listened in outraged disbelief, then wailed, "Ain't I going to see the shooting?" Oliver caught him by the hand and told him to hush. Then he and the Curtises bade farewell to lawyer Elias, and Andy led the way downstairs.

They paused in the foyer. Warily Andy cracked the door and peeked out; Judge Curtis, standing close behind him, laid a loving hand on his back. Glancing from one to the other, Oliver saw how the fret had gone from the judge and how solid Andy had grown, in the time since he'd seen them. The sight heartened him; it was good to see his friends begin to heal. Syl tugged at his hand, trying to get free. Andy opened the door, and they filed outside and turned away from the square. And just then Syl wrenched himself out of Oliver's grasp and ran like a deer across the street and straight into the middle of the square.

Rage and dread tore Oliver. "*Sylvester Price!*" he cried, starting to run. But his bad leg, which he'd forgot, gave way under him, and he fell headfirst into the street; his cowhide grip and Syl's case went skittering. As he fell he saw Andy dart past him into the square. Oliver stood; Judge Curtis came to steady him and then scooped up the bags Oliver had dropped. At the edge of the square they watched as Syl crossed through the fringe of the crowd toward Hennessee's corner with Andy in close pursuit. Some in the mob turned to stare, and a little black dog chased after Andy, barking. Once more Oliver called Syl's name, which was a pointless act, he knew; he'd sooner call back the sun from its rounds in the heavens.

Then with the judge's strong hand on his arm he set off hobbling. He went past a man with a rifle and another checking the loads in a big revolver. Some jasper whose breath was fruity with the smell of peach brandy was singing the song "I'm a Good Old Rebel." The bell was still tolling in the distance.

At the northwest corner of the square Syl stopped in the sudden way boys do when they see they've gone too far in their mischief. With a surge of relief Oliver saw him meekly turn and wait for Andy. Judge Curtis said, "He's all right now," and they hurried on. Andy caught the boy up under the arms and whirled him laughing, and Syl laughed too. The black dog circled them and jumped up at Andy, wanting to play.

Oliver and the judge were only a rod or two away when Oliver saw a man standing just beyond Andy and Syl jab a pistol into the breast of another man and shoot him. It was a small-caliber pistol, and muffled in the shot man's clothing it made a dull pop that only a few people heard. The shot man reeled, the front of his coat afire from the powder flash; Andy pushed Syl into the grass and dropped down over him; the shot man toppled over sideways with one arm flung out over the backs of Andy's legs. The black dog ran up wagging its tail, still wanting to play, but then saw the fire and slunk off. As the man lay there ablaze Syl twisted his head out from under

Andy to see; he looked as if somebody had just given him two pounds of horehound candy.

On all sides people dropped flat on the ground, except for the man who'd shot. Oliver and the judge lay down too, and Oliver watched as the jasper with the pistol cocked it with a shaking hand and looked down at the shot man, as if considering whether to shoot him again. More and more folks were lying down around the shot man now, and presently the biggest part of the mob over by the courthouse noticed this and divined what had happened. There was a lot of yelling and cursing, and then somebody over there fired—it sounded like a military musket to Oliver, and made everybody lying on the ground flinch. Oliver heard the ball whistle overhead. It hit the jasper with the pistol while he was still pondering whether to shoot his man a second time, and knocked something off the side of his head into the grass right in front of Syl. It was a part of an ear, and Syl lay regarding it with grateful wonder.

The jasper with the pistol—it was Jim Morrow, they would later learn, and the man he'd killed was lawyer Boone, as promised—clapped his free hand to his ear and with the other started shooting over toward the courthouse. He shot right across where Oliver and the judge were lying and peppered them with powder sparks. The fellows by the courthouse shot back, and for a minute or so Oliver was reminded of some of the battles he'd been in and recalled why he'd disliked them. Then Morrow turned and ran for the hitch rack in front of Hennessee's and picked himself a chestnut horse and swung up on it, and Oliver saw a bullet hit him in the back and two more strike the horse as he wheeled and rode off.

After he'd gone the shooting petered out, and for an instant the only sounds in the whole town of Murphy were the bell ringing in the distance and that little black dog barking as it dashed madly around the square. Powder smoke smelling of rotten eggs hung thick in front of the courthouse. Pigeons startled from their roosts in the eaves and gables off the square were wheeling overhead. But every-body knew the affair wasn't done—this was but the lull before the storm. Andy cried, "Let's go!" and jumped up, dragging Syl after him, and Oliver and the judge followed, hurrying past the body of lawyer Boone with the fire burning on its chest. They got to the corner by Hennessee's house before the shooting broke out again.

Some days later, when lawyer Elias got to Hayesville with Miz Balm In Gilead Quillen in tow, they heard how matters turned out. Morrow got clean away, although the horse he'd taken—which belonged to a man named Whitaker—threw him and returned to the square and dropped dead there. In the subsequent shooting Perd Tatham and Fate Morrow were killed and Captain James Cooper wounded. Altogether it was an awful tragedy. But it was also a tale that Syl Price would tell with relish till the end of his long life.

Lawyer Elias had engaged lodgings for himself and Miz Balm In Gilead Quillen in the hotel at Hayesville, but Miz Curtis wouldn't hear of them putting up in public rooms amid the hubbub of court week and insisted they stay at the farm instead. In making the invitation Miz Curtis acted as if Miz Quillen was every bit as refined as the Curtises, instead of being the coarse and common sort she was, and Oliver was struck with wonder to think Miz Curtis's Christian charity was such that no distinctions of that sort would occur to her.

Lawyer Elias consented to stay, but it was plain to see that Miz Quillen had her doubts. After all, as she saw matters, these same Curtises had helped get her menfolk murdered. Although she was ready to testify in their behalf she didn't feel easy about sleeping under the same roof with them. Yet she had a dread of towns and clearly didn't want to take a room there. In the end she compromised by sleeping on the gallery rolled up in blankets and a quilt——an arrangement that offended Miz Curtis's notion of hospitality but seemed to leave Miz Quillen tolerably content.

But still the poor woman couldn't rest altogether at peace. It wasn't just the bushwhacker killings standing between her and the judge that made her restless. She lived in a hovel and was staying in a mansion; she was trash while the Curtises were quality. She hardly knew how to behave, and Oliver could see that the whole experience was an ordeal for her. Yet she bore up as best she could. She'd worn her best linsey-cloth dress, that she'd washed in the creek at home and beaten clean with a stick against a stump. She'd bathed her neck and braided up her hair. Although the presence of Hamby McFee was very plainly obnoxious to her, she spoke no word of abhorrence. She forbore to dip snuff. She tolerated the rude questions of Syl and the Cartman boys. But so misplaced did she feel that she took her meals apart and kept mostly to herself.

The judge was as gracious to her as Miz Curtis. The day she arrived he begged her pardon for the fate of Old Mose and her boys, but she was shy and couldn't speak, though she showed in looks that she bore him no malice. Oliver was the only one in whose company she seemed to feel at ease. Oliver was more or less her kind, and he'd been the one to seek her out and treat her decent and make her see the right thing to do. But everyone was relieved——Miz Balm In Gilead Quillen most of all——when court day finally came.

Lawyer Elias went into town early that morning in Uncle Amos's rockaway. Oliver, the judge, Andy and Miz Quillen drove in later in lawyer Elias's surrey. As they rolled into Hayesville they saw several whiskey wagons drawn up among the maples in the square and long lines of men winding among the trees leading up to them. Hard women lounged about hoping to ply their charms. The covered wagons of the farmers were parked at a decent distance from these goings-on, and with their tailgates down they laid bare all kinds of produce, from the finest pink-eye Irish potatoes and turnips and peas to leatherbritches, bunch beans and the fat sweet potatoes called Indian Spanish. Other wagons sold treats like ginger cakes, maple sugar, dried apples and tarts. The stores were busy trading with the country people for salt, coffee, medicines and tools. Buggies and carryalls of every sort lined the edges of the square, and mules and horses were at all the hitch racks, drowsing and whisking their tails at the flies. In the livery corrals oxen bawled mournfully. Womenfolk and younguns were everywhere. The place smelt of wood smoke and manure and scorched hoof rind from the blacksmith's. The usual bunch of idlers roosted on the courthouse steps smoking, dipping snuff, chewing and spitting tobacco, whittling, telling lies. In the space before the courthouse forty or fifty others stood in a gaggle, and here and there among them the sun gleamed on the barrel of a weapon. In this bunch there was some shouting, some cursing, some pushing and shoving.

Looking on, the judge expressed a wish there wouldn't be a fuss in Hayesville such as had spilt blood in Murphy. But he didn't sound hopeful. There were grudges aplenty pending on the docket in Clay, just as there'd been in Cherokee, and there were no fewer men on this side of the line willing to take desperate steps for vengeance. Some of them—old-time tories and Union men—even felt hard against the Curtises in behalf of the Pucketts and Quillens. It was less safe here for a Curtis than it had been at Murphy. This was why Oliver and Andy both had brought their pistols.

They parked the surrey as near to the courthouse as they could get and passed around the square to avoid the revelers among the maples. Approaching the courthouse, Andy recognized Colonel Coleman going up the steps and hailed him. As court solicitor the colonel was preoccupied and in a rush, but graciously if somewhat coldly he paused to greet them and say how pleased he'd been to hear of the end of the Bellamy matter. In turn Andy made introductions, then he and the judge thanked the colonel for his counsel and for his recommendation of lawyer Elias, whom they praised.

The colonel rested a hand on Andy's shoulder and gave him an earnest look. "Go to the clerk's office. Seek out an attorney there called Johnston Barrett," he said. "He is the advocate for the Puckett family. Elias is probably with him. Barrett has news for you which I think you will welcome. You will know him by a very distinctive hairy mole, just here." He pointed to the spot between his eyebrows. Then quickly he excused himself and hurried inside.

Lawyer Barrett was easily found at a small table in a corner of the clerk of court's office. Lawyer Elias sat with him, and they were busy signing a mess of documents. Barrett's mole was large and hairy indeed. Also he was long and rangy and wore a shabby-looking wig and had a disconsolate air. Lawyer Elias, however, was beaming.

Then they all trooped outside, and standing by the doorway lawyer Barrett announced without ceremony that both the Puckett women had recently perished of natural causes—apparently the dreaded hydrophobia—and since they had died without heirs no one remained to press their suit against Judge Curtis. The action, therefore, was at an end.

The judge bowed his head and whispered, "Praise be."

Miz Balm In Gilead Quillen gaped at lawyer Barrett. "You mean I come all this way to give evidence and there ain't a-goin' to be no trial atall?"

Lawyer Barrett said that was right, and so did lawyer Elias, running his hands down his silk lapels like a bird preening itself. "The matter is entirely closed, concluded, wound up, finished," lawyer Barrett declared. "And I must say it is as great relief to me as it must be to you." He sighed with exasperation. "I was drawn into this matter on a point of principle as a Union man, only to find my chief sponsor branded an assassin and shot down while in the act of an attempted homicide, and my complaining witnesses a pair of degenerates scarcely capable of reasoned thought. The entire affair may have considerably damaged my reputation; I regret exceedingly having got caught up in it."

After this outburst nobody but lawyer Elias could think of anything to say; as always the child was ready with his tongue. "You're all free to go," he assured them with a wave of his hand, "although I must remain to try some other cases which have not turned out so well as this. Madame Quillen, if you don't mind returning to the Curtises', I'll arrange transportation back to Sweetwater for you by tomorrow."

Miz Quillen stood glaring as lawyer Elias shook hands all around. Then she announced that by God she could make her own way home, and damn a bunch of lawyers anyhow. But Judge Curtis gave her a commiserating pat and said he hoped she'd reconsider, and she stood fuming but did appear to take second thought.

Lawyer Barrett wasted no more time. He clapped on his stovepipe hat and bade them good day and walked off crisply toward the livery, presumably to claim his horse, return to East Tennessee and endeavor to forget he'd ever heard of Clay County, North Carolina.

By now Oliver had started in thinking about Nancy. Like Miz Balm In Gilead Quillen he'd traveled a far piece to no purpose on earth, and it irked him. But it was far more than irksome, what he'd risked with Nancy. She could be gone this very instant, passed on, while he stood here doing no good at all.

Once more, he bitterly reflected, he'd fallen short. Instead of giving what he owed his dearest Nancy he'd abandoned her to go off and do favors for the sake of others, or to keep his word, or for some other notion equally empty, while the flame of her poor life flickered out. Just as he'd chosen to go away to war when most hadn't, again he'd put Nancy aside in favor of a cause. What was this force inside him that drew him always away from what he ought to love, to do service for people not of his blood, to act in causes not his own? It seemed an impulse of the devil that tempted him beyond his power to resist; it must be an awful sin, so easily to turn away from one's own and tend the needs of strangers.

But then he remembered Nancy speaking to him of his honor—the honor she thought he owned when few others did. She was proud of that honor in him, which made him always keep his bond. And after that he thought of what the Lord Jesus said in Holy Writ about loving one's neighbor as oneself. Maybe it was immodest to conjure an idea so lofty, yet, truly, love was what had moved him. He did love Judge Curtis and Miz Curtis and the two Cartman boys and the girls. He saw too how the love he felt had sprung in turn from the love they'd showed him. This, he thought, was the way the world might be saved in the end, so perhaps it wasn't wrong after all to partake of a transaction so charitable.

And next he recalled the saying of the Savior's that had always puzzled him with its terrible sound, about Jesus having come to bring not peace but a sword, to divide a man from his mother and father, from his wife and his child, in the name of redemption. For the first time he grasped what that might mean—not just that the Redeemer must have first place in the heart but also that those not of your own kin were worthy also, sometimes worthier even than the ones you held close, if their need was larger. Maybe he aspired to that without knowing. Maybe all his study of the Bible and his prayers to God, which had borne him safe through the war, had carried him on to this, so that he could glimpse how the world might be saved. In this idea he found a measure of comfort—a very small measure, that tasted of the iron of sorrow.

But even so, right then, that very minute, he wanted to go home. What he did instead was take Miz Balm In Gilead Quillen to one side and hold her hand in both of his and say how grateful he was she'd come to do right by the judge. Judge Curtis himself stepped up too and took off his hat to her. She relented then and agreed to stay over at the farm till tomorrow. And for the first time since arriving she smiled, exposing her one front tooth. "I reckon hit would make Old Mose laugh," she said.

Just then a rattle of gunfire erupted around by the front of the courthouse, and they all flattened themselves against the log wall.

It was Murphy all over again, but without the fatalities. Some Unionists and some ex-Rebels traded shots without hitting anybody. That brought a hundred or more jaspers boiling into the square, ready to do battle. But Judge Augustus Merrimon, who was hearing cases that day, ordered the sheriff to deputize sixty trustworthy men from each faction, arm them and tell them to shoot the first man guilty of a violent act, and that brought an end to the trouble. So as things turned out no one was hurt.

On the way home Judge Curtis extolled Judge Merrimon for a fine gentleman who'd always served the state in honorable and impartial fashion, both in the Union and out. He'd voted for him, he said, in last year's election for the state convention, but Merrimon lost and an extreme Unionist served instead. "Extreme opinion," he lamented, "has carried the day on all sides, I'm afraid."

The judge brought the matter up again the night before Oliver was to depart for Georgia. He and Andy and Oliver were relaxing in the parlor after supper, and the leave-taking put them all in a melancholy frame of mind. The judge spoke of Daniel McFee, of his regard for Daniel, of how after returning home Daniel became estranged and even hostile but then in the end sacrificed himself so his former masters might be saved.

He stared for a time into the blaze on the hearth. Then he said, "Extremists carried the South to war in defense of slavery and led us to defeat and ruin, and because of this at war's end they were entirely discredited. Most men from the South saw the error we'd fallen into and recognized the wrong of slavery and were ready to end it. I even heard men of property—not just Union men either—admit after the war that the nigra deserved his freedom and his rights.

We all had a glimpse then of what should be done. Of a future that might be. If we'd reached out to grasp it, if we'd listened to our hearts, there could've been a reconciliation of the black man and the white, and the Union could've been quickly composed."

Sadly the judge shook his head. "But we let the moment pass. The president and the old Rebels and others appealed to our worst prejudices, told us that only whites should govern the South, reminded us that the nigra longed to ravish our women, warned us of the mongrelization of our race. Now the legislatures of all the Southern states are busy passing Black Codes meant to mostly reenslave the nigra, and all through the South the old extreme Rebels rise once again to power. Nigras are beaten and tortured and killed by whites gone mad with hate and fear. And at Washington City the Radical Republicans gain strength from the revulsion of the rest of the country against the wrongs we commit."

He paused, drew a long breath. "I see nothing ahead of us now but division and hate, the suppression of the nigra, the degradation of the white. I fear the two races can never be reconciled but instead will be forever at odds. And the pity of it is that we might have averted it, had we only been men of better character."

Oliver had no opinion to offer on the future of the races but was sure of one thing, and that was the goodness of the character of Judge Madison Curtis. Here Oliver sat, a poor shoemaker without a prospect in the world, warmed in the bosom of a man of means and station who valued him not according to wealth or blood or learning but according to the quality of his soul. Oliver wanted to say something to the judge, to thank him for that, to tell him of his fond regard. But Oliver wasn't given to such talk and so said nothing. Instead he lazed by the fire thinking of the time to come when he would realize his dream and move to Clay County and take up land and farm, and be a neighbor to his friends the Curtises.

But in fact it would be ten long years before that happened. One thing and then another would delay him. There would be many shoes to make and many crops to grow. There would be his marriage to Emily Henslee, and there would be her children to provide for, along with Syl and Martha and James Littleton. There would be four new younguns, all boys, one of whom, Caleb, would die of milk-sick before he was two years old and be buried in the cemetery at Head of Tennessee Baptist Church near what would become Dillard, Georgia. Oliver's mama would pass away, and he and Lit and Mac and Archie would help dispose of her estate, and he would work a long time paying off the debt he owed her. When at last he came to Clay County in 1876 Madison Curtis would be two years dead.

As he drove up the lane toward the wagon road to carry Oliver and Syl back to Murphy, Madison turned in the rockaway to get a look at Daniel's grave yonder by the poplars. At first his view was obscured by the crown of the apple tree standing where the old servants' quarters had once been. Three straight seasons he'd thought that tree dead, but now, curiously, it was at full growth and flourishing, something he wouldn't have thought possible.

He craned to see past it, and at last as the rockaway gained the road the red mound of the grave and the tall headboard he'd carved out of good oak came into view. He was too far away to read the inscription, but he didn't need to see it to remember what it said:

DANIEL CURTIS MCFEE
1829–1866
BELOVED COMPANION
Greater Love Hath No Man Than This
That He Lay Down His Life For His Friend

The rockaway turned into the road and rattled on, and soon the grave was lost to view. Madison squared himself on the seat and settled in for the trip. In the rear seat Syl was asking question after question—Whose cows were those? Why did that ram have only one horn? What kind of bird was that?—and Oliver, who sat next to Madison, was patiently answering.

Madison smiled. He felt himself in a state of grace, and so guilt no longer plagued him as it once had. There was grief for his lost friend, and some fear of what might befall him and his in the uncertain times to come. But no guilt. God had washed that away. Still, he kept remembering the words Daniel spoke to him the day before giving himself up to death: *If the Lord's forgiven you, why do you need me to?* Madison had longed to be reconciled, but Daniel would not extend him forgiveness. Yet Daniel had died in his stead. Like much else about Daniel it was a mystery, and Madison very much wanted to solve it. It seemed to him that if he could solve it he could begin to understand not just Daniel alone but a great many other things as well.

But then he called to mind a notion he'd once expressed to Daniel, that if in times gone by they'd shared love—even amid the wrong of bondage—it was possible now to hold onto that love, nourish it and eschew the hate the times seemed to call for. If they did that, maybe it could save them. That was what he'd argued. The old love was a foundation they could build on. But to Daniel that was a mystery as deep as the one Madison now confronted. At least it was a mystery on the day Madison said it. But now as Madison reflected, it occurred to him that in yielding up his life Daniel had done precisely what he had urged. At the end he'd chosen love. And what was love if not forgiveness?

When Oliver got home Nancy was still alive but so weak that her pulse felt like the twitch of the wings of a butterfly resting on a leaf.

In the candlelight he bent close over her and said, "I come to claim that kiss you promised me." She stirred faintly and her dry lips parted, but she didn't speak or open her eyes. Leaning down he kissed the parched mouth. When he rose back up she was looking at him with her clear blue eyes but didn't seem to see him, so he said her name and she stirred again, and this time he thought she might have smiled a little, though he couldn't be sure. Then she slept.

Still in his traveling clothes he waited by the bed all that night holding her hand. When dawn came she opened her eyes again, but still he didn't think she could see him. So he drew closer and laid his head on the pillow next to hers and quietly sang some of the songs he knew she favored. He sang "Sourwood Mountain" and "Old Uncle Joe" and "The Huckleberry Bush." Then he sang "Blest Be the Tie That Binds."

When he finished the last song she whispered something, but he couldn't hear it, so he put his ear down next to her mouth, and she said, "I'm cold." So he went to the crib and fetched up James Littleton and brought him to the bed and laid him in the crook of her arm beside her, and he called in Syl and Martha and told them to crawl up close next to her, and last of all he laid himself gently over her and enclosed them all—his dear Nancy and the children she'd borne him—in his arms. And warmed by the flesh of all her loved ones Nancy slipped out of this world and into the next.

AFTERWORD

This book, like *Hiwassee* its predecessor, is a work of fiction founded on some fact. The Madison Curtis and Oliver Price families were real, and their menfolk served in the Confederate army during the waning months of the Civil War, as recounted here. The Curtises and most of the Prices lived and worked in the places I describe.

However, I have taken liberties. I have changed some names to respect the sensitivities of living descendants. In the absence of certain knowledge, some causes of death were invented, although the causes I chose are plausible for the time and the dates are approximately correct. Certain events of the final military campaigns of the war have been telescoped for the sake of clarity. Jane Sims Price actually lived in Gilmer County, Georgia, rather than at Rabun Gap, where I found it convenient to situate her. While Kope Elias was in fact a prominent western North Carolina attorney during and after Reconstruction, I have him practicing law five years before he was actually admitted to the bar. And in portraying all historical personages I have of course drawn freely on my imagination to supplement what we know of them—which in some cases is precious little.

Daniel McFee is invented, but there was a mulatto named Hamby in the Curtis household. Colonel Hiram Willoughby and Captain Whitney Callendar are fictional; Colonel David Coleman and Captain William Patton Moore are real. The Pucketts and the Quillens are imaginary but represent a certain type common in the mountains during and after the war. Nahum Bellamy is also fictional. His wartime career as a pilot is based on that of an actual person, the intrepid Union guide Daniel Ellis, but the real Ellis was innocent of the atrocities I attribute to Bellamy.

The names of Bellamy's victims—those of Folk's Battalion who hanged Unionists in East Tennessee—are fictitious, but the events at Dugger's Ford on the Watauga River are factual. The identities of the men who actually handled the rope are not known, insofar as I can tell. It is a matter of partisan opinion whether the hangings were crimes or justifiable acts of war. Captain Roby Brown existed and, regrettably, behaved as he does in these pages, but as far as I know the time and manner of his death have gone unrecorded. The circumstances of the Civil War in East Tennessee were pretty much as I relate them.

The names of Oliver Price's messmates in Company G of the Thirty-ninth Georgia Infantry are taken from the actual roster of that unit, and for the most part their fates during the war were as I report them. The same may be said for Andy Curtis's friends in Company E of the Thirty-ninth North Carolina Infantry.

The organization of the army of occupation in western North Carolina during 1865 and 1866 was as I describe it. I have, however, made free with the structure of the Bureau of Refugees, Freedmen and Abandoned Lands. In reality the Franklin office of the bureau had no branch in Hayesville; apparently the area west of the

Nantahalas was covered, if at all, from the Franklin station. The bureau agents I name—Oscar Eastmond in Asheville and George S. Hawley in Franklin—were in place in 1866 and 1867, but it is unclear from the spotty bureau rosters for 1865 whether they were on duty in that year as well; I have assumed they were. The bureau had no post such as I have Nahum Bellamy holding. Otherwise my account of the bureau—its structure, personnel and policies—is faithful to the historical record.

The shootout at the spring 1866 term of court in Murphy occurred pretty much as I tell it, and so did the skirmish on court day in Hayesville, although I have moved these events later in the year than they actually happened in order to accommodate the story line. The lynching of a Unionist by the men of Murphy which I describe did occur, though the date is uncertain.

For other events of 1865 and 1866 in Clay and Cherokee, the record is largely silent. So is my family tradition. Consequently I have felt free to invent the story of Bellamy's vendetta against the Curtises and the troopers of Folk's Battalion. But I have tried as best I could to portray accurately the events of the first year of Reconstruction in the border South.

ACKNOWLEDGMENTS

Once again I must thank my nephew David C. Galloway for his genealogical studies of the Price family and my sister Wanda Price Galloway of Bald Creek, North Carolina, for her early research into the history of the Curtises and the Prices. Without their work I would never have been inspired to undertake my own.

In addition thanks are due Fred J. Hay, librarian, and Dean Williams, assistant librarian, W. L. Eury Appalachian Collection, Appalachian State University, Boone, North Carolina, for their work as stewards of a matchless repository of historical material about the mountains and the records of the Freedmen's Bureau in North Carolina; James Price of Clay County, who advised me on agricultural lore; Dorothy Wells of Asheville, my consultant on mountain flora; Frances Curtis Bogy of San Antonio, Texas, genealogist of the Curtis family; Frank Lloyd, for talking to me about bygone days as a black man in Clay County; and John Corn of Clay County, for arranging my meeting with Frank Lloyd. I especially want to thank Mr. Lloyd for sharing with me the story of the two rednecks at the bridge, an experience I gave to Daniel McFee in 1866 but which actually happened to Mr. Lloyd in our own day. He also told the story of how one of his ancestors made a deal with a white farmer to buy farmland on credit, paying off the loan with a colt a year, which I also appropriated for the freedman McFee.

For the few memories of the Madison Curtis family that survive I have drawn on a private memoir set down in 1928 by Nellie Walker, daughter of the Curtises' sixth child Sarah; I am grateful to Jamie Fields Ghantt for transcribing the sometimes illegible typescript.

My deepest gratitude is reserved for Ruth Perschbacher, who closely read and astutely commented on the entire manuscript. If not for her this would have been a poorer book indeed. I am deeply indebted as well to Natalie Frost and Margaret Hartman Abbott of Asheville and to John Bradford of Brevard, North Carolina, for reading and critiquing the manuscript.

Thanks go to Carolyn Sakowski, Steve Kirk, Anne Holcomb Waters, Debbie Hampton and all the other fine people at John F. Blair, Publisher, for their faith in this work. Thanks also to Liza Langrall, formerly of Blair.

Various volumes of the *Foxfire* series were indispensable for capturing the details of old-time mountain life. As I did in writing *Hiwassee*, I drew upon the invaluable series *North Carolina Troops, 1861–1865: A Roster*, published by the North Carolina Division of Archives and History, and I am once again grateful to its generous editor Weymouth T. Jordan, Jr., for providing me a copy of out-of-print material about the Sixty-fifth North Carolina Cavalry Regiment (Folk's Battalion). The series *North Carolina Regiments, 1861–1865*, edited by Walter Clark in 1901, was a valuable source as well, as was volume 4 of *Roster of the Confederate Soldiers of Georgia, 1861–1865*, edited by Lillian Henderson.

The following works were also very useful in recreating the time and place of this book: *A Curtis Geneology*, by Frances Curtis Bogy; *A History of Clay County, North Carolina*, by Guy Padgett; *The People of Cherokee County, North Carolina, 1546–1955*, by Margaret Walker Freed; *My Folks Don't Want Me to Talk about Slavery*, edited by Belinda Hurmence; *Thrilling Adventures of Daniel Ellis, the Great Union Guide of East Tennessee . . .*, by Daniel Ellis; and *Reconstruction: America's Unfinished Revolution, 1863–1877*, by Eric Foner.

One other work which came late to my attention deserves special notice—*The First American Frontier: Transition to Capitalism in Southern Appalachia, 1700–1860*, by Wilma A. Dunaway. This groundbreaking study overturns much of conventional scholarship about antebellum Appalachia and deserves a wide audience.

If I have made errors of fact or interpretation in drawing on these or other works the fault is mine alone.